Dagger in the Sleeve

Dagger in the Sleeve

Deanna Maclaren

W. H. ALLEN . LONDON
A Howard & Wyndham Company
1979

Printed and bound in Great Britain by
Butler & Tanner Ltd, Frome and London
for the publisher, W. H. Allen & Co. Ltd,
44 Hill Street, London W1X 8LB

ISBN 0 491 02358 8

In memory of my father

Contents

My grateful thanks are due to the following for their help in the research and preparation of this book: Anna Cooper, Michael Godfrey, Janice Gravett, Andrew Hewson, Dr Bruce P. Lenman (University of St Andrews), Eileen Piggford, Pamela Simpson, Dr Elspeth Wilson-Kay.

Staff at the British Library, Drummond Castle Estates, Scottish Record Office, National Library of Scotland, Scottish National Portrait Gallery, National Gallery of Scotland and Farnham Public Library.

DM

PART ONE
Margaret Drummond

One

Have good day, now Mergerète,
With grete love I thee grete.
I wolde we mighten us ofte mete
In halle, in chaumbre, and in the strete,
Withoute blame of the contré –
God grant that so mighte it be!

Anon

'The King's brains,' bellowed the Earl of Angus, 'appear to have sunk to his balls.'

'It's outrageous,' choked the Earl of Lennox, gazing sourly through the window at the couple whispering together in the May twilight. 'You'd think the King would show more discretion, with the Spanish ambassadors here to offer him the hand of the Infanta.' He accepted a goblet of wine from Bella, the serving girl. 'I can't see the Queen of Spain smiling with imperial indulgence, Angus, at the news that the prospective bridegroom was observed dallying with another woman. *And* unchaperoned.'

Bella Kyle took her tray across to the High Table and began collecting up the greasy platters. Her sea green eyes glittered with amusement as she watched the Court squawking and hopping like hens on a hot griddle at the latest amorous adventure of their King. Even the two new Spanish ambassadors, huddled behind her near the blazing fire, had been reduced to an undiplomatic fit of sulks over the astonishing behaviour of the Scottish sovereign.

Not that you could blame the ambassadors for feeling aggrieved, reflected Bella, jumping out of the way as two servants raked the spitting pine logs in the vast fireplace. They had journeyed all this way to the chilly Palace of Falkland bearing gifts, goodwill and the offer of marriage to a daughter

3

of Spain. In return the King of Scotland had appeared distinctly underwhelmed.

Serving the four-course dinner at the High Table, Bella had heard the ambassadors gamely endeavouring to engage the royal attention. They had chattered about a magnificent painting of the Madonna by a brilliant Italian artist ... and how it was rumoured that the lusty French soldiers were spreading the pox across Europe, which even the Pope –

But the King had gone. Pausing only to cleanse his hands in rosewater, he had crossed the candlelit Great Hall to one of the two long trestle tables stretching from the royal dais. And he had led away into the scented gardens the beautiful dark haired young woman whose laughing eyes had captivated him all evening.

Bella nibbled a piece of roasted peacock breast. The poor Spaniards must be famished, she thought. The ambassadors had been so intent on ingratiating themselves with the King that they had waved away the servants bearing succulent cuts of peacock, venison and goose. Now it was too late. Bella crammed a couple of custard tarts into her mouth. For once, she felt glad to be a mere common servant who was not compelled, as were the lords and ladies of the Court, to finish eating the moment the King laid down his knife.

On the High Table, the spun sugar which cobwebbed the almond flan was drooping in the heat of the fire. Bella giggled as she watched the spirits of the Court sagging with it. She hoped the neglected Spaniards would glean at least a measure of spiteful consolation from the dismay of the Scots as they choked on the indigestible fact of the King's new romance: James IV, King of Scotland and Lord of the Isles, was in love. And with the wrong woman.

'Bring me more wine, girl! And hurry.'

Bella wiped her sticky hands on her dress and took across a flask of the King's finest burgundy to Lord Lennox.

'The King should be out hunting a wife, not fawning over another mistress,' muttered the dark, wiry Lennox, tearing at a loose thread in the wall tapestry. 'Scotland needs a Queen.'

The Earl of Angus cast a glance of contempt at the Spanish ambassadors grouped despondently against the great carved mantel. 'Can't say I relish the thought of a mincing little Spanish filly as Queen of Scotland. Prefer my women more red blooded.'

'Then you have no cause for alarm. There will be no Spanish Queen.'

Recognising the voice of Bishop Elphinstone, the King's most trusted adviser, Bella hovered in the juniper-scented shadows, eager to hear more.

'I understand that King Ferdinand of Spain has already betrothed his daughter to Philip of Flanders. The King knows of this. His Council knows of it. In fact,' the Bishop's smile was razor thin, 'the only people left unaware are the two Spanish ambassadors.'

'God's teeth!' exploded Angus. 'The wretched Infanta is being bartered round Europe like a string of Spanish onions. Are you *sure* of this Flemish alliance, Elphinstone?'

The Bishop nodded. 'Letters of instruction from King Ferdinand to his ambassadors arrived in Edinburgh ahead of the Spaniards. Naturally,' said the Bishop blandly, 'the King opened them.'

'Naturally,' chorused Angus and Lennox, having never in their lives entertained a qualm about reading someone else's private correspondence.

Bishop Elphinstone continued calmly. 'The letters ordered the ambassadors to say nothing about the Infanta's betrothal to Philip. They were to offer the lady to the King, and in return Scotland was to withdraw her support from the Pretender.'

Angus' scarred fist smashed against the stone windowseat. 'I have *already* withdrawn my support from the Pretender!' he roared. 'I'll happily go to war with the English to defend my country, my lands, my family and my tenants. But I'll be damned if I'll get myself hacked to death for the sake of a hot-headed young impostor like Warbeck.'

'Unfortunately, the King does not regard him as an impostor,' murmured Bishop Elphinstone.

For once, Bella was in agreement with the peppery Earl of Angus. In the streets and back alleys of Edinburgh she had heard nothing but derision for the Pretender, one Perkin Warbeck who had arrived in Scotland claiming to be a surviving 'Prince of the Tower', and therefore the rightful King of England. He alleged that while his brother had perished in the Tower of London, he had escaped to France and lived with a family called Warbeck, whose name he had adopted.

'Warbeck!' snorted Angus. 'How can he claim to be King of England with a name like that? Can you imagine the illustrious crowned heads of Europe – Ferdinand, Isabella, Maximilian – accepting to their hearts a King *Perkin*?'

Bella hurried to pour more wine as an uneasy silence fell. She knew that no one, least of all Angus, needed to be reminded that Warbeck had already enslaved one heart. He had captured one of Scotland's great beauties, Catherine Gordon. She had been contracted to Angus, but had married the Pretender instead, with the King's blessing, in a blaze of public merrymaking and national expense. All Scotland was aware that Angus, a man of stubborn pride, had never forgiven the King for encouraging the woman he loved to marry a penniless adventurer.

Lennox said, with uncharacteristic tact, 'Well he isn't King yet, Angus. He knows full well his only hope of gaining the English crown is with a Scottish army at the back of him.'

'How typical, my lords! Skulking like a parcel of petulant soothsayers, and prophesying war, while your ladies crave your attention.'

Bella dipped a curtsey and smoothed her tangled golden hair at the approach of the elegant Elizabeth, Lady Drummond.

Bishop Elphinstone bowed. 'You malign us, my lady. In truth, we were merely divining that your lovely daughter may catch a chill if she lingers much longer in the cool night air.'

He glanced towards the gardens, where Margaret Drummond laughed with the King.

'I find your concern for the Lady Margaret most touching,' purred Lady Drummond. 'But rest assured – if she is shivering, it is merely with delight at renewing her acquaintance with the King. You will mind, my lords, that they were much in one another's company some years ago, when my daughter was lady-in-waiting to the King's poor departed mother.'

Lennox hastily assembled an expression of suitable reverence at this mention of the late Queen, and murmured, 'It seems to me the King has found the Lady Margaret somewhat . . . transformed since they last met. Permit me to express my compliments, my lady, on your most effective instruction in the feminine art of persuasion. Your daughter has clearly learned her lessons well.'

Lady Drummond's voice was honey sweet. 'My dear Lord Lennox, I regard myself as a capable woman, but really, I must confess it beyond even my powers to train a virtuous eighteen-year-old girl to engage the affections of a king. Margaret's charm, you see, lies in her naivety. And her good name. King James, you must agree, is too much surrounded with guile. It surely sickens him to look on his Court and see the stains of past treachery tainting those who now pretend to fawn and flatter. We Drummonds, my lord Lennox, have *proved* our loyalty.'

As she swept away, Elizabeth Drummond beckoned a ringed hand at the hovering servant girl. For a moment, Bella found herself mesmerised into an involuntary tally of amethysts versus age spots.

'Wake up, girl! I said I'd like some sweetmeats. No,' she called, as Bella turned towards the High Table, 'not those which have been lying near the fire all evening. They'll be covered in wood ash by now. Fetch me some fresh from the kitchen. And make sure they're nice and soft.'

Bella ran off, glad to escape from the prickly atmosphere surrounding the three men who had remained at the window. Lady Drummond's barb about loyalty had clearly gone home. Bella recalled that even the Spanish ambassadors had been heard to remark that 'the trouble with these Scots is that so many of them consider they are King'.

Bella thought it a fair, if tactless comment. They lived in a turbulent age when kings were more likely to die by the sword than in their beds, leaving behind a Court nigh strangulated by the ties of intermarriage, and a clutch of ambitious nobles who bitterly resented the twists of fate and blanket that had deprived them of the crown. In the front rank of this mutinous field stood Lennox. A year after James IV's coronation, Lennox had led a rebellion against the King.

Bella spat on a silver dish, rubbing it to a shine with the cambric sleeve of her dress. She cut off the crusty edges of the almond sweetmeats and arranged them on the polished salver, a grim smile on her face as she remembered the humiliating defeat Lennox had suffered. Although the King had been lenient and eventually restored Lennox's title and lands, it was common knowledge that the Earl still harboured a grudge against both the King and the Drummonds. For the latter would never let Lennox forget that it had been Lord John Drummond who had led the final annihilating rout on the rebels. Judging by Lennox's crabbed face as she returned to the Hall, Bella guessed he was wishing that the entire Drummond family had been boiled and strained through cloths at birth.

She placed the sweetmeats beside Lady Drummond, wondering if the lady's sharp ears had caught Angus' amused comment: 'Proud bitch, that. Plump as a partridge. Just how I like a woman. Her daughter, now, is too thin. I prefer them meatier myself.'

'Unfortunately,' retorted Lennox tartly, 'it's King James the Fourth's taste we are concerned with, not yours. But I suppose we should at least be grateful that it is *women* the King is interested in. If he'd inherited the vices of his father, it could have been you or I, Angus, out in that garden submitting to the King's caresses.'

Angus' shout of laughter silenced the tattling Court for a moment, and Bella grinned as she collected up the last dishes from the High Table. In the Edinburgh fishmarkets she had heard many times the story of why they called the Earl of Angus *Bell-the-Cat*. Of the horror and scandal when it dawned on the elegant ladies and gentlemen of the Court that their revered James III had preferred the company of hand-some young men to that of women. What a rage had beset the aspiring, conspiring mothers of pretty daughters whose charms had failed to win the favours of the sovereign. What disgust and terror had consumed the King's lords, especially the old warriors like Angus whose overwhelming fear of being labelled effeminate drove them to prove their manhood to the world by noisily pleasuring the serving girls on the back stairs.

The affronted Court had argued for weeks about who was to confront the King and make an example of his simpering, limp-wristed friends. They likened their situation to the fable of the mice who, fearing the cat, proposed that one of them should slip a warning bell around its neck. But which of the mice had the courage to perform the deed?

Angus had volunteered. As a result, James III's favourites had been strung up like broken puppets over the Bridge of Lauder, with the unhappy King himself compelled to witness the grisly spectacle. Angus' sole reward for the bloody deed was the nickname, *Bell-the-Cat*.

A mountain of a man, he seemed to Bella to stand head and shoulders above the rest of the Court as they flocked to the windows of the Great Hall. Minstrels played unheeded in the timbered gallery and jugglers performed feats of in-credible dexterity unnoticed by the agitated nobles. The attention of Scotland's greatest families was focussed exclu-sively on the palace gardens. Even the King's dogs sat whining by the window, waiting for their master to return.

Bella threw them a few goose wings as she slipped from the Hall, out down the turnpike stair that led to the gardens. Her face alight with expectation, she wriggled through the rosebushes nearer the couple who stood by the trellised wall. The air was filled with the fragrance of May blossom and the strains of the minstrels' lutes floating out from the palace. It was a night, Bella thought, made for lovers. And she alone

9

was in a position to hear what the Court would have given their jewelled right hands to know.

Bella, anticipating the sweet words of romance murmured by lemans since time began, was brought sharply back to reality. Into a world of duty and of death. A climate too harsh for gentle lovers.

'I was crowned that day with murder in my heart, Margaret. You saw me in black, mourning for my father, still swearing revenge on those who killed him. I remember faithful Bishop Elphinstone insisting that I wore a short red mantle over my drab robes. He said if I wanted to make myself miserable that was one thing, but it was unfair to inflict my suffering on the people.' King James smiled. 'Elphinstone was right, of course. He always is.'

Margaret's amber eyes danced. 'With respect ... you seemed at your coronation to be having a little trouble with your crown.'

James threw back his auburn head, and the sound of his laughter hypnotised the frenzied Court waiting in the palace.

'That monstrous crown was made for Robert the Bruce. He must have had a head the size of an outside cannonball. I was terrified in case it fell off. Can you not imagine the scene? Lennox rushing to snatch the crown for himself. The Edinburgh fishwives wailing *bad omen*. And miserly Henry Tudor bellowing across Europe that he wouldn't have to bother conquering Scotland, for James IV had thrown his kingdom away.'

Margaret played with the fringed belt girdling her pink silk gown.

'There was talk,' she said diffidently, 'of a marriage being arranged for you with the English Princess Margaret.'

'She is but a little girl,' replied James shortly. 'And I have no desire for an alliance with the English. Besides, we are now committed to assist the Pretender regain the throne of England.' The King shrugged, unwilling on this enchanted evening to dwell on the cursed English, and the prospect of an ill-starred marriage to a foreign princess. He took Margaret's

10

hands in his. 'Oh Meg, I can't tell you how happy I am to see you again. Do you remember the picnics we used to enjoy under the willows on the River Tay? And my poor attempt at verse for you ...

> *The river through the rocks rushed out*
> *Through roses raised on high*
> *The shene birds full sweet 'gan shout*
> *Forth from that seemly shaw;*
> *Joy was within and joy without*
> *Where Tay ran down with streames stout*
> *Right under Stobbeshaw.'*

Margaret said softly, 'Of course I remember.' Then a wry smile touched her lips as she nodded towards the palace. 'But there is little *joy within* tonight, I fear. How young we were when you wrote those lines to me, James.'

'Such carefree days, before I was King,' said James wistfully. 'Since then, from the moment I was crowned, I seem to have been constantly in armour. The country was divided, with the people forever at one another's throats. Then came Lennox's rebellion, and the Highlanders' uprising. I didn't realise how alone I've felt until tonight, when your father led you into the Great Hall.' His long fingers traced the delicate line of her throat. 'You looked more beautiful than ever, Margaret, moving with such grace and dignity ... and yet, there was laughter in your eyes. I always loved that about you. When I saw you, Meg, it was as if I recognised a friend in a Hall full of enemies.'

'I know,' murmured Margaret. 'I stood amidst a crush of courtiers and curtseyed to my King. But when I lifted my head, it was as if you and I were suddenly alone.'

He drew her to him.

At least a hundred people witnessed the kiss. The Court, silently thronging the windows of the Great Hall, stood aghast, furious, jealous, resentful or disappointed according to their rank, sex and expectations. Only two women smiled on the lovers: Lady Drummond and Bella Kyle.

Bella, her legs tingling with pins and needles, began to edge

11

her way out of the bushes, then scrambled hastily back as she saw the King lead Margaret Drummond towards her hiding place.

'Tell me we shall meet again soon, Meg.'

'It shall be as you wish. You are the King.'

'No, Margaret! I am not commanding you to come to me. You are no serving woman, to be used and disposed of at the royal whim. When ... if you consent to come to me, I wish you to do so because it is your will.'

Bella held her breath, wondering how the Lady Margaret had the nerve to keep the King of Scotland waiting like this. She herself would have swum to France and back if the King demanded it.

At last, the Lady Margaret Drummond said softly. 'It is my will.'

James embraced her, and for a moment she rested her dark head against the purple velvet of his cloak. 'Then we have all the time in the world, my Margaret. But now we must return.' Laughing, he gestured towards the palace windows. 'I fear the Court feels neglected. And I must ask those poor Spanish ambassadors more about that Italian, da Vinci. Do you know, he has drawn a picture of a marvellous machine that actually flies!'

Margaret smiled. 'So you *were* listening to the ambassadors as we dined?'

'Of course. But it is what they omitted to tell me that I found most revealing. I am afraid I shall shortly have to inform them that their mission is fruitless – that I have discovered the Infanta is already betrothed.'

Margaret said drily, 'You sound desolate.'

By way of reply James drew from his belt an elegant jewelled dagger and, reaching up, sliced it through an over-hanging sprig of May blossom. With a flourish, fully aware of the sullen eyes staring from the palace, he presented Margaret with a spray smothered in white flowers. Then, hand in hand, the couple walked slowly back to face the Court.

As she emerged scratched and dirty from the rosebushes,

12

Bella's sharp eyes picked out something gleaming in the grass. Swiftly she knelt, and her roughened fingers closed around a cool, small pearl. It must have fallen from the Lady Margaret's dress, she realised, slipping the pearl into the purse at her waist and scuttling back up the turnpike stair.

In the Great Hall, she found the mood switching from reverie to revelry as the Court hastened away from the windows and affected to be convulsed at the antics of the jugglers.

'Damn it all, Lennox,' barked the Earl of Angus above the din, 'it's not as if the King feels the need to prove his manhood. He had a couple of bastards by Marion Boyd. The lad's shown the nation he's got it in him.'

Lennox leaned against a trestle table, oblivious of the spilt burgundy staining his costly silken hose. Bella mopped up the wine, suddenly nervous of the wintry expression in Lennox's ice-blue eyes. 'He shouldn't be prancing about after yet another bitch on heat, Angus. The country needs an heir. He should find himself a Queen.'

'Perhaps,' interposed the mild voice of Elizabeth Drummond, 'he has already found one.'

As the two Earls gulped for breath, the Lady addressed her next remark vaguely in the direction of the large oriel windows above the royal dais. 'You will mind, my lords, that the Drummonds have already given Scotland two Queens. David II and Robert III were both blessed with Drummond wives. It is something to reflect upon, is it not?'

She smiled and drifted away.

'So that's her game,' growled Angus, an expression of begrudging admiration in his bloodshot eyes.

Lennox was clearly struggling to control the rage that consumed him. When at last he spoke, the malevolent tone of his voice made Bella flinch.

'No! By God! I swear to you, Angus. While I live, there will be no third Drummond Queen!'

Two

No man can ever dream what that joy
Is like, neither by wishing nor desiring
Nor by thinking nor imagining.
Such a joy can never be equalled ...
Guillaume of Aquitaine

Drummond Castle was plunged into an unprecedented state of chaos. Sweating servants scurried up and down the stone stairs, bearing huge chests overflowing with dresses, robes, cloaks and fine linen. Tailors, dressmakers and embroiderers toiled through the night by the light of spluttering mutton fat candles, lashed by the caustic tongue of the mistress of the castle.

Lady Drummond had been out of temper for a full ten days. Over breakfast she was unburdening her woes onto the padded shoulders of her husband.

'... And to cap everything, I can get no sense out of your other daughters! They just giggle and giggle like a gaggle of silly geese. Margaret, of course, won't tell me a *thing*. She goes her own sweet way regardless of all I'm trying to do for her. I'm surprised she even condescended to mention that she was going to Stirling Castle at *all*. She's having twenty new dresses made and won't stand still one moment for a fitting, and as if that's not enough, that shovel-footed ostler of yours tripped and dropped a bale of Bruges lace outside the byre. Now it's covered with cow dung and will have to be cleaned before I can give it to the seamstress. You'll have to speak to that ostler, John. John! For pity's sake. You aren't even listening!'

Lord John Drummond downed his pint of ale and murmured soothingly, 'I'm sure you have everything well under control, my dear.'

His wife sighed. 'I would wish for a little more of your sup-

14

port, my lord. It isn't every day your daughter leaves home to take up residence with the King at Stirling Castle.'

John Drummond's hawk-like face was a picture of civilised regret.

'My dear. I have three hundred lambs to inspect, a shipload of wine coming from Burgundy and a party of tenants out in the courtyard waiting to complain that their roofs have blown off. Two of my new falcons died last night, the gelding is lame and I have a strong suspicion that that rogue Sam Bollow overcharged me for my new armour. With all this to attend to, can I reasonably be expected to involve myself in the romances of my daughters as well?'

Elizabeth Drummond was not deceived. She knew that her husband's ambition fully matched that of the Earl of Lennox. But they pursued their goals in vastly different ways. Lennox, spurred by an egoistic, misguided sense of his own destiny, made no secret of his aspirations. 'But a bladder full of wind is speedily deflated by the sharp point of a needle,' John Drummond had mocked after quashing Lennox's last rebellion against the King.

Where Lennox resorted to bluster, Lord Drummond employed guile. A master at the art of achieving his ends through others, he had no hesitation in exploiting the renowned charms of his six beautiful daughters to further the Drummond family star. Had not three of the girls already been united with the most powerful families in Scotland? Eupheme had married Lord Fleming, Annabel the Earl of Montrose and Elizabeth the Master of Angus, old Bell-the-Cat's son and heir. Their dowries had been crippling, and without exception the girls loathed their husbands. But that was a small price to pay, reflected their father, for the prestige with which they had endowed the House of Drummond.

And the best was yet to come. Margaret, his eldest daughter, was undoubtedly the brightest jewel in the family crown. The allusion pleased John Drummond. He only hoped the King would find the notion as engaging.

He pushed back his heavy oak chair and laid a hand on his wife's shoulder. 'Now you must go to Margaret. Talk to the girl. Impress upon her that it is imperative for us to learn the King's true feelings and intent towards our daughter.'

'John, you don't know what you're asking,' protested his wife. 'If you mention the King to Margaret she behaves as if she has never heard of the man, let alone lain with him.'

As if she had not spoken, Lord Drummond went on quietly, 'Margaret will not be the first of the King's mistresses. And she will not be the last, even if she does become Queen. You would do well to remember that, Elizabeth.'

And, calling to his dogs, he strode out into the courtyard.

Lady Drummond remained at the table, absently dipping pieces of hard barley bread into the jug of ale. Normally her teeth pained her, making even soft food an agony to eat. But today her aching jaws took second place to the nagging problem of what to do about Margaret.

Of course she wanted her daughter to marry James IV. As Queen, Margaret would become a woman of property, and considerable wealth. Stirling Castle, the Palace of Linlithgow and vast, valuable estates would become hers for her lifetime. She would have her own state apartments, hung with cloth of gold, and a train of attendants to dress her and adorn her in the priceless crown jewels which the First Lady alone was privileged to wear.

As the father of the Queen, Lord Drummond would be rewarded with honours and titles certain to make him one of the most exalted men in the land. While she, Elizabeth Drummond, would be known to future generations as the grandmother of James V of Scotland.

The prize was breathtaking. And it was within their grasp, if only Margaret could be persuaded to reveal the extent of her hold over the King. The fact that they had shared the royal bed at Falkland Palace told Lady Drummond nothing. She knew only too well how little that meant in terms of influence. She certainly had none over Lord John, and they had lain together for over twenty-one years.

It was all very well, thought she, for John to feign disinterest, to cloak the fact that, once again, she was doing his dirty work. He didn't appreciate the stubborn nature of

16

their eldest daughter. Which was ironical, since it was from her father that Margaret inherited her obstinacy. Her sisters had tried. She, Lady Drummond had tried. But Margaret had refused to say a word, beyond a disdainful comment about declining to engage in salacious Court tittle-tattle.

Briskly, Elizabeth Drummond stood up, her intentions clear. She would instruct the new cook on the best method of salting beef, and then she proposed to confront Margaret once more. She would be firm. She must make the wretched girl talk.

At the door, Lady Drummond stopped a serving girl. 'Agnes. This floor looks disgusting.'

The girl pouted. 'The rushes were changed only last week, my lady.'

'Well change them again,' snapped Lady Drummond. 'They smell as musty as funeral clothes.'

Margaret's sisters were, quite naturally, as eager as their mother to learn the details of her romance with the King.

'Come now, Margaret,' urged Sybilla, sprawled comfortably on Margaret's feather bed. 'Tell us what it's like to lie with the King.' She giggled. 'Does he wear his crown in bed?'

Margaret sat on the windowseat, sketching the view of the rolling green hills of Perth. Of her five sisters, Sybilla and Eupheme were closest to her. From the cradle they had laughed, played and cried together, sharing their toys, their dresses, their secrets. But the love of a king, Margaret had discovered, was something she could bring herself to share with no one.

'See how her face changes when you mention her nights with the King,' declared Eupheme, adding slyly, 'They say he is an expert lover.'

'He is everything a King should be,' replied Margaret coolly, holding up her drawing to the clear May light. She would take the sketch with her to Stirling, she decided, to remind her of home.

Sybilla wrapped the damask bed curtains around her feet. 'You are mean, Margaret. You might at least tell us if his nightshirt —'

The door was flung open. Lady Drummond swept in, her back straight, her jaw, Margaret noticed with foreboding, set as square as a dice.

Elizabeth Drummond ignored the unseemly spectacle of Sybilla scrambling to disentangle herself from the bedcurtains. 'Eupheme, Sybilla!' she rapped. 'I wish you to go to the kitchens and supervise that new cook salting the beef. The last batch stank as high as a goat, and if he goes on like this he'll poison us all.'

'But we wanted to talk to Margaret,' protested Eupheme.

'You will do as I say,' her mother instructed tartly.

Eupheme reddened. 'You can't speak to me like that any longer, mother. I'm Lady Fleming now, remember, with a husband and a household of my own.'

Lady Drummond smiled a sweet smile, 'My dear Eupheme, I had no idea you were pining so for your beloved John. No doubt you will wish to leave for home immediately. Pray do not allow us to detain you.'

The last thing Eupheme desired was an untimely return to her pompous husband.

'Oh, come on, Sybilla. Race you down to the kitchens,' challenged Lady Fleming, dragging her sister from the room.

From the high padded seat of the tapestry armchair, Lady Drummond came straight to the point. Margaret took one look at her mother's determined face and wished fervently she were salting beef with her sisters.

For two hours Lady Drummond wheedled and whined, poked and probed, badgered and bullied. Margaret said nothing. Calmly, she gazed from her window and drew the bake-house, the buttery, the stables and the willow trees round the castle lake.

'I don't know what's the matter with you, Margaret,' sighed the older woman hoarsely. 'Don't you want to be Queen of Scotland?'

At last, Margaret lifted her head from her drawing. The matchless amber eyes of mother and daughter mingled in expressions of confusion and distaste.

'No,' said Margaret Drummond clearly.

18

Lady Drummond's bosom heaved in disbelief. 'Nonsense. Every girl wants to be Queen.'

'I'd rather be loved than Queen.'

'You can be both.'

Margaret shook her head. 'Queens are never loved. They are unhappy, pitiful objects, bought and sold one nation to another, nurtured like prize cows until the investment pays off and they produce heirs. Once the succession is assured, the Queen is discarded and condemned to a life watching the King besport himself with younger, prettier women. She is not even allowed the solace of her children. They are taken away, to be reared by nurses and tutors, until their mother becomes nothing to them but a distant, carping figure. A nuisance.'

Such cynicism from a mere eighteen-year-old girl dismayed Lady Drummond. 'It need not be, Margaret. I have borne many children, but your father has been a fine, faithful husband to me.'

'You are not Queen,' said Margaret simply.

'And you won't be the King's only mistress!' her mother lashed back, remembering her husband's warning.

Margaret shrugged her slender shoulders. 'No matter. I'd rather be a cherished mistress than a neglected Queen.'

Lady Drummond stood up and moved restlessly about the room, searching for reassurance. 'Oh, you are just a lovesick girl. One should not expect you to be capable of thinking clearly at such a time. Why, just look at the midden you've made of this room.' She snatched down a forlorn bunch of herbs from the bedpost. 'What's the point of Agnes hanging wormwood to sweeten the air when you let it wither and die?'

Her face impassive, Margaret moved aside, allowing her enraged mother to hurl the offending wormwood through the window.

'Nothing more to say for yourself? My word, if the King could see what a sullen baggage you really are. It's lucky for you that he doesn't know you as I do.' Lady Drummond rustled to the door. 'Wait till you get to Stirling Castle, my girl. Once you've tasted the tempting fruits of power, I'll wager you'll have second thoughts then about being Queen.'

The door slammed.

With an unqueenly oath, Margaret flung herself on her bed. Gazing up at the dull damask canopy, she allowed her thoughts to drift back to those enchanted nights in the royal bedchamber at Falkland, with its decorated ceiling of azure, vermilion and gold.

Arranging a tryst with a king, Margaret had discovered, was no simple matter. James could not come to her room, for if the King's chamber had been discovered to be empty, the resulting hue and cry would have been too appalling to contemplate. Alternatively, the notion of Margaret slipping quietly along to James' apartments was equally fraught with stumbling blocks, in the shape of the attendants constantly surrounding the King. Even when he went to bed, his chamber was thronged with young noblemen, jostling for the honour of bringing his napkins and washing basin, competing for the privilege of undressing him or fetching his night-shirt, freshly warmed from the fire. There was no question, either, of Margaret concealing herself in his garderobe before he retired: James had flatly refused to submit her to such a humiliating game of hide and seek. Besides, his chamber was thoroughly searched each evening for potential assassins, and sentries stood guard throughout the night outside the royal door.

Paramount in James' mind was the need to shield Margaret from embarrassment. Conscious of the watchful eyes of the Court, he was determined to do nothing which would cause her to be regarded as one of the Court serving girls: a mere object of royal pleasure, to be sniggered over, laughed at, despised.

Margaret appreciated his sensitivity. But when it became clear to her that James' chivalry stood between them and the consummation of their love, she decided to take the initiative. One night, soon after the Court had retired, she slipped down the stair to the King's chamber, and before the guards could stop her, swept in, without knocking.

She found James, in a silk shirt and breeches, surrounded by his attendants. Margaret curtseyed gracefully, and then addressed his astonished young noblemen. 'My lords, you may leave us,' she commanded, her face flushed, her voice steady. 'I shall attend to the King.'

The Earl of Mallaig laid the King's embroidered surcoat on an oak chest. 'But my lady, it is hardly seemly...'

'Kindly do as the lady says, Malcolm,' interrupted the King, his hazel eyes brilliant with mirth.

Beneath heavy black brows the Earl of Mallaig broodily surveyed the fragile, beautiful woman who had dared to invade the all-male stronghold of the King's chamber. Margaret Drummond stared unflinchingly back. The King leant negligently against the carved bedpost, savouring the scene.

It was no contest. With the most cursory of bows to his monarch, Malcolm Laxford, Earl of Mallaig, turned and led the royal attendants from the chamber.

Margaret and James collapsed into one another's arms, helpless with laughter.

'My God. Did you see young Mallaig's face?' cried James. 'He was aflame with anger, yet his eyes were as cold as ashes. *But my lady, it is hardly seemly!*'

'He'll be scuttling now to tell the Earl of Angus how brazen I am,' smiled Margaret.

'Let him,' said James adding drily, 'knowing Bell-the-Cat, you'll have gone up ten points in his estimation. He admires spirited women. I hear he's laying siege to that hellcat Janet Kennedy, but so far all she's done is spit in his eye.'

As he talked, James moved round the room, snuffing out the candles. When just one candle flickered in the niche beside the tiled mantel, he returned to Margaret, and swiftly, expertly began untying the fastenings on her dress. Soon she stood naked and lovely before him. Firelight rosed the pearly translucency of her skin as she lifted her arms, and taking a long golden pin from her hair, allowed the glorious black waterfall to tumble free to her waist.

Margaret opened her eyes, and stretched now, luxuriously, at the memory. Eupheme had been right. The King was, indeed, an accomplished lover. But Margaret no longer thought of him as King. He was the man she loved.

As night followed night, they had lain in each other's arms on the scented pillows and whispered, as lovers do, of their innermost secrets, desires and fears. She had learned more of his lonely childhood spent, after the death of his mother, almost exclusively in the austere company of books and bishops. For the first time, too, she heard him speak frankly about the nobles' rebellion against his father; of their adoption of the fifteen-year-old James as King, a move which had culminated in the bloody battle by Sauchie Burn.

'It was there that my father was forced to flee the field,' James told Margaret, holding her tight as dawn broke over Falkland. 'He was thrown from his horse and carried, semiconscious, to a mill. One of the rebels found him there.' James paused, and Margaret felt him swallow, hard. 'My poor half crazed father, mistaking the rebel for a priest, asked for the last sacrament ... *That I shall do hastily*, declared the man ... and stabbed my father through the heart.'

Although James had refused to take part in the battle, Margaret knew the shock of his father's murder had left a scar on his soul which would never heal. Nor would James want it to. Seeking to punish himself further, he insisted on wearing a heavy iron chain belt round his waist. It served as a permanent reminder, he explained, of his duty as King and as his father's son, never again to allow any noble to plumb the dark well of bloodshed, bitterness and treason which had poisoned his country's affairs for so long.

Anxious to divert her lover from such brutal recollections, Margaret talked of the security he had brought to Scotland. 'You have given your subjects peace of mind by restoring order to an unruly, divided country,' she told him. 'The people are proud of Scotland now. And proud of their King. They desire nothing more from you than that.'

Nothing except, they both knew, a Queen and an heir.

Every morning, Margaret would slip away early from the

royal bedchamber, before the handbell was rung and the four most privileged servants surged in to tie back the bedcurtains and wish the King goodday. James often told her how he laughed to see the clutch of eager faces peering expectantly through the silken hangings, each hoping to be the first to discover the Lady Margaret lying there in wanton disarray.

Margaret arose from her own lonely bed now and returned to the window. A commotion in the courtyard heralded the arrival of visitors to Drummond Castle. With a sinking heart Margaret recognised the gilded arms of Lady Lennox blazoned on the tunics of the attendants shouting orders at the Drummond stableboys. Already, Margaret could hear her mother feverishly issuing commands to the servants for wine and sweetmeats to be brought to the Great Hall.

Margaret resigned herself to a day of shrill interrogation by Lady Lennox. She would want to know everything, from the King's true opinion of Lord Lennox, to what style of underwear James preferred Margaret to wear. Lady Lennox would, of course, be disappointed on all counts. But for a moment, Margaret was tempted. Of Lennox, James had commented acidly: 'A beggar's appetite is always fresh.'

As for her underwear. . . . Margaret dearly wished she could tell the spindle-shanked Lady Lennox that the first time James had seen her in a shift, he had stripped it from her and flung it on the fire, forbidding her ever to wear one again.

When Margaret Drummond walked down to the Great Hall to greet Lady Lennox, her face was very properly demure. Her body, under the soft silk of her dress, was deliciously naked.

Three

None may pass down your principal streets,
For the stink of haddocks and skates
For the shrieks of the women swearing and scolding
And the deafening din of the brawling ...

William Dunbar

While Lady Drummond called for fiddlers to entertain her guests, Bella Kyle was washing her clothes in the icy water of one of the lochs that girdled Edinburgh. She wasn't hurrying. It was pleasant to linger on the fresh spring grass, far from the stinking streets of the town.

Even more than the smell, Bella loathed the noise and bustle of Edinburgh. She could still vividly recall the horror of arriving here two years earlier from her village in the Highlands. There on the wild western coast, the familiar sounds of Bella's childhood had been the cry of the curlew, the roar of the sea and the song of the wind through the trees in the night.

Nothing had prepared her for the strident clamour of Edinburgh. The vendors bawling their wares from canvas stalls. Women haggling loudly in the fishmarket. Gipsies screaming to tell her fortune – cursing when she refused. And toothless beggars clutching at her skirt, whining for the price of a pint of ale.

Her brother Robert had been reluctant to bring the thirteen-year-old Bella to Edinburgh at all. But with the death of the woman she knew as Aunt Lilith, there had been no one left to care for Bella.

'It won't be like the village,' Robert had warned, as they fled from the Highlands by night on stolen horses. 'Edinburgh is a big town. Over ten thousand people, so they say. And none of them will understand the Gaelic, so we must remember

24

to speak in lowland Scots. I'll try to keep an eye on you, of course, but I'll be busy learning a trade ... I rather fancy myself as a saddler ... so I can't be with you all the time. You'll have to take care and watch out for yourself.'

Intent on not falling off her horse as they careered through rocky mountain passes, Bella had been too frightened to understand what Robert was trying to prepare her for. But she learned. Two years in Edinburgh had transformed her from a shy country lass into a flint-sharp young woman. She used her elbows to fight off the shrieking women who competed with her for the best cuts of cheese as they were weighed in the Tron Market. She screamed fearful abuse at the poultry dealer for selling month-old chickens. She bribed the water carrier to bring her the first drawing of water from the public well before it was tainted by the reeking dross the townsfolk hurled from their windows. Bella learned to brew ale for her brother and his friends ... and not to ask questions when they disappeared at night in the direction of Leith Port, returning before dawn with chests of precious saffron, casks of Rhine wine, bolts of Flanders velvets. Scrupulously honest by nature, she nonetheless accepted the compromise that hardship brings. Robert had told her often enough: 'These are difficult times. And a man must make a living where he can find it.'

Bella bundled the wet washing into her basket and reluctantly turned away from the loch, back towards the town. She walked briskly, the rush basket balanced on her hip. In half an hour she had reached Edinburgh's broad High Street, where the saddler's sign on Robert's shop still gave her a thrill of pride. Dumping her washing there, Bella hurried back down the street, past the perfumers, wigmakers and goldsmiths, to the barber-surgeon's shop, with its distinctive striped pole. Inside she found Sam Bollow, the armourer, reluctantly having his gums leeched.

'It's to stop them hurting so much, Bella,' Sam explained, opening a mouth that smelt like a charnel house.

Bella's stomach lurched. 'Poor Sam. I'll send you round some broth later on,' she promised, hastily looking away. She kept her eyes on the barber-surgeon, busy selecting his leeches, as she said, 'Robert sent me with a message. He says the candlemaker's wax is ready.'

Sam nodded his comprehension, but declined to answer Bella's enquiring lift of the eyebrows. Not that she minded, particularly. She was accustomed to passing on information from Robert which she didn't understand. Though in this instance she grasped the obvious reference to Candlemaker's Row, that notorious haunt of thieves, beggars and witches.

The leeches which the barber-surgeon was preparing to apply to Sam's suppurating mouth were really quite pretty, thought Bella. They were about three inches long, with blackish brown backs marked with two vertical lines enclosing yellow spots. Bella wondered idly if the barber-surgeon ever played dominoes with them.

Fascinated, in spite of her feelings of revulsion, Bella stared transfixed as the barber-surgeon used a swan's quill to pick the leeches from the pot and delicately stroke them onto Sam's inflamed gums. Once gorged with blood the leeches would, Bella knew, drop off – unless the barber-surgeon decided enough blood had been let and hastened their departure by sprinkling them with salt.

Sam groaned. Bella headed for the door, to avoid hearing Sam choking then screeching when, inevitably, a leech fell down his throat.

Out in the High Street a baying crowd had gathered at the Market Cross, the traditional central meeting place of the town. Bella, unable to see over the heads of the yelling mob, scrambled up the outside stairs of the goldsmith's shop where its owner was also craning for a better view. At the Cross, in the shadow of the great Cathedral of St Giles, a naked woman stood, trussed into an ox cart.

'Can you see who it is?' asked Bella, wincing as the shrieking crowd hurled abuse, stones and horse dung at the shivering woman.

The goldsmith peered short sightedly over the wooden balcony. 'I think it's Nan the bawd. But it's hard to tell with

her clothes off. She was caught again in the Lawnmarket trying to entice some soldiers to go with her.'

'I shouldn't think they needed much encouragement,' commented Bella, shouting to make herself heard above the
outraged citizens of the town.

The goldsmith shook his head reprovingly. 'That may be,
Bella. But harlotry is a sin and it is just that a bawd should
be punished.'

'Sanctimonious old goat,' muttered Bella, pushing her way
down the stairs and away from the scene. She knew Nan well,
and sympathised with the woman's struggle to feed herself
and three young children after her husband had been
slaughtered at Sauchie Burn. But there was nothing Bella
could do to help her now. Later, when Nan had been freed,
she would take her a chicken pie, and a jug of her best
ale.

The episode made Bella thankful that she was quick witted
enough to earn a few pence by sewing and running errands
for the ladies at Court. She sold her talents well, yet in these
grim times she felt only pity for a woman who had nothing
to offer but her body. What was the practical difference, reasoned Bella, between being skilled with a needle and dextrous
between the blankets? Good luck to Nan for exploiting her
sole saleable asset while she was still healthy and attractive.
One thing was certain: no one stayed healthy and attractive
for long. It was commonplace to see men bearing the bloody
legacy of Sauchie Burn and the unremitting Border warfare,
with half their faces hacked away or severed limbs. Bella was
well aware that anybody could be scarred by the pox, maimed
by a drunkard or thief, and dead from the plague, all in the
space of a week. Bodies, to Bella, were cheap commodities.

Yet she herself, against overwhelming odds, had remained
untouched by any man in Edinburgh. She was glad of that.
Few other fifteen-year-old girls could say the same. Not that
she was unaware of the covetous glances cast her way by stall-
holders, soldiers and even the fine young lords up at the
Castle. But she would have no truck with any of them. Over
the years they had learned to respect the golden-haired girl's

acid tongue, and the nimble feet that carried her so swiftly out of trouble.

Above all, the men had acquired a wary admiration for Bella's greatest asset. Her brother. Robert the Red they called him, after his birthplace (all Highlanders were dubbed as Redshanks by lowlanders) and for his shock of carroty hair. The play of his sword and the lethal glitter of his dirk had earned him an enviable reputation as a fighting man. It was rumoured, too, that he was a smuggler, though none dared say so to his face. There was something indefinable about Robert Kyle and his sister, a steely quality that set the young saddler and the serving girl apart from the rest of common folk. Some cited the couple's remote Highland origins as the cause, mutting resentfully about the Kyles' irritating habit of talking to one another in the unintelligible Gaelic. Others whispered darkly of a savage Highland murder from which, it was said, Robert Kyle had been fleeing ever since. Whatever the truth, on one point at least everyone agreed: it made good sense not to cross Robert the Red. As for his bonny sister, well, you may look at her, even lust after her, but touch her you may not.

Robert's brotherly protectiveness reaped another reward for Bella. It meant she would never have to marry solely for security – at least while he lived. They were not rich, far from it, but when Robert had acquired the money to buy his own saddlery, he had also bought Bella peace of mind. No longer was the future marred by the spectre of a gross, boorish husband extracting his conjugal levy in a marriage bed curtained with her loathing and disgust.

That Bella was free to marry for love instead of money was understood implicitly by brother and sister, although Robert teased her unmercifully whenever he caught her engaged in any of the traditional fortune telling rites.

'I confidently predict all you'll get from that is a black mouth and stomach ache,' he had warned Bella last Shrovetide, finding her resolutely chewing a soot-cake to conjure a dream of her future husband. 'You know Sam the armourer has offered to marry you, Bella.'

Bella had shuddered. 'Sam Bollow is forty if he's a day and what's left of his teeth looks like black pudding.' She had tossed her hair. 'I've seen those ladies up at the Castle, Robert, going to their joyless arranged marriages with faces as long as scabbards. I'll not have that. When I marry, it'll be for love.'

'Knights on white chargers,' Robert had laughed, 'only happen in fairy tales, Bella.'

In the same way that beautiful ladies only fall in love with common saddlers in fairy tales, thought Bella. But she had kept her silence, just as she had avoided asking where Robert had found the money to set up the saddlery. It was mere co-incidence, she smiled to herself, that Robert had come home with gold in his purse after the last in a series of clandestine meetings with Lady Catherine Gordon. Ten days later, the lovely Lady Catherine had married Perkin Warbeck, the Pretender to the English throne, and Robert had never mentioned her name again.

Bella hiccuped. And hiccuped again. And again. She swore, cursing these embarrassing attacks to which she was unaccountably prone. Hiccups, she had discovered, was a malady that aroused laughter rather than sympathy. Particularly when they occurred at the Castle as one of the elegant ladies of the Court gave her instructions for an errand. The young lords invariably took advantage of Bella's distress, shoving cold keys and clammy hands down her bodice, and staining her only clean dress by making her drink a goblet of wine upside down.

Fastidiously Bella picked her way through the fishmarket. Her face was scarlet with the effort of holding her breath, to restrain the hiccups and blot out the stench of the rotting fish trimmings strewn at her feet. Engrossed in sidestepping the muck, she collided with a couple of women fish sellers and received in return a torrent of abuse. Bella responded with a staccato stream of apologetic hiccups. One of the women looked at her closely, shot out a gnarled hand and clutched at the pearl Bella wore on a velvet ribbon round her neck.

'What's a common serving girl like you doing with a costly bauble like this?' she cried. 'I'll wager you stole it, Bella!'

'I did not!' shouted Bella, outraged. 'Listen you old hag, this pearl was given to me, yes, *given* by the Lady Margaret Drummond herself. So don't you tar me with your own stinking brush you –'

A cackle from the other crone cut Bella short. 'Got rid of your hiccups for you, though, didn't we?'

'*Cailleacha sith!* '* cursed Bella. But already her anger was dissolving into laughter. It was the oldest hiccup cure in the world, and it had worked.

The incident had caught the attention of a small, swarthy skinned man with a black patch shielding one eye. Close and silent as a shadow he followed Bella until she turned into a narrow, quiet close.

He pounced, gripping her arm tightly. 'What have you got there, Bella?'

Bella tried furiously to shake him off, as his bony fingers bit deeply into her flesh. She fought, too, to keep the fright from her eyes. Everyone feared Blackpatch. Part gipsy, pickpocket, cattle-thief, poacher, Blackpatch was a bungling rogue whose poor success rate was apt to drive him to desperate acts of violence.

Bella played her ace: 'May the Devil help you, Blackpatch, when Robert comes looking for me.'

Blackpatch merely grinned and Bella recalled with sinking spirits that he was one of the few men in Edinburgh who seemed unafraid of her brother. She suspected that Robert found Blackpatch a useful ally on his smuggling expeditions. Certainly, Robert was the only person she knew who could offer any explanation of Blackpatch's missing eye. 'He went on a cattle raid down on the borders,' Robert had told her. 'And rather carelessly left an eye behind. I hear one of the Borderers has it pickled in vinegar as a souvenir.'

Now Blackpatch's one good eye was fixed covetously on the pearl at her throat.

* 'Fairy hags!'

'Where did you say you acquired this, Bella my dear?' he enquired softly.

'It dropped off the Lady Margaret Drummond's dress in the garden of Falkland Palace. I picked it up and took it back to her. But she very kindly told me to keep it. Leave me be!'

She twisted sideways, but Blackpatch had a firm hold on the pearl and held on to the velvet ribbon as if it were a bridle restraining a frisky pony.

'Do you think it's wise to wear your pearl openly like this, my dear? This is a valuable jewel. Anyone might steal it,' leered Blackpatch, his face close to hers.

Recoiling from his sour breath, Bella stamped hard on his foot, trying to wrench herself away. Blackpatch hung on. The ribbon tore. The pearl was gone. And so was Blackpatch, slipping eel-like through the close towards the crowded market.

'Thief!' shrieked Bella, giving chase. 'Wait till I catch you, you one-eyed cur! Give me back my pearl!'

The mob in the market, eager for a diversion, took up her cry, agog at the sight of the swarthy black-patched man and the golden-haired girl, her skirts raised to her thighs in hot pursuit and screaming loud enough to be heard in Glasgow. The young man riding through the market on an imposing white stallion had a better vantage point than most.

'Come on, lass! You've nearly got him,' he called encouragingly, as Bella sprinted down a cobbled sidestreet, hurdling over the middens dunged at either side. The crowd were greatly enjoying the chase, and if no one moved to help Bella, it was simply because they had seen her run before . . . usually *away* from a man. Knowing Bella's past form, they had every confidence that she would outpace and overtake Blackpatch.

She would have caught him. He was a fingernail from her grasp, his yellowy face contorted with the effort of such unaccustomed exercise. Bella reached out to grab his shirt, skidded on some sheep's entrails a flesher had flung into the street, and fell headlong onto the cobbles. The onlookers groaned in disappointment.

Blackpatch, sensing a reprieve, gained a second wind and made off towards the shelter of the stalls in the Lawnmarket.

He would probably have got clean away but for the young man on the white stallion. Without a word he spurred his horse in pursuit of the flying one-eyed villain. The mob cheered. It was a fine horse, fit for a nobleman. Yet the young man's simple clothes marked him out as a commoner, one of their own kind. They liked the honest look of his cheerful, tanned face, flushed with excitement as he steered the horse skilfully through the maze of stalls.

Blackpatch ducked and weaved, dodging this way and that past cascades of Flemish tapestry, heaps of sweet-smelling spices and the brilliant cobwebs of Spanish shawls. Wherever he went the young man followed, causing the gipsies to drop their trays of charms, and the men at the brew-stands to raise their mugs and roar him on.

Frantic, Blackpatch blundered into the poultry market. For a moment he stood bewildered, defeated by the cackle of geese, the squawking of hens and the clamour of the townsfolk as they haggled for the best bargain. Then he scuttled into the labyrinth of vennels, the dark dank passages that ran narrowly between the houses. The young stranger swiftly dismounted and shot after him.

Seconds later someone shouted: 'Up there! Look!'

Blackpatch had climbed onto a balcony connecting the outside staircases of the timbered houses. He scrambled down a flight of stairs and out into the street. His young pursuer scorned the staircase and, with scarcely a moment's pause, leaped from the balcony to the back of his waiting horse.

Bella, catching up with the buzzing crowd, found them wild with delight. 'Come on!' they urged her. 'The rascal's making for the churchyard.'

Suddenly, it was all over. The stranger had cornered Blackpatch in a churchyard heaped with the fly-blown filth daily tipped there by the townsfolk. The thief crouched by a tombstone, whimpering and pleading for mercy.

The young man snatched the pearl from Blackpatch's quivering fingers and tucked it safely within the purse at his belt. Blackpatch tried to slither away, but he didn't move fast enough. Two tanned hands shot out, seized him by the scruff of the neck and the tail of his shirt, and lifted him clean off the ground. Blackpatch whimpered.

His captor glanced round. 'Where is the fair-haired lass?' he asked.

The crowd pushed Bella forward.

'What would you like me to do with him?' The young man shook Blackpatch like a rat catcher jostling a bag of ferrets.

The mob were not slow to voice their opinion: 'Call the bailie ... Don't let him get away with it, my girl! ... He'll get twenty lashes at least ...'

Bella hesitated, undecided.

'I'd be glad if you'd hurry up,' urged the young man. 'He is rather heavy, you know.'

Bella stared at Blackpatch, dangling four feet above the ground, helpless. His face was brick red and streaked with sweat. In the scuffle, his patch had slipped, revealing the grisly cavity which once had held his left eye.

She made up her mind. 'Let him go.'

'Are you sure,' asked the stranger, as the crowd mumbled its disapproval.

Bella nodded.

'Well,' the young man glared at Blackpatch, 'after all my trouble, you rascal, the lady says I'm to let you go. But she hasn't specified *where*.'

He spurred his horse towards a reeking midden strewn with rotting fish, fruit and offal, teaming with maggots and scavenged by grunting hogs.

'Let me go! Let me go!' squealed Blackpatch.

'A pleasure,' replied the stranger, and opened his fists, allowing Blackpatch to plummet face down into the heap.

Satisfied, the mob roared its approval, and began to disperse into the gathering twilight.

Slipping easily from the saddle the young man bowed, with a hint of mockery, to Bella. 'Tom Fraser, at your service.'

Bella gazed up at a weatherbeaten face topped by a mass of unruly chestnut hair. 'I'm Bella Kyle. I can't begin to thank – ' she hiccupped.

Tom waved aside her thanks. 'Yours, I believe,' he said,

drawing from his purse the pearl, still attached to its torn ribbon. Bella nodded, hiccupping helplessly, furious with herself.

'May I put it on for you?'

Tom didn't wait for a reply, and Bella was in no fit state to offer one. Yet at his touch on her neck, her hiccups miraculously disappeared. Who was this gallant stranger, she wondered. No nobleman, certainly, for these were no pampered, manicured hands tying the velvet ribbon.

'I'm an ostler,' volunteered Tom. 'I've just come down from Aberdeen to work up at the Castle. But if the last hour's anything to judge by, I think I'm going to enjoy Edinburgh.'

Bella flushed, uncomfortably aware of the clear blue eyes surveying her. What if the young man demanded a reward for saving her pearl? Darkness was beginning to cast eerie shadows across the tombstones. The crowd had melted away. Even the reeking Blackpatch had scuttled off into the night, no doubt to indulge in his first bath of the year.

Through rising panic Bella heard Tom say, 'Perhaps you can help *me* now, Bella. I've just been to have this horse shod, and the blacksmith suggested I should seek out a saddler they call Robert the Red. It seems he might be able to tell me where to find lodgings.'

'Robert!' cried Bella, her voice shrill with relief. 'He's my brother.' Her mind raced. 'And if you wish ... that is, if you don't mind sharing a room with Robert, well, you would be welcome to lodge with us.' She watched Tom anxiously. With the extra money she might be able to afford a new shift for the winter...

As Tom considered her offer, Bella went on quickly, 'We live very simply, you understand, above the saddlery. But the rooms are clean, and there's a neat little garden. We have honey from my bees. I'm a fair cook, and even my brother admits I brew a fine jug of ale.'

In an instant Tom had swung her up onto the white horse. The ostler leapt into the saddle behind her. 'Well, that seems to be settled then, Bella!' he laughed.

As she rode home, conscious of Tom's muscular arms

around her waist, Bella wondered what Robert's reaction would be. Knights on white chargers only happened in fairy tales did they? Bella was glad Tom couldn't see the look of triumph on her face. It would be pleasant, she thought, just once in her life, to prove her superior older brother hopelessly wrong.

Four

Their high feast was Love, who gilded all their joys...
                              Tristan and Isolde

'All right, Lennox,' shouted James IV. 'I accept that as a loyal subject you are worried, nay, gravely concerned about my singular failure to provide Scotland with a legitimate son and heir. But is it my fault that there happens to be a dearth of suitable European princesses?'

The unfortunate Lennox shifted stickily in the stifling heat of the tapestry-lined Presence Chamber. He wished he had never come to Stirling. Especially since the King clearly had no intention of inviting him to sit down. Lennox glanced hopefully at Bishop Elphinstone, willing him to come to his aid. Instead it was the Earl of Angus who said, with unaccustomed control,

'Sire, it is not merely we who are concerned. Your people, too, are anxious. If you remember, we have already levied a heavy Marriage Tax on them for the express purpose of sending ambassadors to search Europe for a princess.'

'With no success,' interrupted James, throwing morsels of meat to the hounds crouched beside his chair. 'For the simple reason that there are no available princesses. Unless, of course, Lennox here would care to deck himself up in one of his wife's dresses and pose as my fairy godmother?'

Lennox's smile was glacial. The King went on briskly, 'Besides, I have neither the time nor the inclination to go a-wooing just now. I would remind you that we are preparing for a war against England, to set the Pretender on the throne. He's active over in Edinburgh at this moment, getting together an army.'

Arousing hostility amongst the people more probably, thought Angus sourly. The Warbeck lad was strutting

36

through the streets, bragging that as the rightful King of England he would soon send old Henry Tudor packing. Though they hated the English, the men of Edinburgh could summon little confidence in this swaggering boy.

'He has neither the breeding nor the bearing of a King,' Angus had heard Robert the Red proclaim in the Wild Boar tavern. 'He talks too much, plunges headlong into skirmishes entirely of his own making, and then blames his own supporters when he ends up bleeding in the gutter.'

For once Bell-the-Cat was inclined to agree with the young saddler. The old Earl would have cut his throat rather than admit that his antagonism towards Warbeck was rooted in the Pretender's abduction of Angus' beloved Catherine Gordon.

Angus mopped his face. Lennox, with the self-righteous air of one determined to be seen doing his duty, was rashly returning to the volcanic question of a Queen.

'If I might venture to suggest, Sire, I understand the Emperor Maximilian of Austria has a daughter.'

Bishop Elphinstone cut in quickly before the King could erupt. 'I fear, my Lord Lennox, that the lady is already betrothed to Spain.'

A storm-laden hush heightened the suffocating atmosphere of the Presence Chamber. The King, grimly regal in his high-backed oak chair, glared at his lords, daring them to mention the one name he dreaded most.

Lennox cleared his throat. 'Of course, there is still the possibility of the Princess Margaret of England...'

The storm broke. 'Lennox! Have you grown harvest ears?' demanded the King. 'I should have thought it would have penetrated even your uncomprehending skull that we are about to wage *war* on England. I can hardly go prancing down to Richmond to court the Princess Margaret, with a lute in one hand and a dagger in the other, ready to plunge into her father's heart!'

Lennox winced. The lords fell silent. The King arose.

'I am surprised,' he went on, his tone edged with ice, 'since you have all clearly devoted a great deal of time to the matter of my matrimonial affairs, that none of you seem to have considered the wisdom of choosing a *Scottish* Queen for Scotland.'

He left them choked with dismay, and went to seek fresh air, solace, and Margaret Drummond. He climbed first up to the rampart wall that crested the jagged slate grey cliff, the impenetrable rock of Stirling upon which the castle was built. Margaret often sat there with her sketch board, attempting to capture in charcoal the elusive patterns of the clouds as they drifted over the far hills, casting gigantic shadows on the sun-soaked plain below.

But today, instead of Margaret, there were four soldiers throwing dice on a worn hollow of the castle wall. They snapped to attention as the King approached, and he paused, insisting that they finish their game. At last James was unable to resist trying his luck. He rolled the dice, lost, and cheerfully flung the men some coins before strolling on down the path that led to the Knot Garden.

There he found Margaret. Enclosed by the formal, clipped hedges of box and yew, Margaret sat surrounded by her ladies, the ambitious young men of the Court, and the new Spanish ambassador, Don Pedro de Ayala. James hesitated for a moment, taking pleasure in the scene: his elegant black-haired mistress, exquisitely framed under an arch of deep pink roses . . . and the gay colours of the ladies' dresses, rivalled only by the flamboyance of Ayala's crimson shot-silk doublet. But Kings are never allowed to remain peacefully unnoticed for long. Within seconds of James' arrival the commotion and curt-seying began, until James was seated in the single wicker chair, with his Court fluttering around him like butterflies in the warm August sun.

James, his temper restored after a few laughing words with Margaret, called for his favourite falcon to be brought while he talked to Ayala. He was glad to see the Spaniard. After the first two ambassadors had been hurriedly withdrawn, along with the offer of the Infanta's hand, James had antici-pated with dread Ferdinand and Isabella's next offering to-wards Scottish-Spanish *détente*.

He had been pleasantly surprised. Ayala, with his proud, lithe bearing and wryly intelligent face had proved a companion of considerable merit. James gathered that Margaret shared his liking for the ambassador, taking joy in his wickedly perceptive comments about this fractious Scottish Court.

Catching sight of the young Earl of Mallaig, still smarting from his undignified dismissal from the King's bedchamber at Falkland, Ayala had likened his thick brooding brows to clumps of sedges on the mire. Margaret had laughed out loud. Mallaig, though out of earshot, had sensed that he was the target of their amusement, and flushed poppy red under his downy black beard.

James, his hooded falcon perched on his arm, was conversing in faultless Spanish with Ayala about the ambassador's mission to Scotland. It was a subject both men were reluctant to pursue, as Ayala had been sent to try to persuade Scotland to abandon her support of the English Pretender, Perkin Warbeck.

'The problem is,' Ayala explained diffidently to James, 'that the hand of Princess Katharine of Spain has been promised in marriage to Prince Arthur, the elder son of Henry Tudor. Naturally, King Ferdinand would not wish to see this marriage threatened by a Pretender usurping the English throne.'

'Naturally,' echoed James drily. 'I can see that from your point of view it would be most inconvenient for Perkin to claim the crown. As he is already married, it would mean your Spanish princess finding herself thrown back into the market place. Most demeaning.'

He glanced across the garden where sat his lovely Margaret, her graceful head bent over her embroidery. Ayala followed his gaze and shrugged. 'Ah, what does it matter? In the end, you will do what you want to do. I have said what I was told to say. They can ask no more. Besides, why haggle over such trivialities when there are more important matters to discuss.'

He stroked the sleek feathers of the bird on James' gloved

wrist. 'Tell me, is it true that you paid a hundred and eighty nine pounds for this falcon?'

Two hundred candles illuminated the feast in the Great Hall that night. Margaret Drummond, now openly acknowledged first lady of the Court, sat ankle deep in rose petals at the King's right hand on the royal dais. James fed her by hand the choicest pieces of pheasant in red wine, roast swan and sugar frosted date pastries. He held his cup steady at her lips for her to drink the sweet malmsey wine, while the fiddlers in the gallery played solely the tunes she had chosen. The banquet over, James took up his lute and sang to her. He chose romantic verses from the French poems of the *Chansons de Geste* and, to the delight of Ayala, the lyrical *Cantar del mio Cid*.

As the haunting melodies of the bitter sweet songs lingered in the perfumed air, not everyone sat as rapt as Margaret Drummond.

'Ridiculous,' spluttered the Earl of Mallaig, his beard matted with food and wine. 'Setting themselves up as some sort of latter day Arthur and Guinevere.'

'Is that so very terrible?' enquired Ayala, resplendent in leaf green watered silk.

The young Earl wiped his mouth, regarding the shimmering figure of the Spanish Ambassador with disbelief. 'God's teeth, Ayala!' he said thickly. 'This is 1496, not the dark ages. It's the New World people like your man Columbus are seeking now. Not the bloody Holy Grail.'

Ayala moved aside as Mallaig slumped drunkenly across the table, scattering a dish of sugared almonds. Listening to snatches of gossip from the sabre tongued ladies of the Court, Ayala sensed that the edge of their jealousy towards Margaret Drummond had been blunted by relief: now she was patently mistress of the King, it was tacitly assumed that she could never be Queen. In Scotland, Ayala gathered, a woman was either one thing or the other.

As Lady Drummond had predicted, Margaret was enjoying her new elevated position in Court society. Her life with James had fallen into a most agreeable pattern. Together they rode, read, sang, danced and made love. But however much James insisted that he wanted her with him every moment of the day and night, Margaret was careful never to take advantage of her influence over him. While the King presided over Council meetings, the Edinburgh Assizes and meetings with foreign embassies, Margaret tactfully kept to her own apartments. As the King's mistress, she had neither the right, she felt, nor the desire to participate in affairs of state. Instead, she busied herself with drawings and embroidery until the King came to find her, to show her his new white courser, to play skittles or take her hawking.

Hawking was the only form of hunting Margaret was able to tolerate. It consoled her that the herons and bitterns flapping across the sky were used merely as quarry for the chase. The falcons were never allowed to kill their prey.

This was how Margaret loved James best. Out on the moors, freed from the cloistered atmosphere of the Court, his eyes alight with expectation as he unleashed the falcons ... the air filled with the jingle of their bells, the furious, swift flurry of their flight ... then James, the wind in his face, racing headlong after the birds across a plain ridged with firs and starred with tufts of white bogcotton. She had tried to sketch James with his beloved falcons, but he would never stand still long enough for her to complete the picture.

Her days at Stirling were proving a far cry from the sedate, uneventful life she had led at Drummond Castle.

'If I were at home now,' she confided to Ayala that evening, when the King had laid down his lute, 'I'd be sitting dutifully with my sisters, listening to my father complaining about the hot weather, the price he'd had to pay for that new bull and how those smugglers got away with twelve casks of his fine Rhine wine.'

'And your mother?' asked Ayala. 'What would she be doing?'

Margaret's eyes danced. 'Moaning that my father wasn't listening to her.'

Ayala laughed, and excused himself to play backgammon with the King. From her seat on the dais, Margaret surveyed the rich assembly representing the most influential families in the land. They were all here, the Montroses, the Homes, the Bothwells, the Douglases, the Gordons. Names engraved deep on the soul of Scotland. Though not, Margaret thought acidly, as Lady Lennox sidled into the seat beside her, carved always with pride.

'I've been talking to the King's astrologer,' Lady Lennox confided. 'He's that strange looking man watching the jugglers.' The long nose wrinkled. 'Really, such odd clothes. I'm surprised the King allows it.'

The 'odd clothes', Margaret recognised, were a flowing rough wool skirt and plaid mantle – the proud traditional dress of the Highlander.

'And what lucky sign were you born under, Lady Lennox?' Cancer, clearly.

'Oh my dear, I wouldn't dream of troubling him with my boring life,' fluttered Lady Lennox. 'Now *you* are far more interesting. Tell me, I asked him, will the Lady Margaret marry, and have children, and live a long and happy life? That's a fairly easy question I should have thought. But guess what he told me?'

To mind your own business. 'I cannot imagine.'

Lady Lennox leaned forward, and hissed, 'He merely said, "The Lady Margaret will reach the goal of her desires." Just that. No more. I offered him a gold piece, but he wouldn't tell me even the initials of the man you will marry.'

'I'm not surprised,' said Margaret. 'The work of astrologers, Lady Lennox, is to prepare intricate charts incorporating the signs, good or ill, that prevail at your birth. They do not purport to tell fortunes like gipsies at the fair.' Margaret, unruffled, bit delicately into a candied borage flower. 'As for my immediate future, I can confidently predict that I shall shortly have to rescue the King from the backgammon table before he hands the Spanish Ambassador a promissory note for the Scottish crown jewels.'

The smooth brow and amused amber eyes were deceptive. Not by the flicker of an eyelash would Margaret Drummond allow herself to reveal her fury with Lady Lennox. For the first time, Margaret realised the vulnerability of her position. If she were Queen, Lady Lennox would never have dared to bribe the astrologer and then report such an impertinent conversation. *If she were Queen*. For a moment, Margaret allowed herself to dwell on what might have been ... what still could be. Then, firmly closing the shutters on a world that she had long ago decided could never be hers, she stepped down from the rose-strewn dais to join the King.

Despite losing heavily to Ayala at backgammon, James was in good spirits. Ayala rose as Margaret approached, his shrewd dark eyes noticing her pallor.

'Come my lady,' he said, taking her arm, 'sit here. We are trying to persuade the King to tell us more about his most unusual ambassador to the King of Denmark.' Margaret joined gratefully in the shouts of laughter.

James, enjoying himself, swept aside the carved pieces on the polished walnut and yew of the backgammon table.

'I sent the ambassador,' he began, 'with a letter of introduction from His Grace the King of Scotland to the most Sovereign King of Denmark. The letter stated that the bearer was an Egyptian Prince and was to be accorded all the civilities due to a person of that rank. The Danish King just couldn't do enough. He turned his entire Court upside down. There were banquets, hunting parties and jousts. He recruited Venetian rope dancers and even some Russian dancing bears. Only when one of the bears trod on the ambassador's jewelled foot did the truth come out ... with a vengeance. The poor fellow screamed and let out a stream of most unEgyptian oaths that exposed him as the poor Glasgow gipsy whom he was.'

As the Court exploded into laughter, James smiled ruefully at the memory. 'The Danish King paid me back. He sent home my "ambassador" along with a shipload of Scottish pirates whom he said had been captured in Danish waters. He'd be pleased, he said, to receive their heads after I'd executed them. He never got them, of course. I sent him a barrel of Scotch herrings in lieu.'

'I gather the King of Denmark enjoyed your joke – and the herrings,' said Bishop Elphinstone. 'He is a civilised man. Apparently he is most impressed with your new law, Sire, making education compulsory for the sons of our knights and gentlemen.'

James smiled wrily, 'Unfortunately, it seems the new law has come too late to benefit the knights themselves. My lord Lennox, here, evidently has great difficulty remembering for two minutes at a time that we are about to wage war on England.'

Having lost at backgammon the King, Ayala realised, was about to indulge in a spot of good-natured Lennox baiting. Regrettably, Lennox possessed neither the wit, humour nor sound sense to parry the King's verbal thrusts. But before the King could impart the next blow, Bishop Elphinstone interposed smoothly,

'About the war, Sire. Perkin Warbeck has asked me to raise with you the matter of funds. He says he needs –'

A disturbance at the end of the Hall interrupted the Bishop. Two servants appeared at the main door, leading a roughly dressed man whose agonising shrieks aroused even the Earl of Mallaig from his drunken slumber.

'It's Sam Bollow, the Edinburgh armourer,' Bell-the-Cat informed the King.

'He has toothache, Sire,' said the servant.

'So I gather,' replied James, reeling from the pungent smell of oil of cloves dribbling from the hapless armourer's mouth. 'Bring my instrument,' he instructed the servant.

Ayala was trying to imagine such a drama being enacted within the confines of the Court of Spain. Impossible to contemplate the hauteur, the incredulity frosting the imperial faces of Ferdinand and Isabella at the sight of a common armourer bursting into the glittering Hall. To complain not of famine, or pillage or murder. But toothache.

The King laughed at Ayala's astounded expression. 'I'm afraid aching teeth take precedence over ambassadors and bishops in this Court, my friend. I must confess I take considerable pride in my reputation as an amateur surgeon. The

44

Court physicians know I'm interested in medicine and often seek my advice on difficult cases. My people, too, understand that they are free to come to me when they are in pain. No one is ever turned away. Though I suspect they only seek my help as a last resort.'

Last resort was right, thought Sam, reflecting bitterly that it was Bella Kyle who had finally driven him to seek aid from the King. When the barber-surgeon's leeches had failed to alleviate his pain, Bella suggested an old Highland remedy. She would, she said, put a dead man's finger in his mouth, and chase him all the way to the graveyard. By the time Sam tripped over the first tombstone, Bella had promised, he would have forgotten all about his toothache.

Sam had scrambled onto his horse and set off in a panic for Stirling. Barbarous, Highland bitch. And to think he'd actually offered to marry her. God knows what she would have prescribed for the pain in his groin.

James took the pair of silver pliers, a smaller version of the type used to extract nails from horseshoes and, urging Sam to be brave, ordered:

'Open your mouth, my friend. I shall be quick.'

A turn of the royal wrist, a moan from Sam, and the drama was over. James triumphantly held up the tooth for all the Court to see.

Sam stuffed a piece of rag in his mouth and, holding his jaw, stuttered incoherent thanks. Margaret Drummond whispered in the King's ear, and he nodded.

'Take him to the kitchens,' he told the servants. 'Make sure he doesn't leave until the blood has stopped flowing and he's had a jug of ale to restore his spirits.'

The incident offered but a brief respite from the talk of war. Margaret listened intently as Angus cast doubts on the credibility of the Pretender. The fighting men of Scotland, he asserted, had no love for Warbeck and no faith in his cause, but they were loyal to their King. If the King proclaimed that the Pretender's claim was legitimate, then their misgivings would be allayed. They would fight. The Scots, thundered Angus, had always been a nation ready to defend a principle.

Margaret listened with mixed feelings as James stoutly upheld the Pretender's claims. She knew that he himself was prey to doubts. He had thought long and hard before sending his people to battle; he was not certain that Warbeck's cause was as just as the young man claimed. But James had given the Pretender his word, and he would not go back on it. Right or wrong, the Scots were committed.

War was declared on England in September. As the Scottish army massed on the Burgh Moor of Edinburgh, ready for their long march south, their women barred and bolted the doors of their crofts or castles, and waited.

As Margaret Drummond sat alone on the ramparts of Stirling Castle, her thoughts were drawn to another Margaret. A child, still too busy playing with her toys in Richmond Palace to pay much attention to her father's latest war. Her brothers would be far more interested. One day one of them would be King of England himself, waging war on his own account. Yet Margaret Drummond realised that for Margaret Tudor, the stamp of soldiers outside the palace, the talk of strategy and the shouts of command meant nothing more than an irritating commotion beyond her nursery door. Her supper might arrive a little late, borne by an unusually harassed maid, but otherwise she would remain in ignorance of the fearful threat of the Scots pouring over the border.

It was ironical, thought Margaret Drummond, that Margaret Tudor could not know how, in a far distant land, a woman she had never met recognised her with chilling certainty as an innocent, though dangerous, hostage to fortune. For every instinct warned Margaret Drummond: if Scotland lost this war, then the little princess playing happy families with her dolls would unwittingly have won herself a husband, a king, a crown and a country.

Five

And loud the warden's war-note rang,
Oh! 'Wha dar meddle with me?'
Battle-cry of the Borderers

'Cheer up, Bella. It'll be over in a fortnight.'

Bella smiled grimly at Robert as he and Tom saddled the horses that would take them to join the Scottish forces gathering on Edinburgh Moor.

'Men have been saying that about wars since time began,' she said. 'I wish you would not go.'

Tom pretended to check the provision packs. He had learnt the hard way not to intervene between this high spirited brother and sister. Apart from the sea green eyes and the determined set of the chin, they were little alike to look at, thought Tom, surveying the red head and the gold. But they shared the same capacity for loyalty, the same quick wittedness and a certain natural poise that made Tom feel clumsy, even oafish, by comparison. He'd have given a week's pay to learn the secret of that Kyle self-assurance. It would certainly take longer than the four months in which he had lodged above the saddlery.

In that time, Tom had grown closer to Robert than any other man in his life. Robert the Red had accepted his friendship wholeheartedly, drawing him into the exclusive, if raffish, circle which had made the Wild Boar tavern notorious throughout southern Scotland. Bella, brave, beautiful Bella, had remained friendly enough, but to Tom's acute distress, a little reserved, a trifle wary.

Tom had loved Bella from the first moment he had seen her in full fiery cry after Blackpatch. But, uncertain of Robert's reaction and mindful of Bella's guarded attitude towards him, he was careful to conceal his true feelings. He was

47

prepared to wait. He knew that, like a nervous filly, she would learn to trust him in time.

Meanwhile he established a bantering relationship with Bella, which pleased her and appeared to satisfy Robert, who now slipped an arm round his sister.

'Stop being selfish, Bella. Tom and I have a duty to fight for the King. You know that.'

Tom grinned his agreement. 'Besides, we want to see if our young Perkin – I beg his pardon – the nearly King of England, is as ready with his sword as he is with his tongue.'

'Oh! This war is just a game to both of you!' flared Bella, her eyes luminous. 'You see yourselves as bold brave knights riding fearlessly to a glorious battle. But from where I stand you look like reckless children, rushing into a silly, dangerous game with borrowed horses and stolen armour.'

'*Dùin do bheul!*'* hissed Robert, glancing anxiously round the crowded street. 'Would you have us face the English halberds like the rest of the common soldiers, with nothing more than faith and a thin vest between them and the Almighty?'

Bella fell silent. In her heart she could not condemn the theft. What was five hundred pounds worth of steel and leather compared with the lives of the men she loved?

'Don't worry, Bella,' Tom reassured her. 'I'll bring him home safely. And meanwhile you'll have Blackpatch to look after you.'

It was true, though even now Bella could scarcely believe it. Robert, hearing the story of the stolen pearl, had set off at once to find the one-eyed thief. What passed between them Bella never discovered. But the next day Blackpatch had sought her out, grovelling apologies, and presented her with the fine gold chain which now held the pearl safe at her throat. Since then, Blackpatch had become almost embarrassing in his devotion to Bella. He brought her presents, mended her broken spindle, and appeared, wraithlike, from the shadows to escort her whenever she was out alone after dark. Now, with Robert and Tom away at the war, Blackpatch would stand sentinel until their return.

* 'Shut your mouth!'

Robert bent from the saddle to kiss his sister. 'Take care, Bella.'

She clung to him for a moment. Then, turning to Tom, she briefly brushed her lips against the ostler's burning cheek. Her farewell blessing was brisk, to mask her tears: '*Beannachd leibh.*'*

As they sped away from the saddlery, Tom stole a backward glance, hoping to catch a glimpse of the girl with the saffron coloured hair. She had gone.

Instinctively, Bella flung herself into an orgy of housework to purge her mind of bloody thoughts of war. With holly branches she raked the soot and grime from her chimney. She scrubbed the floors and laid down fresh, sweet smelling rushes. Broom from her garden was cut and tied into neat bundles, ready to fuel the kitchen range throughout the winter. She took long walks in the September sunshine, gathering pine-cones for kindling, digging berberis root to boil for its yellow dye, and picking blue and white clary flowers to strengthen the celebration ale she would brew when Robert and Tom returned.

'They *will* come back, won't they?' she asked the bees humming in the wooden hives among the chamomile flowers at the end of her garden. Bella firmly believed in conversing with her bees. She told them everything. Back in the Highlands, Aunt Lilith had always said that bees only make honey when they are trusted with your secrets. So she gave them the thoughts she trusted to no one else, and they repaid her with generous combs of honey. Aunt Lilith, Bella recalled, had been right about most things.

She even told the bees the truth about Blackpatch's missing eye. Robert had given her the authorised version of the story to cheer her up on their last evening together.

It appeared that Blackpatch had been caught by a Borderer, making off with two of his prize calves. Instead of filleting Blackpatch on the spot, the Borderer had decided to give Blackpatch a sporting chance.

'We'll have a friendly wager,' the Borderer had informed

* 'Goodbye – a blessing on you.'

a whimpering Blackpatch. 'If you win, you go free. And if *I* win, I shall claim something tasty for my pickle jar.'

Blackpatch, resigned to a bloody duel by sword or dirk, had brightened when the rugged Borderer named his unexpected choice of weapon.

'Poor old Blackpatch didn't laugh for long, though,' Robert had grinned, 'for not till the Pope turns cartwheels is Blackpatch going to admit that he lost his eye on the turn of a card.'

Robert was proved right. The war was soon over. Less than three weeks after they had ridden forth in pride and hope, he and Tom limped back to Edinburgh, caked with mud and dried blood. They were tired, hungry and furious.

'It wasn't a war. It was a fiasco,' raged Robert, throwing his stolen armour in a clanging heap on the kitchen floor. Bella scurried to rake up the fire. Robert's livid face and Tom's brooding silence had already told her the worst.

Robert took the pot of ale she offered, and spat out his story.

They had, Bella learnt, crossed the border into the wind-swept moorlands south of the River Tweed. A hostile wilderness with, apart from the Scottish army, not a soul in sight. The English had retreated for safety inside the forbidding black stone towers of their feudal lords. These gaunt shuttered fortresses, rising like monstrous tombstones from the boggy morass, had survived a century of savage attack from the Scots borderers.

'We were determined to show them,' said Tom, 'that this was no mere border scuffle. The King ordered the cannon to be brought up, and we blasted through the outer gates of the towers.'

'All hell broke loose,' went on Robert. 'The explosion sent the women and children screaming from the tower, clutching blankets, chickens, pots and pans, anything they could lay their hands on. The cattle broke loose from their enclosures and stampeded, just as the barns went up in flames. By this time we'd abandoned our horses and were fighting hand to hand with the enemy. But what with the smoke and cannon shot, it was impossible to see if you were struggling with a hairy Englishman or a terrified sheep.'

Tom broke in grimly. 'It was a shambles. And to make matters worse, the English and Scots borderers threw down their weapons and took advantage of the confusion to start rounding up cattle. You'd think in a war they'd give up this senseless raiding and plundering of one another's land. But no, show them a stray goat and they're blind to the most glorious cause in the world. You'd have thought it was market day rather than a full scale invasion of England.'

He sniffed appreciatively as Bella ladled boiled mutton spiced with cinnamon onto wooden platters. 'God, this looks good, Bella. All we've had to eat for two days were some dingy fungus your brother insisted were mushrooms. They did a damn sight more to empty my stomach than fill it.'

Bella watched the men wolfing their food. 'What about the Pretender. Did the English rise to his support?'

'That they did not,' mumbled Robert through a mouth full of mutton. 'The English regarded him with the same horrified disbelief they reserve for a haggis. He was furious at the lack of support, and rode off in high dudgeon back to Edinburgh.'

'Leaving the King to fight his war for him,' added Tom hotly.

Bella topped up their tankards. 'I fancy we shan't be hearing much more of Mr Warbeck.'

Robert lunged viciously at the hunk of mutton. 'I've heard enough of that milksop to last a lifetime. He steals our most beautiful women, and squanders our best men. God help him if our paths cross again!'

In the privacy of his chamber at Stirling Castle, the King was giving vent to *his* displeasure with the young Pretender.

'Two days! Just two days our young warrior lasted,' he ranted to Margaret Drummond. 'He sat on the horse I'd given him, watching my gallant Scots army routing out the English from those stony black towers. And then when the whole fiasco was over, he dared to accuse me of slaughtering the English. His *very own people* he had the gall to call them.'

Margaret held his trembling hands in hers as the King went on, 'I told the arrogant young whelp, "you seem to worry yourself over what does not concern you. You have called the English your subjects, yet not one of them has offered to help in a war waged on your behalf." He was speechless. His face went as white as his shirt and without a word he turned tail and galloped back to his castle . . . the castle he borrowed from me, leaving me to make a very patchy peace with Henry Tudor.'

Margaret's delicate face was thoughtful. 'What will happen to the Pretender now? The Scots are hardly likely to throw flowers at his feet. And the English will clearly have no truck with him.'

'I neither know nor care what becomes of the upstart,' James spat. 'He's neither fish nor fowl nor good red herring. For the moment, it is enough to know that we are at peace.'

Margaret kissed him. Peace. There would be little of that for her. Not while the young Margaret Tudor was growing daily towards maturity, and her role as a Queen, a wife and a mother.

'Why so pensive?' James' slender fingers traced the much-missed outline of Margaret's face. 'It is all this talk of wars, and treachery and deceit. No more, I promise you, Margaret. We'll have music, and song, and you must tell me all your news. I want to know everything that has happened in my absence.'

Margaret Drummond lifted her fine amber eyes to his. 'I am with child,' she said.

March was traditionally a time of rejoicing for the Scots. They sang of the advent of Spring, *Lenten is come with love to toune*, and like generations before them, welcomed the start of their New Year. At the Palace of Linlithgow the ladies of the Court added the finishing touches to a tapestry almanac, their annual offering to the King. Their stitching, however, was lackadaisical, a reflection of their conviction that nothing they could give the King would compare to the gift he awaited so eagerly from Margaret Drummond.

It was at the end of March, with a gale gusting the grey waters of Linlithgow loch into rippling pleats, that Margaret Drummond's daughter was born. James was delighted. He named her, with what Lennox declared a singular lack of originality, Margaret. She was to be known, James announced, silencing the buzz of speculation, as the Lady Margaret Stewart, the daughter of the King.

For James and Margaret, those few months at Linlithgow were among the happiest of their lives. James, reliving fond childhood adventures, showed her where he had practised his archery on the bow-butts, learnt to catch perch in the loch, and lost to the Head Keeper at bowls. To James, Edinburgh was the royal capital, Falkland an impressive state palace, and Stirling an important strategic fortress. But in Linlithgow, with its air of soft tranquillity, he found a much-needed refuge.

Margaret, too, had fallen in love with the palace. She was enchanted by the specially tinted yellow window glass James had imported from Holland. Even on the greyest days it conveyed a welcome illusion of sunlight through the elegant lancet casements, and her abiding memories of the palace were to be of gracious, golden rooms where the sun was ever shining.

With the safe delivery of her daughter, Margaret was able to bask, too, for a time in the warmth of the Court's approval. Caught up in the excitement of a royal birth, the Scottish nobility channelled their peevish energy into vying for the honour of admittance to the King's Presence Chamber, to pay homage to Margaret and her infant daughter.

Bella, accompanied by Tom, was one of the many common folk who journeyed to Linlithgow that spring to congratulate their popular King and his beautiful mistress.

'What do you think of it?' asked Tom, setting Bella down from his horse onto the fresh young grass within the palace wall. 'Not as imposing as Edinburgh Castle, I admit. But not as forbidding either, is it?'

Bella's eyes brightened as she gazed for the first time on the sandstone palace, with its gabled towers and carved buttresses mirrored in the placid waters of the loch below. Her voice was distant. 'It reminds me of Kinleven.'

Tethering his horse, Tom followed Bella up the grassy bank circling the palace. 'What's Kinleven?'

'In the village where I grew up,' Bella told him, 'if you climbed the highest hill you could see two castles standing at either end of a sweeping bay. One was built of bluish-green slate. There was something evil about that castle. I always think of it lashed with rain and sea spray in a storm, when it seemed as cruel and full of menace as the sky. But if you looked the other way, right to the end of a stretch of silver sand, you could see the other castle. Like Linlithgow, it was built of sandstone, and seemed to radiate light and warmth, and a kind of mellow brilliance. That was Kinleven.'

'Who lived there?' asked Tom.

'Just a keeper and a handful of servants. Kinleven belongs to the King. But it's so far away, he seldom goes there.'

Tom felt elated. This was the first time Bella had spoken to him of her childhood. He wanted her to go on. 'Don't you miss the Highlands, Bella?'

'I miss the sea. And I miss the ceilidhs. We used to gather on winter nights in one of the crofts, and sing, and play the harp, and tell outrageous tales. I remember the men sitting mending their nets, while the women carded and knitted, and we children asked each other silly riddles.'

'Sounds fun,' said Tom wistfully, remembering his own joyless childhood scratching for food in the barren farms around Aberdeen.

Bella shook her head. 'It was a hard life too, Tom. When the gales beached the fishing boats, I remember children crying with hunger as their mothers begged from croft to croft. The fishermen could do nothing but wait for the storms to pass, their faces blackened by wasted hours spent brooding over the peat fire.'

'Will you ever go back?' asked Tom.

Bella's voice was as cold as the water of the loch. 'Never.'

Swiftly, she changed the subject. 'Are you coming into the palace with me, to see the baby?'

'Not me, Bella. I'm not one for kissing babes. A friend of mine works in the stables. I'll pay him a surprise visit. Meet me there when you're done.'

Bella joined the long good-natured line of citizens winding up the dank turnpike stair which led to the Presence Chamber. It was dusk when, hours later, the guards motioned Bella to enter. As she stepped forward, a wave of warmth and kindly light swept over her. Bella caught her breath. Confronting her was a magnificent stained glass window stretching the entire length of the chamber, each of its fourteen recesses illuminated by candles which cast a roseate glow on the carved and painted ceiling. Her eyes shining, Bella moved slowly across the green glazed tiles towards the fireplace, where Margaret Drummond sat with the King and her ladies, rocking a wooden crib draped with white lace.

Bella curtseyed nervously to the King, and laid a small soft bundle on Margaret Drummond's lap.

'I made a present for the baby,' she said anxiously.

Margaret Drummond bent forward to look more closely at Bella. 'We've met before. Aren't you Bella, the girl who found my pearl?'

Bella smiled at the recognition, and Margaret Drummond unfolded her gift.

'Oh, but it's exquisite!' she exclaimed, holding up the delicately crocheted shawl for the ladies of the Court to admire. 'But wherever did you find all these richly coloured wools?'

'I dyed the wool myself, my lady,' Bella explained. 'I used lichens for the scarlet yarn, sloes for the blue, heather for the green and walnut bark for the black. My aunt in the Highlands taught me how to crochet the crossed tiretaine pattern as a child.'

She thought this was hardly the place to add that the orgy of boiling and dyeing, with its accompanying pungent odour, had driven Robert and Tom to take refuge in the Wild Boar tavern, complaining that the saddlery kitchen stank higher than a whore's pallet.

She saw the King had suddenly taken an interest. '*Slàinte*, Bella!' he cried.

Automatically, Bella returned his greeting: '*Fàilte!*' adding shyly, 'I didn't know you spoke the Gaelic, Sire.'

'I believe a King should speak the language of his people,' James told her. He took the brightly coloured shawl from Margaret and fingered it admiringly. 'You appear to have gone to a great deal of trouble to make a present for my daughter, Bella. To what do we owe such kindness?'

Bella's neck burned. Clearly, she could hardly admit that her fascination with the royal couple stemmed from the evening she had eavesdropped on their romantic reunion at Falkland Palace.

'It . . . it's a token of friendship,' she stammered. 'The Lady Margaret was once generous enough to give me a pearl. I wanted to give something in return.'

'Ah . . .' The King reflected for a moment, and then murmured, as if to himself,

There is no worth in mantles or furs
Nor wealth in coins, in mules or asses . . .

'. . . . *But riches lie in friends and kindred.*' Unable to stop herself, Bella took the lines on, drawing a surprised glance from Margaret Drummond.

James let out a sharp breath. 'Exactly, Bella. It occurs to me that King's daughters have plenty of attendants, and even more enemies. But very few friends.' He paused, frowning, and then leant forward and said urgently to Bella, 'If there should come a time when my little Margaret has no friends or kindred to shield her, will you be her friend? Will you promise to find her, stay with her, protect her?'

Bella stared uncomprehendingly at the King. What did he mean? How could she, a mere serving girl, presume so intimate a relationship with the daughter of a King? Surely he was aware of the gilded palisade of etiquette, protocol, title, position and privilege that divided them?

Bella felt Margaret Drummond's cool hand on hers. 'Please,' she said quietly.

For the first time Bella looked closely at the black-haired child lying in her crib. She had imagined the baby to be sleeping. Instead she was wide awake, her eyes of cornflower blue gazing up at Bella, innocent, defenceless, dependent.

'*Ma gh eallas mi sin co-gheallaidh mi e,*' Bella told the King.

He arose, and laid a grateful hand on her shoulder. '*Dia gu d'bheannachadh,*' he said softly.

'You're talking in riddles, both of you,' laughed Margaret Drummond.

James bent for a moment to look at his daughter. 'Bella says she will fulfil her promise. And I replied, God bless you.'

Bella curtseyed, and ran back to the stables, eager to blurt out to Tom her extraordinary conversation with the King. But she found him merry with drink, swapping scurrilous stories with the stable lads. Wisely, Bella elected to keep the promise she had made, like her pearl, close to her heart.

Lady Drummond, sweeping into Margaret's private apartments half an hour later, cast but a cursory glance on her new grandchild. It was not that she was being callous, or even that she had more pressing matters on her mind. But as the mother of six daughters, in an age when boy children were all important, she recognised that to the chosen woman of the King, be she Queen or mistress, sons were not merely desirable: they were paramount.

'You don't look well,' Elizabeth Drummond informed her daughter, throwing off her new ermine-lined cloak.

Margaret Drummond sat listlessly in the cushioned windowseat. Below, in the lamplit courtyard, she could see Bella surrounded by a joking crowd of stableboys. Her face tightened. 'You might show a little more interest in your granddaughter. You've hardly looked at her.'

Lady Drummond settled herself next to her daughter. 'Forgive me, Margaret. She's a delightful child. A woman's first baby is always the most beautiful, the most treasured.' She sighed. 'But your baby is a girl, and illegitimate at that. Where does that leave *you*?'

When Margaret didn't reply, Lady Drummond followed her daughter's gaze down to the courtyard, where a rapidly sobering Tom was hastily lifting Bella to the safety of his horse.

'It's no use casting cow's eyes at them, Margaret. Life is easier for the lower orders. They may marry whom they choose. But you are the King's mistress. The mother of his bastard. And for you, time is running out.'

Margaret's voice was warped with strain. 'Mother. Once and for all. I have no wish to be Queen.'

'You'll be nothing but the King's abandoned mistress if you go on like this,' snapped Lady Drummond. 'Don't you realise that once the crows of the Court have tired of cooing over your new baby, they'll be pecking at the King again to find himself a wife. Angus, Lennox and Mallaig are already sharpening their claws.' She rested her head in her hands. 'If only you'd borne a son you'd be in such a powerful position. But a *girl* . . .'

'It's not my fault, or his that I had a girl,' retorted Margaret. 'You act as if I did it deliberately.'

In a dramatic gesture, Lady Drummond flung her arms around her daughter, her amethyst rings digging into Margaret's back. 'Please listen to me. I beg you to take a mother's advice. The King is desperately in love with you. I can see it in his eyes, in his whole bearing towards you. Believe me, your hold over him has never been stronger. But it won't last. It never does. You must use your influence to make him marry you. Soon. *Now.*'

Argument, Margaret knew, was useless. She was familiar enough with the veiled aspirations of her father to realise that it was he goading her mother into such a tyrannical role. Misinterpreting Margaret's silence, Lady Drummond patted her hand as she arose.

'There's a good girl. I knew you'd see sense in the end. Even if you have left it this late. Now I must go. And I shall expect to hear some good news from you very soon.'

Close to the edge of despair, Margaret closed her eyes and leant her throbbing head against the cool yellow glass of the window. She had survived a difficult birth, an inquisitorial Court and a week of close inspection from the curious crowds who had flocked to Linlithgow. And she had, she felt, conducted herself throughout with grace, dignity and good humour. Now, suddenly, she could smile no more. Tired, overwrought, and reeling from her mother's latest onslaught, Margaret Drummond gave way at last to the tears she had held back for so long.

James found her slumped on the windowseat with her face pressed against a velvet cushion to mask the sound of her sobs. He had never seen her cry before. Alarmed, he quickly dismissed his attendants and comforted her, drying her eyes and bringing sugared wine and sweetmeats.

Margaret made no mention of her mother. Merely, 'I'm sorry ... it's just the excitement.'

James brushed the damp strands of hair from her brow, his eyes searching hers. 'No, Margaret. It's more than that. We have known each other for a long time. We can, we must be honest with each other.'

Lightly, she touched his lips with her fingers. 'There are some things best left unsaid.'

'Not between us, lovedy.' He sat beside her, holding her close. 'We must talk. Of our future. Of this wretched caprice of fortune that makes me a king, and you my mistress, and little Meg there my illegitimate daughter instead of my Princess.'

'I am happy as I am, James,' Margaret insisted wearily.

'But I am not,' declared the King. 'I would have you as my wife, Margaret. You know that.'

She nodded. 'But it is not possible. The Court, your Council and your Bishops would sleep with the Devil rather than see you marry anyone but a woman of royal birth.'

'And at one time I would have accepted their strictures,' said James softly. 'But no longer. I love you, Margaret. More than a woman, my woman, you are my life. In my heart and soul you are already my wife and Queen. And I am resolved to make the crowned heads of Europe celebrate you as such.'

She sighed. 'My lord, I deeply appreciate what you are trying to say. But you must understand and accept *my* position. I am truly happy to love you ... to be with you as ... as we are now. I want nothing more.'

'Well I want more,' said James, his voice rising. 'What use to be King if I can't exercise the pauper's right to marry whom I choose? I *will* marry you, Margaret!'

He caught the glimmer of a smile dance across her face, and the storm gathering in his eyes broke as laughter. 'You are right, Margaret. This is no time for the regal command. I meant what I said at Falkland: that I would never take you against your will. But I can, surely, hope to change your mind.' He sank gracefully before her. 'Margaret. My dearest love. I ask you, I beg you on bended knee. Will you marry me?'

Margaret Drummond looked with love and longing into the imploring eyes of the man who knelt before her. When she bent her head and kissed him, her face was wet with tears.

Six

Let us strive with all our might
To love Saint George, our Lady's knight.
                    A carol of St George

'*No?*' screamed Lady Drummond. 'The King asked you, on bended knee to marry him? And you said *no*, as if you were refusing a bowl of rennet?'

She had barely stopped berating her daughter for a month since Margaret had returned home to Perth with her baby daughter early in May. Even in her bed, to which Margaret had retired, exhausted, there was no escape from Lady Drummond's remorseless tongue.

'You didn't fool your father for one minute with all that high and mighty talk of *duty* and *not wishing to cause dissent amongst the Council.* Though I must confess it was clever of you to confront your father with your folly while he was ensconced with old Bell-the-Cat and Mallaig. With their ears yawning like pitchers he could hardly tell you what a bone-headed, meddling little bitch you really are. Do you realise what you've done? You've accomplished in one act of wanton stupidity what generations of our enemies have failed to achieve. Your father is extremely displeased . . .'

Later that evening, Sybilla Drummond crept softly into Margaret's room. She found her sister alone, singing a sad, lilting song to her baby:

I loved myself a falcon through a year's long days.
When he was safely tamed to follow all my ways
And his plumage shone golden, painted by my hand,
With powerful wingbeats rising, he sought another land.

Since then I've often seen him, soaring in fair flight
For on his feet my silken jesses still shine bright

And his plumage gleams with scarlet and with gold.
May God grace lovers and reunite them as of old.

Sybilla let out a long sigh. 'Don't be so forlorn, Meg.'

'But I miss him so.'

Sybilla's childish face puckered. 'Then why did you leave him? He would never have sent you away.'

'No,' Margaret agreed. 'That is why I chose to leave. I knew that while I was with him he would never summon the courage to accept the Queen whom the Council will urge upon him: Margaret Tudor. The hostile atmosphere between the King and the Court was thicker than curdled milk. The King knew what should be done, but in the end, I realised that I was the only person capable of taking action. Which is why I am here.'

The shadows under Margaret's eyes deepened as she recalled that last aching night with James ... how they clung together in a fever of despair, waiting hopelessly for the dawn that would tear them apart.

Sybilla said, with the careless pragmatism of youth: 'Oh Meg, don't be disheartened. Father will find you another husband. The Earl of Mallaig has called at the castle twice since —'

'No!' Margaret's amber eyes flashed. 'For the King, there will be other women. But for me there will be no other man.' She gazed fondly on the baby asleep in her crib. 'One thing at least I shall ensure, Sybilla. When this little daughter of the King is old enough, she shall marry for love, or not at all.'

Sybilla regarded her sister uneasily. 'Love! How many women in our position can marry for love? We are desired for our lands, our titles, our dowries. You don't seem to realise your unique position, Margaret. It isn't given to most of us to win the heart of a King.'

'Thank heavens it's hardly likely to happen to my little Meg,' said Margaret. 'And I fancy there's no man more unattainable, or unsuitable she could fall in love with than a King. But when the time comes and the young men of Scotland come to court her the choice shall be hers. She will never be forced to marry against her will.'

'I think motherhood has addled your brain,' muttered Sybilla. 'The only women I know who are allowed the luxury of marrying for love are the castle serving girls.'

Margaret tucked the multi-coloured shawl securely round her daughter. On its deckled edge she had embroidered, in fine gold thread, her own personal motto: *Mérite*. Sybilla was right, of course. She remembered the serving girl who had made the shawl – what was her name ... Bella – galloping away into the night with the young man on his horse. It was absurd to envy the girl, Margaret realised. Her cloak had been threadbare, her hands chapped and she probably led a wretched life, while she, the Lady Margaret Drummond, was wealthy, richly dressed and well fed. All the same, as she picked up her lute and sang again of her lost falcon, Margaret could not help but reflect that there was more than one kind of poverty.

'Jump in the loch?' demanded Bella. 'Are you quite mad, Robert?'

Robert ignored her question, his lean face creased with laughter. Bella, crouching by the light of a fitful moon in the reeds of Edinburgh's Nor' loch, was not amused.

It had taken all Robert's considerable powers of persuasion to make her agree to his crazy plan in the first place. But, her mouth tinder dry with fear, she had done as he asked, and brought the horses down to the deserted lochside at midnight. Meanwhile Robert, Tom, Sam and Blackpatch had ridden to Leith dock, to plunder a secret supply of arms the French had sent to Perkin Warbeck. With the muzzled horses securely tethered, Bella had stood knee-deep in mud among the rushes, holding aloft a lamp to guide the four men and their boatloads of stolen swords to the safety of the shore.

Now the men worked feverishly unloading the boats while Robert argued with his sister.

'It's not my fault that several things went wrong tonight. How was I to know that Warbeck himself would be at Leith to take the arms off the ship? It's as well for us that he had only a handful of men and not a whole army. I suspect he's having an uphill task drumming up support amongst our kin-folk after that border fiasco. But it meant Tom had to waste precious time stampeding their horses.'

Bella nodded grudgingly, shivering in the chill wind that sliced across the water. 'So Warbeck couldn't ride back along the Leith Road and cut you off on this side of the loch?'

'Exactly.' Robert reached into the boat and shoved a long, heavy package along the muddy bank to Sam. 'As if that wasn't enough, once we were on the ship our armourer friend here was so overwhelmed by the quality of Milanese work-manship, that he frittered away precious minutes just stand-ing *admiring* the bloody swords.'

Bella sensed Sam Bollow's prickle of embarrassment. 'Do you think they recognised us, Robert?' he asked, heaving the package to Blackpatch, who was loading the horses.

Robert said grimly, 'I think our pretty friend Warbeck would know us again. We gave him something to remember us by all right! But he's got to catch us first. *And* in possession of the goods.'

'He's having a damned good try,' grunted Blackpatch. 'I can see lights coming this way across the water.'

They stared anxiously across the loch, where two torchlit boats were approaching at furious speed. 'Right.' Robert's voice was urgent. 'Are the horses loaded?'

'Buckling at the knees,' muttered Sam.

'Where are you going to hide the swords?' asked Bella. 'The first place they'll look will be Sam's –'

'It's taken care of,' said Robert shortly. He gripped her arm. 'What we need now is a diversion to give us time to get clear away.'

Bella's heart sank. 'Robert, I thought you were joking about me jumping into the loch.'

'You won't come to any harm. The water's lovely,' he assured her. 'You're a strong swimmer. All you have to do is make your way up to the place where you usually do your washing. Tom is waiting to pick you up there. With any luck, Warbeck will spot you and fall in the water with shock.'

Bella rebelled. 'Why me? Why can't Blackpatch do it? He needs a bath.'

'I can't swim,' said Blackpatch hastily.

'Besides, he's not as pretty as you,' laughed Robert. 'The object of the exercise is to play on Perkin's renowned weakness for a beautiful woman.'

Bella was justifiably suspicious of any compliment coming from her brother. 'And how am I supposed to swim in all these clothes? I'll sink faster than a cat in a weighted sack.'

'I was not proposing,' said Robert sweetly, 'that you should plunge in the loch fully dressed. Clearly, for your own safety and the added rapture of Mr Warbeck, it would make sense if you wore as little as possible.'

'*Mallachd!*' The curse died on Bella's lips as she gazed across the water at the fast approaching boats. They were near enough now for her to recognise Warbeck, torch in hand, goading on his men. She glared at the grinning trio standing by the loaded horses, awaiting her answer.

'Well turn round then, the lot of you,' she snapped, tugging at the fastenings of her dress.

In less than a minute a bundle of cambric hit Robert squarely on the back of his head. He shoved the dress into his saddle-bag, and glanced sideways into the reeds, where his sister, wearing only the briefest of shifts, her golden hair streaming round her shoulders, was wading stoically into the murky water of the loch.

The hard lines of his face softened. 'Thanks, Bella,' he called quietly. 'Good luck.'

'Think nothing of it,' she muttered through chattering teeth as the water lapped icily around her thighs. 'I always did fancy myself as Aphrodite.'

Robert whirled round on the two men beside him. 'Blackpatch, if you don't stop staring at my sister I'll make her a present of another gold chain . . . with your one remaining eye strung on it.'

Blackpatch hurriedly spurred his horse. 'I wasn't . . . it just occurred to me that Warbeck might catch her. What then?'

'He won't,' grunted Robert. 'The only toys Bella had as

a child were the fish she chased in the western sea. I'll back her to leave Warbeck and his men floundering. If she doesn't,' he drew out one of the finely worked Milanese swords and slashed at an imaginary foe, 'we might have cause to use these sooner than we anticipated!'

That night marked Perkin Warbeck's final disenchantment with the Scots. A year later, pacing the Tower of London as he waited for Henry Tudor to sign his death warrant, Perkin was to acknowledge that soggy pantomime on the Nor' loch as the first leg of his nightmare journey to the gallows. Everything had gone wrong. The swords he planned to use to hack his way to the throne of England had been pirated by a gang of Scottish cut-throats. His horses had been unbridled and set loose, forcing him to pay that villain of a ferryman a small fortune for the hire of two boats. Even then, he would have caught the thieves if it hadn't been for that yellow haired mermaid suddenly rising up from the muddy waters of the loch.

His men, who until then had been rowing with determined efficiency, were plunged into disarray at the sight of the near naked girl. Warbeck too, to his undying shame, fell victim to her charms. At the very moment when he should have been rallying his men, he found himself distracted, confused, enchanted. A careless second or two had been enough. The boats collided, oars floated away, and discipline disintegrated as the men began berating one another, knocking the torches into the loch in their fury.

Before the flames died, there was a last tantalising glimpse of white limbs and glittering hair. Then darkness. Shout and rage as he might, Warbeck saw no more of the mysterious Aphrodite. What he could see, all too clearly, was that his hopes, his plans, his dreams were – like his boats – hopelessly scuttled.

Bella was swimming underwater to avoid the debris of oars and spent torches littering the surface. When at last she came up for air, she shook the water from her eyes and looked back on the shadowy outlines of Warbeck's bedraggled fleet adrift in the reeds. The Pretender's voice echoed loudly across the water, casting quite unwarranted aspersions on the birthright of a certain man with red hair whom, nevertheless, he seemed anxious to meet again.

Bella grinned, and struck out towards the stony inlet where, on warm summer days, she did her washing. There was no sign of Tom. No light, no token, nothing at all to guide her. She swore as she stubbed a bare toe on the shingle before clambering on all fours across the smooth rocks beyond the waterline. As she stood upright, dripping and wary, a dark shadow moved, a cloak enveloped her and Tom's welcome voice was sounding, faint and far away, in her waterlogged ear.

'We must hurry. When they fail to catch Robert, Warbeck will come looking for you. I know a good hiding place.'

He took her hand and they ran back into the town, swerving down paths and lanes and passages until they reached a covered yard. In one corner, bathed in watery moonlight, stood an oxcart, brimful with rushes. Tom pushed the breathless Bella deep into the cart, burrowed in beside her and pulled the rushes over them until they were completely covered.

'Why can't I just go home?' Bella complained.

'You can, later. When Admiral Warbeck and his jolly sailors have given up the chase. They'll never think of looking here.'

'How did you know where to come?'

'I helped to cut the rushes this afternoon,' said Tom. 'The ostlers are mounting a Moses pageant for the Corpus Christi parade tomorrow. The Saddlers Guild are doing the wicked kings. Robert is going to be Herod.'

'Type cast again,' sniffed Bella. 'He —'

Tom's rough hand closed over her mouth. His sharp ears had picked up before Bella's could the sound of a man's firm tread on the cobbled yard. He flung himself on top of her. Their hearts beat in wild syncopation as they heard the steps drawing steadily nearer ... then stop. Silence. For a minute Bella and Tom lay, scarcely breathing, in the dark womb of the rushes. The one sound, when it came, seemed as loud as a whipcrack: Bella hiccuped. Instantly, the rushes were torn apart and the blazing light of a lamp swept over them.

Bella's nervous hiccups received a shock cure as, peering round Tom's shoulder, she met the anguished eyes of her confessor. 'Father Duncan!'

The man in the long coarse woollen robe regarded the bare-limbed girl and the tousled young man with a mixture of surprise and pious dismay.

'I heard voices,' he said severely, 'and assumed someone was trying to tamper with the Moses cart. I never dreamt that I should discover you lying in sin, Bella. And among the blessed rushes, too! God himself may be forgiving. But,' he held the lamp nearer and peered closely at Tom, 'I cannot vouchsafe the merciful instincts of your quick-tempered brother, my girl.'

Bella sat up, hastily pulling the cloak tight around her damp shift. 'Father Duncan, I can explain. It's not ... we weren't...'

The breath was squeezed out of her by the full weight of Tom's warning arm pressing on her stomach.

'There is no sin, Father,' Tom said clearly. 'Let me reassure you. Mistress Kyle and myself are handfasted.'

Bella blushed rose red at the lie. Handfasted indeed! Thank heavens for the dark. Father Duncan would have no choice but to recognise the convenient traditional custom which enabled a man and woman to share bed and board for a year while deciding if they were suited for marriage. If they then chose not to marry, but went their separate ways, the handfasting left no stigma on the woman, and any child she conceived was declared legitimate.

Father Duncan's eyes bored into Bella. 'Is this true, Bella? You are handfasted to this man?'

Bella abandoned her childish dreams of heaven, and embraced the fires of purgatory. 'Yes, Father.'

'Then you have my blessing,' said the priest, adding blandly, 'I must seek out your brother first thing in the morning, and congratulate him on finding so resourceful a groom for his little sister.'

His fading footsteps rang like a death knell on the cobbles. Tom mopped his brow. 'I'm sorry. It seemed the best way to put the old fox off the scent.' When Bella made no reply, he went on, 'Of course, there's no question of me keeping you to the letter of our, er, agreement. We can be handfasted in name only, just for appearances. After a year, you'll be free.'

Still no word, no gesture from the woman at his side. Yet Tom could have sworn she was holding her breath. He reached out and touched her still wet hair. 'I want you to know, Bella. I love you. More than anything on this earth I want to marry you.' Silence. 'Bella?'

Again, Bella blessed the shadow of night that veiled her face, masking the conflict that consumed her. She loved him. Of course she loved him, this handsome chestnut-haired man who for twelve aching months had made her blood pound with desire. She had always imagined that when she fell in love, revealing the truth about herself would be easy, or even un-necessary, with a brother like Robert to act as her spokesman. But now, tonight of all nights, Robert wasn't here. She would have to tell Tom herself. And in telling him, she realised with a sick chill of terror, she would risk losing him.

'Tom, I *do* love you.' The words came out in a rush. Yet even as his hands gripped her shoulders, she forced herself to twist away from the kiss she longed for. 'But there's some-thing you must know.' She kept her head turned away from him. 'I'm ... I'm not a virgin.'

Tom said nothing, his mind skeined with conflicting emo-tions. He was, essentially, a practical man. Of all the women he could have chosen to marry in Edinburgh, he would have expected less than a handful to be virgins. But Bella ...

His question, when at last it came, was not the one Bella had anticipated.

'Does Robert know?'

Bella almost laughed with relief. Dear Tom. How she had underestimated him. And how typical, now she thought about it, that his reaction should be not one of shock, or resentment, but curiosity.

'Yes,' she said. 'Robert knows.'

Tom's voice was quite deliberately detached. They might have been discussing the theft of a pot of honey from Bella's bees.

'It doesn't make any difference to us, Bella. Not to the way I feel. But ... do you want to tell me about it? You don't have to.'

She would have told him everything if he had insisted. For him, she would have relived what the kindly mists of time had contrived to obscure. Instead, she whispered: 'No. I don't want to talk about it. Except ... it wasn't by my wish.'

Understanding raged through Tom. It explained so much. Bella's reserve. Robert's steely surveillance. And when at last Tom kissed Bella, his passion was tempered with an infinite, loving tenderness.

'I'll make it up to you, Bella,' he promised.

Edinburgh rang the next day with the sound of tambours, flutes, fiddles and pipes as the Corpus Christi procession wound noisily up the High Street towards the Castle. It was led by the Guild of Hammermen. In full armour, and with drums beating, they bore the proud Blue Blanket, the standard of the Incorporated Trades of Edinburgh, woven with its legend *Fear God and Honour the King*. Crowds milled good naturedly by the roadside and thronged the balconies, applauding the Glover's Resurrection float, and the Goldsmith's Nativity. Only Father Duncan closed his eyes in sorrow at the Armourer's offering, with a bright-eyed Bella enthroned as the centrepiece in the Coronation of the Virgin.

Everyone was in good spirits. Everyone, that is, except Perkin Warbeck. He stood, hollow-eyed and sullen, with the King's entourage up at the Castle, scorned by the monarch and ignored by the Court. The amusement, the laughing whisper that ran round Edinburgh that day failed, strangely, to reach Warbeck. But every other man, woman and child of

70

the city knew within hours about the consignment of stolen swords, and where they were hidden.

Had Warbeck been glaring less intently at the red-haired Herod in the Saddler's pageant, he might have noticed something gleamingly familiar about the burnished sword held aloft by the Tailor's St George – and understood the special cheer the crowd reserved for the scarlet and gold dragon he rode.

Robert, listening to the rattling of the swords in the dragon's hollow belly, bared his teeth in a Herod-like smile at the gloomy Warbeck as the procession circled the Castle courtyard. The King ordered refreshments to be brought out and the citizens' good humour increased as the rumour spread that James had furnished Warbeck with a 'ship and a boot up the arse'. He was to depart by July at the latest ... and the name of his ship was the *Cuckoo*.

Tom, however, was in no mood for jesting. Clad in a knight's regalia, he marched beside the oxcart of rushes carrying the infant Moses, muttering anxiously to himself. He had been rehearsing opening gambits ever since his beautiful Bella had stirred in his arms in the cart that morning, opened her sea green eyes and enquired, 'Whatever is my dear brother going to say?'

Tom waited until Robert had consumed enough of the King's ale to make him expansive without being explosive, before embarking on his man to man talk. Robert, he reasoned, could hardly attack him in full view of the King and his Court ... could he?

'Robert. About Bella. I think you should know ... I hope you don't mind ... Well, the fact is, we're handfasted.'

He watched anxiously as Robert turned to gaze for a long moment at a radiant Virgin Mary stuffing her sacred mouth with currant buns. Iron fingers clasped his shoulders. He braced himself.

'What took you so long?' laughed Herod, his gaudy paper crown tipping crazily over one mocking aquamarine eye.

71

Seven

When I see hir forrow me,
that is fulfillit of all bounte,
and I behald hir colour cleir,
hir hair, that to fine gold is feir,
hir cheke, hir chin, her middle small,
hir fare-hede and her fassoun all,
I am sa movit throw that sicht
that I have nouther strenth nor micht
to heir, to see, na yit to fele.
As man suld de, this wait I wele,
thus am I staid before that fre,
for hir that all my lufe suld be.

The Buik of Alexander

'I promise to be faithful, in mind and body and spirit, to the end of my days,' Bella assured an inscrutable Father Duncan and a stiff-backed Tom.

They had not waited the full year from their handfasting, for Bella was anxious to be married in April, on her seventeenth birthday. She gripped Tom's hand hard, fearful that she might faint, as the priest anointed them with holy water and declared them man and wife. The cause of her breathlessness was not so much the excitement of the day, as the tight fit of her magnificent blue silk wedding dress.

Robert, insistent that his sister should marry in style, had disappeared for three days, returning in triumph with a dress of shimmering harebell blue silk – from whence, Bella neither knew nor, at that moment, cared. She did not need to try it on to realise that it had been made for a woman anatomically far less well endowed than herself. A woman of quality, too. For the law laid down that the cloth worn by common folk must not cost more than forty pence per yard, ensuring that the expensive imported velvets, silks and satins were strictly reserved for the nobility.

An acquisition even more intriguing than the dress was the delicate white lace petticoat presented with a flourish by Robert.

Bella had never before seen anything so fine, so French, so flagrantly feminine.

'I didn't steal it,' said Robert, forestalling Bella's protests. 'I promise you it was given ... er ... very freely.'

At least, Bella reflected, as they knelt for Father Duncan's blessing, the ring Tom had slipped on her finger was legitimately her own. The simple circle of chased silver had been a gift from Aunt Lilith shortly before she died. It was the one possession, apart from the clothes she stood in, that Bella had brought with her from the Highlands. Mercifully, Tom had remembered to bring it with him to the church. Father Duncan was notoriously unsympathetic towards nervous bridegrooms who requested the church doorkey as a token in place of a forgotten ring.

Hand in hand they ran from the church, pursued by Robert, Sam, Blackpatch, Nan and all the other friends who had come to celebrate with them. In the April sunlight, the men fought to snatch lucky bridal trophies from Bella: the white wedding ribbons on her dress, and sprigs of forget-me-nots and myrtle from her bouquet. One bold stable lad even delved under the froth of her petticoat in a bid to steal her garter.

'Enough,' said Tom, stepping firmly on the boy's hand and lifting Bella to safety on a white horse bedecked with pink laces. The laughing crowd surged ahead, strewing the cobbled path that led to the saddlery with rosemary, lavender and primrose petals.

They were to continue living above the saddlery. Robert had insisted. 'After all,' he said, 'I need someone to cook my meals and practice my Gaelic on!' It did not need stating that the newlyweds could never have afforded to rent rooms elsewhere.

The walls of their simple lodgings had been garlanded with boughs of yew, and on Bella's new pine table were sweetmeats and the bridal cake. She was proud of the table, bought with the profits from the bride ale she had brewed and sold to friends a week before the wedding.

Long after the sun had set that night, when the revelry in the festive kitchen was at its height, Robert brought out the sack posset. He had made it himself, from milk, wine, egg yolks, sugar, cinnamon and nutmeg. Tom drank first, while Nan winked at Bella and cackled: 'Mark my words, Bella. Sack will make him lusty, and sugar will make him kind. You've a good man there.'

'I know,' said Bella, flinching as the women of the party descended upon her for the climax of the evening's entertainment.

They bore her off to the tiny room she and Tom shared, and stripped her down to her shift and stockings. Once she was settled, laughing self-consciously on the straw mattress, the men ushered in Tom, in a similar state of undress, to join Bella on the bed. The crowd cheered and stamped their feet, until even Robert, choosing to remain alone in the adjoining kitchen, felt a passing stab of sympathy for the woodlice deafened in the rafters. At last to a chorus of 'Off, off, off' Bella and Tom pulled off their woollen stockings and threw them over their heads. The man and woman who caught them, so it was said, would be the next to marry.

A skirl of delighted disbelief rang round the room as the stockings landed in the outstretched hands of Blackpatch and Nan. The party was over. Pausing only to pelt the couple on the mattress with bryony root to guard against barrenness, the whooping crowd ran from the room, leaving Tom and Bella alone.

Tom promptly brushed the fertility herbs from the bed, and, ignoring Bella's protests, threw them on the fire. 'Superstitious nonsense,' he muttered. 'And what's that rolling pin doing hung over the fireplace? Don't tell me you're thinking of making a chicken pie for breakfast?'

Bella straightened the glass rolling pin, painted with flowers and her and Tom's initials. 'It's a charm. A witch coming down the chimney is compelled to count all the flowers and seeds and leaves on the glass before she is free to harm us,' she told her incredulous bridegroom.

Tom choked as, eyes streaming, he consigned the last sprigs of bryony to the flames. 'Any witch,' he gasped, 'who can survive a perilous journey down a soot-filled chimney, suffocated by the smoke thrown up by a spurious fertility root, deserves all the spiteful fun she can get.'

He was talking to an empty room. He dashed through the door, skirting the kitchen and the cruel amusement Robert would derive from a man losing his bride less than ten hours after his wedding. He eventually found Bella in the garden, talking to her bees. She had trellised their straw skeps with white ribbons, and was whirling round them in the moonlight, showing off her silk wedding dress.

Bella laughed when she saw Tom's flushed face. 'They get very upset if you don't tell them what's going on in the household,' she said seriously, her flowing hair silvered in the moonglow. 'And you must never quarrel with me in front of them, or they'll sting you and fly away.'

'Blackmailed by bees, is it?' murmured Tom, seizing the dancing girl round the waist. 'Come here, Mistress Fraser. I've a mind to teach those bees how to sting in places they never knew existed.'

Two weeks after Bella's wedding, the plague struck Edinburgh. As the terrified people fled to their houses and clamped tight the shutters, the city took on the appearance of a ghost town. The markets were closed, and all incoming travellers were halted at the city gates until they could prove themselves clean. Stray dogs and pigs were rounded up and driven into hastily erected pens, a lunatic performance that under less tragic circumstances would have provoked considerable hilarity. But no one laughed. Upon the normally bustling streets of the city fell a strange, alien silence, broken only by the mournful toll of the church bells, and the clatter of the cleaners' carts as they bore away the dead.

Edinburgh had never been famed for its fragrance. Yet with the coming of the plague the stench of the fish and urine, of horse droppings and rotting wood was washed away in the frantic daily scrubbing of street, wynd and vennel. Instead, the air of Edinburgh was permeated with two new scents that spring. The perfume of juniper being burnt day and night in all the public squares to cleanse the atmosphere. And the throat-catching, sickly smell of death.

But every disaster, be it war, famine or plague, throws up its maverick spirits adept at profiting from the misfortunes of others. One such was Robert the Red. He arrived back at the saddlery at dawn one day, dripping wet and clutching an oilcloth stuffed with precious saffron and cloves.

'You've been up to your tricks at the docks again, Robert,' Bella said crossly, hastening to bring him dry clothes.

Robert sank down wearily on the stone floor of the kitchen, and poked the embers of the fire. 'Aye. But with half the population of the city about to die like flies, the other half will be setting about burying them. And once the funerals are over, and the crying and wailing is done, the good folk of the town will need saffron to sprinkle over their funeral clothes before they pack them away in their musty chests. I shall make a fortune out of this plague, Bella.'

'You'll get caught and branded more like,' put in Tom, appearing bleary-eyed in his nightshirt.

Robert was quick to defend himself. 'I'm not the only one making money out of the plague. What about the carriers, blackmailing entire families with the threat that if they don't pay up, they'll declare the household diseased, and cast the lot of them into the plague house, and certain death? Or the gravediggers, so greedy for their wages that they'll bury the sick, alive?'

'All right,' said Tom. 'But you know full well they've declared we may enter or leave the city only by the main gates. So how did you get back in?'

'I swam,' replied Robert, shaking the moisture from hair that resembled wet bracken. 'Blackpatch rowed me across the loch. Sam was supposed to meet me there and smuggle me through the main gate in his cart. But he didn't come. It was beginning to get dangerously light, so I had no choice but to go underground.'

'But the only underground passage is the sewer pipe that runs into the loch!' cried Bella.

Robert nodded. 'Correct, my dear sister. And most unpleasant it was too. But,' he silenced Bella's indignant protest, 'I took the precaution of drawing water from the public well and cleansing myself before I set foot in your castle.'

Bella wasn't satisfied. 'Really, Robert! What were you thinking of? You could catch the plague!'

Tom watched her ostentatiously flinging sage leaves onto the fire to disinfect the air. 'I shouldn't worry about Robert,' he advised lazily. 'If he fell down a well he'd come up with a salmon.'

The fire hissed as Robert shook out his sodden shirt. 'I wonder what in God's name happened to Sam?' he asked.

Bella discovered the answer the following day. She had ventured out to the Market Cross, hoping to find someone who would sell her some resin. She intended to stuff the resin with Robert's stolen cloves, and sell the pomanders to the few remaining ladies who were too petrified to flee the castle.

She found Sam lurking by the door of St Giles cathedral. He had bought a load of tawdry charms and amulets from a gipsy who, standing at a safe distance, was assuring him that they would ward off infection.

Bella took one look at Sam and realised it was too late. He was shivering with fever, and on his neck the tell-tale boils had swelled to the size of duck eggs.

'Come on, Sam,' said Bella softly. 'I'll take you home.'

Sam gazed at her fearfully, his eyes heavy with aching fatigue.

'Don't come near me, Bella. For your own sake, keep away.'

Bella knew the risks. Even if she escaped the plague, the punishment for anyone rash enough to associate with a victim was death. If they caught her with Sam, she would be dragged to Castle hill and burnt like a bundle of faggots.

But she took him home all the same. She stuffed his mattress with birch leaves to make him sweat and ease the fever. She fed him weak broth and barley bread. She watched the black spots break out all over his body as she cleaned up the vomit flecked with his blood. And three days later, she watched him die.

News of the plague had not yet reached the King. He had been forced to leave Edinburgh a few weeks before to quell a rebellion amongst some of Robert's more excitable compatriots in the Highlands. Behind the King's banner rode the lords Drummond, Lennox, Montrose, Hume and Mallaig. The Earl of Angus, his sword arm broken in two places after strenuous tilting practice with his son, was refused permission by the King to join the army on this expedition. A week after the King led his men through Edinburgh's West Gate on the long march through the mountains, the ladies of the Court were to be observed streaming out of the South Gate. Frothing with panic over rumours of the plague, they had all suddenly found urgent matters to attend to on their lords' neglected country estates.

With the plague-infested city deprived of its rarified blue blood, Bella was surprised one May morning when a peremptory banging on the saddlery door revealed the florid face of the Earl of Angus. But this was no Bell-the-Cat, the weathered man o'war. Today, despite the broken arm still strapped in its splint, the old Earl's step was light as a boy's. He wore a fine cloak lined with scarlet silk, a hat plumed with ostrich feathers, and on his arm rested the gloved hand of Lady Janet Kennedy.

Bella smiled to herself as she admitted them. So old Bell-the-Cat had landed his catch at last. And not, she imagined, without some considerable difficulty. Janet Kennedy was a petite red-head with green eyes and a scorching temper. She also possessed an enviable reputation for knowing exactly what she wanted. And getting it.

Certainly, no one was left in any doubt that what she required today was the finest saddle for her new jennet. It must, she declared, be lined with softest sheepskin and covered with silk-trimmed velvet. Only the very best would do.

Especially, thought Bella, since Bell-the-Cat was paying. Janet, now smoothing the folds of her emerald green riding dress, was setting out to make the greatest possible fuss of the old man. Bella followed the pair into the street, listening carefully as Robert fitted the chosen saddle onto the back of the Spanish horse. There was something about Janet Kennedy, perhaps the flash of green eyes, and the throaty, intimate note to her laughter, that alerted Bella. Robert, for his part, got on with his job as if it were any other, treating the demanding, insistent lady in green with a cool, diffident politeness. Anything Robert had to say was addressed matter-of-factly to the Earl. At last, Janet was satisfied with her new purchase. With a final long, lingering smile at Robert she joined her lover, their bridles clinking in harmony as they rode away, laughing, up the deserted street.

Bella shut the doors and said casually, 'Trust Janet Kennedy not to fear the plague.' Her brother did not take the bait. She was on the point of adding a witty, speculative remark about the cause of Bell-the-Cat's broken arm, when Robert's face silenced her. The two saddlery apprentices, however, were less inhibited. Apparently absorbed in boiling up glue for Robert to use on the joints of the beech saddle trees, they fell to gossiping like two old women over a stewpot.

'Bell-the-Cat'll need more than a saddle to tame *that* little filly.'

'He should sit her on something that'll give her a bairn instead!'

'Nay. 'Tis said she uses candle grease to stop the bairns.'

'Hush, man! The Pope does not allow that.'

'The Pope hasn't met Janet Kennedy.'

'I mind even he would recognise her type. You know what they say: *No need to hang a bell on a bitch's tail...*'

The other boy opened his mouth to laugh, then closed it again as Robert seized him. A moment later he was nursing a bruised ear which roared most unpleasantly with the sounds of the wind and the sea. His companion found himself being trussed like a fowl on a beam above the fire, with a glue-soaked rag stuffed in his protesting mouth.

Bella, rhythmically sweeping the floor, behaved as if nothing untoward had occurred, and ventured innocently, 'Janet Kennedy is a most attractive woman, don't you think?'

'I hardly noticed,' Robert replied.

'Such a shame she chose to wear emerald green today. It reflected so poorly on her lovely white skin. I thought,' went on Bella sweetly, 'she would have looked so much more becoming in blue. Harebell blue silk, perhaps, with a hint of white petticoat...'

She dodged the bar of saddle soap that whistled her way, and ran, laughing, into a street still heavy with the scent of smouldering juniper.

By the summer, Edinburgh's putridly familiar smells had returned. The plague had mysteriously run its course, and life in the city began to return to normal.

For the first few years of her marriage, as the myrtle from her wedding bouquet took root and flourished in her garden, Bella settled into a life of routine domesticity with Tom. The days were peaceful, but never dull, punctuated as they were by Robert's nocturnal adventures and dawn homecomings. There was one memorable wild party when Blackpatch finally summoned enough courage to ask Nan to marry him. And, in the midst of the bonfire-lit revelry which heralded the turn of the century, Bella celebrated the New Year 1500 by giving birth to a son. They named him Douglas, after Tom's father.

Occasionally, sitting in the garden at twilight after the day's work was done, the fragrant drift of May blossom would remind her of an evening at Falkland Palace ... and a later time when she had made a promise to the King. How strange and remote that hour in the Presence Chamber of Linlithgow Palace seemed to Bella now. For Bella had heard nothing more of Margaret Drummond since she had taken her baby and fled from the Court three years ago. She might just as well be dead.

Eight

By day mine eyes, by night my soul desires thee,
Weary, I lie alone.
Once in a dream it seemed thou wert beside me;
O far beyond all dreams, if thou wouldst come!
                                                    Anon

It was a hard, lonely road that Margaret Drummond had chosen.

'For me there will be no other man,' she had told her sister, in the year her baby was born. And she had kept her word. She passed the summers of her early twenties walking and sketching with her growing daughter on the soft lush hills around her home in Perth.

Like any woman who is lovely yet alone, rich yet sad, Margaret found herself enveloped by an air of mystique that for a time made her one of the most sought-after women in Scotland. The most persistent of her admirers was Malcolm Laxford, the darkly intense Earl of Mallaig. He devoted an entire summer to a courtship so insistent that Margaret was finally forced to ask her father to refuse him entry to Drummond Castle.

A more welcome visitor was the flamboyant Spanish Ambassador. Sent by James ostensibly to enquire into the health of the King's young daughter, Ayala enlivened many of Margaret's long days with witty gossip from the Court. When he told her, at last, that he had been recalled to Spain, Margaret felt the wrench of losing a true friend. James, too, she knew, would regret the departure of the elegant, shrewd young ambassador more than he might care to admit.

If the summers were tolerable, then the winters wrought a bitter revenge. The gentle hills turned bleak and inhospitable under a snow-laden sky, the moat froze over and even the great blazing fires were no match for the icy winds that whined through the draughty castle.

Each succeeding winter seemed to bring a harvest of bad news borne with ill-concealed malice by Lady Lennox. It was she who 'felt Margaret ought to know', in the last December of the century, that the King had stolen Janet Kennedy from old Bell-the-Cat.

'*Venus despicit senes*,' murmured Margaret, offering her guest a cup of spiced wine.

Lady Lennox, who had neither Latin, nor beauty nor opportunity to mock at any man, young or old, prattled on: 'Of course, we all know that the King and Angus have always had it in for one another. And Janet's no fool. After all, who could blame her for grabbing the chance to be the King's mistress?' The wine splashed onto the floor. 'Oh, my dear. How tactless of me. I'm sure I didn't mean...'

'Of course you didn't, Lady Lennox,' said Margaret coolly. 'You must know how grateful I am that you should spare the time to ride through all that snow to entertain me with the latest diversions of the Court. Especially when you must have so many household worries of your own to attend to. I trust Lord Lennox is keeping well?'

Bull's eye. Margaret guessed that Lady Lennox's festive flush had started somewhere around her waist at this reference to Lord Lennox's flagrant affair with one of his wife's linen maids.

But time was on Lady Lennox's side. She waited. And two Christmasses later she was once more seated before the massive carved fireplace in the Great Hall of Drummond Castle. She rattled through the courtesy enquiries after Margaret's daughter, her parents, her sisters, her sisters' husbands, their children and her own health. Margaret's response was detailed, lengthy and extremely boring. Lady Lennox contained herself only with considerable difficulty, her thin sparrow-like face pecking the air with impatience.

When her moment came, she threw it away, gabbling her news so fast that Margaret was obliged to ask her to repeat it.

Lady Lennox took a calming sip of wine, wondering if Margaret Drummond was being deliberately obtuse. 'I said, Margaret, that the King is to marry. My Lord Lennox informs me that arrangements have finally been made for an alliance with the Princess Margaret of England.'

A small, sad smile flickered across Margaret's pale face. Poor James, she thought. For all these years he had dreaded the spectre of that unseen wee girl down in England. She considered the unwanted prospective Queen, and the unwilling bridegroom, and couldn't make up her mind for whom she felt more sorry.

'When will they marry?' Margaret asked.

'In January by proxy,' Lady Lennox told her. 'But of course, the marriage will not be official until the Princess is able to come to Scotland, and a church ceremony has taken place. As the girl is so young, I doubt if her father will allow her to leave the Palace of Richmond for a while yet.'

Margaret stared into the crackling fire, her face impassive. So James had another year or so of freedom. She had no doubt that he and Janet Kennedy would make the most of it.

'It is well that Scotland is to have a Queen,' was Margaret's single comment, to Lady Lennox's eternal disappointment.

The following spring, with her former lover now married, if only on parchment, to the English Princess, Margaret Drummond resumed her lonely hillside walks with her lively five-year-old daughter.

She was glad of the child's company, and not at all resentful that the little girl demanded so much of her time and attention. From the moment she had been carried under the Drummond Castle portcullis, the young Lady Margaret Stewart had proved a wilful, spirited child. She had inherited her mother's raven hair, her Danish grandmother's cornflower blue eyes and her father's distinctive Stewart nose. Plus his legendary charm and unquenchable restlessness. Margaret alone was able to control the child. If left in the care of anyone else, pandemonium was certain to break out. Time after time the cry rang through the castle that the young Lady Margaret was lost. After a frantic search she would be found gluing a stinking fish to the underside of the cook's spotless kitchen table .. or up on the castle ramparts, playing soldiers ... or careering across the courtyard on the back of Lord Drummond's prize ram.

'I just don't understand that child,' Lady Drummond complained to Margaret. 'She behaves more like a boy than a girl. You and your sisters were such quiet, docile little creatures. This one doesn't act like a Drummond girl at all.'

'She *isn't* a Drummond girl,' Margaret retorted. 'She's a Stewart. And the daughter of a king.'

Lady Drummond paused. When she spoke, her tone was one of thoughtful concern. 'Of course you are right, Margaret. But it seems such a pity, does it not, that the King has been deprived of the opportunity of seeing his daughter for all these years? She's five now, and such a pretty child. I'm sure, Margaret, that no one could consider it amiss if you took the girl to visit her father. It would be ... only natural.'

Margaret's dark amber eyes narrowed in distrust. Lady Drummond hurried on, artlessly. 'No – it is foolish of me to suggest it. Naturally, such a meeting would cause you too much pain. It is not fair to ask you to give the King and his daughter the joy of meeting, at the cost of so much suffering to yourself. Forgive me, my dear, for an old woman's fanciful, silly thoughts.'

Late in May, Margaret told her parents that she intended to take her daughter to Edinburgh to meet her father.

Lady Drummond's ringed hands flew to her face. 'No, Margaret! Not Edinburgh! Your father has just brought word that the city is once more struck with the plague.'

Lord Drummond confirmed the bad news. 'It would be unsafe for you to venture into Edinburgh at this time, Margaret. It isn't just unhealthy, it's a joyless city now. The priests have frightened the people into believing that their evil gambling has angered God into sending the plague. All the dice makers found they were going out of business, and have turned to carving rosaries instead.'

His abstracted wife was pursuing another train of thought. 'Surely the King will not stay in Edinburgh? It would be foolish of him to place himself unnecessarily in danger. He is sure to go to Linlithgow. Why – Margaret can take little Meg *there* to meet him.'

Margaret shook her head. 'You are wrong, mother. The King will not flee the city. He will stay in Edinburgh with the people who need him the most.' Through her disappointment, she heard her mother ask what was being done for the afflicted.

John Drummond laughed. 'Well, I hear the good Bishop of Dunkeld is affecting a cure. He's anointing people with holy water in which one of St Columba's bones is said to have been dipped. One shameless wretch was heard to mutter that he wished the holy water had been a pot of strong ale. He died the next day.'

Margaret fretted through the long hot weeks of that early summer. Now that she had finally made up her mind to see James for one last time, the enforced delay was almost unbearable. Every day she expected Lady Lennox to arrive and impart the sorrowful news that the King had been stricken with the plague ... or that Margaret Tudor was travelling north for her marriage. But the days dragged into weeks, and Lady Lennox did not come. At the end of June, Lord Drummond announced that the worst was over in Edinburgh. The King, having seen the city through its crisis, was travelling to his palace at Falkland.

Falkland! The very name spelt magic for Margaret. It had to be a favourable omen, a sign that it was right for her to take this step and visit the King. It was at Falkland, after all, that her romance with James had begun. How fitting that at Falkland, six long years later, she would kiss him goodbye for the last time.

Although she sent no word, Margaret Drummond was aware as her entourage travelled the road to Falkland, that James would have been advised of her approach: Kings are not permitted the luxury of unexpected visitors. If he chose not to see her, it was an easy matter for him to decide that pressing matters of state demanded his presence in Edinburgh, Stirling or Linlithgow.

Margaret tried not to dwell on the riptide of despair that would engulf her if the only message she found at Falkland was the one declared by James' absence. She could well imagine the thinly masked triumph of Lady Lennox, the caustic reproach of her mother and, worst of all, the corrosive rasp of her own crushed pride at having invited such wilful humiliation.

Fearfully, she began the long ascent up the hill that would bring her within sight of the Palace. On the crest, she ordered her train to halt while she looked down across the river valley and beyond the forest to the sandstone Palace glimmering in the heat of the summer sun. Margaret smiled. It was like a homecoming. Turning, she hugged the blue-eyed little girl who had ridden doggedly beside her all the way from Perth.

'He's there, Meg. He's there!' High on the flagstaff on the topmost Palace rampart, the gold and red lyon-rampant royal banner was signalling proud welcome to Margaret Drummond and her daughter.

James was not, of course, waiting at the Palace gates to greet her. Kings are not accustomed to lurking behind their own front doors. Besides, it was understood that when ladies had journeyed a considerable distance, they were anxious to change their travel dresses, and refresh themselves before venturing into the perfumed jungle of Court society. Even so, Margaret was surprised by the silence that pervaded the Palace. It seemed strangely bereft of the chatter of courtiers, the plucking of lutes and above all the laughter that usually attested to the presence of the King.

The serving maid who showed her to a chamber answered her question.

'The Court is out hunting, my lady. They will be away overnight. Except for the King. I believe you will find him walking in the Palace gardens.'

86

Margaret felt limp with relief. Of course. Dear, clever, romantic James. He had disposed of the tattling Court. He had remembered. He was waiting. Hurriedly she cleansed herself with rosewater and changed into a dress of pale violet silk. Then taking her daughter by the hand, Margaret Drummond, her graceful head high, stepped out into the rosegarden to bid farewell to James Stewart.

Years later, when Bella questioned Margaret Drummond's daughter about this legendary meeting, the girl was maddeningly vague. All she could remember was curtseying to a tall dark man she knew to be her father, and pulling his funny pointed beard. Then he had said he wanted to talk to her mother, and she had wandered away to chase the spiders up the trellised garden wall.

The child would have had no recollection of the look that passed between her parents as they gazed on one another for the first time in five years. It was an expression of raw enquiry. A contemplation that encompassed all the echoes of the past, of what had been and what might have been. It spiralled them back through the aching years, deepening in intensity as in that one short minute, Margaret and James relived their past passion, their present pain, their mutual defeat.

When at last their lips met on that golden summer afternoon, they knew in an instant that this could never be a kiss of farewell. Their every nerve sang with the answer to their unspoken question. Yes, they still loved. More, in the crucible of that fiery embrace was forged an unyielding declaration of faith in their future together. The minutes fled past, unheeded by the couple who clung to one another in the midst of the buttercupped grass, appalled at what they had set in motion, yet helpless to prevent it.

They slept little that night. As the sky began to lighten, James looked down into the glowing eyes of the woman beside him, and murmured: 'This time, Margaret, I'm not asking you. I'm telling you. To the Devil with the consequences— I *shall* marry you!'

She kissed him. James slipped from the bed and pushed aside the window shutters, revealing a sky gloriously streaked

with crimson and with gold. The Stewart colours. Turning
to Margaret, the King sang exultantly:

> *The shadows flee, the light draws near;*
> *The sky is calm and clear,*
> *The dawn no longer hesitates,*
> *The day in fair perfection waits.*

To the Court, returning in merry mood after a hectic two
days' hunting, it seemed as if they had stepped back in time
five years. They choked in disbelief as the King led Margaret
Drummond into the candlelit Great Hall, sat her in the chair
next to his own and fed her the choicest cuts of meat from
the royal silver platter. In the presence of the King, even Margaret's sworn enemies had no alternative but to swallow the
bitter pill of betrayal. But when the King rose, and bidding
them all goodnight, calmly led Margaret from the Hall, the
pent up fury of the Court was unleashed.

'It's scandalous!' blazed the Earl of Lennox.

'It is certainly unwise,' mused Bishop Elphinstone.

'*Unwise?*' barked Bell-the-Cat. 'What does the man think
he's doing? It seems to me he would trade our country's future
for a night or two rutting with that ... that ...'

'Sorceress,' replied the Earl of Mallaig, brooding over his
wine. 'It's unfortunate that the English Princess has been so
long delayed. If it would speed our King to the altar I'd go
and cart her up here myself, but –'

'At this moment,' interrupted Bishop Elphinstone gravely,
'the Princess is in mourning for her late mother. It will be
another six months at least before King Henry will release
her from the grief-stricken English Court.'

'By which time,' stormed Angus, 'our merry monarch may
have changed his mind about the marriage. Or had it changed
for him. God damn it – why in hell does he want to go and
saddle himself with yet *another* woman?'

Most of Angus' companions sympathised with his sense of
injustice. He was still smarting at the manner in which the
King, while in the midst of negotiations for the hand of the
Princess Margaret, had spirited Janet Kennedy away from

him. A bleak smile flickered across Angus' drawn face. Not for all the virgins in Scotland, he decided, would he like to be in James' fur lined boots when the news of his renewed liaison with Margaret Drummond reached the ears of Janet Kennedy.

James was mentally armoured against trouble on all fronts: his ex-mistress, his Court and his Council. To the latter he drily announced that there had been a change of plan. Instead of completing his proxy marriage to the English Princess, he intended to wed the Scottish Lady Margaret Drummond. As he had anticipated, the Council raged, bleated and pleaded. Finally, in desperation, they sent for Bishop Elphinstone.

The man of God talked diplomatically to James, emphasising the desirability of an immediate alliance with England, a *rapprochement* which could be permanently secured only by the marriage of James IV to Margaret Tudor. He cautioned the King about the dissent at Court, the feelings of outrage, and the rash of family feuding that would break out if James were to marry Margaret Drummond.

James liked and trusted the Bishop. He knew his friend was saying what he sincerely believed to be true. But James found it impossible to convey to such a pious and unworldly man the depth of his feelings for Margaret. He could talk, in truth, of an alliance of minds, a union of two lonely spirits. What he could not bring himself to explain to this gentle celibate was the consuming desire he and Margaret triggered in one another. For how could a man who had forsworn the body's hunger understand an appetite which could not, even after five years' absence, be contained a moment longer? Instinctively, James knew that by marrying Margaret Drummond he would make Scotland a finer King than if he were forced into an unhappy partnership with an English Princess whom he had never even seen, yet alone met.

In the end, all James felt able to tell the Bishop was that he felt the deep relief of having made the right decision. 'My conscience, my lord Bishop, is at peace.'

Bishop Elphinstone, unconvinced, nodded and silently retired.

Janet Kennedy, stalking the tapestried halls of Darnaway Castle, was not the silently retiring type.

'So, you condescend to come at last?' she spat at the King, who had given her the castle.

James addressed her mildly, noting with disinterest that she offered him neither refreshment nor embrace. 'I thought it only honourable to pay you a last visit.'

The green eyes glittered. 'I gather that other, *older* friends are claiming your attention this summer.' She paused, but the King refused to be drawn. 'They say you intend to marry her. Is this so?'

'I think that is my affair, Janet.' James' voice was as splintered ice. 'In any case, you know full well that our liaison would have had to end in the event of my marriage to Margaret Tudor.'

Janet's pert face flamed with scorn. 'But now you are going to wriggle out of this marriage to the pudgy English Princess. You prefer to marry one of your mistresses instead. I wonder why Margaret Drummond has been singled out for this honour. Why not Marion Boyd? Why not me? All Scotland knows there have been plenty of us to choose from.'

James gripped her by the shoulders, his fingers branding the bare, white flesh.

'Margaret Drummond has never been *one of my mistresses*. She is the only woman I have ever loved. She is the woman I intend to marry. And nothing you can say or do, Janet, is going to change that.'

The second he released her she sprang, clawing, at his face. As her painted nails grated his cheek, he flung her hard against the stone windowseat.

Like a wounded wild animal, Janet crouched there, watching the storm of dust from the King's horse until he was out of sight. Then, shaken but determined, she sat down to write some letters, her quill spiking the paper and her hot furious tears falling as drops of acid on the wet black ink.

Nine

Gang Warily
Motto of the House of Drummond

A mantle of expectancy lay over Drummond Castle. The Court, still smouldering with indignation, had sourly accompanied the King to Stirling. James, fearful of exposing Margaret further to the vitriolic jibes of his courtiers, sent her and their daughter back to Perth. He visited them there frequently, ignoring the uproar he left in his wake up on Stirling Rock, where the harassed Council was even now concocting elaborate plans aimed at stopping tidings of the King's untimely romance from filtering through to Henry Tudor. For once, Bishop Elphinstone blessed the bad roads, hostile hills and autumn rains that slowed the dissemination of news over the four hundred miles between London and Edinburgh.

A twenty-four hour look-out had been posted on the Drummond Castle ramparts to warn of the arrival of the King. Lady Drummond had thrown her servants into a turmoil, instigating a fresh scourge of cleaning and burnishing. The flagstones were scrubbed and the courtyard brushed. Fresh straw was laid each day in the stables. Every piece of castle brass and silver was polished with a mixture of onion and damp earth. Elizabeth Drummond personally attended to the priceless salver, ewer, salt cellar and two cups that graced the oak sideboard in the Great Hall. She smiled as she worked, peaceful in her proud reflection that the heirlooms had originally been a gift to her husband's ancestor, John Drummond, from his sister, Queen Annabella.

Once again, the seamstresses were called on to work through the night on a trousseau for a wedding that most of the Court were still insisting should not take place. But at

Drummond Castle nobody could talk of anything else. Nobody, that is, except for the prospective bride.

It was as if, complained her mother to Margaret one dull October morning, a stranger's wedding was being planned.

'Really, Margaret, you might show a little more interest. I thought you were extremly rude to Lady Lennox yesterday when she called with the Earl of Mallaig. She only wanted to know if she could be of any assistance to you at this busy time.'

Margaret was unabashed. 'You know as well as I do mother, that the only assistance Lady Lennox would ever wish to render me would leave me with a broken limb, or a broken heart – or both.'

'Hush, Margaret!' Lady Drummond glanced a warning at her granddaughter sitting at the top of the stairs. 'I'm taking young Meg for a walk. Meanwhile, Eupheme and Sybilla are waiting in the Hall to have breakfast with you. They're squabbling over which one of them should borrow your emeralds to wear at the wedding.' She frowned. 'Can you imagine what the Earl of Mallaig was doing accompanying Lady Lennox here yesterday? *Her* intention was clear – to nose her way into your marriage preparations. But why, I wonder, was Malcolm so interested?'

Margaret shrugged. 'Perhaps he wanted to be bridesmaid.' And pausing only to kiss her young daughter, Margaret Drummond hurried down to join her sisters for breakfast.

For the rest of her life Margaret Drummond's daughter was to dread the coming of autumn. It meant soggy brown leaves. A smell of decay. And three chilling screams piercing the morning mist that wreathed Drummond Castle.

Frozen suddenly to the bone, young Margaret Stewart picked up her skirts and ran blindly back through the gardens and up the turnpike stair that led to the Great Hall. Her grandmother, who had arrived a second before her, turned to bar the way. But Margaret shot past, and almost stumbled over the upturned breakfast table.

Margaret ignored the terrible groans of her two aunts lying writhing on the floor. She was aware only of her mother crumpled beside them, her dark hair falling loose, her fingers desperately clawing the strewn rushes. Her mother, who had moved in beauty and grace, who had smelt of rosemary and rosewater, was lying with bulging eyes and foaming mouth, her lustrous skin stained black. Her mother, who had never raised her sweet voice to her, was shrieking ... in a high-pitched shrill whine of agony.

Margaret Drummond squirmed frantically, as if in a last frenzied effort to escape whatever evil possessed her. Then, with the vomit streaming from her mouth, she pitched forward, to lie at her daughter's feet.

'Murder!' Lady Drummond's stark, screaming accusation shattered the shocked silence of those who had flocked in the next few days to comfort her.

'Murder! They have poisoned my daughters!' The cry of anguish rebounded as a hundred unearthly echoes from the cold stone walls of the castle.

Lady Lennox knelt by the sobbing woman's chair. 'My dear. Why assume the worst? It is dreadful. Horrible. But poison ... surely not. The meat Margaret and her poor sisters ate must have been bad. It happens frequently.'

'Bad meat!' exclaimed Lady Drummond, anger stilling her tears. 'Never. I taught that cook myself how to salt meat. Members of your household may be accustomed to giving up the ghost over Grace at your table, Lady Lennox, but I can assure you, it is not common practice in mine.'

Elizabeth Drummond, suddenly straight-backed and in command of her dignity once more, glared round at her husband, at Lady Lennox, at her ladies and at her weeping servants. 'I declare before you all. My daughters, Margaret, Eupheme and Sybilla, were poisoned. By whom we can only conjecture. But we all of us know why.'

Nobody dared demur. Lady Lennox asked the obvious question. 'And little Margaret, your granddaughter?'

'She is safe,' said Lord Drummond.

The grief-stricken King had himself galloped the fifty miles to Drummond Castle and, pausing only to change horses, had snatched up his daughter, bearing her to the fortressed shelter of Stirling Castle. He had shut himself away in his chamber, eating nothing, admitting no one. Even Bishop Elphinstone found the door locked against him. For the King, there had been no confidant with whom he could share the joy of his passion for Margaret. And now there was no single person with whom he could share the depth of his despair at her death. Margaret Drummond had been the sole woman in the world with the power to melt his gilded chains of office and free the soul of the man beneath. He trusted her. He loved her above all others. Now she was gone, James knew that for the rest of his life he would remain a king cluttered by courtiers, yet utterly alone.

There was one person in Scotland who would have understood. Who could have offered the genuine touch of comfort James craved so much. But she would never have been allowed to throw even a flower of sympathy to the mourning King. Instead, Bella wept all night in Tom's arms. He comforted her as best he could, puzzled by her distress over the death of a lady who had, after all, given his wife nothing more than a pearl from her dress.

Margaret Drummond and her sisters were buried at the Abbey of Dunblane. Later, Tom took Bella and their two-year-old son to kneel before the three blue slate stones that formed the Drummond sisters' monument. Over the centre stone, someone had placed a cloth of purple velvet, and stitched across it in crimson and gold silk Margaret Drummond's personal legend: *Mérite*.

While the King issued orders that for the rest of his life masses were to be sung at Dunblane in Margaret's memory, controversy still raged over who had killed the woman the King had loved ... the woman he had been willing to abandon a princess for ... the woman who could have plunged Scotland into civil strife, and another bloody war with England.

Lady Drummond's scalding interrogation of her kitchen staff revealed that a scullery maid had disappeared on the morning of that tragic breakfast. After an intensive search of the Perth hills, the girl was found in a ditch by the castle guards. She had been stabbed in the back.

Lord Drummond, thirsty for revenge, cast his accusing eye further afield than the domestic confines of the castle. Suspicion had already fallen heavily on Janet Kennedy and her family, though they were vehement in their denials. Unable to restrain himself for a moment longer, John Drummond ordered his men into armour and set off at full gallop towards Darnaway Castle.

'I'll drag the truth from that green-eyed bitch,' he swore, lashing his terrified horse, 'and then I'll tie her long red hair round her treacherous white neck, and strangle her with it.'

With Darnaway Castle in sight, Drummond was overtaken by a breathless Bishop Elphinstone.

'I bring word from the King,' gasped the Bishop. 'You are to turn back. There must be no more blood spilt.'

'Let me pass!' exploded Lord Drummond. 'In the name of my dead daughters I demand justice.'

Elphinstone stood his ground. 'In the name of God and the King I order you to return to Drummond Castle. It is not justice you seek, but revenge. Another murder will not return your daughters to you. And the King will not thank you for using your grief as an excuse for renewed bloodshed amongst Scotland's most noble families. That is not how he would wish Margaret Drummond to be remembered.'

The two men stared at one another for a long moment. Then without a word, Lord Drummond wheeled round his horse and led his men back to Perth.

The King, whatever his private thoughts and inner accusations, let it be known through Bishop Elphinstone to the entire Court that there was to be no witch-hunt. He would not raise, nor could he face, a holocaust of interrogation, denials and festering distrust. Margaret was dead. The light had gone from his life. Let the dark remain as solace.

Openly relieved, his Council once more took up the delicate threads of the negotiations that would bind King James with Margaret Tudor. And on 10 December, 1502, at St Mungo's

Abbey in Glasgow, James IV of Scotland finally signed his marriage treaty with England.

The following summer, word reached Edinburgh that Margaret Tudor had at last begun her journey north. The King, whose heart would remain forever alongside the woman he had buried at Dunblane, awaited his bride's arrival with dutiful acceptance and resignation. To escape both the bleak lethargy of despair, and the gaunt grey towers of Edinburgh Castle, James ordered a new palace to be built, next to the Abbey of Holyrood.

What the King remembered, his people forgot. To most of them, the death of Margaret Drummond was now but a romantic memory, a bitter-sweet tale they would tell to their grandchildren. They had suffered and survived a harsh Scottish winter, and rejoiced now in the notion of a royal wedding, with its welcome promise of feasting, pageantry and merrymaking.

Naturally, they were eager to set eyes on Margaret Tudor, to assess her beauty and test her mettle. There were many who were already well disposed towards the English Princess. The new Palace of Holyrood was to be her home, and its construction had created desperately needed work for hundreds of Edinburgh artisans. Others, Bella, Tom and Robert amongst them, were more cautious, for in their souls they still loathed and feared their old enemies over the border.

The Scots take no one easily to their hearts. But they are a nation renowned for their sense of justice. She may be English, they said, in the taverns, the markets and the public squares, but it was only fair to give the lass a chance.

So it was, that in a spirit of optimism tempered with wary reserve, Scotland awaited the coming of her Queen.

PART TWO
Margaret Tudor

One

Nor hold no other flower in life so dainty
Like the fresh Rose, of colour red and white,
For if thou dost, hurt is thine honesy,
Considering that no flower is so perfite,
So full of virtue, pleasance, or delight,
So full of blissful angel-like beauty,
Imperial with honour and dignity.

William Dunbar

The Rose of England and future Queen of Scotland lay face down on the bed, her plump young face blotched with tears.

Lady Guildford, her lady-in-waiting, calmly wrung out a muslin cloth in cold water and pressed it against the girl's hot, flushed cheeks. 'Come, my lady. Your procession is waiting to leave Berwick. We can delay no longer.' She brushed away the tangle of red gold hair from Margaret's freckled brow. 'Just imagine! In a few hours' time you will cross the border into Scotland, where the people will greet you as their Queen. Aren't you excited? Aren't you eager to see the new land that is to be your home?'

Margaret Tudor clutched the damask bedcurtains and howled. Three weeks ago she had bidden farewell to her beloved father. She knew, instinctively, that she would never see him again. And less than seven months had passed since she had watched her mother die, in pain and silence, after the death of her ninth child. Now Margaret was being forced from her homeland into an alien country that her brother Henry said was cold, unfriendly and downright barbaric – there to marry a man she had never met.

Drawing her knees up to her stomach, Margaret gave way to another storm of weeping. She was, after all, only thirteen years old.

99

'Queens do not cry,' said Lady Guildford tartly.

The tears dissolved as Margaret's eyes blazed. 'If I'm Queen then I can do as I like, Guildford!'

Lady Guildford, who had attended the girl since she was a baby, hid a smile as she observed the famous Tudor temper beginning to take effect.

'I shall be Queen of Scotland,' declared Margaret fiercely, sitting upright, arms akimbo and fists clenched. 'Queen! While brother Henry is still only a mere prince.' She laughed. 'Do you remember when the marriage papers were signed, Guildford? Poor Henry turned purple with rage when my father told him that in future he must give precedence to me. And now he's stuck behind at Richmond in a dreary Court still stiff with mourning.'

Lady Guildford, accustomed to these lightning changes of mood, took Margaret's childish hands in hers. 'While you, my lady, will travel forth today in a litter lined with blue velvet and cloth of gold.'

Margaret scrambled off the bed. 'Is it really that splendid, Guildford? Cloth of gold . . . how we shall impress the Scots! What shall I wear? My orange and white silk, or the yellow? My emeralds would look dazzling on the yellow. Oh, hurry and decide, Guildford. I can't wait to get started!'

Despite the girl's brief bout of self-pity, Lady Guildford knew that this was a journey for which Margaret Tudor had been prepared all her life. As an English princess it had always been made clear to her that when she married, she would have to leave the beautiful Palace of Richmond and travel to a foreign land, and the bed of a royal stranger.

Her entire education had been devised with this objective in mind. While learned scholars instructed her brothers in the classics, mathematics and the art of warfare, Lady Guildford taught Margaret to dance and sing, to play the lute and cards with equal dexterity; gentle accomplishments, calculated to amuse and entertain him who would win her, the prize of an English alliance. Now Margaret's training was complete. In a week's time, Lady Guildford would see the girl she had cared for from the cradle, crowned Queen of Scotland.

The first part of Margaret's journey, through Newark, York, Durham and Newcastle, had done much to alleviate her despair at having to abandon her family. In every town church bells had rung in greeting. Cheering crowds lined the roads, the common people thronging to see their young princess on her fine white palfrey, eager to give her fruit and nosegays, and wish her well. Margaret was delighted, unable to resist such total indulgence of her vanity as, for the first time in her life, she found herself the sole centre of attraction.

While the consort of musicians, proudly liveried in Tudor white and green, filled the summer air with her favourite tunes, Margaret threw the red roses that decorated her saddle to the children who danced before her procession. Escorted by her uncle and aunt, the Earl and Countess of Surrey, Margaret's splendid progress had continued through a blistering July. Every day, there were new dignitaries to meet, speeches to listen to, gifts to be received, formal banquets to be consumed. The pace was exhausting, but not once had Margaret shown signs of fatigue. A robust girl, with glittering red gold hair brushed to a fine sheen every morning by the patient Lady Guildford, Margaret had basked in the pomp and pageantry, feeling at last, like a real Queen.

Only at the grim border fortress of Berwick had Margaret given way to the pangs of homesickness. But now, with her tears dried, emeralds round her throat and yellow ribbons in her hair, Margaret faced the future with confidence once more. At the beginning of August, 1503, armoured with her tough Tudor spirit and the knowledge that she was the first lady in the land, Margaret crossed the border into Scotland, blissfully unaware of the lukewarm reception that awaited her.

It was at the Castle of Dalkeith, just outside Edinburgh, that Margaret's nerve finally broke. An anxious Lady Guildford had seen the crisis coming for the past three days, as the four-hundred-strong royal procession made its cumbersome way across the treacherous Scottish hills and marshy bogs, where even the surefooted pack mules stumbled on the furrowed, unmade roads. In this wild, unfriendly country, progress was unbearably slow. Margaret's English retinue, accustomed to the soft, lush meadows of the south, gazed appalled at the craggy, hostile terrain of moorland and mountain that surrounded them. They complained constantly: about the mud that splashed their elegant clothes; about the jolting roads that lamed their horses and made for hard riding; about the swarms of gnats which feasted on their fine English skins.

As the salt marshes stained her cloth of gold litter, Margaret heard the whining voices, and said nothing. But her eyes, Lady Guildford noted, were everywhere. For a girl who had grown up believing that Richmond Hill was an arduous climb, Lady Guildford sensed Margaret's foreboding as she gazed for the first time on the lowering Scottish hills.

The yellow ribbons, tossed by a lashing wind, whipped against Margaret's face, as uncontrollable as the storm of fear beginning to rise within her. She was destined to be Queen of this country. Yet already she felt threatened by the unfamiliar, sombre landscape and the scattered groups of impassive peasants who watched her from the tops of dry stone walls. Outwardly serene yet inwardly in turmoil, Margaret smiled and waved. But while she acknowledged the occasional muted cheer she was studying the Scotsmen with a mixture of curiosity and apprehension. How un-English they were. How unlike the Earl of Surrey and his well-bred compatriots in the procession.

The Scots were like no men she had ever encountered before. It was not merely that they were smaller, more compact and swarthier than the English with whom she had grown up. There was something about the expression in their eyes – a flinty wariness that to Margaret smacked of disrespect, insolence, even contempt. They were like the very countryside itself, bleak, harsh and unyielding. Yet, on the rare occasions that a Scotsman smiled, it was like the sun sweeping away the dark shadows that clothed the stubbled fields, bringing the relief of gold bright light and longed-for warmth.

But they smiled so infrequently. Unlike her English party who fawned and flattered and smiled continually with the practised ease of professional courtiers. At least, in England they had. Now, as carts overturned and the procession struggled along the rutted Scottish roads, the English were finding less and less to smile about. Everyone was relieved when they reached Dalkeith.

Once alone in her chamber with Lady Guildford, Margaret said little as her travel stained dress was removed. Then at last came the question her lady-in-waiting had been expecting.

'Guildford. What will he be like?'

'You mean the King, my lady?'

Margaret sighed. 'Of course I mean the King. What other man is there?'

Lady Guildford, unclasping Margaret's emeralds, chose her words carefully. 'They say he is a fine man, madam. He is extremely devout, he is widely read, he speaks five languages and is well loved by his people.'

Margaret shook her head impatiently. 'But is he *handsome*, Guildford? He never sent me a portrait. Henry said King James was too frightened to show me how hideous he is. He said . . .' Margaret's voice quavered, 'he said James would look as ugly as a toad.'

Lady Guildford delivered a silent curse in the direction of Prince Henry. She felt genuinely sorry for Margaret, obliged to travel four hundred miles to marry a man she would not yet recognise if he passed her in the street. And through all the long journey, despite the cheers, the flowers, the bands that had played and the bells which had rung for her, Margaret had been sick with fear that her future husband would revolt her.

'Your brother has misled you, madam. All our ambassadors report that King James is exceedingly handsome.'

Margaret's childish face was still clouded. 'Will I please him, though, Guildford? I can't wait for the days to pass until he greets me in Edinburgh. But perhaps . . . perhaps *he* is reluctant to meet *me*.'

Lady Guildford put her arms around the girl. 'I am sure the King is only too anxious to greet his Queen, my lady. And

103

I think you may well find that meeting will be sooner than you think. We are but a short ride from Edinburgh. It would not surprise me if the King found himself unable to restrain his impatience to see his young bride.'

'You mean, he might come to Dalkeith, today, to visit me?' exclaimed Margaret.

Lady Guildford nodded. If he doesn't, she thought grimly, then King or no King, he'll receive a piece of my mind.

'I suppose,' said King James dryly to Bishop Elphinstone, 'I'd better do the gallant thing.'

'It will certainly impress the English,' said Elphinstone.

James sighed. 'Ah ... the lusty King, overwhelmed with desire to set eyes on his lovely virgin Queen, gallops at breakneck speed to Dalkeith. What a surprise! What consternation! What are they all doing sitting waiting in their best dresses?'

The Bishop's laughter echoed round the bare walls of the Great Hall. 'You will carry it off perfectly. The Earl and Countess of Surrey are sure to write glowing reports to King Henry of your manners, style and wit.'

'Not to mention my unbounded enthusiasm to catch sight of his precious daughter.' James' tone changed. 'Poor wee thing. I'll wager she'd give a kingdom to be safely back at Richmond with her brothers and young sister.'

Elphinstone nodded. 'We must do all in our power to make the Queen feel that Scotland is now truly her home.' He surveyed the newly finished Great Hall of Holyrood Palace, still redolent of fresh limestone, pitch and seasoned wood. 'The Queen can't fail to be enchanted with the palace you have built for her.'

The King kicked a piece of rubble into the gaping fireplace. 'I hope it pleases her. Though I can't say I've observed my nobles bruising their hands in applause for my efforts. I don't think they'll ever forgive me for moving the Court a mile down the road to Holyrood, when they've spent fortunes building themselves houses in the fashionable area near Edinburgh Castle.'

'I shouldn't lose any sleep over them,' counselled Elphinstone. 'They'll sell their houses at fat profits to the rich burghers, and come scurrying down the hill after you. In fact, I hear that the young Earl of Mallaig is half way through building a house in the Canongate, just outside the Holyrood gates.'

'I know. He's already stolen my Master Carver,' said James testily. He sighed. 'So much upheaval, all for one English princess. I can build her palaces, seat her at my right hand and lay the Crown jewels at her feet. But I can never love her. You know that, Bishop. And you know why. I can't even promise I'll be faithful to her. But I swear I'll try to be a considerate husband and a good friend to the girl.' He picked up his cape from the windowseat, and shook off the film of sandstone. 'Right! Now let the Prince of Love descend with music and musk onto the unsuspecting English bower.'

Elphinstone could not resist a smile as, that afternoon, he watched the King and sixty of his Court sweep dramatically through the cobbled courtyard of Holyrood Palace. James, indulging to the full his sense of theatre, was dressed for the hunt, in a dashing crimson jacket with the lion of Scotland embroidered in silk on the shoulder. He would, Elphinstone guessed, spur on his gleaming black courser and leave his companions in a cloud of dust, to thunder down alone on Dalkeith to greet his bride.

'The King! The King of Scotland has arrived!' The cry rang through the ancient castle as James leapt from his horse and hurried through the courtyards, towards the great chamber.

Margaret, freshly dressed in a richly embroidered green velvet gown, had spent a fraught afternoon playing the worst game of cards of her life with the Earl and Countess of Surrey. As the oak door of the chamber was flung open, she clasped her diamond necklace for luck and reassurance, and led Lady Guildford and her ladies into the deepest of curtseys.

It occurred to the terrified Margaret then, as she gazed on the rush-strewn floor, that the King had no means of recognising her. They had never met. He had not even seen her portrait. Suppose – oh, it would be too unbearable – but suppose

105

he came forward and greeted not her, but the prettiest of her ladies as his Queen?

She heard footsteps, saw polished leather boots, black velvet breeches and a ringed hand extended towards her.

'Margaret. May I claim a kiss from my lovely bride to be?'

She took his hand and arose, trembling, to look for the first time on the sensitive face, the auburn hair, the amused hazel eyes of the man her father had chosen for her. As his lips brushed her burning cheek she closed her eyes, dizzy with relief and gratitude. Relief for his good looks, and gratitude for his timely arrival. By coming to meet her, instead of waiting for her Entry into Edinburgh, the King of Scotland had shown them all, the cynical English and the wary Scots, the extent of his yearning for her.

As Margaret breathlessly presented the Surreys and her ladies, James gazed upon his bride with well concealed dismay. He loathed plump women, especially those, like Margaret, still prone to adolescent spots. When he had entered the chamber and surveyed the confusing array of unfamiliar heads bent before him he had, as he told Elphinstone later, trusted to his gambler's instinct and approached the girl bedecked in the most jewellery.

But if, as he gazed on his bride, James glimpsed for a moment the slim elegant vision of another Margaret, he gave no sign. As the rest of the Scots party burst noisily through the oak door, James left the Surreys to entertain them, and drew Margaret aside.

He gestured towards the green baize card table. 'I see we already have an interest in common?'

Margaret laughed nervously. At least, observed James, none of her teeth had fallen out yet.

'Lady Guildford taught me to play as a child,' said Margaret, 'but for the last few years my father has forbidden card playing. He said it was the work of the Devil, encouraging the Court to neglect their archery skills.'

James stored away this seemingly innocuous nugget of information. If the English alliance weakened, the Scots could well take advantage of the rusty archery prowess of Henry

106

Tudor's army. He smiled at Henry Tudor's daughter. 'Well now you will be able to play cards as often as you wish. And in your own castles. You have become a woman of property, Margaret. Has my lord Surrey told you of my wedding gift?'

Margaret nodded, chanting like an obedient child repeating her rosary: 'You have given me the castles of Doune, Newark and Stirling, and the palaces of Methven and Linlithgow.'

James' face creased with amusement. He said kindly, 'Our strange Scottish names mean nothing to you yet. But they will. I'll take you myself and show you all your castles, your palaces, your forests. And,' he glanced at the diamonds studding her throat, 'you shall wear a rope of matchless pearls from the Scottish crown jewels. Would you like that?' His own Margaret had always refused to wear the pearls, declaring that it was not her right to do so.

From the delight in Margaret Tudor's face as he mentioned the pearls, James knew he had found the avenue to her soul. And now he understood the nature of the chubby girl who stood twisting her hands before him, he deliberately set himself to disarm her. By the time he left Dalkeith that evening, with a whispered promise to Margaret that he would return the following day, he knew he left behind not a frightened young girl but a woman in love.

Margaret slipped peacefully into sleep that night. She dreamed of a man with laughing eyes who had listened sympathetically as she talked of her childhood, her love for her father, her rivalry with brother Henry. He had been attentive, charming and witty. James. He was King. He was kind. He was handsome. He was hers.

Two

Welcome the rose both red and white,
Welcome the flower of our delight,
Our sprite rejoicing from the spleen,
Welcome in Scotland to be Queen.
                    William Dunbar

'Fire! Wake up, my lady. *Wake up!*'

Margaret clung frantically to her fading dreams as Lady Guildford wrenched apart the bedcurtains and shook her roughly by the shoulder.

'The castle is on fire, madam! You must come with me. Quickly!'

Fully alert, as the scent of burning wood filled the air, a terrified Margaret allowed Lady Guildford to bundle her into a blanket. Singed by red hot flying ashes, they raced through an unfamiliar maze of smoke filled chambers, illuminated by livid patches of flaming timber, to the safety of an outer courtyard.

'How did it start?' choked Margaret, watching with horror as servants passed buckets of water hand to hand towards a castle blazing orange against the night sky.

'In the stables, my lady,' said the Earl of Surrey, ignoring Lady Guildford's warning shake of the head.

Margaret's blackened face crumpled. 'Oh no! Guildford, my palfrey! My beautiful white palfrey. I must rescue it!'

Lady Guildford grabbed the hysterical girl, holding her firm while she kicked, lashed and struggled. 'It's no use my lady,' she said quietly. 'The stables are already burnt out.'

The Earl of Surrey pushed back his embroidered nightcap. 'I am afraid none of the horses was saved,' he said gently. 'I am so sorry.'

An inconsolable Margaret was moved for safety to nearby

108

Newbattle Castle. All the way there she lay in Lady Guildford's arms and sobbed for the splendid white horse, the parting gift from her father, that had carried her so faithfully all the way from London. Only when Lady Guildford reminded her of the King's promised visit did Margaret brighten, dry her eyes and remember she was Queen, not a grizzling child.

On hearing of the disaster, James promptly ordered not one but three replacement palfreys to be sent to Margaret.

'Typical Stewart excess,' was Lennox's reaction as he whipped his horse in an attempt to keep up with the royal courser on the way to Newbattle.

The Earl of Angus disagreed. 'Whatever else you may say about the King, you must admit the man is a master at the art of laying siege to a lady's heart. And remember, the more he manages to enslave the Princess Margaret, the more good Scottish mud he's flinging in the eyes of the carping English.'

Events proved the old warrior Bell-the-Cat right. An impressed English herald reported back to Henry Tudor that James flew 'as the bird seeks her prey' to console his bride at Newbattle. James' second visit was, if anything, a greater success than his first. Disarmingly at ease in a black velvet jacket bordered with crimson braid and white fur, the Scottish King appeared entranced as Margaret and the Countess of Surrey performed an intricate *basse* dance for him. After the most commendable display of modesty, James was persuaded to play the clavichord. As Margaret sat on a silken cushion at his feet, James ran his hands over the delicate keys and filled the scented chamber with music from the great love ballads that he knew would haunt the memory of all who heard them. Even the sourest of the English party, who, since crossing the border, had done nothing but sneer at these savage Scots, had to admit that here was a monarch endowed with rare style and grace.

Only the Earl of Surrey said nothing. He rested his domed head on his clenched fist, and absorbed every move, every gesture, every word of the King of Scots.

James had not yet finished with the English. As they accompanied him into the courtyard to say farewell, he turned, and very tenderly kissed Margaret. 'In four days we shall be wed, my little one.'

Margaret flushed. 'The day cannot come soon enough, my lord.'

James delivered the most elegant of Court bows, turned, and spurning the stirrups, took a running leap onto his black courser. Fully aware of the admiring gasps of the English, he called to his nobles and, blowing a kiss to Margaret, galloped away at full pelt through the castle gates.

A slow sarcastic handclap from the Earl of Surrey broke the stunned silence. Margaret was the first to turn away.

'Why so sad?' fussed Lady Guildford. 'Are you not pleased with your dashing, handsome husband?'

Margaret's eyes were shadowed. 'I like him well, Guildford. Too well. Last night I went to sleep with love in my heart. And when I awoke the castle was afire and my precious palfrey burned.'

Lady Guildford looked confused. 'But the King is very generously sending you not one, but three new horses, my lady. And surely you are not suggesting that your feelings for him could in any way have caused the fire?'

'I believe he is a man who attracts fire to those around him,' said Margaret thoughtfully. 'And if you love a man like that, you must be prepared to lose much else that you cherish.'

For Margaret's State Entry into Edinburgh, the city took on an appearance that for once justified its position as one of the royal capitals of Europe. With the streets cleared of the customary fly-infested filth, six cartloads of rose petals were strewn onto the newly washed cobbles. The people, delirious at the prospect of a week's holiday, flung tapestries over the woodwormed balconies and decorated their windows with plaited ribbons in Tudor green and white, Stewart crimson and gold. Edinburgh was en fête, the centuries old hostility towards the English forgotten in a euphoria not entirely unconnected with the promise of free meat and unlimited wine from the King's own cellars.

A mile outside the city, all was not well with the royal party.

The Earl of Surrey and Lord Lennox were engaged in a tight-lipped diplomatic wrangle over the question of precedence. Margaret had turned her back on the Scottish ladies, declaring in a loud whisper to Lady Guildford that their dazzling display of jewellery was not merely ostentatious but downright vulgar.

Lady Lennox was hardly listening, distracted by the throbbing of a bruised *derrière*. The King had asked her to mount behind him on his horse, explaining that he wanted to test the black courser's reaction to a second rider before inviting Margaret to travel with him. With the temperamental animal's violent rejection of Lady Lennox, the matter was settled.

At last, with Surrey and Lennox riding grimly side by side, and Margaret seated behind the King on a docile white palfrey, the trumpets sounded, the band struck up and the royal procession set forth for the capital. Pageants, mock jousts and dancing enlivened their route. Margaret, enchanted, at first regarded the spectacle as a welcome repetition of her joyous journey through England. She accepted the ringing of bells, the fanfares, the shouted greetings of the people as no more than her due. It was only natural that the Scots should want to show their admiration for her, their new Queen.

But with the city gates in sight, Margaret's contented smile began to stiffen. Like the slow penetration of summer rain came the realisation that the cheers of the crowd were not so much for her, as for their King. Her expression hardened as she observed their eyes turning first to James, with love, then to her with a look Margaret miserably interpreted as disappointment. On that glorious month through England she had been the star attraction. It was galling, now, to be relegated to a supporting role: a mere satellite to James' sun.

Lady Guildford, riding a discreet pace or two behind the royal couple, raised her eyes to heaven as she perceived the mood that had settled on Margaret. Nothing would please the girl now.

Margaret dismissed with a glance the turrets of the gatehouse, lavishly gilded in her honour. She received the keys of the city from the Lord Constable with limp, indifferent

111

hands. And she positively glared as, from an arch of golden vine leaves, four young boys clad as angels raised their sweet voices and sang in her praise:

> *Now fair, fairest of every fair,*
> *Princess most pleasant and preclare,*
> *The loveliest one alive that been,*
> *Welcome to Scotland to be Queen.*

'*Fairest of every fair?*' exploded Tom as the royal procession passed by. 'They must be joking, Bella. You're ten times more beautiful than that podgy lump. Old Willie Dunbar knows the King has no time for him, so now he's trying to woo the Queen with his pathetic simpering verse.'

Bella studied every inch of the girl in the lustrous dress of cloth of gold and black velvet. 'She has lovely red hair ... and that sapphire pendant must be worth a fortune. But she's too plump, and her expression *is* a trifle sullen.'

Tom squeezed her waist. 'You'd look more than a trifle sullen if you knew that after your wedding tomorrow you'd be bedded with the King in front of the entire Court.'

'Oh, I don't know. The King is *so* handsome, and – Tom!'

He kissed her in the middle of the milling, jubilant crowd. Bella flung her arms around him. 'Oh, Tom, I'm so happy. A week's holiday! I give you fair warning, I intend to enjoy every minute of it. Just think, no serving sucking pig to over-stuffed courtiers, no running errands, no yes sir, no sir, tickle me too sir.' She dragged Tom towards the High Street. 'Come on, let's find Robert.'

'Knowing your brother, he'll be up by the Market Cross,' predicted Tom. 'They say the fountain there is gushing wine instead of water today.'

Robert was not at the Market Cross. But he was soon for-gotten in a day of dancing, feasting and drinking with their friends, and it was not until late that summer evening that they wandered hand in hand back to the saddlery.

'If he's not here, Tom, we'll know for sure he's up to no good.'

'Probably out burgling the Earl of Surrey.'

'And when we do find him, we'll have no horse talk,' warned Bella. 'We're on holiday, and I don't want to hear any more boring gossip about the King's white horse that he's trained to – '

She froze as Tom's warning hand touched her lips. Hurrying out of the saddlery were two richly dressed men.

'I've seen the Earl of Angus here before,' breathed Bella, 'but who's that with him?'

'The Earl of Huntly,' said Tom, 'One of the wealthiest landowners up in the north. He must be down here for the King's wedding. Strange – you'd think he'd be with the royal party.'

Bella shrugged. 'Perhaps he wanted to buy a saddle.'

'On a public holiday? With all the shops and markets closed?' Tom took her arm. 'Let's go in. Pretend you've seen nothing. Robert's business is his own, remember. If he wants to tell us anything, that's up to him. If not ...'

Robert was sitting at the kitchen table, his carroty head bent over a roughly drawn plan.

Bella said, with forced gaiety, 'What's this Robert? You're not still working at this hour? It's a holiday ... we're supposed to be having fun!'

Robert looked up. One glance at his face told her the festival was over.

'I wanted to talk to you both,' said Robert gravely.

'I was afraid you might,' murmured Tom. 'What is it this time? Are we to steal the Queen's wedding dress? Or is it just a straight case of gatecrashing Holyrood Abbey?' Tom had recognised the plan on the kitchen table.

Robert sat back on his stool, his thumbs tucked into the heavy leather belt at his waist. 'Tomorrow the King marries the English princess. And at some point during the ceremony, or the banquet afterwards, the English are planning to murder Margaret Drummond's daughter, the Lady Margaret Stewart.'

Bella sat down, her face white.

'Tell us what you know, and what we are to do,' said Tom quietly.

113

Robert sighed. 'I know very little. Angus and Huntly uncovered the plot. That bastard Surrey, of course, is behind it. Evidently word has reached the English party of the King's strong attachment to Margaret Drummond. The English feel it is important that no word of their love affair should inflame the delicate ears of the *fairest of the fair*, who is well known for her jealous nature.'

'But the King has had other mistresses,' protested Tom. 'There was Marion Boyd, Janet Kennedy ...'

'But he didn't want to marry them,' said Bella.

Robert nodded. 'Exactly. What's more, he wasn't planning to wed them when he was already married by proxy to the English princess.'

'And with Margaret Drummond already conveniently poisoned, the English intend to perform a vanishing trick on little Margaret Stewart as well,' muttered Tom.

'It's more complicated than that,' explained Robert. 'It's not just the English who are embarrassed by the existence of Lady Margaret Stewart. Certain of our Scottish nobles feel that if Henry Tudor learns of the Drummond romance, he might be incensed enough to use the affair to justify cutting a hefty slice from the Princess' dowry – you've heard how miserly he is. Now with King James pouring money like water on this wedding to impress the English, the Scottish coffers are well nigh empty. If we don't receive Princess Margaret's dowry in full, the country could go bankrupt. And without money to raise arms, we'd be ripe for invasion by the English.'

'God's teeth, how ignoble are our nobles,' cried Bella bitterly. 'Killing Margaret Drummond wasn't enough. Now they're thirsting for her daughter as well.'

'It's tempting, of course, to suspect the Lennoxes and Kennedys,' mused Robert, 'but Angus and Huntly have no proof that they are involved in the plot. We suspect the English will have inside help from certain – interested – Scots, but what we don't know is who the traitors are.'

Instinctively, Bella's thoughts flew to her own three-year-old son, who was being looked after for the day by the reliable

114

Nan. 'Why can't the King send little Meg to Stirling for safety? If the guard was doubled – '

'I suggested that,' interposed Robert, 'but Huntly says the child begged the King to let her attend the wedding. He will refuse her nothing. And increasing the guard at the Abbey would only draw unwelcome attention to the girl.'

'Does the King know of the plot?' asked Tom.

Robert shook his head. 'Apparently not. The King is so involved in the wedding rehearsals, courting Princess Margaret and impressing the English, that Huntly is unwilling to burden him with this fresh crisis.'

A frown creased Tom's freckled brow. 'Presumably Huntly will have his men stationed discreetly around young Meg.'

'Of course,' said Robert. 'But he felt some less conspicuous precautions might be more effective.'

'I wonder why Angus brought Huntly to you?' mused Tom.

Robert grinned. 'I imagine because a few of Perkin Warbeck's swords found their way into Angus's armoury. When he asked me to explain where they came from, I took a risk and told the truth. Old Bell-the-Cat roared with laughter, and said he'd long been an admirer of my powers of persuasion.'

Bella smiled. If Robert could charm the vixen Janet Kennedy, ex-mistress of both Bell-the-Cat and the King, into giving up one of her finest silk dresses, then it was easy meat for him to unearth a murderous plot from a parcel of squabbling nobles.

Tom turned to Bella. 'How reliable is Margaret Stewart's nurse?'

'I don't know. The nurse she'd had since childhood died recently. The new one is Mistress Monroe. I'd recognise her, but I've heard little about her, good or ill.'

'Find out,' instructed Robert, 'tonight. And tomorrow, you will offer your services at the wedding feast. That way, you can keep an eye on the Lennox crowd.'

'And what, pray, will you be doing?'

'Tom and I will be with you at the Castle,' said Robert. 'You will recognise us, though I hope to God no one else does.'

'And what about the Abbey?' pondered Bella. 'Don't tell me your dear admirer Angus gave you an embossed invitation to the wedding?'

Her brother smiled. 'Hardly. But there are more ways into Holyrood Abbey than through the front door.'

Three

Go, my song, and bear my greetings to good wine;
Many a man it tumbles in the swamp,
And many another it sends to bed in his clothes,
And trips up many another on the smoothest path.
A man employs his money well who spends it on good wine.

Anon

By the morning of the royal wedding the disdain of the
English had disintegrated under the hammer blow of a massive
collective hangover – the sorry consequence of the previous
night's vain attempt to drink the Scots under the table. And
the ebullient mood of King James as he led them on a tour
of Holyrood Palace served only to increase their ill humour.

The King had laid his plans well. Since the beginning of
the year a stream of merchants had arrived from Europe,
bringing tapestries, silver plate, satins, silks, velvets and furs.
James had personally supervised the hanging of lustrous red
and blue velvet in the Queen's apartments, along with the
cascade of cloth of gold for the canopy and curtains of her
bed of state. That not a yard had been paid for was a trifle
James left his Council to squabble over.

The English clutched their throbbing heads, surveying the
dazzling splendour of Holyrood through aching, half closed
and wholly unappreciative eyes. They had not asked to come.
They neither liked the Scots nor understood their strange
accent. They loathed the wild uncompromising countryside
and the chilly grandeur of this city built around a granite rock.
They wanted to go home.

More immediately, they prayed for those confounded bells
to stop. Since dawn all the church bells in Edinburgh had
been ringing out in triumph – and every chime had reverberated like a gong in the fragile heads of the English.

The clangour was even worse in Holyrood Abbey as they gathered to celebrate this long awaited, long debated marriage of the Thistle and the Rose. Amidst a deafening tumult of fanfares Margaret entered the Abbey. Every woman craned to catch sight of the ornate wedding gown, of shimmering white and gold damask, bordered with lush crimson velvet. In the charming traditional style of royal brides, Margaret's glittering hair fell loose to her waist, crowned with a circlet of eighty-three gold coins. The King, moving up the aisle to greet her, was an equally spectacular figure, adorned in a cloth of gold shirt, scarlet hose and a long jacket slashed with crimson satin. Over his shoulders was draped a robe worth six hundred pounds of white damask figured with gold.

The Earl of Surrey, not to be outdone in sartorial splendour, had chosen a long gown of cloth of gold, over which was laid his collar of the Order of the Garter.

'My lord Surrey is slipping,' whispered Robert to Tom, from a vantage point high in the Abbey gallery. 'Surely the Countess could have lent him her gold earrings, and a brooch or two?'

Taking advantage of the masons' still unfinished work on the Abbey, the pair had entered, precariously, through an opening in the roof. Now, perched on a beam high above the nave, they concentrated their attention on the child who watched, wide eyed, as the Archbishops of Glasgow and York married her father to a woman only seven years older than herself.

The English were observed to wince as, to a thunderous fanfare of trumpets, James and Margaret approached the altar. Margaret whispered her marriage vows, unaware that at the very moment she received the crystal sceptre as Queen of Scotland, two men knelt above her, their bows taut, their eyes and arrows seeking to protect not her own crowned head, but the raven haired daughter of the King.

Throughout the *Te Deum laudamus* and the long mass, the vigilance of the two men never wavered, although they had agreed it was unlikely that any attempt on the girl's life would be made while she was within the sacred Abbey.

118

'Surrey wouldn't be such a fool,' muttered Robert. 'Besides, in the ensuing fracas he might get blood on his precious cloth of gold.'

Tom had cramp. Not for the first time, he wondered what quirk of fate had led him to marry the sister of the irrepressible Robert the Red. There was a score of other women with whom he could have led a quiet, uneventful and, it had to be admitted, boring life.

'I sometimes think women have the better deal,' he complained, feeling the muscles knotting painfully in his thighs. 'I'd much rather be Bella at this moment, wheedling the Castle cook into giving her titbits of wild boar. Why ever didn't you train your sister to break into abbeys and take on half of England with a bow and arrow?'

'She probably could if she had to,' grinned Robert. 'But, knowing Bella, she'd have hiccuped and given the game away long ago.'

Bella, methodically searching Margaret Stewart's room for traces of poison, eyed the girl's canopied bed with longing.

It was all very well for Robert and Tom, she thought furiously, capering like monkeys across the Abbey roof, and loving every reckless minute of it. They hadn't been up half the night. *Find out about Mistress Monroe*, Robert had instructed. It had taken Bella, with the resourceful Nan's help, until nearly two in the morning to discover the link between Margaret Stewart's new nurse and the threat on the child's life. The trail had led to a wetnurse who, roused from her sleep in a fetid room on the other side of Edinburgh, said irritably that yes, she knew of Mistress Monroe. They had both been employed together ... in the service of Lady Lennox.

Bella had already ransacked Mistress Monroe's small room next to that of Margaret Stewart, convinced she would unearth the poisonous herbs she sought there. But she found nothing. The child's room, too, yielded nothing of interest. Except, Bella was touched to notice, the multi-coloured shawl she had made as a christening present for Margaret Drummond's daughter. Bella had heard that since the day when

119

the King had snatched the girl to safety from Drummond Castle, Margaret Stewart had refused to sleep without the shawl cuddled for comfort in her arms.

Hurrying back to her duties in the kitchen, Bella found the steaming cavern of a room echoing with the feverish commands of the Master Cook, the clanking of well buckets drawing up the spring waters, and the grunts of sweating boys slowly rotating the spits over a heap of blazing oak logs. Bella stood for a moment, savouring the aromatic smells of honey, almonds, mulled wine and fresh pounded spices sprinkled over roasting joints running with succulent juices. It would, she realised, be impossible for anyone to poison Margaret Stewart's food here in the kitchen, without murdering the Queen and all the English into the bargain. So if Margaret Drummond's daughter died tonight, it was more likely to be by the knife.

By six that evening, Edinburgh Castle was ablaze with light, music and laughter. In a Great Hall adorned with brilliant tapestries, and the High Tables trellised in roses, vine leaves and scarlet ribbons, the wedding feast had begun.

Scurrying to and fro with dishes of wild boar, stuffed sucking pigs, roast partridge and syruped quinces, Bella kept an anxious eye open for Tom and her brother. Robert had promised her she would recognise them. But as she scanned the faces of the acrobats, jugglers, dancers and tightrope walkers waiting nervously to entertain the Court, Bella began to wonder if this was merely one of Robert's more elaborate jokes. Her husband and brother were nowhere to be seen. Knowing Robert's sense of irony, she looked hard at the tightrope walkers. But even a master of disguise like her brother, she decided, could never have grown a veined hook nose and spindly chicken legs.

As she waited, Bella concentrated on memorising the prominent members of the Court in their respective places. It was vital, Robert had emphasised, that she should be instantly aware if anyone suddenly defected from the feast.

At the High Table, conversing with the King and Queen, sat the Earl of Surrey. Huntly was at his side, whispering confidences to Bishop Elphinstone. Margaret Stewart was tucked away with the other children of the Court in a small alcove, out of the Queen's sight. Bella glanced across to the opposite side of the Hall where the Lennoxes and Kennedys laughed with the Earl of Mallaig. They all seemed completely relaxed and at ease. Yet at this moment, she knew, one or more of them was contemplating murder.

Two hours passed before the King laid down his knife. In that time, the illustrious company had drunk fifty casks of French wine and consumed more than forty courses served on silver plate, ending with a magnificent jelly quivering with the royal arms of Scotland and England. Bella had watched the cook matching his creation shake for shake when first it had failed to turn out of the mould.

Now it was Bella's turn to feel rising panic. In the alcove, several of the children had fallen asleep on the floor, heaped like puppies on top of one another. Young Margaret Stewart's bright blue eyes were still wide open, but Bella felt it was only a matter of time before the dreaded Mistress Monroe arrived to claim her.

The King turned to his radiant Queen and asked whom he should call to entertain her. Without hesitation she chose the two jugglers sitting waiting near the children's alcove with a basket of silver balls and clubs. Dressed in jesters' costumes, with cap and bells and painted smiles, they looked anything but happy to Bella. In fact, they appeared to be quarrelling. In fact . . .

'Robert, there's something I have to tell you,' said Tom urgently.

'There's no time,' replied his companion, pulling Tom to his feet. 'The King has commanded us to perform – now.'

'Robert. *I don't know how to juggle*!'

'Good. I shall shine all the brighter by comparison.'

'You said,' hissed Tom, gingerly picking up two silver clubs, 'that we wouldn't have to *do* anything. And it's as hot as horse piss in this idiot costume.'

Robert, bowing low to the High Table, whispered from the side of his mouth, 'How was I to know the Queen has a weakness for jugglers? Cheer up, it could be worse. We could have disguised ourselves as tightrope walkers.'

Robert selected six silver balls and threw them into an arc over his head, catching and throwing them again with a dexterity that brought delighted murmurs from the Court. Uttering a silent prayer, Tom cautiously hurled a silver club into the juniper scented air. It crashed to the floor. As the eyes of the Court turned uncertainly towards the High Table, Robert pelted his luckless partner with silver balls, loudly berating him for his incompetence.

The Queen giggled. Relieved, the Court laughed with her. Robert pitched more balls up over the cross beams, pantomiming: *look, it's easy, this is how you do it.* Tom, falling easily now into the role of buffoon, flung up his clubs, caught one with both hands and narrowly avoided being brained by the other. The crowd roared. Robert feigned anger. In an exaggerated gesture of helplessness, he tossed a silver ball towards the Queen. She caught it, smiling, and threw it playfully at the butterfingered Tom. In minutes, all the ladies of the Court were clamouring for the silver balls.

Out of the corner of her eye Bella saw the white aproned figure of Mistress Monroe urging a protesting Margaret Stewart to her feet. The child obviously wished to stay and see the end of the fun, but her stifflipped guardian had other ideas. Grasping the King's daughter firmly by the ear, she marched her from the Great Hall, though not before Margaret had directed a well-aimed kick at her nurse's shin. At the same moment, the air was filled with silver hailstones, as all the ladies pelted Tom with the shiny balls. With a breathtaking series of cartwheels, Tom vanished from sight after Mistress Monroe, leaving Robert to perform a finale with the silver clubs.

Bella knew that time was running out. Setting down her tray, she took one goblet of wine and hurried out up the back stairs towards the Lady Margaret Stewart's room.

As the dancers took the floor, Robert lingered amongst the revellers, slowly gathering up the silver missiles scattered around the garlanded tables. Yet all the time his eyes were scanning the glistening faces in the Hall, vigilant for one suspicious move, one untoward look. He was sweltering in the jester's costume, and plagued by the accursed tinkling of the bell on his cap. Drawing his dagger, Robert sent the jangling object rolling to the floor. Which was how, when it happened, Robert was looking the wrong way.

It was Lord Huntly, ostensibly on his way to pay the dancers on behalf of the King, who murmured to the still kneeling Robert: 'I believe our man has just left.'

Furious with himself, Robert fled from the Hall, up the stairs to the stone gallery leading to Margaret Stewart's apartments. As he expected, the candles in the gallery had been doused. His hand dropped to his dirk as, cat-like, he inched his way through the gloom towards the young girl's chamber. A thin, high shriek of terror, instantly muffled, stopped him in his tracks. Seconds later, the barest change in the shadow of darkness warned Robert that Margaret's door was opening. For a moment, the figure of a man stood silhouetted. Robert's mind hammered . . . too far to throw the dagger . . . but he had another weapon. The juggling club shimmered like a flying silver fish as it flew, hard and true through the murk to strike the running man smartly on the back of the head, bringing him crashing down. Robert sprang, crouching over him, dagger poised. The man was conscious, but too stunned to offer any resistance. Robert seized him by his embroidered collar, and dragged him to a window.

For several minutes he gazed down on the man's face. But a contemptuous, *'get out!'* was all Robert said as he flung the man towards the stairs. Only then did he open the door to Margaret's room. He walked with unhurried steps towards the bed. The white damask cover was soaked with blood. Gently, he turned it back and looked dispassionately on the butchered body of Mistress Monroe.

That night, bonfires blazed in every civic square, and all over Scotland people danced till dawn in the streets. Up at the Castle, the mood of the Court was distinctly sour. The King had indicated that the time was now opportune for him and his Queen to withdraw to the bridal chamber at Holyrood. Eagerly the Court surged forward, each lord and lady determined to witness this ultimate consummation of the Scotland–England alliance. The King raised his hand, and courteously bade them goodnight. Ever a warm hearted and sensitive man, he saw no reason why this young virgin should be subjected to such a public ordeal. Taking Margaret by the hand, he led her to their bedchamber, alone. If the Court felt cheated of their vicarious pleasure, for Queen Margaret it was a reprieve, an act of kindness she never forgot.

At midnight, Robert and Tom were to be found sprawled on Bella's kitchen floor, dedicated to the estimable task of getting drunk. They felt they deserved a celebration. For somehow, their audacious scheme had succeeded ...

When Tom and Bella had left Robert juggling in the Great Hall, both had followed Mistress Monroe. As they anticipated, her actions that night could hardly be interpreted as in the best interests of the little girl in her charge. After putting Margaret to bed, the nurse had left the child's door unlocked and deliberately snuffed out all the candles in the gallery. When Tom pounced, Mistress Monroe was slipping on her cape prior to fleeing the Castle.

Tom was a powerfully built man and had no trouble forcing the frightened nurse to drink the wine Bella had prepared. The potion, laced with selected herbs from Bella's garden, speedily reduced the woman to a state of docile drowsiness.

Bella's next task was more difficult. Somehow she had to persuade a six-year-old child to leave the imagined safety of her cosy bed, and accompany her, a perfect stranger, to another part of the Castle. There was so little time. From Mistress Monroe's treacherous actions it was clear that the murderer was ready to strike at any moment.

Margaret Stewart, still haunted by the chilling screams of her dying mother, had learned long ago to trust no one lightly.

She sat hunched in her bed, fear pinching her young face. 'I don't know who you are. If you don't go away, *now*, I shall call my nurse and the guards.'

Bella knelt beside her. 'My name is Bella Fraser,' she

said quietly. 'I knew your mother. Look, she gave me this pearl.'

Margaret eyed the pearl suspiciously. 'Anyone could have given you that.'

Bella controlled an urge simply to seize the girl and bundle her from the room. She thought of the unknown assassin mounting the stairs, and Tom supporting the drugged nurse outside the door, ready to throw her into Margaret's bed. Her heart raced as she caught sight of the shawl clutched tight in the girl's hand.

'That shawl! Did your mother ever tell you where it came from?'

Margaret nodded. 'She said it was made for me by a woman who would one day be my friend.'

'That's me! I made it. I gave it to your mother at Linlithgow, just after you were born.'

The bright blue eyes of the child widened in disbelief. 'How do I know you are telling the truth?'

'No one else in Edinburgh, in all southern Scotland could crochet a shawl like that,' Bella told her. 'It's a Highland art, and I'm a Highland girl, born and bred.' Suddenly inspired, Bella jumped to her feet and lifted her skirt. 'Look. There, you must believe me now!'

Margaret peered down at Bella's shift. The worn cambric was edged with a deep frill, crocheted in exactly the same intricate pattern as Margaret's multicoloured shawl.

The doubt melted from the girl's face. She put her hand into Bella's, and said, 'Shall we go?'

'So the Lady Margaret is safe,' said Tom, raising his cup for Bella to pour more of her heather ale.

Bella smiled. 'She's in seventh heaven, sitting on the Castle kitchen table and scraping out the jelly mould. The cook will care for her tonight. But tomorrow, she will require a new attendant, and I shall apply for the position.'

'If that's what you want. It'll be convenient with both of us working for the King's household.' Tom turned to Robert, who was gazing into the embers of the kitchen range. 'What happened to the murderer?'

'He got away,' said Robert shortly.

Tom masked his surprise. 'But didn't you see who it was?'

Robert was looking straight at Bella. 'Yes. It was Malcolm Laxford, Earl of Mallaig.'

Tom whistled. *'Mallaig?'* But when neither Robert nor Bella made any further comment, he stretched, and said lightly, 'Well I don't envy that young man when Huntly and his armed guards get hold of him.'

'They won't,' said Robert. 'I intend to tell Huntly that I didn't get a proper look at the man's face.'

Perplexed, Tom glanced at Bella, but she was busy throwing wet pine cones onto the glowing fire. Robert stabbed at the embers with an iron poker. 'I want the pleasure of dealing with Mallaig personally ... in my own time ... and in my own way.'

Four

My sickness comes, oh! Love, you know it,
From loving a false friend
Who promised me that he would always be
My faithful lover; alas for me, poor wretch,
I trusted him, and so my heart is breaking;
For his falsely charming words
And his courteous loving manner
Made me believe that he spoke truthfully;
And he did not: the thing is fully proved;
And thus he robbed my heart of all its joy.

Christine de Pisan

If Lord Huntly was surprised at the ease with which the King was persuaded to appoint a common serving girl as attendant to the Lady Margaret Stewart, he was a wise enough diplomat not to show it. But he was careful to counsel Bella of the King's express wish that to avoid upsetting the Queen, on no account must the first lady be made aware of the presence of the child. At least, thought Bella wryly, until she is safely delivered of a child, a legitimate heir, of her own.

Somehow, against overwhelming odds, the conspiracy of silence was maintained. There were those, Bella knew, who would have been only too willing to drop a timely word in the young Queen's jewelled ear. But for the moment they had been effectively gagged by Huntly's swift intervention over the murder plot on the Queen's wedding day. Although there had been no official reprisals, both Huntly and Robert Kyle had let it be known, in their respective circles, that the would-be assassin had been recognised and was under surveillance. Next time, went the carefully nurtured rumour, his head would be not just sore: it would be severed.

Bella quickly established an excellent relationship with the

King's young daughter. The girl delighted in a new name Bella had given her – Mairead – the lovely Gaelic version of Margaret. She was intelligent, goodnatured towards those she liked, and spirited enough to enjoy the game of cloak and dagger to which she was subjected whenever the panic call went out that the Queen was approaching. Although Mairead was lodged in Edinburgh Castle, a mile away from the Queen's apartments in Holyrood Palace, Huntly had ordered Bella to take no chances. If the Queen was in Edinburgh, then Mairead must be somewhere else.

Bella saw no sense in keeping the truth from Mairead. How else could she explain the hurried departures from Edinburgh to Stirling to Linlithgow and back to Edinburgh again? To Mairead it was a great game. To Bella, a nightmare. Even with Tom, Robert and Blackpatch waiting with horses, disguises and delaying tactics for the approaching royal party, Bella felt like a hunted animal, destined always to be on the run.

The situation was further aggravated by the restless nature of the King. He grew irritable and discontented if he resided at one palace for more than a few months, and liked nothing better than to leap on his horse and gallop off with his Court to yet another of his castles. For James, travelling was a simple matter. But his Queen, eager though she was to accompany her new husband, turned each trip into a full scale expedition. She could not, would not embark on a journey without her full retinue of ladies, her chests of dresses, her baskets of fine linen and her large collection of jewels, to which she was passionately attached. James, who travelled light, regarded his wife's luggage train with exasperated resignation. Inevitably, something vital was mislaid, some other essential left behind, and Margaret was forever complaining that her maids had failed to pack clothes suitable for the prevailing conditions at each particular palace.

For Bella, the Queen's love affair with her possessions was a blessing. If she had ridden, like the King, unencumbered, free and fast, Bella would have had no time to hustle young Mairead out of sight. But when more than thirty wagons were required to transport the Queen and her personal effects, Bella could be sure of receiving plenty of warning.

Even so, there were times when Bella's blood ran colder than spring water. Her worst moment came one gusty autumn night when two lame horses had delayed Mairead's departure from Linlithgow to Stirling. Robert found masks and torches, and as the royal party swept across the draw-bridge, the Queen and her courtiers were greeted by a group of Hallowe'en revellers. The meeting would have passed without note or incident, had not Mairead suddenly kicked her pony and, holding aloft a grisly turnip head, cantered round the Queen, shrieking:

> *This is the night of Hallowe'en,*
> *When the witches can be seen,*
> *Some are black and some are green*
> *And some the colour of a turkey bean!*

Before the astonished Queen could call for the guards, Tom caught the reins of the girl's pony and dragged her to safety beyond the palace gates. Bella, racing in the direction of Mairead's shrill screams of laughter, reflected that the child had been born at this very palace, in the middle of the March gales. Sometimes it seemed as if her soul was possessed by the wind's wild, uncontrollable spirit.

Catching up with Tom and the unrepentant Mairead, Bella snatched down some berries from a rowan tree, and threw them into the child's flying black hair.

'You foolish girl, bringing yourself to the attention of the Queen like that! And you *know* it's unlucky to mock at the witches.'

Mairead pushed back her mask, shaking her hair free of the scarlet fruit. 'Oh, *Bella*! You're so superstitious. As if a few rowan berries would scare off a witch. Anyway, they're such stupid creatures, pretending they can go to sea in sieves and egg shells. How silly.'

'Haven't you heard the story,' asked Robert gravely, 'of poor Agnes Simpson? She was about your age. She confessed at the Assizes that a witch had helped her to sail out of Berwick on a chimney, and led her to a wonderful ship, loaded with the most magnificent feast you ever saw. Well, Agnes and the witch tucked into the food. But when it was finished, the ship sank and the witch disappeared, leaving the wretched Agnes and her chimney to find their own way home.'

This cautionary tale, told by the ghostly light of the moon, reduced Mairead not to a frightened silence but to fits of giggles. All the way to Stirling she drove Bella mad trying to find a rhyme for chimney.

For the Queen, the two years following her marriage were unlike anything she had known in the cloistered Court of Richmond. Determined not to be left behind whenever James' wanderlust took hold, Margaret gamely followed wherever he led. She went hawking with him in Falkland, smiled through what she privately regarded as an excruciating performance on the bagpipes by the burghers at Dumfries, and returned to Edinburgh in time to play her part in the Easter celebrations. She insisted on rowing at James' side across the water to Anstruther and endured agonies of self-deprivation lodging with him in half-ruined castles and abbeys, where well intentioned monks and nuns provided a feast for the spirit but precious little in the way of bodily sustenance.

Through bleak, mountainous countryside, in lacerating winds and lashing rain, Margaret, whose father had often declared her to be a delicate girl, stuck firmly to her husband's side. She dreaded the inclement weather, and feared the dark, stark hills. But she loved James. The more she learned of him, the more she delighted in being the wife of this brilliant, amusing man who could hawk and hunt, dance and play the lute with a skill and fire that inspired everyone around him. And when at last the rain stopped, and the skies cleared, James showed Margaret a different Scotland ... a land where the sun brought scented steam from hedgerows twined with honeysuckle and wild rose, as he took her hand and sang:

> Now the fields are laughing,
> Now the maidens playing,

130

The face of earth is smiling,
Summer now appearing,
Joyous and lovely with all flowers beguiling.

James' unquenchable curiosity fascinated Margaret. At haymaking time, he was unable to resist asking a harvester to let him try his hand with the sickle. The King stood in the middle of the sunsoaked cornfield, surrounded by his richly dressed Court and laughing ragged peasants, laying about him with the reaping hook like a carefree lad of twelve ... until he hit a patch of cornflowers whose tough stems blunted the tool. Abashed, James reached into his silk purse and gave the reaper a gold piece worth the price of ten new sickles.

It was an act of generosity characteristic of James. He showered Margaret with jewels, dresses and costly trinkets. On the rare ocassions when he made a pilgrimage to a shrine without her, he always returned bearing an exotic present, like the white peacock which strutted beneath her window at Linlithgow.

In their lovemaking, too, Margaret found James sensitive to her slightest change of mood. When they married, three years ago, she had been little more than a child, and his attitude towards her had been benevolent, almost paternal. But now, at sixteen, Margaret had ripened into a physically mature woman, with a Tudor passion which equalled that of her red-blooded Stewart husband. They were well matched, thought Margaret. The marriage was a success. Such was the Queen's confidence in herself that she severed the last tie with her childhood and despatched Lady Guildford back to Richmond to care for her young sister Mary.

Margaret had only one regret: she had not yet conceived. Knowing how James longed for an heir, she was desperate not to disappoint him. But, she consoled herself, there was plenty of time. And meanwhile, there was still enough of the child in Margaret for her to look forward with bubbling excitement to Christmas.

It was a particularly pixillated Christmas at Holyrood that year, a festival no one ever forgot. Margaret's furrier remembered it as a work marathon during which he and his harassed assistant toiled for four days and three nights preparing the Queen's new gowns. The merry Court talked for months afterwards about the morris dance performed under the auspices of the King's favourite Moorish drummer, who indulged his wry sense of humour by dressing the dancers in striking coats of half black and half white. The King, helpless with laughter as the Abbot of Unreason led the entire Court in a game of catch-me-and-pinch-me across the yew laden trestle tables, was to look back on the holiday as a time of peace. His nation was united, his alliance with England was holding firm, his Queen was content. And for Margaret, entranced by the acrobats, the mummers and the cornucopia of gifts James laid before her, it was the last happy Christmas of her life.

'This palace stinks worse than a pig pen!' shouted the Queen.

Patiently, the Master of the King's Household explained that he had done all he could. The rushes on the floor were changed daily, sweet laurel had been hung in every chamber, and all the windows were sealed against the damp January air. About the odours from the kitchens the Master admitted nothing could be done.

The King had left Edinburgh, leading an army south to put down a border revolt in Eskdale. Margaret, deprived of his lively company, was finding the winter months at Holyrood intolerable. It was not merely that she missed James. There was the harsh Scottish weather to contend with as well: the mornings when her bowl of washing water froze over, the driving sleety rain battering against the windows, and the howling winds that invaded every cranny of the palace. Even the great roaring fires proved ineffectual against the bitter cold, for the wind swept down the vast chimneys, sending acrid smoke billowing into the chambers. The smell and sooty grime clung to the tapestries and woodwork, making everything greasily unpleasant to touch.

The Queen's ladies tried valiantly to distract her. They sang, danced, told stories and spent hours either admiring her

132

latest finery or dutifully losing to her at cards. Margaret, sullen and discontented, would be mollified by none of these diversions. Even her beloved jewels brought her little pleasure. Roaming restlessly round the evil smelling palace, she began to understand and appreciate James' constant craving for change. By moving home every few months he at least escaped the dank, chicken-coop atmosphere that built up after the Court was confined for too long in one place.

At the end of February Lady Lennox made a suggestion to the bored and fretful Queen.

'Why not remove to Stirling, madam? A fresh outlook would revive you, I'm sure. If we left early tomorrow, we could be dining in the clean sweet Hall at Stirling by nightfall.'

Margaret hesitated. In all the years of her marriage she had never before moved anywhere without James. 'But my dresses, my linens ... it will take days for my ladies to prepare ...'

'We'll have everything sent on.' Lady Lennox was at her most persuasive. 'Think, my lady – it will be such an adventure. Just a few of us setting out for Stirling. And I *know* the King will approve. Having spent Christmas in Edinburgh he is bound to welcome a change of residence for the spring.'

Margaret proved an easy conquest. Secretly, the idea of making such a move on her own initiative excited her. She hoped James would not be angry, but after all, she was Queen, and presumably free to travel wherever she wished.

Exhilarated by her new sense of freedom, Margaret enjoyed her journey to Stirling, despite the icy weather and rough roads. Wrapped in ermine, she chose as her travelling companions Lady Lennox, whose company she found increasingly agreeable, and the Court poet, William Dunbar. Dunbar, one of the Scottish emissaries who had journeyed down to Richmond to escort her on her journey north, was a particular favourite of the Queen. His poems in lavish praise of London had soon endeared him to the English Court, while his verses in equally copious adoration of Margaret herself had done much to gratify her voracious sense of vanity.

She could never understand James' hostility towards

Dunbar. He had been indignant, almost angry, when she had told him Dunbar was renowned in London as Scotland's greatest poet.

'I always knew the English had no taste,' James had exploded. 'The only reason I sent the balding old fool down to London was to get him out of my hair — fawning, talentless creature.' He had wagged a jewelled finger. 'Don't be misled by his flattering verses to you, Margaret.'

Margaret had hotly defended her bard. 'It's not his fault if he has to rely on the patronage of the Court for his pension. And he doesn't just write verses about me. There are poems about you, and the shocking dirty streets of Edinburgh, and . . . oh, all sorts of things. He's a poet of our time.'

James had laughed then, and kissed her, and told her how pretty her new gown looked. She knew he had favoured another poet, one Robert Henryson, a weird, uncouth fellow who had dared to refuse to appear at Court. But Henryson was of no interest to Margaret: he had died years ago, and could hardly write charming verses to her from his grave. Now, with James away, Margaret was able to indulge her patronage of Dunbar to the full.

The royal party, led by a flushed, laughing Margaret, arrived at Stirling at dusk. At the Castle gates, the Keeper greeted her with open-mouthed dismay. 'My lady! We are unprepared. We did not know . . . we had no word that you were coming.'

Margaret, huddled in her furs, was astonished at the commotion she had caused. Servants scurried across the courtyard, lighting torches, shouting orders and bumping one into the other as the Castle household erupted into confusion.

It was Lady Lennox who soothed the aggrieved Keeper and issued concise instructions to the harassed servants for the preparation of the Queen's apartments, and the Queen's supper. This done, she motioned to the chastened Margaret. 'Do you hear the sound of violins within the Castle, my lady? Perhaps while the good Keeper is making ready for you, we should while away a pleasant hour listening to the fiddlers?'

Margaret clapped her gloved hands. 'Oh yes! And Master Dunbar can set some words to the music.'

Led by the lively tune of the fiddlers, the trio crossed the courtyard, stumbled up unlit stairways and crossed empty chambers, until at last with an extravagant flourish, William Dunbar flung open the door from whence the music came.

Smiling, the Queen entered a bare room where a dark haired child was in the middle of a dancing lesson. The music stopped abruptly. The fiddlers, the dancing master, the child and her attendant bowed, curtseyed, waited. The atmosphere was strangely tense.

Bella recovered first. Hustling Mairead towards the door, she murmured respectfully, 'Excuse me, madam. The child was merely practising some simple steps. We were unaware that you had graced the castle with your presence.'

Margaret, the smile wiped from her face, stood square in the doorway. She ignored Bella.

'Who is this child?' she asked Lady Lennox.

'I should imagine, madam, she is one of the daughters of the Keeper of the Castle,' replied Lady Lennox unconvincingly.

Margaret surveyed the dancing master. 'You are William Tabroner, are you not?'

The man bowed.

'And what,' the Queen demanded of the room at large, '*what* is the King's dancing master doing, giving lessons to a mere child of the Keeper of the Castle?'

No one dared reply.

For the first time, Margaret gazed fully at the child. To her surprise, the girl stared coolly back.

'What is your name?' rapped the Queen.

The girl dipped the briefest of curtseys. Then her eyes met those of her father's wife. 'I am the Lady Margaret Stewart,' she said clearly.

The Queen had been trained from birth never to register surprise or dismay in public. Though her blood was beginning to race, her face was impassive as she enquired, 'And who is your father?'

135

'My lady,' interceded Lady Lennox. 'If I may suggest –'

The Queen whirled on her. 'We are beginning to distrust your suggestions, Lennox. Be silent.' Again she demanded, 'Who is your father?'

Mairead glanced uncertainly at Bella who nodded, murmuring, *'Gu dearbh, Mairead.'**

'My father is King James IV of Scotland.'

The temperature in the room seemed to drop ten degrees. Bella fully expected to see frost icing the royal brow as the Queen said, her tone glacial, 'And have I the good fortune to be acquainted with your mother?'

Mairead's dark head was held high. 'My mother is dead.'

'How was she called?'

'Her name . . .' the childish voice wavered. *Don't cry*, prayed Bella. Please, my brave *leanaban*, don't cry. The girl's voice steadied, then sang out proudly, 'Her name was the Lady Margaret Drummond.'

The Queen's face was as blank as her fogged mind. Drummond? No one had ever mentioned a Margaret Drummond. She knew Lord John Drummond, of course, an ambitious though well-respected member of the Court. And she recalled that his wife, Elizabeth, was excused attendance at Court on the grounds of failing health. Or so she had been told.

The Queen indicated that she wished to sit down. Knees creaking, Dunbar stumbled forward with a chair. Once more, the Queen addressed young Mairead.

'I have interrupted your lesson. I have a fancy to see how well the daughter of the King dances. Pray continue.'

Terrified, Mairead looked to Bella for help. Bella hiccuped. 'Excuse me, madam. The child is tired. She would be glad, some other day, after more preparation – '

The Queen's eyes blazed. 'She will dance for me *now*!'

Bella smiled encouragingly at Margaret Stewart as the girl walked slowly to the middle of the polished wooden floor. Hesitantly the musicians struck up a gentle, lilting tune and with regal grace, Mairead lifted her arms. Although the dance

* 'Certainly Mairead.'

136

she had chosen to perform was one of the most difficult in her repertoire, not once did the girl's blue eyes leave the frigid face of the woman who sat, straight backed, watching her. Anyone less well acquainted with the King's daughter might have been tempted to interpret that look as one verging on insolence. Only Bella appreciated the rare control the girl was exercising over her feelings. Margaret Stewart, Bella realised, was furious. There was nothing this free spirited creature resented more than the knowledge that she had been out-manoeuvred. Forced to perform like a dancing bear, she was being humiliated, publicly, and for once in her indulged, royal life, there was nothing she could do about it. Her habitual weapons of screaming outrage and stormy tears were useless before the implacable, tightlipped presence of the Queen. At least, thought Bella, her fingers tightly crossed, the girl has enough sense to know when she's caught. A tantrum now, with the King away could result in the Queen clipping Mairead's wings by packing her speedily off to France or, worse, England. But Mairead was doing nothing to provoke. The gliding movements, the set of her head, the demure curve of her mouth were all icily correct. Only in the depths of those clear blue eyes fastened, unwavering, on the Queen, could one detect a hint of the rebellious, unbroken spirit that flamed her soul.

Danish eyes, decided the Queen, recalling the portraits of James' mother. While the nose, and the firm chin were unmistakably Stewart. But the raven hair and flawless translucent complexion held an echo of someone else. The Drummond woman.

Two spots of colour stained Margaret's cheeks as the full implication of this child's existence flooded through her. James had made a fool of her. The entire Court, the whole of Scotland must have been aware of this Drummond mistress, this Stewart daughter. And how many other mistresses and their byblows were lurking in the castle closets? Everyone had known, laughed, and whispered behind her back. And for nearly three years she had sincerely believed that James was as much in love with her as she was with him.

A kaleidoscope of memories dizzied her . . . James serenading her amidst a field of poppies . . . a farmer's harvest-home feast, when she and James had disguised themselves as peasants and joined in the games, the teasing, the kissing . . . the lovemaking . . .

Now it was all spoilt. Nothing could ever be the same again. And all because of this pert brat of a girl. God, if only the child would stop staring at her like that. There was something knowing and unsettling in those brilliant blue eyes. Even her choice of dance, the *basse*, seemed calculated to cause most hurt. For by some eerie coincidence, the girl was demonstrating, extremely ably, the same rhythmic, flowing movements that Margaret herself had performed for James when he had come courting her with such *élan* at Newbattle.

As the hot tears stung her eyes Margaret's overwhelming instinct was to rush from the room and bury herself in the comforting warmth and darkness of her curtained bed. But she was the Queen of Scotland. Dignity was paramount. She must swallow her sobs, suffer Dunbar's fawning, tolerate Lady Lennox's illconcealed smile of satisfaction, and compliment the musicians. She allowed herself the luxury, however, of ignoring Margaret Stewart. Instead she turned to William Tabroner.

'Your pupil is a credit to you, Master Tabroner. The positioning of her feet and arms is perfect. But I think she would be wise to pay a little more attention to her expression.'

She swept from the chamber, raw from the effort of sustained self-control. She told herself she was imagining that, from the room she had just left, she could hear the sound of a child's mocking laughter.

Five

Most honoured lady, your splendour fair
Has overwhelmed me, and I am yours
I shall not waver, I yield me quite;
Thus say they all, and yet it's never so.
                              Jean le Seneschal

'Marion Boyd. Janet Kennedy. *Margaret Drummond*!' The Queen spat out the names like mouthfuls of dirty water.

James, returning to Stirling tired and out of temper after a successful, though debilitating expedition against the Eskdale rebels, had looked forward to an excellent dinner in the company of a laughing, solicitous, dutiful wife. Instead, he was confronted by a screaming harridan, her face contorted with selfrighteous rage and indignation. James had already gathered the gist of the crisis from Bishop Elphinstone, who had ridden to meet him at the city gates to warn the King of the domestic holocaust awaiting him at the castle. Elphinstone had indicated that with her pride dented by the discovery of Margaret Stewart, the Queen had lashed herself into a fury by compelling certain ladies of the Court to yield everything they knew of the King's licentious past. James was sure that Lady Lennox, for one, would have required little persuading to spill out, in sympathetic whispers, the names and details of all his past mistresses, plus a liberal sprinkling of salacious anecdotes for good measure.

Exhausted though he was, James made an effort to calm his distraught Queen. He sat her down beside him in their chamber, took her hand and talked to her gently, as if she were a frightened little girl seeking reassurance.

'Margaret, my love. Listen to me, now. You say I have deceived you. But when we were first wed, you were no more than a child. You had come to be Queen of a foreign land,

139

and to marry a royal stranger. I thought they were burdens enough for one so young. I sought to protect you from that which I believed you would not understand. So, naturally, I kept from you the fact that before I met you I had mistresses, and children too. Surely you would not have expected me to remain celibate all those years before my marriage?'

Margaret bit her lip. In truth, she had never given the matter a thought. Vain, self-centred Margaret. Not for a moment had it occurred to her to pause, and wonder about James' personal life before her own arrival in Scotland. But although she was forced, now, to concede that there had been other women in his life, she saw no reason to suffer a continual reminder of one of those mistresses, impertinently taking dancing lessons in one of her own castles.

'But you wanted to marry this Margaret Drummond,' the Queen burst out. 'In fact, they say you *did* wed her, secretly, in a little village church in Perth.'

James rested his head in his hands, shielding his eyes from Margaret's accusing gaze. 'What *they* should also have told you,' he said acidly, 'is that Margaret Drummond was a woman of grace, honesty and integrity. She would never have consented to a hole in the corner marriage. Anyway, all that was a long time ago. It is over and,' the lie did not come easily, 'forgotten.'

Margaret's eyes narrowed. 'How can it be forgotten when you keep her daughter near you?'

'Of course young Margaret Stewart is very dear to me,' said James patiently. 'I cannot forget that she watched her mother die an excruciating death. I feel the least I can do is to provide her with all the love and security within my power. You of all people should understand that, Margaret. You've told me how you wept at your own mother's deathbed. Can you imagine how much more desolate you would have felt without a father's arm to lean on?'

Margaret was silent. James pressed on, 'I am married to *you*, Margaret. It is *you* who is the Queen of Scotland, not a poor dead woman.'

Sensing victory, Margaret demanded, 'As Queen, I insist

that you send the girl away. I will not have another woman's child cluttering up my castles.'

The King's voice was level. 'She is not another woman's child, Margaret. She is my daughter. If you do not wish to set eyes on her, then that is easily arranged. But send her away I will not.'

Margaret plucked at the tassel on her silken girdle. Deep down, she knew that James was right. Margaret Drummond was just a box of bones, now. It was foolish to fear the past. A dead woman could not harm her, and a nine-year-old child, though a nuisance, could surely be dealt with.

She put the niggling problem of the King's daughter aside for later consideration, and turned her attention to the other names on her black list. Marion Boyd, she knew, had been a mere youthful infatuation. She may not be dead like Margaret Drummond, but the flame of passion had been extinguished long ago. Which left the red-haired Janet Kennedy who, Margaret had been told, was still very much alive ... and capable of kicking.

Margaret, like her brother Henry, had still to master the art of the subtle campaign. 'You've been seeing that Kennedy woman again!' she flared.

James sighed, suddenly bored. 'Of course I have. What of it?'

His indifference took some of the steam from Margaret's attack. 'What of it?' she blustered. 'But you've been lying to me. You've said countless times that you were going to pray at the shrine of St Ninian. I know full well it was only an excuse to bed that carroty-haired strumpet.'

'For the daughter of a King, Margaret, you are extraordinarily naive,' James sipped his wine and regarded his wife calmly. 'Did your father not have mistresses?'

'No!' Margaret's face was scarlet. 'He and my mother were *devoted*.'

James rolled his fine hazel eyes. 'That explains your outraged attitude, then. Well, my English rose, here in dear old barbaric Scotland, things are somewhat different. Scottish Kings have always taken mistresses. I suppose they always will. You seem blind to the fact that most of the Court – including your tattling ladies – are unfaithful to their respective spouses. It is just the way of life here. And like it or not, you will have to accustom yourself to it.'

Margaret's voice faltered under James' stinging honesty. 'Are you telling me you're not going to stop bedding this Kennedy bitch?'

'If I wish to see Janet Kennedy, or any other woman, then I shall,' shrugged James. 'But I will attempt to be discreet. I would not wish to cause you hurt, or undue embarrassment in the eyes of the Court.' He raised a hand. Margaret flinched. But the fingers rested under her chin, tilting up Margaret's sullen, uncomprehending face to look into the searching eyes of her husband.

'I don't understand why you are so upset. You are my wife. You are Queen. You are the first lady of the land. Every woman in Scotland envies you. You have castles, palaces, forests, hundreds of dresses and a matchless collection of jewels. What more do you want?'

'I want you,' muttered Margaret.

'But you have me. Are we not married?'

'I am not willing to share you.'

'But you have to share me, as you put it, with the people. I am King as well as your husband. If you accept that I have a duty to my subjects, that I have to give myself to them, surely you can concede that occasionally I will sleep in the bed of another woman.' As the tears welled up again in Margaret's eyes James slammed his fist against the carved bedpost. 'Damn it, Margaret, I'm a restless man. I crave change. Sometimes I seek the company of a different woman. But you always come first. Always. Can't you understand that?'

He stood up, lines of weariness etched on his weatherglazed face. 'I am hungry. Will you come and eat with me?'

She shook her head. James stroked her hair, and said softly, 'It is time you grew up, Margaret. Time you accepted the world as it is. If you try and fight the accepted order of things, it is you who will end up the loser. We have been happy

142

together. Why allow this trifling matter to spoil our contentment?'

To Margaret, left alone to sulk, the notion of other women in her husband's life was a great deal more than a *trifling matter*. Her pleasure with James had been based on the premise – false, she now realised bitterly – that he loved her solely. For Margaret, possession was all. From the nursery, she had fought her brother Henry, and from him she had learned that to accept half shares only put you in a weak bargaining position. Let the Stewarts and the Scots adopt lukewarm compromises. She was an English Tudor. And Tudors took all.

The call of the first cuckoo, the splashes of yellow gorse flowers and drifts of forget-me-nots did nothing to gladden Margaret's heart that spring. The rift between the King and Queen widened as Margaret began to listen to James more attentively, laying verbal traps, sifting his words for possible untruths, seeking to catch him in a lie. When he returned from hunting or hawking she cross-examined him mercilessly, shrill in her conviction that he had made a detour to call on Janet Kennedy at Darnaway Castle. Nor were the ladies of the Court above suspicion. Let one of them laugh too loudly at James' jokes, or avoid looking Margaret straight in the eye, then she would receive a curt note from the Queen, authorising the lady to take immediate leave of absence from Court.

Never had Margaret felt so alone. Consumed with jealousy and mistrust, she felt there was no one in whom she could confide. With her ladies all now condemned as possible rivals, Margaret turned for light relief to Malcolm Laxford, the darkly attractive Earl of Mallaig. The only time she forgot her misery over James was when Mallaig amused her with tales of his Highland childhood ... poaching ... fishing in the wild western sea ... midnight feasts on the silvery sands ...

'He remembers a surprising amount, my lady, considering his father sent him to France as a boy,' said William Dunbar sceptically. 'He finished his education there and came straight back to Edinburgh from Paris.'

143

'Did the old Earl of Mallaig ever come to Court?' asked the Queen.

Dunbar shuddered. 'Thankfully, no. The first Earl was never one to cultivate Court manners and gentle ways. He was a raw, brash man. His coarseness would have repelled a lady of your sensitivity, madam.'

Margaret, gratefully absorbing all the flattery Dunbar had to offer, regarded him as her champion against the amorous adventures of her husbad. With Margaret's encouragement, Dunbar even dared write verses rebuking the King for his neglect of 'that sweet meek Rose'.

'Dunbar could do with some sweetening himself,' muttered James to Bishop Elphinstone. 'The man smells as high as a compost heap.'

'I understand Sire,' said the Bishop, 'that Mistress Bella Fraser advised him to rub his head with garlic, as a cure for baldness.'

The King exploded into laughter. 'A sure way to gain a few hairs and lose what few friends he had. I could tolerate him more if the wretch was totally loyal in his devotion to the Queen. But he hedges his bets. Writes me pathetic little verses saying he'd be much nicer about me if only I'd increase his pension.'

The King, tired of Margaret's reproachful looks and bored to tears by the constant cringing presence of Dunbar, took refuge in a new interest. A man of eclectic tastes, the new, the weird and the wonderful had always fascinated James. He had already aroused Margaret's scorn by involving himself in experiments with alchemy, medicine and printing presses. Now, with the arrival at Court of a Frenchman, Jean Damien, James fell in love with the idea of flying. The notion had intrigued him for years, ever since he had learned of Leonardo da Vinci's drawing of a flying machine. But Damien promised to go one better. He would, he insisted, take to the air like one of James' beloved falcons, without the aid of any machine.

Supported by the faith of the King, and more essentially, Scottish treasury funds, Damien embarked upon a secret training programme. At last, he announced to a cynical Court that he was ready. Two French ambassadors were due to return home from Stirling. Damien declared that while they lay groaning with seasickness on a Channel boat, he would soar overhead, and reach Paris days before them.

With only the Queen conspicuous by her absence, the entire Court trooped onto the gap-toothed battlements of Stirling Castle to watch Damien's historic launch. In awed silence, the crowd gaped as Damien buckled on a pair of feather wings, bowed to the King and, with a blood-curdling cry, flung himself from the topmost rampart.

'Of course, he plummeted like a stone all the way down the castle rock,' Mallaig reported later to a giggling Queen. 'He was lucky to get away with just a broken thigh.'

'That'll teach the King to indulge in such nonsense,' said Margaret smugly.

Mallaig shook his head. 'Damien excused the disaster by complaining that hens' feathers had been used for his wings. Hens, as you may know, have a considerable struggle just flapping up into a tree, let alone skylarking across the Channel. He says he'll use eagles' feathers next time.'

'*Next* time?'

Mallaig spread his hands in a gesture of despair. 'I'm afraid the King is still enough in thrall to lavish yet more money on the fellow for fresh experiments.'

The King was less than enthralled, however, when Dunbar wrote a satirical poem about the affair, describing a flock of indignant birds swooping down to peck and mock their human rival.

The Court grew increasingly concerned about the deteriorating relationship between the King and Queen. Bickering privately and publicly, encouraging contesting groups of friends and courtiers, the couple seemed irreconcilable. Even the launch of Scotland's latest warship, named in honour of Margaret, aroused more royal marital disharmony when the Queen overheard James boast to John Barton, the captain, 'My streamlined *Margaret* is a modern miracle of engineering compared to Henry Tudor's fleet of medieval floating castles.'

But in June came the only news capable of reuniting the royal pair. The Queen, at last, was with child. That summer, an elated James remained constantly at his wife's side. He even forced himself to tolerate the insufferable Dunbar, and his nagging verses urging James to more tender attention of his Queen.

Then, at Christmas, it occurred to James to increase the poet's pension. In reply to Dunbar's annual verse pleading for more funds, James penned the reply:

> *After our writing, Treasurer,*
> *Take in this grey horse, Old Dunbar,*
> *Which is my aid with service true,*
> *In lyart changed is his hue.*
> *Go house him now against this Yule!*
> *And adorn him like a bishop's mule*
> *For with my hand I have endorst*
> *To pay whate'er his trappings cost.*

The biter bit. The freshly robed Dunbar took the hint, and the gold, and troubled James with his poems no more.

Margaret promised James repeatedly that their child would be a boy. 'I will give you an heir. And when you look on him, you will forget your curtseying, mealy mouthed Drummond daughter. My son will be the only child who matters to you then.'

Forty days before the birth Margaret retired, as was the custom, to her apartments in Holyrood Palace; only her ladies were admitted. At dawn on the morning of 21 February, 1507, her pains began.

Margaret screamed.

'*In sorrow thou shalt bring forth children,*' intoned Lady Lennox mournfully.

Lady Huntly pushed her away from the bed and sponged Margaret's sweating face, arms and bosom with cool chervil water. The Queen had been in labour for twelve hours. Despite Lady Huntly's efforts, the perspiration still streamed from her, until the bedlinen was soaked and her fine red hair

146

lay matted like hessian across the embroidered pillows. Even so, Lady Lennox ordered a servant to stoke up the roaring fire, re-pin the thick blankets across the windows and make sure the keyhole was blocked up. The room must be insulated, she insisted, against evil spirits, the unhealthy night air, and the prying eyes of the guards outside the door.

No one needed to tell Margaret that all was not well. Through her groans she could hear the midwives muttering dolefully together by the fire. Terrified, she listened to the two older women passing on their wealth of experience to a younger, novice midwife.

'It's taking too long. We may have to hurry it up by tossing her in a blanket. Or maybe the baby's head is not pointing downwards. We'd be forced to hang the Queen up by her arms and knead her stomach very hard. Oh, it really tires you out doing that.'

'The worst thing is if the baby won't come at all. I had to cut the last one to pieces in the womb to get it out. Even then, it had been in there so long it had gangrene, and its skin flayed off. And the stink ...'

Margaret clamped her hands over her ears, writhing as another spasm of pain convulsed her. No one had told her it would be as bad as this. She was going to die. She knew it. Her mother had died in childbirth. Those midwives would butcher her and the baby and it would serve James right for being so unkind.

As the stabbing in her swollen stomach intensified, Margaret clutched at the bedpost. But Lady Lennox had anointed it with lavender oil against bedbugs, and her hands slipped.

'*See much, say little and learn to suffer in time*, madam,' murmured Lady Lennox.

'I'm suffering *now*, Lennox, you flannel faced fool!' shrieked Margaret, tipping Lady Huntly's nourishing caudle of egg, nutmeg and sugar over the bedcurtains.

One of the midwives stopped scratching the lice from her grey head long enough to suggest, 'Why not let one of your ladies share your bed, my lady? If you pretend that she is the one having the baby, you will find that it is she who bears the pain, not you. I've known it work before.'

Before Margaret could gasp out a suitably acidic reply, a loud explosion shook the room.

'The Queen has fainted with shock,' shouted a midwife. 'Hurry, squirt the *aqua vitae* up her nose.'

Margaret opened her eyes. 'No! I'm all right. But what on earth was that dreadful noise?'

'Merely the King, your husband, madam,' said Lady Huntly soothingly. 'He has acquired a new shooting machine, and is distracting himself by engaging in a contest with Monsieur Damien.'

Tears coursed down Margaret's flushed cheeks. 'Oh, how can he play his juvenile games, when I'm lying here in agony giving birth to his son? It *will* be a boy, won't it, Huntly? It *must* be a boy ... Huntly! Something's happened. Oh my God, I'm all wet! *Do* something quickly!'

Lady Huntly motioned to the midwives. 'Her time has come. Be gentle.'

Margaret watched in helpless horror as the three midwives, smearing their hands with butter, approached the bed. 'Don't hurt me! Huntly, don't let them hurt me!'

The baby was born two hours later. It was a boy. The King, the Court, the nation went wild with joy. But the Queen never heard the bells, the songs, or the first cry of her first child. As the bonfires blazed and the people danced in the streets, Margaret lay unconscious in her bed, close to death.

Six

When she is decked out in her finest dress,
She has the appearance of a huge tar-barrel.
When she was born the sun was in eclipse,
And the night most fairly gave up all fight,
My lady with the big fat lips.

No point in contesting for her with lance and shield,
Trying your strength with courage in the field,
When you should only kiss and squeeze her
To win and evermore possess her,
My lady with the big fat lips.

William Dunbar

For two months Margaret clung desperately to life, tormented by fragmentary glimpses of her past, that splintered her dreams like jagged pieces of a shattered looking glass. James was by her side day and night, seeking to find in her feverish chatter a key to that which would give her the will to live. Then, listening to her babbling of her childhood at Richmond, of the festivals, the pageants, the processions and tournaments in which she had played a leading role, James knew he had found his answer.

'Listen, Margaret,' he whispered. 'When you are better, I shall organise the most spectacular tournament in your honour. It will be such a splendid occasion, that people all over Europe will talk about it for years to come.'

She opened her eyes. 'You promise?'

'I promise.'

By the end of April, Margaret had recovered sufficiently to attend her son's christening. And when she smugly informed James she knew for a fact that Janet Kennedy dyed her hair red with a lotion of box leaves, he realised her recuperation was complete.

Meanwhile, the Scottish heralds had been sent abroad, to proclaim the forthcoming tournament to the noblemen of Europe. Every young foreign knight had heard his grandfather tell of the last great European tournament, René d'Anjou's famous *Pas d'Armes de la Bergère* when he had dressed his beloved mistress as a shepherdess, and seated her in the middle of the tiltyard. Two valiant knights had guarded her, and her flock of bewildered sheep, through the heat and fury of the lists. Since then, tournaments had been banned by the respective governments of Europe on the grounds that they represented a possible breeding ground for rebellion. But now, with their imaginations fired, the young bloods clamoured round the Scottish heralds, eager to enter their names and recapture the glory of those legendary days when chivalry, honour and truth were all.

In Edinburgh, aspirations were centred on a less elevated plane.

'The King is presenting a golden-headed lance as one of the prizes in the jousting,' Robert told Tom and Bella, as they relaxed in the saddlery garden one Sunday afternoon.

'That's nothing,' said Tom, throwing a ball for his son Douglas to catch. 'Have you heard about the main prize? It's an amazing woman, with a skin as dark as soot. The Queen calls her Black Ellen and parades her round Holyrood on a leash with that pampered Persian cat of hers.'

'Where did Black Ellen come from?' asked Bella, keeping a wary eye on seven-year-old Douglas, as he bounced his ball on her beehives.

'One of the Barton brothers brought her back from a trading mission to Portugal,' said Tom. 'She was a slave.'

Robert nodded. 'Some slave! Robert Barton told me all about her one evening at the Wild Boar tavern. He said he'd rather put down a mutiny than have Black Ellen on board again. Slave she may have been, but it would take a man and a half to master her now. She created merry hell on the voyage because she had to share the boat with a bear destined for the King's menageries.'

'Well, she might meet her match at the tournament,' Tom said. 'They say there's a mysterious Wild Knight entering the lists with the intention of claiming her. No one knows who he is.'

Bella peered suspiciously at her brother. '*Robert?*'

His sea green eyes were beguilingly innocent. 'Rest in peace, my dear sister. For once, *non mea culpa*. I shall be contesting, of course, but for the prize of the golden lance, alone.'

'Don't you fancy Black Ellen, then?' grinned Tom.

Robert crushed a sprig of thyme between his calloused fingers. 'As a matter of fact, through the courtesy of Robert Barton I am, as you might say, already acquainted with the lady.'

'You would be,' muttered Bella. 'And those Barton brothers are nothing but common pirates. You could land up in jail associating with them.'

'Then I'll be in illustrious company,' replied Robert. 'They've already presented the King with a lion, two bears and a Portuguese horse with a red tail. Not to mention the Queen's exotic little pussy cat.'

'It's got an exotic little bite, too,' warned Tom, rubbing his ankle. 'If the Queen finds out you've been tampering with her new tarry toy she's likely to set that vicious ball of fluff onto you.'

'Don't alarm yourself on his account,' said Bella dryly, 'My brother has vast experience in taming wild cats.'

Robert said loftily, 'I am particularly interested in acquiring the golden lance, because I am informed that a certain Earl of Mallaig has set his milky apology for a heart on winning it.'

'That may be,' said Bella, 'but you have first to gain acceptance to the lists. You know as well as I do that the joust is open only to noblemen, not lowly saddlers. Mallaig would have you publicly discredited and barred from the tourney in seconds.'

'My dear sister, I don't intend to turn up reeking of saddle soap,' retorted Robert. 'The invitation to combat has been relayed all over Europe. Edinburgh will be clanking with titled foreigners in armour and vizors. In all the confusion, it will be impossible for the heralds to check the credentials of every competitor. Which reminds me,' he reached into his doublet, 'I have prepared some sketches of my livery. If you wouldn't mind, Bella, fetching your sewing basket...'

Bella groaned, and prayed the tournament would be rained off.

'Why don't ladies joust?' demanded Mairead, as Bella led her into the tournament field below Edinburgh Castle.

'It's a man's sport,' said Douglas Fraser firmly. 'Women would only faint and fall off their horses.'

James IV's daughter regarded him with a mixture of scorn and triumph. 'Not so,' she said. 'Joan, the Maid of Orléans, was a skilful tilter. She beat scores of men.' Her chin lifted. 'When I am old enough I shall enter the lists, and if I fall off my horse, Douglas Fraser, then it will be to land on top of some overweight, overconfident – '

'Oh look! Isn't that pretty!' interjected Bella. Following her pointing finger the children fell silent, dazzled by the sight of the Tree of Esperance.

The tree, traditional symbol of chivalry, truth and honour, was decorated with eighteen dozen silver and gold leaves, six dozen silk flowers and thirty-seven brass pears. Skulking among the foliage were all manner of fabulous beasts from heraldic legend, dragons, unicorns and gryphons, brilliantly encrusted with precious stones.

'How beautiful,' whispered Mairead.

'That it is,' agreed Bella, 'though I'll wager you'll find it harder to climb than the almond tree in the garden at Falkland.'

Mairead laughed. 'We'll see about that. Come on, Douglas!'

Their progress across the bustling tournament field was slow. By royal decree, all workers had been given the day off, and they responded by flocking in their hundreds to this, the first Royal Tournament in Scotland since James IV's succession. A few lucky commoners had wheedled a place in two specially constructed wooden stands flanking the royal box, and now sat smugly alongside the wealthy burghers, merchants and their families. But most either sprawled on the grass around the tilting barrier or sat on moss-filled cushions and wooden stools brought from their homes. In the hours before the tournament started they were kept busy by the musicians, tumblers and fortune tellers who had swarmed onto the twelve acre field, looking for rich pickings. The yeasty aroma of warm pastry wafting from the braziers of itinerant piemen mingled with the smell of newly-mown grass, cut specially short and dressed with gravel to ensure a firm footing for the horses.

The prospect for a good day's sport looked promising. In the shadow of the royal pavilion – a gigantic marquee topped by the King's crimson and gold standard – the tents of more than eighty competing knights had mushroomed. As the sun rose higher in the clear blue sky the wine sellers' cries of 'all you can drink at one draught for tuppence' proved increasingly irresistible. Boisterous spectators began cat-calling the knights in their tents: 'Come out! It is time you gave us something to watch!' A demand which caused an embarrassed flutter among the knights' ladies, perched like exotic birds in the three tiers of seats below the royal box.

At noon precisely, with the crowd in a fever of impatience, a phalanx of heralds and trumpeters, resplendent in uniforms of red and green silk, assembled in front of the royal box. Seconds later, to deafening cheers, the King and Queen took their seats on a raised podium surrounded by the flags of a dozen nations. Piemen, jugglers and gipsies were forgotten as the crowd surged closer to the tilting arena, craning for a better view.

Mairead, clutching a brass pear plucked from the Tree of Esperance, screamed with excitement as a mailed figure, astride a strawberry roan, thundered into the arena.

'The *Chevalier d'Honneur*,' said Lord Huntly, shepherding Mairead and Douglas to a splendid vantage point in front of his own tent. 'He acts as arbiter. You see the scarf he is carrying on his lance? Well he uses that to touch any knight who is in difficulties, and so prevent any further attack upon him.'

'To stop him being killed, you mean?' asked Mairead.

'Good heavens, no,' said Huntly, appalled. 'These are civilised times, my child. We have progressed far from the days when a knight was expected to fight to the death to protect his honour. In any case, it would be wasteful to kill off the cream of our fighting men. That is not to say,' he swept on, seeing Mairead's faintly disappointed expression, 'that there is not the occasional . . . accident. But generally it is considered more in the interests of chivalry to allow an opponent to live and fight again, rather than to despatch him to the hereafter.'

'So it's not real fighting at all?' said Mairead scornfully.

'Oh, it's real enough,' Huntly assured her, with Douglas vigorously nodding support. 'You just wait and see, my girl. The lances may be blunt, and blows may not be aimed to kill – but the cuts and bruises are real enough.'

A roar from the crowd drowned their conversation. The Lord Constable had asked the King's permission to start the Tourney, and two opposing teams of knights, chosen at random by James, were poised at either end of the tilting barrier.

'Silence!' cried the chief herald, a hush fell on the milling throng, broken only by the snorting of the knights' horses, and the clanking of steel as vizors were tugged down.

A lace-edged handkerchief, dropped by the Queen, fluttered to the dusty ground beneath the royal dais. '*Laissez-aller*' shouted the herald. Shields raised, lances lowered, the knights dug in their spurs.

'The poor horses!' cried Mairead. 'They'll all be slain!'

'Don't worry,' yelled Tom above the crowd's excited clamour, 'They're better armoured than the knights, and anybody seen striking a horse is out of the contest for good.'

The opposing forces met in a thunderclap of steel against steel as lances splintered against shields that reverberated like gongs. The war cries of warriors competed with the screams

154

of steeds armoured so heavily that for them to raise a canter was difficult enough, and a gallop, impossible.

For ten minutes, while the crowed bayed itself hoarse, the mock battle raged, until, at a signal from the King, the royal herald sounded the retreat.

Douglas turned to Mairead who was standing, hands to mouth, appalled yet exhilarated by the scene. 'There. Nobody's been killed.' He pointed to a victorious French knight, happily acknowledging the cheers, 'See how his armour is designed like the scales of a fish. No blunt lance could pierce such a strong defence.'

Bella ran across from the fortune teller's tent to announce: 'Black Ellen is coming! She's riding in a chariot.'

The jousting was momentarily forgotten as every man, woman and child, peasant, lady or lord strove for a better view of the strange black creature from the lands across the sea.

Black Ellen stood proudly erect, in a chariot drawn by four white horses and flanked by twelve blue-liveried pages. The spangles on her pale silk damask dress sparkled in the bright sunlight as, led by the Lyon King-at-Arms, the colourful cavalcade swirled twice round the field and up to the royal dais. To the delight of the spectators, the King bowed graciously to Black Ellen and indicated that she should take her place not at his feet but on his improvised throne. 'You look to my kingdom for a while, Mistress,' he said. 'I have a mind to look to the horses.'

The Queen, apparently entering into the spirit of the jest, dropped a deep mock curtsey before waving the ebony-skinned woman into the carved chair next to her own.

As the King strode towards the horses' enclosure, a fanfare of trumpets heralded the start of the contest for the golden spear. Rivalry was intense. Knights from all over Europe, determined to uphold their tradition of chivalry and honour, had made the perilous journey across the Channel to challenge for the coveted trophy, with its shaft of elm and tip of purest gold. After four hours of fierce combat under the roasting sun, all but two contenders had been eliminated. One was Malcolm Laxford, Earl of Mallaig. The other, Count Roberto Reger d'Avila, had already won the hearts of the crowd with his bold, unorthodox technique.

Never in his life had Robert Kyle felt so uncomfortable. His dyed black hair itched with sweat, and he was sure his magnificent false moustache was coming unstuck in the suffocating heat.

The prospect of jousting against Mallaig did little to restore the saddler's characteristic coolness. Fine swordfighter and horseman though Robert was, he realised that against a tilter of Laxford's experience his chances must be slim. Natural ability, a few devious ploys acquired in practice sessions with Tom, and more than a little luck had seen him safely through the preliminary rounds. But the swarthy earl who sat confidently astride his black stallion at the opposite end of the tilt presented a far greater challenge than the Burgundian baron and Italian count whom Robert had earlier sent tumbling into the straw.

'Put on your helms,' ordered the herald.

Robert grunted with the effort of lifting the twenty pound steel helmet onto his head. Hell's teeth! What a price the nobility were willing to pay for chivalry. Under the sweat-soaked fustian shirt and sixty pound suit of borrowed armour the saddler felt like a partridge in one of Bella's cooking pots. Small wonder, he mused, that the Duke of York had died at Agincourt not of wounds sustained in battle but of heatstroke and exhaustion.

'Ready, sir?' enquired the herald.

Robert snapped the vizor shut, and blinked the sweat from his eyes. There were, he knew, three ways of winning the contest – by unhorsing Mallaig, by breaking his lance or by thrice striking his helm. Under any circumstances, it was a daunting task, but Robert faced an additional, unforeseen hazard. Mallaig, he had discovered that afternoon, was left handed. Robert had never before fought a sinistral opponent, or even trained for such an eventuality. Now it was too late...

The Queen rose from her seat. Robert tightened his grip on the shield and lowered the eleven-foot lance, tucking the butt under his right arm so the shaft lay along the horse's neck.

A butterfly of white lace drifted earthwards. *'Laissez-aller!'* cried the herald.

Robert dug his spurs into the chestnut's flanks, his mind firing instructions to his body as the animal lurched into a canter. *Lean forward. Chin in to protect the throat. Hold that shield well up. Backside deep into the saddle, feet hard into the stirrups.*

Ten ... twenty ... twenty-five miles an hour. Christ, I can't see much of Mallaig through this damned vizor. Just his helm and shield behind the horse's head. Where shall I aim? Helm? Too small a target. I could easily miss. Shield? A firm blow might unseat him. Lord, he's coming fast. Watch that lance. It's aimed high, for my helm. The bastard's out to knock my head off! Well we'll see. Only thirty yards between us now. Think. Decide. Yes ... I'll feint to the left, just before he reaches me. Try to get him to strike early. Then lunge late for his shield. He's practically on top of me now. I can see the whites of his stallion's eyes. Steady. Concentrate on his shield — the four studs near the middle. Grip that lance. Get ready to lean now. God, the exhilaration! Strength. Speed. Power. Thrust ... NOW!

Bella couldn't look. She heard the thunder of hooves, the clang of steel meeting steel and a wild burst of cheering. When she opened her eyes, the Earl of Mallaig was lying helpless as a beached turtle on the straw mattresses that lined the tilt.

As Robert was led away by the heralds to receive the congratulations of the royal party, Douglas turned to Tom. 'Aren't you in charge of the horses today, father?'

Tom shook his head. 'Tournament horses have their own trainers, Douglas, because they have to be able to react in a special way. If you look at any ordinary horse you'll see that it always tends to lead with the same leg — it doesn't matter which. But when a horse is running in a joust, he must never swerve to the left, inwards towards the opposing horse. So tournament horses — they're called destriers — are taught always to lead with the right leg. Some destriers can perform the most fantastic tricks for their riders. I've seen —'

'Wheesht!' cried Bella, as a steady drum beat resounded

over the great field. 'It's the Wild Knight!' The mysterious challenger, splendidly arrayed in a complete coat of chain mail, was seated on a white stallion and brandished a gilt battle axe and dagger. He was closely attended by two Bavarians clad in cloth of gold and velvet, and a motley collection of fierce looking bearded men wearing hairy goatskin coats, with harts-horns fixed to their bucklers.

'He's keeping his vizor closed, so we can't recognise him,' said Mairead, beside herself with excitement. 'Who on earth can he be?'

'My guess is Bell-the-Cat,' replied Bella, 'Or the Queen's brother Henry. Nothing would please Prince Henry more than to boast how he'd beaten the Scots on their own ground.'

There was no shortage of challengers for the Wild Knight. The most skilled of Europe's fighting men had entered the lists, determined to deny this impertinent stranger the prize of the fabulous Black Ellen. But the mail-clad figure proved peerless. One by one the foreign knights fell, 'like corn before the scythe' murmured Robert, shaking his dyed head in unstinted admiration. By St Ninian, the Wild Knight could joust.

Lady Lennox appeared at his side in the royal pavilion. 'Count d'Avila, I hope you will understand if I speak Scots. My French is poor and I have no Spanish.'

Robert said, in broken Scots, 'Madam, a lady with such beautiful eyes as yours has no need of mere words.'

Lady Lennox simpered. 'You are too kind, my lord. I trust your gallantry will be no less unstinting to my lady the Queen. She begs you to enter the lists against the Wild Knight.'

Robert bowed deeply to the Queen, hiding a smile as Black Ellen winked at him. He called for his horse and entered the field, wasting no time on ceremony. Before the herald's cry of *'Laissez-aller!'* had died, he was hurtling down the tilt, lance point aimed at the Wild Knight's shield. The Wild Knight spurred his stallion to meet Robert's rush, but before surging forward, the animal performed a strange side stepping movement. A split second before they clashed, Robert remembered ... only one horse in Scotland possessed this particular idiosyncrasy, and there was only one man whom he would allow to ride him.

The Wild Knight's lance struck Robert's shield. It was only a glancing blow. Robert hardly felt it. But he fell from the chestnut and lay still on the straw.

Bella shrieked. The Earl of Mallaig, nursing a bruised shoulder, cheered. And Mairead jumped up and down with joy. 'I know who the Wild Knight is! I know, I know!'

'It was obvious all along,' said Douglas, as the Wild Knight threw off his helmet and acknowledged the delirious cheers of the crowd. 'Look at the dogs leaping up round the white stallion. They follow the King everywhere.'

'You're a perverse woman, Margaret,' James commented, watching his wife feed Black Ellen choice sweetmeats at the banquet that night. 'You throw one hell of a tantrum if anyone so much as mentions the name of my dead mistress. Yet you open your heart to a black slave woman I am supposed to have won in a joust.'

Margaret licked almond paste from her fingers. 'The two are not the same at all. Mistresses frighten me because they are real. Even if they lie stiff in their graves, there are still hurtful reminders.' She glanced across at the alcove where Mairead was engaged in a cushion fight with the other Court children. 'Black Ellen is merely a symbol, part of the play acting of the tournament. Everyone knows that the helm represents the knight's defence of the Church, and the two edges of the sword show that the knight serves both God and the people. The rules are clear. You fight a man in the lists, but you do not kill him. And when you win a woman as a prize, she is a token only. You do not take her to your bed.'

James laughed. 'You were born in the wrong age, Margaret. I can just imagine you as Guinevere at the last great tournament at Winchester – the one when she commanded Lancelot to do badly. She didn't relent until the very last day, by which time poor Lancelot was a laughing stock, and had practically to turn cartwheels in the joust to regain his reputation.'

Margaret took his hand. 'You certainly enhanced *your*

reputation today, my lord. Those poor foreign knights must dread going home, to confess that they were all tumbled into the dust by James IV of Scotland.'

The King could afford to be generous. 'They're probably a little short of practice, that's all. Don't forget that in places like France and Italy, tournaments are forbidden. The so-called great brave rulers of Europe are terrified that such a gathering would bring together too many skilled fighting men who might be tempted to start a rebellion or settle some old scores.'

'How absurd,' declared the Queen. 'Someone should tell them about the code of chivalry. No knight ever bears malice against one who has defeated him in a joust.'

Beneath the royal dais, the Earl of Mallaig ran his thumb across the tip of the golden spear resting by the side of the Spanish nobleman.

'Count d'Ávila,' said Mallaig, in halting Spanish. 'I much admired your display today. You are clearly a man of rare fighting talent. I wonder, would your sporting instincts allow me to redeem myself? I should be honoured if you would accept my invitation to a friendly duel . . . with the golden-headed lance as the prize.'

Robert, who was enjoying his dinner, didn't bother to look up from his plate of roast swan.

'My dear Mallaig,' he said loudly, in Scots, 'If you went in for a two-man race, I fear you'd be lucky to come in third.'

Mallaig's hand flew to his dagger. 'You impostor,' he hissed. 'You have no choice but to fight me now.'

Robert dipped his fingers into the bowl of rosewater, and carefully wiped them dry on a linen napkin. He stood up. He had the advantage of an inch, no more, over the bearded man blocking his route to the door.

'Mallaig, you are a liar and a cheat. You would have murdered an innocent child in her bed. Like your father before you, you have dishonoured the title you bear. I would be delighted to fight you. I intend to fight you. But,' a slow, hard smile lit Robert's face, 'when I do, it will be for your lands, your name, your title. For all you possess.'

160

Mallaig's eyes glittered with hatred. 'Ah . . . a man of vision. A dreamer of dreams. How unfortunate then, that I intend to expose you now to Lord Huntly as an impostor. When he learns of your trickery at the royal tournament, he will have you broken, bone by bone, on the rack. And I shall be there to watch.'

He turned towards the High Table and was within four paces of Huntly when a cloud of black smoke began to envelop the royal dais. Remarkably, not a single member of the Scottish Court was thrown into panic. It was only Jean Damien, they explained to the alarmed foreign nobles, seeking by alchemy to conjure gold from the Great Hall fireplace.

True to form, a disappointed Damien found no gold within the palace grate. But when the smoke cleared, Robert the Red had gone. There was no sign, either, of the beautiful Black Ellen.

Seven

Let no man come into this hall,
Groom, page, nor yet marshall,
But that some sport he bring withall,
For now is the time of Christmas.

Anon

The gaiety of the Queen expired the following summer, along with her baby son. Another child, a daughter, was born in July, but died almost immediately. Commonsense told Margaret that this was the natural order of things. Her own mother had borne nine children and lost five of them. Margaret, though healthy and robust, fully expected to breathe her last with each confinement. That she herself could live through those long days of lacerating pain was wonder enough. For her child to survive as well would be nothing short of a miracle.

All this Margaret accepted philosophically. Yet she remained engulfed by an overwhelming sense of failure. Scotland needed an heir. James, she knew, yearned for a lively son to succeed him. It was a perfectly normal desire, aggravated by what Margaret regarded as his morbid obsession with the notion that he had not much longer to live. 'The hourglass of my years is running out,' he warned her.

'Superstitious rubbish,' Margaret snapped. 'You are only thirty-five. There is plenty of time for me to bear you a dozen sons.'

As if to prove her words, by the time the almond blossomed in the palace gardens, the Queen was once more with child. But, as so often happened with Margaret, her triumph was to be tempered with grief. It was James who came to her, and gently broke the news that her adored father was dead. Through her tears, Margaret smiled only once, wryly pictur-

162

ing her brother's jubilation at his succession as Henry VIII of England. At last he had overtaken his older sister.

Burdened by her pregnancy and the heavy grey mourning clothes, Margaret found little solace in James' company during that long, hot summer. Increasingly, she found herself regarding James' informal style of government with distaste. Having grown up in an English Court crusted with nobles and starched with etiquette, Margaret frowned upon the motley assortment of artists, sculptors, physicians and astronomers whom James invited to Holyrood. She could not condone the King her husband's practice of dining with the wealthy merchants in their flamboyantly vulgar houses up near the Castle; drinking with the common artisans in the Wild Boar tavern; and mixing with the common workfolk. 'A king's hands should be reserved for dealing with affairs of state,' she told him scornfully, after he had spent an enjoyable afternoon setting type at the printing workshop in Blackfriars Wynd.

Margaret found an unexpected ally in old Bell-the-Cat, a man renowned for his fierce advocacy of a more rigid form of monarchy. If nothing else, Angus and the Queen shared the belief that the social tone of the Court was deteriorating. When she asked the Earl why he was named Bell-the-Cat, Margaret listened attentively to his story of James III's favourites.

'You mean my husband's father was also friendly with such lowly creatures as a shoemaker, a tailor and his *fencing master*?' cried an appalled Margaret, completely missing the point. 'You were quite right to hang them, my lord Angus.'

It was not only James' friends who aroused Margaret's resentment. She also felt aggrieved that the King refused to heed her advice on the growing problem of her brother Henry. With the accession of the politically ambitious Henry VIII, James was attempting to intervene as peacemaker in the young king's squabbles with the crowned heads of Europe.

'Henry is determined to wage war on France,' Margaret told the Earl of Mallaig. 'And James will insist on sending him letters full of fatherly warnings and advice. James just won't listen to me when I tell him that the one thing sure to send my brother into a towering rage is the suspicion that he's being patronised. Sometimes,' she sighed, 'I feel the King regards me as no more than a breeding machine.'

Mallaig nodded sympathetically, reflecting that Scotland's first lady might also be feeling a little piqued by the increasing amount of time the King was devoting to his daughter, the young Lady Margaret Stewart.

The Queen could not imagine what the King found to talk about for so long to a twelve-year-old girl. They spent hours together, walking in the knot garden at Stirling or feeding the animals in James' private menagerie at Edinburgh Castle. Margaret loathed the animal house. Especially now, in the sweltering summer months, when the wild cat stank and the lions' coats took on the mottled appearance of a moth-eaten tapestry.

The menagerie was one of Mairead's two private havens: the other was the Castle chapel. She had chosen both solely on the grounds that they were never visited by the Queen. The English Rose found the menagerie offensive and when it came to communing with her Maker, she preferred the more sumptuous surroundings of Holyrood Abbey.

For her own safety and peace of mind, Mairead had learned to avoid the Queen. Since that day at Stirling when she had been forced to dance to the royal tune, Mairead had come to recognise her father's wife as a petty, vindictive woman. Although Mairead normally lodged in Edinburgh Castle, out of sight and, she hoped, out of mind of the Queen at Holyrood, their paths still occasionally crossed. Should Mairead be careless enough to get in the Queen's way during the revels accompanying a royal banquet, she could be sure of a deftly twisted arm or boxed ear as Scotland's first lady passed by.

Bella too, was unhappy, disturbed by a spate of mysterious thefts from Mairead's apartments. An ermine lined cape, an Italian lute and a kitten, all of which Mairead was particularly fond, had disappeared within a few weeks. Naturally, it was unthinkable to suspect the Queen herself of burglary. But there were many at Court, Bella knew, only too willing to interpret and act upon the Queen's lightest remark.

The Earl of Mallaig, for instance, had become a frequent visitor to the Castle. Unable to prove that he was behind the thefts, Bella then imagined that Mallaig might be using her to gain some useful information about his enemy, Robert the Red. Yet it soon became clear from his conversation that he knew her only as Mistress Fraser, the wife of Tom the ostler. He had never seen her with Robert, and was not aware that they were brother and sister.

Mallaig was attentive, too, to Mairead, teaching her the songs he had learnt in France, taking her riding, bringing her a tabby kitten to replace the one that had been stolen. Much to Bella's annoyance, Mairead found Mallaig entertaining company.

'He told me a lovely story about swallows,' enthused Mairead. 'Do you know, they pick a sprig of celandine and rub it on the eyes of a fledgling to stop it going blind. Isn't that sweet?'

'No, it's not sweet,' said Bella crossly. 'I use celandine to poison rats. And I've seen beggars rubbing it on their skins to produce highly convincing counterfeit sores. Really, I don't know what you see in that man Mallaig, Mairead. You're usually such a shrewd judge of character.'

Mairead gazed at her with guileless blue eyes. 'I see the same in him as you do, Bella. After all, I haven't noticed you sending him away.'

Damn Robert! It was he who had insisted that his sister must encourage Mallaig's visits to enable them, discreetly, to keep an eye on him. So throughout the autumn she forced herself to turn a pleasant face towards this man, whom she hated most in all the world. She often walked with him in the menagerie, while Mairead chatted to her father.

Both Mairead and James agreed that their favourite animal was the Portuguese horse with the red tail.

'Bella tells me you spend a great deal of time in the chapel,' said James, handing Mairead an apple for the horse. 'I am glad to know you are so devout. You must be following in the footsteps of Saint Margaret. She used to pray there, you know. All Europe admired her goodness and piety.'

Mairead said cryptically, 'I shouldn't think it was too difficult for the lady to set a celestial example, considering her immediate predecessor was Lady Macbeth. Even *I* would shine by comparison –'

'Shame on you, Margaret! I will not have you talking that way about a saint of Scotland. You will light a candle to her in the chapel tonight, and pray for her forgiveness. Now, I was going to tell you why the thistle is the emblem of Scotland...'

'My father was really angry,' Mairead told Bella on their way to the chapel that night. 'I had to pretend I hadn't heard the story about the time the Danes invaded Aberdeen, and took off their shoes for a silent midnight attack, only to find the moat full of thistles instead of water! He cheered up after that.'

'Why *do* you spend so much time in the chapel?' asked Bella. 'I know you don't come here to pray, for I've seen you carving your name on the stall. And it can't be just to avoid the Queen.'

'It's so peaceful and comfortable,' explained Mairead. 'I know my father would think it sacrilegious, but honestly Bella, I'm sure Saint Margaret used the chapel so much purely as a retreat from the noise and clatter of the Castle. All those soldiers marching about, and trumpeters practising on the ramparts – the din is really earsplitting at times. And the chapel is so warm and cosy, with those velvet kneelers and pretty silk hangings. It must have been such a relief for Saint Margaret to touch something soft after the hard stone, metal and wood of a fortress.'

The girl could be right, mused Bella, remembering the services she attended in Edinburgh's St Giles Cathedral. They were packed with common folk who came, not only to pray, but because it was the one opportunity in their drab, poverty-stricken lives for them to be surrounded with the trappings of wealth. For an hour or two, they could forget the flea-ridden pallet bed waiting at home, and glory in being admitted to a place gleaming with crystal, silver and gold, where the walls were covered with embroidered silk instead of mildew.

'Anyway,' Mairead went on, wincing as the hard cobbles struck bruisingly through the thin soles of her kid slippers, 'We are much more devout in Scotland than they are in Europe. The Earl of Mallaig was telling me that the men in France take their hawks to church to accustom them to the clamour and bustle. And at one Christmas show for the Pope, a couple of courtesans danced naked, except for large paper noses in the shape of a male –'

'*Mairead!*'

Shortly before her twentieth birthday, the Queen gave birth to a son. As usual, it was a searingly painful experience for Margaret, who lay ill for over a month afterwards. On her recovery, she and James agreed to christen their child Arthur. For Margaret, the name would be a constant reminder of a beloved brother, long since dead but still mourned. While James cherished the name as a tribute to the Arthurian legends, his favourite reading since boyhood.

It was a source of bitter disappointment to James that his own attempt to emulate the legends by leading a crusade against the Turks had foundered on the twin rocks of foreign indifference and domestic dismay. The rulers of Europe, initially enthusiastic, had abruptly withdrawn their support for the venture, indicating that they currently regarded Henry VIII as a far greater menace than the Turks.

Margaret's first burst of laughter at the proposed crusade had turned to outrage. 'You can't leave me alone to govern the country,' she protested. 'I'm a mere woman. No one would obey me.'

'Rubbish, Margaret. Don't give me that milk and water nonsense. You've got the resilience of an oak barn door.' He called for a Book of Hours and opened it at the painted pages depicting the great ladies of his grandfather's day. 'How do you imagine the wives of knights coped when their lords were away at the war?' he demanded. 'The women had no time then for embroidery, and flirting, and playing chess. They had no choice but to take over the men's work, supervising the estates, mending the walls and defending their homes against a legion of invaders.'

But James did not leave her. As the November mists began to shroud the palace, Margaret decided to take advantage of James' delight with the heir in his crib to demand the removal of the Lady Margaret Stewart from Edinburgh.

'I will not have another Christmas ruined by the sight of that precocious girl,' she told James.

Stony faced, the King heard her out – and refused her demand. Undaunted, Margaret ranted that it would bring bad luck on their infant son if James' illegitimate daughter were to join them at Holyrood for the festivities. James stormed off to fly his falcons, and Margaret Stewart remained in Edinburgh. The Queen was left to vent her anger on Lady Lennox, William Dunbar and the luckless Jean Damien, for whom even a new, expensive furnace had failed to bring forth the elusive gold.

Bella would have been only too glad to take Mairead away to Stirling. The Queen's persecution of the girl had escalated, and even her food was being tampered with. A pie arrived in Mairead's apartments with a dead rat in it. A date slice was found to contain a handful of gravel. True, no attempt was made to kill or seriously maim Mairead, but it was just enough to cause her sickness, or broken teeth. Not for one moment did Bella suspect the Castle cook, who was an old friend of Mairead's. No, the food was clearly being interfered with on its way from the kitchens, which meant that Bella had no choice but to go down and fetch it herself.

Despite the Queen's frosty demeanour, the King and Bella took great pains to ensure that Mairead enjoyed the Christmas festivities to the full. Jean Damien, elected Lord of Misrule, sent the girl into hysterics by ordering the King to leap from a trestle table in a re-enactment of the Frenchman's disastrous flight down Stirling rock. After four days of continual feasting and merriment, Bella sent the exhausted Mairead to bed for a good rest. She was on her way back from the kitchens with the girl's supper, when a figure loomed from the shadows of the gallery.

'My lord Mallaig! You startled me.'

Mallaig took the tray and laid it on an oak side table.

'I was looking for you, Mistress Fraser. You have yet to wish me a happy Christmas.'

Coolly, Bella stood on tiptoe and kissed the earl lightly on the cheek. 'May the season bring you all you deserve, my lord,' she said, turning away to pick up the tray. But Mallaig was too swift for her. His hands were a steel ring, gripping her waist. 'You can do better than that, my dear.'

'No!' She squirmed like a rabbit caught in a snare.

Laughing, he held her firm. As his wine-rimmed mouth clamped down on hers, Bella felt for his hand. She twisted her head away, bent back his little finger and, blessing her wooden shoes, kicked him hard on the kneecap. Mallaig bellowed in agony, involuntarily releasing his prey. By the time the first shock of pain had subsided, Bella had vanished.

So too, she found to her horror, had Margaret Stewart.

'Where *is* she?' demanded Bella, shaking a terrified servant as she surveyed the empty bedchamber.

'In the animal house, Mistress Fraser. She told me she wanted to feed the Portuguese horse,' stuttered the servant.

'*At this time of night?*'

The servant trembled. 'The Earl of Mallaig said it would be all right. He brought her some nuts for the horse...'

Bella fled, racing along the dark gallery, down the stone stairs and out into the freezing night. She hardly noticed the bitter cold, for the hot wave of fear that enveloped her. As she stumbled along the rough path that led to the menagerie, she swore at Mallaig, and cursed even more her own gullibility in allowing herself to be so easily duped. Bella's face flamed in the darkness as she recalled his fleshy lips closing upon hers. Passionately, she wished she was a man, skilled in the use of male weapons.

The iron gate of the animal house creaked as she wrenched it open. Bella rushed along the straw strewn path, frantically

169

calling Mairead's name, until a movement and a dim light caught her eye. The King's daughter was holding aloft a small oil lamp as she tried to entice a cat down from a stable rafter.

'Poor little kitty. You'll catch cold if you stay up there all night. Come with me and I'll give you some nice warm milk.'

The large striped cat crouched above her, ears flattened back and yellow eyes gleaming in the lamplight. Mairead reached up a coaxing hand and the cat sprang, fangs bared, and massive claws reaching for her throat. Before the terrified girl dropped the lamp, Bella realised that this was no stray domestic tabby: it was the wild cat, loose from its cage.

Bella started forward, but a shadowy figure was ahead of her. A split second before the cat struck, Mairead was pushed clear. The animal landed, hissing, on the stranger's shoulder. The man promptly threw himself to the ground, rolling clear of the vicious teeth and claws. In the semi-darkness, Bella could see little of the desperate struggle, which ended with an unearthly shriek and a sickening crack.

Panting, the man relit the lamp and kicked the limp, broken animal aside. 'I think I really prefer the variety that sits quietly by the fire, and purrs,' said Robert the Red. His expression softened as he glanced at Mairead. 'How is she?'

'She'll be all right. I'll put her to bed in a moment,' said Bella, holding the shuddering girl in her arms. She glared at her brother. 'May I ask what kept you?'

Robert dabbed at a scratch on his cheek. 'Sorry I was late, sister dear. As you know, I've had someone watching Mallaig ever since you told me of his sudden fascination with the Lady Margaret. However, the news that Mallaig had tonight visited both Mairead and the animal house was a little late reaching me. I'm afraid my spy lingered too long on one of the castle galleries, entranced by a charming love scene between a beautiful serving girl and a dashing young earl.'

Bella blushed. 'Were you injured?' she asked, taking his hands in hers. They felt sticky with congealed blood, the flesh razored into jagged fillets, in places down to the bone. '*Caraid!* You're cut to ribbons. Come back to the castle, and I'll bandage you up.'

'There's no time,' said Robert. 'I've work to do. I'll see you back at the saddlery later tonight. Then we can talk.'

'Where are you going?' she whispered.

'Home, to collect a sword. Then I shall pay a call on Malcolm Laxford, Earl of Mallaig. I understand his new house is quite magnificent. I'm sure he'll be delighted to conduct me round.'

'Robert, take care. Mallaig's a devious man, and a skilled swordsman. If you should fight him, and lose, he'll show you no mercy. Are you sure it's going to be worth it?'

Robert bent and kissed his sister lightly on the forehead. 'It will be for us, Bella. You, me and Tom. We've waited a long time for this. And I shall have to win, because I can't afford to lose.'

Eight

*To every thing there is a season, and a time to every purpose
under the heaven...*
*A time to get, and a time to lose; a time to keep, and a time to
cast away.*
*A time to rend, and a time to sew; a time to keep silence, and
a time to speak.*

Ecclesiastes 3

The great bell of St Giles Cathedral pealed midnight as
Robert made his way through the deserted streets towards
Mallaig's house. Despite his bold words to his sister, Robert
was by no means as confident as he appeared. He calculated
the odds. As swordsmen, he and Mallaig were evenly
matched. Mallaig, French trained in his youth, was an elegant
fighter, well versed in every sophisticated move, each varia-
tion of cut, thrust and parry. But Robert was Highland bred,
possessed of strength, determination and the raw native cunning of a man who all his life has survived by the ability to
think on his feet. Nevertheless, not for a moment did Robert
underestimate the enormity of his task. For whereas Mallaig
would be out to kill, the saddler knew that it was vital for
him to take the earl alive. And disarming a man, thought
Robert grimly, often took considerably more skill than running him straight through.

Tonight, too, he was challenging Mallaig on the man's
familiar home ground. It was a daunting prospect. Yet the
red-haired man striding swiftly, silently towards the Canongate felt no strafe of fear. Robert had fought in taverns and
castles, on ships, dark roads and hilltops, down alleyways, up
turnpike stairs, and across rooftops. However unfamiliar the
terrain, Robert had taken on the enemy and won – so far. But
in every past instance, Robert reflected, he had enjoyed the

172

advantage of surprise. This time, Mallaig would be waiting for him.

Yet Robert was an experienced enough campaigner to understand that fights are not always won by the most proficient swordsmen. Robert had fought, and beaten, many more technically brilliant men than he. What mattered, he knew, was the will to succeed. And there he had Mallaig by the short hairs. This would be no impetuous, irresponsible skirmish, ignited by liquor and a hotheaded sense of injustice. No, Robert had prepared for this coldly, thoroughly, restraining his natural impatience and biding his time. For Robert Kyle, it would be the fight of his life.

Mallaig could be forgiven for regarding his position as totally invulnerable. Should Robert the Red break into his house tonight, challenge him, and fail, Mallaig could immediately call out the guards and, if the intruder was still alive, have him pitched into jail. Even if Mallaig were to lose, it was likely to be a hollow victory for Kyle. Who would believe the word of a common saddler against that of Malcolm Laxford, Earl of Mallaig? He had the position, the title, the influence, and any allegation of his murderous intent towards the Lady Margaret Stewart was likely to be greeted with incredulity by the Court. The idea was preposterous. Why, hadn't he been seen to cultivate the friendship of the child?

Softly, Robert slipped out of the shadows and stood before Mallaig's impressive house. Tall and narrow, with its great oak door guarded by two stone griffins, the shuttered building gave the appearance that the occupant was asleep, or away. But Robert knew that somewhere inside a light burned, a man waited.

When Robert had gone to buckle on his swordbelt at the saddlery, he had dwelt for some time on the problem of gaining access to Mallaig's house. His gaze had lingered on the heap of ropes and steel hooks he normally employed when tackling disused chimneys, roofs and high back windows. But in the end, he had set off for the Canongate armed with nothing more than his sword.

His damaged hand rested lightly on the hilt as he mounted

the flight of stone stairs to the brass studded door. Robert was counting now on Mallaig's Highland blood. He may have been educated in France, and possess the flowery manners of a trained courtier, but he had been born a Highlander. He would know that in Gaelic there is no word for coward. Mallaig was ruthless, cruel, devious. But tonight, preparing to face a fellow Highlander, he would be anxious to prove that he was no coward. If Robert judged right, he reasoned he would be in the house within two seconds, and confronting Mallaig in three. If he were wrong, in less than a minute he would be dead.

Robert turned the iron handle and pushed the door. It was not locked, but swung open, slowly and noiselessly. A sigh whistled between his teeth. He had judged right. Drawing his sword, Robert walked warily in, waiting for his eyes to adjust to the pitch blackness. With his free hand, he felt his way along the tapestried wall. The silence, like the darkness, was all enveloping. Robert's nerves jangled. At each step he anticipated a shouted challenge, and the cold bite of steel. But the house, the very world, seemed to be holding its breath.

Robert rounded a corner and stopped abruptly. A single lighted candle spluttered on the bottom step of Mallaig's spiral stone staircase.

Robert smiled wryly ... *the moth to the candle.* Crouched in the shadows beyond the soft circle of light, he sensed rather than heard a movement beyond the curve of the stairs. He took a chance.

'Show yourself, Mallaig!'

Silence.

'Mallaig, I know you're there. I can smell you. I fear you'll find fighting me a far more difficult task than enticing a little girl to her death.'

Robert waited. Then Mallaig's voice, cool, detached, self-assured, reached him from the top of the stairs. 'Do you seriously think you can kill me, Robert Kyle?'

Robert said levelly, 'I could, very easily. But I'm not going to. I want you alive, Mallaig. I want, at the very least, your vocal chords intact.'

Mallaig laughed mirthlessly. 'I admire a man with a sense of purpose, Kyle. It will be with infinite regret that I shall ensure you do not leave this house alive.'

Through the gloom, Robert fancied he glimpsed a flash of steel. But still Mallaig made no move. So that was it! Mallaig had decided to engage him on the stairs, taking advantage of his position at the top. Robert smiled, suddenly elated. Mallaig had blundered. Anyone in Edinburgh could have told him that, given the choice, Robert the Red would rather fight on a staircase than a level street. A turnpike staircase was the ideal showcase for his nimble footed, athletic swordplay.

Robert decided on a rush attack. Sucking in a deep breath, he hurled himself through the pool of candlelight into the darkness beyond. Turning instinctively to the right, Robert ran straight into the wall. Knocked off balance, he flung out his hands to save himself from falling – and heard with horror the clattering of his sword spinning down the stone steps. In the second before Mallaig plunged, breathing heavily, towards him, Robert remembered . . . *Mallaig was left handed*. Naturally, he would have had the stairs of his house built with a right-to-left spiral.

Mallaig's sword slashed down, striking not flesh but stone. Furious, incredulous, he lashed wildly around him, hoping for a chance hit against the man he could not see. Once more, his weapon jarred harmlessly on the empty stairs.

Another candle spluttered into life, lit by Robert, who had leapt down the stairwell to recover his sword.

'Shall we start again, Mallaig?' enquired Robert. 'Though I can't say that having you visible this time affords me any aesthetic pleasure.'

Mallaig, at bay on the bottom step, paused, assessing the situation. Robert watched not his sword, but his face. *Know the mind, and you will know the move*. When it came, it was swift, decisive and masterly. Mallaig sprang from the stairway, ducking low, aiming a scything blow not at Robert's chest but at his legs. Robert hurled himself sideways and with the ease of an acrobat, landed on one hand and instantly sprang back to his feet. Mallaig, dragged off balance by the force of the blow, pitched forward.

Robert thrust towards his opponent's side. Mallaig twisted like a salmon and sparks flew as steel met steel. Warily the men circled one another, each searching for an opening. With a roar, Mallaig launched himself at Robert, pinning him against the stairway. As they stood swaying, blade locked against blade, the two sworn enemies stood close as lovers. Robert could smell Mallaig's sweat, and his wine soured breath. The earl's free hand dropped to his waist. Robert, intent on keeping Mallaig's sword from his throat, sensed danger. Of course – the dirk in the earl's belt. Without warning, Robert let his legs buckle then, straightening, drove his right knee deep into Mallaig's groin.

Laxford doubled up, gasping, perspiration showering from his face. His eyes were hot with hatred and pain. Now was the time, Robert knew, for the will to dominate the sword. It was his turn to attack. He sliced his blade towards Mallaig's chest. Instinctively, the earl thrust defensively upwards. Robert forced Mallaig against the wall, their swords locked like the antlers of warring stags. The knuckles of the bearded earl gleamed white. His eyes rolled as Robert increased the pressure. Sensing that Mallaig's fingers were beginning to lose their grip on the sword hilt, Robert summoned his last reserves of strength. Muscles seasoned by years of hard toil in the saddlery swelled and hardened. Mallaig groaned. Slowly, his pale fingers began to uncurl from the pommel of his sword. A second later, the weapon clattered to the stone flagged floor. Mallaig found himself pinned against an oak chest, with Robert's blade ruffling the lace around his throat.

Robert's breath came hard and fast. He felt an overwhelming desire to kill this man, to plunge the sword deep into his thick, treacherous neck.

'For God's sake, Kyle!' Mallaig croaked. 'Have done with me, or tell me what it is you want.'

The storm of hate subsided. Robert bent closer to the sweat-grimed face. 'First, an explanation. Why have you twice

176

tried to murder an innocent child, the Lady Margaret Stewart. What harm could she possibly have done you?'

Mallaig's eyes veiled. 'The Queen. She has taken against the girl. She told me —'

'The Queen told you nothing,' snapped Robert. 'She may be petty, vain, jealous and sly. But she is also a mother. She might persecute Margaret Stewart, box her ears and arrange for her food to be interfered with, but murder — never. So why, Mallaig, *why*?'

Mallaig's fleshy lips were clamped tight. Robert twitched the blade at the earl's throat, and a splash of crimson sullied the lace collar.

'All right! All right, Kyle, I'll tell you.' Mallaig swallowed hard. 'It all started a long time ago, when I was new to the Court. I was a personal attendant to the King when he was wooing Margaret Drummond. On the first night she came to the King's bedchamber she... well, she made me look a fool. In front of the King, in the sight of all the other attendants. They laughed at me. She told me to leave the bedchamber. She, a woman, ordered me to leave!'

'Dear, *dear*,' murmured Robert.

'That was not the end of it. I admit, at the time my youthful vanity was stung. But as the years passed I found myself drawn to Margaret Drummond. I suppose, in a perverse way, I admired her. She was a challenge. When she left Court, and returned to Perth, I followed her. For an entire summer I danced attendance on her. I even offered to marry her. And,' he choked at the memory, 'the bitch spurned me. She had the gall to get her father to bar me from the castle, as if I were a tinker selling pegs.'

'And for that, you poisoned her,' hissed Robert.

'No! Not me!' Mallaig was vehement. 'I knew of the murder plot, sure enough. But the deed was not my doing. I swear it.' He studied Robert's grim face. 'I have told you the truth. What more do you want of me? You must be aware that my servants will have run to fetch the guards by now.'

The sword did not waver from Mallaig's glistening neck. 'Then there'll be quite a jolly party of us. For before I

177

accepted your somewhat churlish hospitality this evening, I sent my messenger for Huntly and his men.'

Mallaig paled, but said nothing. Robert went on, 'What you deserve, Mallaig, is to be split from head to crotch and hung from the city gate like a frog. In fact I'd happily volunteer . . . But in the meantime, I want a confession. You will give Huntly your written word, Mallaig, stamped with your seal, that on two separate occasions you have tried to murder the King's daughter.'

Relief and bewilderment mingled in the bearded face. 'You're a fool, Kyle. You said once that you wanted my lands, my title, everything I possess. But even if the King believes my so-called confession, he is unlikely to hang me. The Queen would never tolerate such a public spectacle over her husband's bastard. No, at worst, I will be sent into exile – to France perhaps. But even with me out of the way, you'd still have no claim, no possible right to my title or anything else that is mine.

Robert the Red smiled. 'Then let me explain,' he said.

The first rays of light were beginning to streak the sky as Bella slipped through the Castle gates and ran down the hill towards the saddlery. There had been time to snatch only a few hours of fitful sleep after settling the overwrought Mairead in her bed.

Edinburgh was just coming to life, with the water carrier's cart already rumbling on its first rounds. As shutters were thrown open, Bella expertly dodged the pails of slops thrown out into the street by yawning householders. She was impervious to the growing bustle all around her – Bella's mind was on Robert, and his encounter with Mallaig.

For if Robert had staked all, and lost, she knew there would be nothing left for her in Edinburgh. With Robert dead, for her own safety, she would have to run, as she had fled once before from her village in the Highlands. But where could she go this time? To Tom's native Aberdeen, perhaps? She might be secure there for a while, before Mallaig found out she was Robert's sister, and came looking for her.

But how could she desert Mairead? It would be impossible to take the King's daughter with her without attracting unwelcome attention and an accusation from the Court of abduction. Yet she had promised Margaret Drummond, in the King's presence, that she would be a faithful friend to the girl. What the King had feared had come to pass. Now, as never before, the young Margaret Stewart was going to need every friend she could muster. And if Robert was dead, and Mallaig remained at Court, Mairead would require more than mere friendship. To stay alive, she would need a miracle.

Bella's pace slowed as she approached the saddlery. The door was barred, the windows dark. If Robert was there, surely he would have lit the candles? Perhaps he was asleep. Bella ran along the vennel skirting the shop, and up the outside back stairs to the kitchen. The door was not locked. As she entered, she sensed she was not alone. Before she could move, or call out, two rough hands closed firmly round her throat.

Like a trapped wild animal, she froze.

'That's right. Keep perfectly still, Bella.'

Terror receded as she recognised Tom's familiar, yet strangely strained voice. Still his hands remained tight around her neck.

'Tom! I can't breathe. What sort of joke *is* this?'

'What sort of joke?' he mimicked. 'Don't fool with me, Bella. I want the truth. I want to know exactly what's been going on between you and the Earl of Mallaig.'

Bella tried to laugh, but the pressure of his hands strangled the sound. 'Mallaig? What are you talking about, Tom? Look, Robert will explain—'

The fingers tightened. 'I think for once it will be my turn to tell Robert a thing or two. Your dear brother clearly doesn't know what I do, Bella. Do you think I haven't seen you, talking and laughing with Mallaig? How do you imagine I've felt? You've been much in his company, and enjoyed every minute of it.' He whirled her round to face him.

Bella massaged her bruised throat. 'Tom... dear Tom. You are mistaken. Mallaig came to the Castle to see Mairead, not me. Of course I was pleasant to him. Robert thought that if Mallaig trusted me, he might let slip any plans he might have for harming the girl.'

'Oh, you've been *pleasant* to him all right,' Tom cried. 'I am informed that you found it extremely pleasant kissing him last night.'

Bella's back was straight, her voice steady. 'The trouble with sneak messengers is that they are apt to run off to their masters with only half the story. The truth is, that I resisted his advances. He has a lump on his knee and a sprained finger to prove it.'

'A lover's tiff. Don't trifle with me, Bella. Mallaig's an attractive man. Many women at Court lust after him. No one would blame you, I'm sure, for feeling flattered at his undoubted interest in you. But –'

'I hate him!' flared Bella.

'You lie. You would be his mistress.'

'Never!' Bella's words fell as splinters of granite. 'For me to lie with the Earl of Mallaig would not only be against my every inclination, but against the law of God and man. It would be unnatural, and illegal.'

Tom stared at her. 'What in Christ's name do you mean, Bella?'

'She means,' said Robert from the doorway, 'that Malcolm Laxford, Earl of Mallaig, is her brother.'

Nine

I myself comprehend not all the thing I am.

St Augustine

'Then . . .' Tom slumped like a stringless marionette onto a kitchen stool . . . '*who are you?*'

'I am the true Earl of Mallaig,' said Robert quietly. 'Now, if Bella can summon the strength to pour us some wine – I have a cask of excellent burgundy, thanks to the unwitting generosity of the Earl of Lennox – I will explain all.'

Giddy with relief, Bella stretched out her arms and pulled both men to her, holding them close.

'Forgive me, lovedy,' murmured Tom. 'I didn't know . . . I thought . . . God, I felt eaten up with jealousy. But why didn't you tell me?'

She kissed him. 'I couldn't.'

'I told her not to,' said Robert, heaping pine cones onto the glowing embers of the kitchen range. 'Selfishly, I was determined to deal with Malcolm Laxford myself, in my own way, in my own time. You're a hot-headed cuss where Bella is concerned, Tom. If you had known the truth your temper might have got the better of you, especially with Bella pretending to find Laxford's company so agreeable. I couldn't run the risk of you getting to him before I did, and killing him. I needed the bastard alive.'

Bella brought the wine, and hunks of spiced cinnamon cake. Warming his scarred hands before the fire, Robert began, 'Bella and I were the first two children fathered by Malise, the first Earl of Mallaig. He was a ruthless, wild Highlander of the old breed – uncivilised, unkempt and unruly. Our mother was Danish.'

'She came across to Scotland with Margaret of Denmark, our own King's mother,' said Bella. 'I don't remember her,

181

but from her portraits she was a beautiful, delicate woman, with long flaxen hair.'

'Why the Devil did she agree to marry a barbarian like Malise, then?' asked Tom, through a mouthful of cake crumbs.

'She didn't,' said Robert. 'Malise was visiting Falkland, saw her riding in the forest and literally carried her off back through the mountains to Mallaig. He forced the local priest to marry them, and a year later, I was born. But it was after Bella's birth that Malise showed his true colours. For no apparent reason, he suddenly turned against his wife. He developed the charming custom of lining up the servants and compelling them to watch him beating her. He'd lock her out of the castle on freezing winter nights and forbid anyone, on pain of death, to let her in.'

'Why didn't she run away?' mused Tom.

'With two infant children, and only a smattering of our Scots tongue?' said Bella. 'She had no money and nowhere to go.'

'In the end, Malise got rid of her,' Robert went on. 'He arranged for them to become the godparents of one of the village children. A cunning move, because under the laws of consanguinity –'

'Hold on. Consan what?' queried Tom.

Bella explained. 'It means you can't wed your sister, or aunt, or cousin. And neither are godparents allowed to be married to one another. So Malise had his marriage declared illegal and secured a divorce.'

'What happened to your mother?'

'That we don't know,' said Bella, pouring them more wine. 'Soon after the divorce she disappeared. She was never seen again, alive or dead. Everyone suspected Malise of murdering her, of course, but without a body, where was the proof?'

Robert propped his feet on the iron fender. 'Malise promptly married again – a Frenchwoman this time. I suspect he deliberately chose foreign ladies knowing they wouldn't have a band of angry male Scots relatives ready to cut him up for maltreating their kin. Anyway, he evidently omitted to mention to her that he had been married before. Which made the presence of Bella and I an acute embarrassment to him. Never a man for half measures, he immediately disowned us. We were dumped, literally, in the arms of a village nurse-maid.'

'Fortunately,' said Bella, 'our plight reached the ears of Malise's widowed sister, Lilith. She was an indomitable woman. Tough, even eccentric . . . she once rescued a wild cat from a trap and kept it in an enormous pen. But she was kind to us. She built a house in Mallaig and took us in.'

'And not just to feed, clothe and love us,' Robert said. 'She educated us, too. Her house was filled with books, music and paintings – it was a revelation after the barren, joyless chambers of Mallaig Castle.'

Tom threw some logs on the fire. Here then, was the explanation for so much that had puzzled him over the years. The cool self-assurance, almost arrogance, of the Kyles. The ability of a common saddler and his sister to read and write. Robert's fluency in French and Italian. And Bella's evasiveness whenever he asked about her parents or her home.

'And Malcolm Laxford?' Tom prompted.

'He was the only child the Frenchwoman bore Malise,' replied Robert. 'When Malcolm was five, she took him back to France with her and, very wisely, never returned. We con-tinued to live with Lilith, which in a perverse way maddened our father. He was obviously close to losing what little sanity he had left. He used to storm up to the house in the middle of the night, crazed with liquor, and demand that she hand us over.'

'Lilith would set the wild cat on him,' laughed Bella.

'I shouldn't think it was very amusing at the time,' murmured Tom.

'It was even less of a joke when Lilith died,' recalled Robert. He paused, apparently engrossed in fishing a dead fly from his wine cup.

'So what happened?' pursued Tom.

Robert looked up. 'I was fifteen, Bella two years younger.

I could see there was no future for either of us in Mallaig. Malise was obviously going mad, and would never leave us in peace. So one night, we saddled the horses and ran away, to Edinburgh.'

Tom glanced at Bella, but her face was turned to the shadows. 'Didn't Malise come chasing after you?'

'No,' said Bella shortly.

'He died,' said Robert, 'some time later. I suppose the drink had finally rotted his brain.'

'And I take it Laxford never knew you were his brother?' asked Tom.

Robert grinned. 'Not until tonight. I can't say he exactly clasped me to his bosom. Mind you, I did have a sword to his throat at the time.'

Swiftly, Robert outlined the night's events to the mystified Tom.

'What will happen to Laxford now?' asked Bella.

Robert shrugged. 'Huntly has him under close arrest. Tomorrow he will be taken before the King, to make a full confession. I have requested an audience with the King in the afternoon. After that, the matter rests in higher hands than mine.'

Tom frowned. 'One thing still puzzles me. Why did Malise's wife return to France so suddenly?'

'Because Malise had acquired a new sword,' said Robert, 'which he was anxious to test. He hung his wife's serving woman by her hands from the Great Hall cross beam. Then he sliced her clean through, from shoulder to hip.'

As Malcolm Laxford had predicted, he was exiled, at the King's command and with the utmost speed, to France. But he took with him his title as Earl of Mallaig, and the right to the revenues from his castle and lands in the Highlands.

'It's a delicate situation,' an embarrassed Huntly explained to Robert after his audience with the monarch. 'The King is anxious that the Queen should not be unsettled at this time. She is already gravely concerned about the poor health of her son. If Laxford were to be publicly disinherited and disgraced, it would draw unwelcome attention to the Lady Margaret Stewart. Attention which the Queen would regard with extreme disfavour.'

But the King did not fail the man who had twice saved his daughter's life. To Bella's delight, he created Robert Earl of Kinleven, giving him the mellow sandstone castle that stood at the opposite end of the bay to Mallaig Castle.

'Kinleven is beautiful,' Bella told Tom. 'Robert would much rather live there than in dank old Mallaig, with all that sinister blue-green slate. The place used to terrify us.'

By midsummer, Robert Kyle, Earl of Kinleven, had begun his nostalgic journey back through the mountains to the Highland shores of his birth. To the lands of Mallaig from which, seventeen years ago, he had fled from a violent past to an unfathomable future. Tom, Bella and their son Douglas moved into Mallaig's imposing house in the Canongate, leaving the saddlery in the erratic charge of Blackpatch and Nan. Robert had steadfastly refused to close the shop and Bella suspected that, Earl or not, her brother had no intention on his return to Edinburgh of forswearing his old friends or, for that matter, his smuggling activities.

The Frasers were now accredited members of the Court, a situation in which Bella revelled but that Tom regarded with mixed feelings. He was proud of his new position as Deputy Master of the King's Stables. But court etiquette daunted him, and he would never become accustomed to hearing his wife respectfully addressed as the Lady Annabella.

The mood of the court was subdued. Prince Arthur, the cherished heir to the throne, had followed the Queen's other two children to the grave. Margaret was attempting to assuage her grief by harassing James about a collection of jewels bequeathed to her by her brother Arthur. Henry, Margaret complained, was refusing to send to Scotland that which was rightfully hers. James, reluctant to ruffle the uneasy peace that existed between the two countries, could not see what all the fuss was about.

'Haven't I given you enough baubles to suffocate yourself in?' he demanded testily.

Margaret would not be pacified. Why should Henry hold on to jewels which Arthur had promised her before he died? James must insist on their return.

Finally, for the sake of domestic harmony, James instigated an exchange of letters and ambassadors between the Courts of Edinburgh and Westminster which was to wax increasingly more bitter. And which would lead, ultimately, not to a jewel box but to the battlefield.

While Henry vacillated over her trinkets, the Queen continued her persecution of the Lady Margaret Stewart. But Mairead was no longer a defenceless child. At thirteen, she was an acknowledged beauty and passionately resolved not to be dominated by any other woman. The Queen, deprived of Mallaig's ingenuity in her petty schemes against Mairead, was further unprepared for the spirited manner in which the girl was determined to strike back. If Mairead's horse bolted on a hunt, as the result of someone placing a thistle under the saddle, then the following day, some small misfortune would befall the Queen: a violent attack of sneezing as she bent to savour the Palace roses (the Cook closed his eyes to his ever diminishing pepper pot) or an itchy rash that made it impossible for Margaret to sleep (Mairead had learnt from Bella about the irritating properties of the hairy little seeds in a ripe rose hip). The Court, fully aware of the feud between the two Margarets, enjoyed the sport immensely, taking bets on which of the royal ladies would emerge the ultimate victor. Finally, the King wrenched himself away from his acrimonious correspondence with Henry VIII, and took a personal hand in the matter.

One late summer day, he took his daughter riding in the gladed woodlands surrounding Falkland Palace. For a while they galloped in silence, Mairead's raven black hair tumbling loose down the back of her green velvet riding jacket. At last, James reined in his courser, and sitting beneath the dappled leaves of an oak tree, watched as she sped across the field towards him. He looked with pride on the girl. Brave, beautiful, carefree, she was his sole reminder of the only woman he had ever loved.

It was impossible not to reflect on what might have been, had Margaret Drummond lived. In the seven lonely years since her death James had continued to mourn her with the intensity of one who knows he must bear his grief alone. He missed her. He ached for her. On occasions he would wake in the night, bathed in perspiration, calling her name aloud. The Queen had discovered him once, by the window at dawn, weeping as he gazed on a shot-silk sky of crimson and gold. In a rare moment of compassion and honesty, she had taken his hand, and murmured, 'I envy her. You had with her what I want with you.'

Now James looked into the brilliant blue eyes of Margaret Drummond's daughter, and said what he knew he had to say. 'You are not happy at Court, Margaret.'

The eyes flashed. 'You know as well as I, Sire, that there is one who bears me ill will. She feels I was created deliberately to draw attention to her own childlessness.'

James sighed. 'I know you have done nothing to aggravate the Queen, Meg. When you were a child, the situation was easier to control. It was simply a matter of ensuring that you and the Queen were never in the same room, the same castle, even the same town together. But now you are a woman, and a member of Court. It is only fitting that as my daughter you should have an entourage, and a position of your own. Yet how are we to achieve this when such bad feeling is being flaunted by the two leading ladies of the Court?'

'The friction is scarcely my fault,' insisted Mairead.

'I know,' agreed the King, twisting the reins round his wrist. 'My wife is not the easiest of women to please.' He paused, groping for the right words. 'It seems to me, it would be better if you and the Queen saw as little as possible of one another in future.'

Mairead grasped his meaning instantly. 'You can hardly send the Queen away. Is it I, then, who is to go?'

Her expression was proud, unyielding. Not for a moment, thought James, would she plead, grovel or beg. She was her mother all over again.

'I intend,' he said, 'that you shall be married. And soon.'

Mairead's mouth tightened. This she had never antici-pated. 'Married!' He was *telling* her, not asking her. The man on the black courser was not just her father. He was also King. Mairead had learned over the years never to argue when James used this particular tone with her. Instead she enquired coolly, 'And who, may I ask, is to be the fortunate groom?'

James repressed a smile. 'I have chosen for you Lord John Gordon, son of the Earl of Huntly.'

A frown creased Margaret's clear brow. 'Lord John Gordon?'

'You have never met him. He is newly returned from his studies in Orléans. But he is gallant and bold. A fine young man, Meg. He will make you an excellent husband.'

'He will make an excellent way of getting me out of the Queen's hair.'

James slipped his arm around her. 'Oh, Meg. Can't you understand? I would much rather have you here, with me, at Court. I dread the idea of you going away to set up home on Huntly's estate in the north. I shall see you so rarely. But I am doing this for your own protection. I shall not always be here to take care of you. With a husband, and a loyal family like the Huntlys, I shall at least rest sure in the knowledge that you are safe.'

Mairead turned away her head. Her voice was wistful. 'My mother always told me to marry for love.'

James drew a hand across his face. 'Your mother died for loving me,' he said. 'Love is a precarious commodity. A luxury few of us can afford.' Abruptly, he spurred his horse forward. 'Lord John Gordon is riding here with his father. They will arrive at Falkland this evening.'

Mairead said not another word, until, back at Falkland, a startled Bella watched her slam the chamber door shut. 'They want to marry me off to a stranger, Bella! A fawning, simper-ing creature with fancy French manners. I'll wager he's drenching himself in cologne at this moment, congratulating himself on landing the Lady Margaret Stewart as a wife.' She flung her riding crop on the floor. 'Oh, damn you to hell, Lord John Gordon!'

After the evening meal, the Lady Margaret Stewart and Lord John Gordon were despatched by the King to stroll in the gardens of Falkland Palace. Bella, hovering nearby as chaperone, felt she was not the only member of Court to sense the irony of the occasion. Everyone, from old Bell-the-Cat to the Lennoxes, would remember that spring evening fourteen years ago when Margaret Stewart's mother walked among the May blossom and fell in love with the King.

There the similarity of the two events ended. Mairead, thought Bella, was no mere watery copy of her mother. Both were beautiful, intelligent women. But whereas Margaret Drummond had possessed an inner tranquillity, a quiet grace, Margaret Stewart exhibited more of the free, wild spirit of a gipsy. There was an untamed quality in the unruly long black hair, the glittering eyes, the quicksilver gestures.

Despite her flare of temper at the suggestion of marriage, Mairead had, Bella guessed, been favourably impressed by Lord John Gordon. Tall, fair and strapping, he seemed blessed with all the Huntlys' renowned good looks and easy, captivating charm. Had not his Aunt Catherine, after all, won the hearts of Bell-the-Cat, Perkin Warbeck and Bella's brother Robert? From the shadows of the trellised wall, Bella kept a nervy eye on the young couple, ready to intervene should Mairead elect to perform her customary trick of hoisting her skirts and shinning up the almond tree. So far, Mairead's behaviour had been unimpeachable, presumably because she feared the lacerating fury of the King if she let him down before the entire Court. But Mairead's demeanour was demure, her step sedate, with Lord John beside her controlling with difficulty his youthful, boundless energy.

The Court was likely, then, to conclude that the King had chosen well for his daughter. The Huntlys were a noble family, staunchly loyal to the monarchy. And Lord John would prove no dull clod of a husband. Quite the reverse. He had a restlessness, surmised Bella, which fully matched

189

Mairead's – a fact that did not necessarily augur well for the forthcoming marriage. Perhaps they were *too* alike. What Mairead needed, Bella realised, was a husband of whom she was a little in awe. A real man. Not a boisterous playmate like the young Lord John Gordon.

The Lady Margaret turned her cornflower blue eyes upon her future husband. 'You have lately returned from France, I believe.'

John Gordon nodded his fair head. 'I was completing my studies there. But now Alexander says I am ready to put my books away, and face the real world.'

'Alexander?'

'Alexander Stewart, brother to the Duke of Albany. He's a great friend of mine. I'll introduce you later.'

'And what is the news from France?' enquired Mairead, eyeing the almond tree with longing.

John Gordon glanced hurriedly round, and lowered his voice. 'They are afraid of your Queen's brother, Henry VIII. They say Henry is drunk with power and are petrified that he will cross the sea and invade Calais. Rumour has it that the Auld Alliance will be signed again between Scotland and France.'

Mairead forgot the almond tree. 'But we have a peace treaty with England,' she protested. 'We can hardly help to defend France against Henry if we ourselves are supposed to be bosom friends with England.'

John Gordon shrugged. 'I am only telling you what I've heard. But I hope we do go to war with England. I'm longing to ride off to battle to the sound of trumpets and a hundred drums.'

Mairead teased: 'And instead of a glorious engagement with the enemy, you've been told you have to marry me.' When he didn't reply, she snapped, 'I would have you know now that I do not wish this marriage. My father the King desires it. I do not.'

'Do you think *I* wish it?' lashed back John Gordon. 'I am a young man, strong and vigorous, with all my life before me. I was planning to travel. I wanted to go to Russia, and to sail across the sea to the New World. Now I'm told that I have to marry, inhabit a gloomy castle, breed screaming children and accept what my dear father keeps referring to as my responsibilities. Do you think I yearn for *that*?'

Silence yawned between them like a dry moat. Mairead swallowed, shocked at the bitterness in the young man's voice.

'I am sorry,' she said at length. 'I realise that because of me, you are forced to give up all that you hoped and dreamed of. Against both our wills, we are being compelled to make a life together. I hope you will grow to like me, and forgive me in time. And in my turn, I will do my best to be a good wife to you.'

John Gordon smiled down on her. 'You have a generous spirit, Margaret. As you say, there is nothing for it but for us to do the best by one another.' He paused, tilted up Mairead's chin and looked her full in the face. What he saw there made his grey eyes glimmer with amusement. 'Frankly my dear, I suspect you are as incapable of being a good wife as I am of proving a responsible husband.'

The Court was surprised and pleased to see Margaret and John returning from their walk hand in hand, clearly in good humour. At a signal from the King, the fiddlers struck up a merry tune, with James and the Queen leading the dancing. After a particularly energetic reel, John Gordon pulled Mairead towards a quiet alcove, where a dark haired man sat in the shadows, absorbed in tuning a lute.

'I want you to meet my closest friend, Alexander Stewart, Dean of Dunbar,' said John. 'Alexander, may I present the Lady Margaret Stewart, my future bride.'

Mairead gazed into Alexander's ice blue eyes, and was afterwards quite unable to explain the excitement she felt at this meeting. It was not as if she made any obvious immediate impression on Alexander. After the usual exchange of courtesies, he seemed hardly to notice her as he and John Gordon became engrossed in a conversation about the good times they had enjoyed in France.

Unaccustomed to being ignored, Mairead hopped from one slippered foot to the other and finally cut through the young men's reminiscences with a blurted: 'Tell me, Dean of Dunbar. Is it true that Rome contains over forty thousand harlots, all kept for the delight of the clergy?'

A slow smile illuminated Alexander's tanned face. 'Now how would a delicate flower of the Scottish Court come by unsavoury gossip like that?'

Mairead tossed her head. 'The Earl of Mallaig told me. Perhaps you were acquainted with him in France?'

A swift glance passed between the two men.

'We have met,' said John Gordon abruptly.

'Did you know he is disgraced?' enquired Mairead. 'He is to make his home permanently in Paris, never to darken our shores again!'

Again the look was exchanged.

'Would you care to dance, Margaret?' asked Alexander.

'My friends call me Mairead.' She hesitated. 'I didn't think it was seemly for a man of God to be seen dancing.'

He swept her onto the floor. 'Tonight, God is looking the other way.'

As soon as they were out of earshot of John Gordon, Mairead challenged: 'What is there between you two and the Earl of Mallaig?'

Alexander executed a graceful turn. 'I have no personal quarrel with the, er, gentleman. But he and John do not exactly see eye to eye.'

'Why?'

'As the future Lady Gordon, I feel it would be hardly proper for me to reveal the origin of the feud.'

'You mean it involves another woman?' demanded Mairead. As his eyes sparkled, she flared, 'You may as well tell me. I'm not the sort of person to be bothered with proprieties. And neither, Alexander Stewart, are you.'

He laughed. 'Very well. The fact of the matter is that some months ago, in Paris, both Mallaig and John Gordon fell in love with the same woman.'

Mairead paused to dip a polite curtsey as the Queen left the Hall. 'Who won?'

Alexander faltered, and missed a step. Mairead's head went

192

up. 'I see. You mean the battle was still raging over this woman when John was summoned home to marry me. What is her name?'

'Diane d'Éste. She's related to the powerful Guise family. John had plans that he and Diane would travel the world together.'

'Is she beautiful?'

'Very.'

'Has she intelligence, wit and spirit?'

'Not to match yours.'

Mairead frowned. 'Poor John. Forced to abandon the woman he loves to Mallaig, in favour of the illegitimate daughter of a King. I am quite resolved that I shall never fall in love, Alexander. It seems to bring nothing but misery.'

He murmured,

'Love begins with care and ends with spleen,
For lady, for wife, for maid, for Queen.'

Mairead hardly heard. She grasped the Dean's hands and swung him into a violent spin to finish the dance. 'Reluctant bridegroom marries reluctant bride,' she chanted. 'It will be amazing if either of us can be bothered turning up at the Abbey at all.'

Ten

And damn the man whose heart admits despair.
                              Chanson de Roland

The autumn wedding of Lady Margaret Stewart to Lord John
Gordon was not graced by the presence of the Queen. She
was absent, too, from the giddy days of feasting and dancing
which followed the ceremony. But Queen Margaret was a
conspicuous figure on the steps of Holyrood Palace as the
Court bade farewell to the young couple setting out for their
northern home on Loch Kinnord. Fervently, the Queen
hoped she would never set eyes on the King's daughter again.
In a year the girl might well be with child. In two, she could
be dead.

Through the spring of 1511 the Queen, never a particularly
devout woman, prayed as she had never prayed before. For
one more child, a son, who would live. Characteristically,
Margaret's spiritual supplication took the form of a straight
bargain: 'Give me a healthy son, Lord, and I promise I will
be good in future.' She was not alone in her excess of devotion
that year. Her husband, kneeling beside her in Scotland, and
her brother in England were both seeking celestial guidance
over the deteriorating relations between the two countries.
But while James simply petitioned respectfully for peace,
Henry addressed his Maker on equal terms as one ruler to
another, demanding that the wayward Scots be brought
immediately to heel.

Having failed to inspire any direct heavenly intervention,
Henry took matters into his own hands. James' sea captain,
Andrew Barton, was spied plundering a Portuguese ship carrying English cargo. After a hectic chase across the high seas,
with Charles Howard, a relative of the Earl of Surrey, leading
the pursuit, Barton was captured and brutally slain.

James promptly demanded Howard's trial, on a charge of murder. Henry not only refused, but created Howard Earl of Nottingham. Throughout the flurry of outraged letters and ambassadors between Edinburgh and London, Margaret alone smiled. *Her* prayers had been answered.

Her son was born the following April at Linlithgow, and christened James. From the moment Margaret heard his first vigorous cry, she knew that this child would live, that this was the son who would one day inherit the throne of Scotland. She had always been sure, she told an unresponsive James, that it was the presence of Margaret Stewart which had cast an unlucky spell over her previous unfortunate children. Now it was proven. Margaret Stewart and her evil influence had gone, and a strong healthy son lay kicking in his crib.

Having supplied James with an heir, Margaret felt secure enough to reopen negotiations with her husband over the vexed question of the jewels Henry had steadfastly refused to return to her.

'You haven't a hope, Margaret,' James told her. 'Your dear, power mad brother has just been defeated in an invasion of France. He knows that Scotland and France are old allies, and he will never give up those trinkets while there is the possibility of my selling them to buy arms to use against him. I would too,' he lashed out, 'in return for the way he scuttles my ships and murders my seamen.'

'Andrew Barton was a common pirate,' protested Margaret.

'He was a brave man,' insisted James. 'I hear that even in the streets of London they sing of him, *He was brass within and steel without.*'

Margaret, confused by all this talk of war, returned to her ladies, and her embroidery. Although she was married to a Scot, and had lived here as Queen of Scotland for nearly ten years, she still regarded England as her mother country, the stronger, inherently more powerful nation. She had been brought up to look upon Scotland as a mere annex of England, and it seemed unnatural to Margaret for James to be acting aggressively towards her brother. Did he not realise that Henry was the most feared and respected monarch in all

Europe? Ever since he was a little boy, screaming himself into a blue fit if he were denied anything, Henry had always known how to get his own way. At all costs, he must be pacified, humoured and flattered. Otherwise, Margaret remembered, he would make your life living hell.

Yet James, writing once more to Henry to demand the return of his wife's jewels, saw fit to add the inflammatory remark that, since Henry and his Queen Katharine were childless, then Margaret was therefore the heiress presumptive to the throne of England. The blistering heat of Henry's rage at this suggestion prompted the wretched courier who relayed it to make a speedy retreat from London hidden in the bottom of a sewage boat.

Undaunted, James renewed the Auld Alliance with France, promising her ships, arms and men if England invaded. Margaret sobbed as the treaty was signed. To her, France, not England, was the enemy. Henry VIII wasted no time on tears. Instead, he exerted his influence as a member of the Holy League and persuaded the Pope to declare that he would excommunicate the King of Scotland if he dared to wage war on England.

For the next twelve months Scotland prepared uneasily for what everyone agreed was likely to be the bloodiest confrontation with England for decades. At Edinburgh Castle workmen toiled day and night manufacturing gunpowder, fashioning brazen cannon, whittling lance staves and arrow heads. James' magnificent new warship the *Michael* was already afloat on the Forth, reinforcing the fleet of twenty-five smaller vessels, including the *James*, the *Margaret* and one captured English ship.

Robert, returning from the Highlands in the spring of 1513, was greeted by Tom with the news that Henry VIII had signed a treaty with the Emperor Maximilian and King Ferdinand of Spain, which committed them to attack France.

'So it's come,' said Robert grimly. 'We are now bound to make war on England. All we have to do is wait for Henry to set one booted foot on French soil.'

Henry, his confidence bolstered by the new alliance, was not one to waste time. At the end of June, he set sail for France. James, in a last valiant bid for peace, despatched his principal herald, the Lyon King-at-Arms, to treat with Henry at his camp at Calais. Henry's reply turned James white with fury.

'Your beloved brother informs me,' stormed James to a weeping Margaret, 'that he *owns* Scotland. That I, James IV, am merely his *vassal*. And that if I rebel against Henry, he will then expel *me* from *his* realm!'

'James, I'm sure Henry didn't mean it like that,' pleaded Margaret. 'He was always hotheaded, and tactless, even as a boy. I'm sure he would have regretted those words almost as soon as he had uttered them.'

'Then it is time our endearing little boy grew up,' said James icily. 'He must learn that men, and especially kings, have a duty to accept responsibility for their words and deeds. As the son of a king, he should know that the leader of a nation can never speak carelessly, can never impugn the prestige, the pride, of another nation, another king.'

'What will happen?' whispered Margaret.

'We shall march on England.'

Margaret had never felt so frightened. The prospect of husband and brother fighting to the death made her blood run cold. She was no longer, she had to admit, as blindingly in love with James as she had been when a young girl. But at twenty-three, she now possessed sufficient maturity to appreciate James' unfailing kindness towards her. He had been a generous husband, both materialistically and spiritually. She had never wanted for money, jewels or clothes, and not once had he blamed her for bearing him children who died. He did not beat her, lock her up or flaunt his mistresses before her. She had been sent to Scotland to marry a stranger, and only now did she realise how fortunate she had been that the royal lottery had provided her with a handsome, intelligent, healthy spouse. Her fate could have been so much worse. Margaret shuddered, remembering that her own sister Mary

197

was betrothed to the drooling Prince of Castile, idiot son of Joanna the Mad.

And James, as well as being a dutiful husband and loving father, was a good King. He had welded a united country from the divided nation he had inherited, and set her on course for a bright future as an international trading nation. James' Scotland was a far cry from the uncivilised, barbaric land the ladies of the Tudor Court had warned her about when she was a thirteen-year-old girl at Richmond. The castles and palaces of Scotland were filled with the works of the writers, artists and musicians patronised by James. The Scottish Court was acknowledged as one of the most brilliant in Europe. And to all this she, Margaret Tudor, had contributed nothing. Except an heir.

With rising panic, Margaret realised that if James was killed in this senseless war, her way of life would die with him. For with her baby son crowned as King, it would be impossible for her, a mere woman, to control single handed the strife, the struggle for power, that would surely engulf the country without James' steadying influence.

For the first time, Margaret fully appreciated her good fortune in marrying James and sharing this lively society he had created. But it could all be lost, at the whine of an arrow, the thrust of a sword. Through her tears, Margaret glimpsed that she could be living in the last summer of a tragically brief golden age ... unless, unless the war could be stopped.

The dreams began quite suddenly and became increasingly persistent. James, immersed in battle plans, listened patiently as Margaret wailed of the awful prophetic visions that came to her at night. In one dream, she said, she had seen him hurled down into a great pit, to lie crushed and broken at the bottom. And she herself had lost one of her eyes. On another occasion she awoke, crying in the night, to tell James how she had been playing with her jewel box – the silver crosses, gold chains and diamonds – when in a flash they had all turned to pearls.

'Pearls!' sobbed Margaret. 'The symbols of widowhood and tears.'

James dried her eyes and told her the dreams meant nothing, she was merely overwrought. As he left her for an early morning meeting with Huntly on the raising of the militia, James reflected that Margaret, like her brother, had never learnt the art of subtlety. Never before had she complained of strange dreams. More important, she was not the kind of woman who would normally attribute dark inner meanings to her nocturnal visions. For all her faults, her jealousy, her vanity, her pettiness, Margaret was above all a realist. She had no truck with superstition. Only in the arena of love did Margaret's realism desert her. In affairs of the heart, she was an unashamed romantic. Here, James knew, he had failed her. In every other way he felt he had made her happy. But to love her in the consuming, exclusive fashion she desired was, in all conscience, more than he had been able to do. Inevitably, when he made love to her, he saw before him another face, with dark hair that spread over the pillow like an ebony fan, and amber eyes luminous with the light of love. But, James consoled himself, if he had failed his wife it was partly because she demanded the impossible. All men would fail her.

But James knew she would make a loyal and devoted mother to his son. In that respect he had perfect confidence in Margaret. Talking of the boy to Huntly that morning, it was impossible for him not to think of another child, his beloved Margaret, now safely – if not particularly romantically – married to Huntly's son. He had not realised how much he would miss Meg at court. Flying across the cobbles to greet him after the hunt, frightening the doves by turning cartwheels, and amusing him with her chatter about her adored Portuguese horse. On impulse, that August, James leapt on his black courser and galloped north. He told Margaret he was going to visit the shrine of St Duthac in Ross-shire, to pray for forgiveness and guidance in the forthcoming campaign against the English. Margaret knew perfectly well that St Duthac would doubtless guide the penitent towards the great fortified Huntly castle on Loch Kinnord. James was going to visit his daughter, and for once, the Queen didn't care. She had her own plans to make.

On his return a subdued James told Margaret that he had paid a courtesy call on the Gordons.

'You found your daughter well?' enquired a serene Queen.

'She is with child,' James said flatly. From his drawn expression Margaret guessed something of the pain he had suffered at leaving his daughter, possibly for the last time. His mood pleased Margaret: a man in low spirits was at his most malleable.

That evening, as James prayed in the lovely chapel of St Katherine at Linlithgow, there was a disturbance in the porch. A scruffy, illclad man of about fifty, with long yellow hair fringing his bald head, was loudly insisting on speaking to the King. James' attendants, assuming the intruder to be a petitioner, motioned him to be silent until the King had completed his devotions. James, wearily accustomed to this kind of interruption, stood, and beckoned the man forward.

The stranger made no bow, no act of obeisance towards his sovereign. Instead, he stabbed a crabbed finger at James, and screamed, 'Heed a wise man's warning. Take not the path to war, or you will be doomed and all Scotland with you. The signs of conflict, disaster and death are writ large in the stars of the sky. Defy the heavens at your peril, oh King, or you will die a most savage and horrible death!'

Before the astonished King could reply, the man slipped behind a curtain which concealed a private staircase leading to the gallery. The guards, stampeding after him, were brought up short by a quiet command from their sovereign.

'This is a house of God, not a border tower to be ransacked in the pursuit of a demented old man. Let him go.'

Later, James rebuked his sulking Queen, 'What a foolish masquerade, Margaret. It had your melodramatic stamp all over it.'

Margaret was not prepared to give up that easily. The following morning an Edinburgh priest, accompanied by Bell-the-Cat, rushed into the Great Hall in a state of alarm.

'Tell the King what you saw,' ordered Angus, his florid face grave.

Wringing his hands, the priest stuttered out his story. 'At

the Market Cross, Sire, in Edinburgh last night ... there appeared a ghostly fiend in the moonlight. His eyes burned like hot coals ... terrible to behold. He renounced the war with England, and then began a roll call of all those who will die. Oh, Sire, I hesitate to tell you...'

'Force yourself,' said James drily, picking his teeth with a jewelled toothpick.

'Your Grace, he called your name. And the names of some of the highest ranked men in the land. You will suffer the most agonising deaths at the hands of the English. Your women will be left defenceless. Sire, believe me, if you had seen with your own eyes this man, this dreadful apparition...'

'I'd be delighted to make his acquaintance,' declared James. 'Where is he now, lurking overhead in a winged chariot?'

'No, Sire. He, well, he just disappeared,' faltered the priest.

'In a puff of blue smoke, I suppose?' James ignored the confused priest and turned to Bell-the-Cat. 'A noble try, Angus. But I can recognise the heavy hand of the Queen in this charade.' He sighed. 'I must say, I feel sorry for the poor people of Edinburgh. They must have been scared half out of their wits.'

Privately, he wondered at this strange alliance between Angus and Margaret. Then it occurred to him that they had a common grievance over his affair with Janet Kennedy. Although James' lust for her had burnt out long ago, Angus had never forgiven him for seducing his mistress. And the Queen never forgave anyone anything.

Despite Margaret's pathetic, though well meant, attempts to prevent the war, James endeavoured to make their last night together at Linlithgow as loving and memorable as possible. Well aware of the fastest route to her eternal heart, he took her into his private chamber, and handed her the key to a large brass chest.

'Here it is, Margaret: my secret treasury. Should anything happen to me in the war, the gold you will find in here is to be used for the safety and education of our son.'

Delighted with this proof of his trust in her, Margaret flung herself into the King's arms.

201

'Not son James – *sons*. I cannot yet be certain, but I believe I am to bear you another child.'

'I am glad, Margaret. A brother for James V.'

She clung to him. 'Oh, don't say that. Why do you talk this way? It is as if you were wishing yourself dead.'

James' voice was remote. 'It is others who wish that, not I.' He stroked her red gold hair. 'Come now, my wife. Let us to bed.'

'You're not going to the war, and that's final!' shouted Bella.

Douglas Fraser beat his fists on the polished dining hall table. 'I'm thirteen, mother. Old enough to fight for my King and country.'

Bella blinked back the tears as she studied the angry face of her only son. She was so proud of him, growing tall and strong as a maypole with Tom's mop of chestnut curls and her own sea green eyes. She couldn't let him go. It would be heartbreaking enough watching Tom and Robert join the army, but the prospect of Douglas leaving her as well – perhaps never to return – was unbearable.

'It's not fair,' muttered Douglas. 'Everyone else is going. Even Blackpatch, and he's not half as brave as me. I shall,' he declared dramatically, 'be the only man left in Edinburgh!'

Tom stood up, and motioned to the waiting serving girl to clear away the breakfast meats. 'Not quite, Douglas. The King has forbidden the Earl of Angus to join the army, on the grounds of his increasing years. The old man is livid about it. He'll need someone here to cheer him up. Besides,' he laid a hand on his son's already broad shoulder, 'with Blackpatch away, Robert will be relying on you to keep an eye on the saddlery for him. And I need you in Edinburgh, to look after your mother and Nan.'

Douglas did not dare say so, but his expression indicated that, judging by all the stories he'd heard, Bella and Nan were more than capable of taking care of themselves.

But a mutinous Douglas was left at home on the day the King led his army into war. Bella watched miserably from

202

a grassy knoll at the edge of the stretch of open country known as Burgh Moor, where the twenty thousand men had assembled, ready for the long march south. Apprentices, farmers, artisans, mercenaries, clerks, clerics and lords stood shoulder to shoulder in the drizzle. Some were clad in complete suits of armour, with gleaming swords and polished shields. Others had been able to afford no body protection at all, but had simply seized axes and shovels, kissed their wives goodbye and rushed to answer good King James' call to arms.

Every able-bodied man and nearly every great name in Scotland was there, Bella realised, recognising the banners of Huntly, Lennox, Elphinstone, Argyll, Crawford, Montrose ... and there was the handsome John Gordon, and a laughing Alexander Stewart sharing a joke with Bell-the-Cat's son George. As Tom, Robert and Blackpatch rode by they dipped their burnished swords in salute to Bella. She matched their mood with a sweeping, elaborate curtsey, smiling with a brittle confidence she didn't feel. Then her husband and brother had gone, leaving Bella to wonder how many of these brave, steel helmeted men were unknowingly feeling Scottish heather under their feet for the last time.

The five massive cannon and twelve culverins rumbled by, on carts pulled by teams of thirty-six oxen. They were accompanied by packhorses, laden with cannon balls; and workmen armed with spades, picks and shovels to clear the rutted roads. Over the men's shoulders were wound two ropes, one to help pull the cannon up hills, and the other to act as a brake going down.

Following close behind the well ordered ranks of the militia, straggled another army: the usual pack of women, astrologers, beggars, jesters and pimps, all jostling for the easy pickings offered since time began by men on active service, far from home. Already, in the streets of Edinburgh, gipsies were selling frightened women lucky gold rings, that in two days would turn their wearers' fingers green.

Bella felt sick. Not merely from the acrid smell of gunpowder carts mingling with the aroma of salted beef, dried fish, wine and cheese emanating from the army's provision wagons. Above all that, Bella scented death.

Hardly had the last banner fluttered out of sight across the moor, than the drizzle intensified into a downpour. Bella lifted her head, welcoming the cleansing streams of water. She sat for a long time, peering vainly through the grey curtain of rain for a last glimpse of the departing men. But all she could hear was a faint echo of the army's marching song:

> *Burn their women, lean and ugly!*
> *Burn their children great and small!*
> *In the hut and in the palace,*
> *Prince and peasant burn them all!*
> *Plunge them in the swelling rivers,*
> *With their gear and with their goods;*
> *Spare, while breath remains, no Saxon;*
> *Drown them in the roaring floods!*

The sound died away. The army, and her men, had gone. It was not until Bella arrived home, soaked and sad, that she realised young Douglas was marching with them.

Eleven

And I looked, and behold a pale horse: and his name that sat on him was Death.

Revelation 6

Like a thief in the night the plague pursued the singing army out of Edinburgh. It struck silently, stealthily, lethally. Men who three days earlier had boasted to their wives that they would cut the English smaller than herbs for the pot, now lay face down, spitting blood and poisonous phlegm into the sponge of mud and horse droppings that ribbed the road. Douglas Fraser, running faster than the plague, caught up with his father and uncle just beyond the English border at Twizelhaugh.

'Your mother will be out of her mind with worry,' raged Tom.

'He must be out of his mind himself,' shivered Blackpatch, shielding their cooking fire from the drenching rain. 'To think, he could be back home, tucked up in a nice warm bed.'

'You have no horse, no weapon, no armour,' observed Robert practically. 'When the fighting starts, Douglas, you'd better stick close to the cannon. I'll have a word with Robert Borthwick, the chief gunner. He'll find you something useful to do.'

Douglas grinned. At heart the three men were, he knew, proud of him. He had been right to leave the nursery and join the war. Head held high, he marched beside his father into a field soggy with rain, where they formed a square, the lords, the clergy, the commoners, facing the King on his great white war horse. There James passed the last piece of legislation before the start of hostilities: that in the event of the bread-winner's death in battle, all widows and orphans would be exempt for life from paying taxes to the Crown.

Blackpatch, who endured an abrasive relationship with his sharp-tongued wife, looked anxiously over his shoulder, fearful that at the last minute Nan had decided to join the camp followers.

'If she got to hear of that new law, she'd be here, slicing me up herself,' he whimpered. 'She always said she'd do better without me.'

'So you think you'll find the field of war more peaceful than your own hearth?' laughed Tom, his eyes on the road where workmen armed with spades and shovels were trying to iron out the deep ruts – inspired by the promise of fourpence a day more than they earned in Scotland.

Blackpatch squatted on his haunches amidst the damp grass. 'I've never volunteered for the army before. I can't think why I did this time. I must be mad.' He shook his shaggy head. 'I'm terrified, if you want the truth. But it's as if this war holds a sort of doomed fascination for me.'

'Cheer up, Blackpatch,' urged Robert. 'You're just cold, miserable and hungry. You'll feel much better when you've tucked into some roast oxen tonight. Apparently, one poor beast was run over by a cannon,' he explained, 'so tonight, my friends, we feast!'

'And tomorrow?' asked Douglas.

'We march on Norham Castle.' Robert ran his nails down Blackpatch's back. 'And the King has ordered that any man caught looting or cattle stealing will get a hundred lashes.'

Riding ahead of his well-disciplined army, through almost incessant rain, the King besieged and captured the English castles of Norham, Etal and Ford. At Ford, instead of pressing on, the Scottish army stopped.

News of the sudden halt brought bewilderment to the face of the Earl of Surrey, commander of the English army, who was leading his men fast through the north of England to head off the Scottish thrust.

He listened with grave attention as the breathless messenger gabbled on, 'It is said, my lord Surrey, that it is not just the Castle of Ford which is under siege from King James. He is so enamoured of the mistress of the castle, the Lady

Elizabeth Heron, that he refuses to allow his troops to advance until the lady,' the messenger giggled, 'surrenders her charms to –'

'Stuff and nonsense!' exploded Surrey, waving the man away and rounding on his son, Thomas Howard. 'The King of Scots is a red-blooded man, but he's no fool. He would never throw all his energies into winning a woman's favours, at the risk of losing his crown. No, King James must be in trouble – deep trouble. My guess is that his men have been stricken by the plague and disheartened by the rain. My spies tell me that already, King James has been forced to send back to Edinburgh for more oxen, ammunition and wheels for the guncarriages. It sounds to me as if the Scots are stuck in the mud, Thomas, like linnets in bird-lime.'

This latest encouraging intelligence about the plight of the enemy helped to disperse the cloud of gloom which seemed always to hover about the lugubrious English warlord. This was the second time in his life he'd been despatched, unwillingly, to this barbaric part of the world. Ten years ago he had escorted Henry VIII's sister to her Holyrood Abbey marriage with the Scots King. He had loathed every diplomatic minute of that journey, pandering to the whims of an adolescent princess, and listening in stony silence as James subtly but relentlessly mocked the English. Now, amidst these soggy northern hills, scarred by peat troughs deep enough to swallow a horse, he was about to face James IV again. While Henry had grabbed all the glory – and all the best English cannon – for his glamorous campaign against France.

With all his heart Surrey had longed to accompany his King to Calais. But at the last moment, Henry had given him his hand to kiss, and charged him with the defence of England against the Scots. Surrey, furious at being left behind, swore to take bitter revenge on James Stewart if ever the opportunity arose. Now his chance had come. Already, as a symbol of their leader's aspirations, Surrey's soldiers wore his white lion on the left sleeves of their uniforms, the beast depicted trampling on the defeated red lion of Scotland.

After some thought, Surrey decided against attacking the

Scots at Ford Castle. Although their forces were of roughly equal size, Surrey calculated that it would be to his advantage to lure the Scots out on to open ground. But how? Then he remembered King James' passion for the tournament: the Wild Knight, gripped by the thrill of the joust, intoxicated with the golden legends of chivalry. Surrey summoned his herald, and gave him a brief message for the Scottish monarch, inviting him to appoint the day and place for a confrontation.

'That should flush the wily fox out,' smiled Surrey.

But what drove James thundering in a white heat out of the gates of Ford Castle was not Surrey's challenge but that of his son, Lord Thomas Howard. Howard had been amongst the party that had chased and slain James' most experienced sea captain, Andrew Barton.

'He has sent a note,' spluttered James to Lord Huntly, 'Defying me to take my revenge for Andrew Barton, *if I can!*'

A livid James promptly despatched the herald back to Surrey. His message was brief and to the point. The Scots would meet the English at noon on Friday 9 September, two miles west of Ford, at a place called Flodden Hill.

By Wednesday evening, the Scots had taken up their position on the highest ridge of Flodden Hill.

'My God, we look impregnable,' Robert exulted. His gaze took in with a fighting man's keen eye the misty Cheviot hills to his right, the flooded River Till to the left, and the marshy, swampy land at their backs. As the last of the great cannon was dragged up to the hilltop, an almost carnival atmosphere infected the encamped Scots. Gypsies were making fortunes foretelling a great victory, while amidst the tents and make-shift shelters pipers vied with ranting friars for the ear of an army jubilantly confident of success.

Certainly, the day had started inauspiciously for the English. Surrey, silently berating himself for allowing the Scots time to entrench themselves, pored over his waterlogged maps, searching for a way to dislodge James' men from the crest. The English troops were in low spirits, demoralised by the long forced marches, short rations and rain. Not only were they fractious and quarrelsome, but worst of all, they had drunk every drop of their ale. All they had left to drink was the filthy river water.

After a peaceful night in his tent, King James was rudely awoken at dawn by Lennox, screeching: 'Sire! The English are on the march!'

He was right. Peering through the inevitable veil of rain, thickened by the smoke of a thousand cooking fires, the Scots could just make out a sideways movement of Surrey's men. The English army was retreating down Flodden Hill, and across the River Till, each man clutching the stirrup leather of the one ahead to avoid being swept away in the torrent.

'But which way are they going?' muttered Bishop Elphinstone, peering into the gloom.

Robert Borthwick flung himself before the King. 'Sire. The guns are ready for firing. At your command –'

'No!' declared James. 'I gave my word we would not fight before Friday noon. We have over thirty-six hours to go. I will not break my pledge.'

'We should strike now, while we have the advantage,' urged Lennox. 'The English are still within our sight, Sire, but visibility is poor. If we lose contact now, the initiative will be with Surrey. He will have the chance to take us at a rush, unawares.'

James glowered. 'This is an affair of honour, Lennox, not a petty cattle raid. We will not move until Friday noon.'

Huntly siezed the dripping pole which supported the royal tent, his hands shaking with anger. 'Your Grace, Lennox is right. We must act *now*. Surrey is not a man to be trusted.'

'Not to be trusted?' shouted the King. 'You presume to cast aspersions on the Lord Treasurer and Earl Marshal of England – a man who at this moment represents his monarch? Do you think Surrey would dare have it bandied about Europe that he had jeopardised the honour of King Henry VIII by leading his men into battle before the appointed time?'

A large forked vein bulged on Huntly's forehead. 'If you

209

do not give the command, Sire, Surrey will be able to bellow round Europe that he won the war because James IV was a laggard!'

'Be silent, Huntly!' James spun round to face his mutinous lords. 'Convey my word to your men. The King's word is his bond. I am a man of honour, leading a noble army. We will fight, on Friday, at noon. Until then, we wait.'

He turned his back on his lords, and the English, and strode away to inspect the munitions.

Lennox flung his dagger into the sodden turf. 'Who does he think he is? Bloody Charlemagne?'

But they waited. All through Thursday and Friday morning they waited, soaked to the skin as the rain leaked under their breastplates and the mist slapped their faces like a damp cloth. The horses' coats were plastered, and all the supplies were turning mouldy, rotten or rusty. Noon came, and went.

'All this hanging about,' moaned Blackpatch, wringing out his eyepatch. 'I thought we were supposed to be men of action.'

No one heeded him. The ears of twenty thousand Scotsmen were tuned to the south, listening for the first trumpet call that would summon them to arms. Shortly after one o'clock, the call came. Robert was amongst the first to spot the English soldiers, in their distinctive green and white livery, marching fast, in well-ordered lines.

'From the *north*!' choked Robert. 'They're coming from our rear – we've been outflanked!'

Tom waited till Douglas, sent running to alert the King, was out of earshot. 'This looks bad to me, Robert. The bastards must have recrossed the River Till and circled back under cover of the mist. That took guts, with the Till flooded and swamps all around deep enough to drown a man.'

Robert was feverishly saddling the horses. 'We should never have underestimated Surrey's determination.'

As a horrified James hurriedly drew up new battle orders, the heart of every Scotsman contracted. Suppose this was just another of Surrey's tricks? The English army now lay between them and their undefended wives and children over the border. Was the phalanx now marching up Flodden Hill merely a token force, a feint to divert James' men while the bulk of the English army attacked Scotland?

Amidst argument, chaos and confusion, the tents were struck and all the rubbish of the camp swiftly set on fire.

'Oh God, what's happening now?' demanded Blackpatch, his one eye streaming with tears as the acrid smoke billowed across the camp. Next moment, flung to the ground by a stampede of horses and madly running foot artillery, he was conscious only of deafening noise and the smell of damp leather, sweat and wet iron.

'On your feet, you old layabout,' said Tom, yanking him up by the collar. 'Your wife would be desolate if I had to report I'd lost you.'

'What's going *on*?' gasped Blackpatch, straining for breath as Tom raced him over the ridge of Flodden Hill.

'The English are advancing from the north,' explained Tom. 'Under cover of the smoke, we're moving further along the ridge to meet them.'

'It's not that I'm afraid to fight, you understand,' panted Blackpatch. 'It's just that I wish they'd make up their damned minds.'

They joined Robert, who was busy mustering a team of pikemen from the Saddlers' Guild. Douglas rapped urgently on his uncle's breastplate. 'Robert. If we're to fight to the north instead of the south – then *all the cannon are pointing the wrong way*!'

'Then get up there and help Robert Borthwick turn them round,' ordered Robert grimly. 'And stay with the cannon when the fighting starts.'

Everything had to be turned round, and in the worst of conditions. The oxen pulling the guncarriages were stupidly stubborn, ropes rotted, wheels stuck in the mud, pikes splintered, horses screamed in fear, tents were sodden and every rainsoaked man felt five pounds heavier in his cumbersome dripping armour.

Yet somehow, from the mayhem, a semblance of military order emerged and the men lined up in diamond and square

211

formations, each a bowshot apart. Robert, Tom and Black-patch joined the far right hand group of Highlanders and Islemen, led by the Earls of Lennox and Argyle. Next to them was the King's party, with James' proud crimson and gold banner slapping loudly in the wind. Robert could see, but not hear, Huntly remonstrating with the King.

'I'll wager he's urging the King to stay out of the front line,' Robert told Tom.

'Then he'll be disappointed,' asserted Tom. 'It's not our King's way to lead from the rear.'

'Aye, he'd not ask us to undertake anything that he'd be afraid to do himself.' Robert's eyes lit up. 'Look! He's sent Huntly packing. He's going to fight at the front.'

This was the largest, the most loyal army ever assembled in Scotland, thought Robert, gazing proudly out over the sea of multicoloured banners held defiantly aloft over the waiting men. They had come from the isles, from the Highlands and Lowlands, from crofts, castles and abbeys: men of the land, men of learning, men of God. Some were more accustomed to wielding a pen or a plough than the sword. Others, merchants and shopkeepers, were more practised at striking bargains than blows. But they had come. From humble apprentice to belted earl, every able-bodied man was gathered here today to fight for the King they loved and the country they cherished.

Robert closed his eyes, summoning the words for a swift prayer. But he had not reached 'amen' when, to a resounding roar from the army, the King's trumpeter sounded the advance. As Robert Borthwick's cannon spat flame and fury, the Scots began their march down the muddy hill towards the English.

The left flank, commanded by the Earls of Huntly and Home, were the first to encounter the enemy. The English foot soldiers had borne the brunt of the cannon fire and the Scots, behind a dense forest of fifteen-foot spears, had little difficulty in forcing back Surrey's men down the slope. But before Robert and the others could draw breath to cheer, fifteen hundred English horsemen thundered into the fray, smashing Huntly's brave hedgehog to pieces.

As the sphere of the battle widened, Blackpatch realised with dismay that Robert Borthwick's cannon were set at too high an angle. Ball and grapeshot were hurtling far above the heads of the enemy. In contrast, the English guns were raking their target with lethal accuracy, the cast iron missiles throwing up mud, blood and dismembered limbs into the faces of frightened men and wild eyed, rearing horses.

It was Blackpatch's last reasoned thought for several hours. To the strident call of the pipes, the Highland contingent to which he was attached were hurling themselves into action. Blackpatch's first instinct was to turn and run. But those behind pushed him forward, and he found himself shrieking a blood-curdling cry – be it of hate or terror – as the foot soldiers bore down on the English. Mindlessly, he smashed, lunged and hacked, aware only of shattering blows and the clang of steel on his armour. He bent low to dodge a hail of hissing arrows, and looked anxiously around. Where was Tom? They had been fighting side by side, but Tom had gone. More than anything, Blackpatch longed to wipe the sweat from his one good eye, but his vizor had him blinkered like a workhorse.

The fighting swirled around and away from Blackpatch, leaving him momentarily becalmed in a sea of bloodstained earth, discarded weapons, wounded horses and dead men. How in God's name, he wondered, was anyone supposed to know what was going on, who was winning or what to do next? It probably all made sense to the noble lords, seated on their horses above the common fray. They, no doubt, had a clear view of the battlefield. But to foot soldiers like himself, all was confusion and chaos. The noise of cannonshot was deafening. Trumpets and drums sent conflicting messages of advance and retreat to both sides, while gunsmoke obscured all but those nearest to him. Blackpatch suddenly saw Robert, to his left, battling with the Earl of Crawford against Thomas Howard and his men. *But where was Tom?*

The smoke cleared for a second, and Blackpatch glimpsed

the King clashing with Surrey's contingent. Behind him, the Scots drove time and again with their long wooden spears against the enemy, only to find their weapons – and the initiative – jarred from their wet hands by the shorter, more flexible English billhooks. And when a spear was broken, a sword was no match for the axe-like blade of the bill. At last, hampered by the slippery, rainsoaked earth, the frantic Scots tore off their shoes, finding it easier to fight in the mud in stockinged feet.

Blackpatch's head seemed to explode. He didn't see who, or what, had hit him. He felt his sword wrenched from his hand and, through the smoke hazed vizor, sensed rather than saw the flash of an English billhook. He was defenceless. The first blow struck his shoulder, spinning him to the ground. Sick with terror, Blackpatch writhed and threshed in the churned-up grass. If he were not killed outright now, he would be trampled to death at any moment by the horses. He shrieked as the Englishman's billhook tore into his armour. My God – he would be peeled like a crab. Blackpatch closed his single eye, and waited. *Make it quick. Dear God, make it quick.* His last recollection was of the peculiarly unwarlike smell of rancid butter.

Douglas knelt in the mud. He was trying desperately not to cry. The battle was over. The Scots had lost. Robert wiped a tear from the boy's smoke-blackened face.

'I saw what you did, Douglas,' he said quietly. 'It wasn't exactly an orthodox tactic, but it worked. You saved Blackpatch's life.'

Douglas managed a smile. Armed with a pound of butter used to grease the cannon, he had thrown the lot into the eyes of the Englishman's horse. The animal had reared, throwing his rider. Douglas had grabbed the billhook and with one frenzied, fearful flow, killed his first Englishman.

Robert ordered his men to take the unconscious Blackpatch to his tent. Then he drew Douglas to him, and told the boy that his father was dead. In the distance, Robert could hear Lords Home and Huntly rallying their men for the retreat.

After a long while, Douglas lifted his head. His lips moved, but his tongue remained a prisoner.

'There are no words,' said Robert gently, surveying the bloodstained hill. 'In time, we will be able to speak of it. But not now. Not yet.'

Together, the man and the boy picked their way across the dead bodies, the severed limbs, the broken arrows, splintered spears and scraps of armour littering the hill. Already, the women followers were trailing across the field, their wails forming a mournful descant to the moans of the injured as the English flung them, unheeding, into pits with the dead. Riderless horses ran free, and instead of the scent of victory, there was only the stench of rotting flesh.

Side by side, Robert and Douglas stepped over the trampled blue banners of St Andrew and St Margaret, and the bodies of bishops, earls and commoners, lying equal, at last, in death. Many Robert had known. Many, back in Edinburgh, he had fought. Many, in different times, he had stolen from. Now the flower of Scottish manhood had been slain in one single, bloody afternoon. He found Montrose, Lennox, Bell-the-Cat's son George, and Crawford. All dead. But he could not find the one he sought.

As a lone piper played the first haunting lament for the ten thousand Scotsmen who had given their lives, Robert glimpsed the crimson and gold banner torn to shreds in the grass. But he did not recognise the King of Scotland. While the white lion standard of the Earl of Surrey flew supreme over the hill of Flodden, James IV, his face hacked completely away, and his body mercilessly slashed, had bled to death in the mud.

PART THREE
Margaret Gordon

One

Where are they whom once we saw,
Leading hounds and bearing hawks . . .
Where is the laughter and the song,
Of all the proud, skirt-trailing young,
Where are the hawks and hounds?
All our joy is gone away;
Singing now is wailing,
In times of much hard trial.

Anon

'The King lives! King James is coming back to us!'

But this was no cry of jubilation that Mairead heard in the spring of 1514 as she returned to Edinburgh for the first time since her marriage. 'The King lives!' The muted plea of yearning told Mairead more about the pitiful legacy of war than all the grim tales of battle recounted by her husband John. Gone was the colourful, vibrant Edinburgh that Margaret Gordon had loved. No one smiled here any more. It was as if the laughter, the irresponsible ebullience that had filled the bustling streets had died with the men on Flodden field. Terrified of an English invasion, and mortified by the memory of their crushing losses, the Scots had hastened to turn their friendly capital into a fortressed walled city. And echoing the gun-spiked barricades, the guarded gates and shuttered houses, the citizens wore a defensive, wary look. The face, thought Mairead sadly, of a defeated nation stricken with fear and shame.

Yet as she collected a brooch from her goldsmith, bought spices, a toy cannon for her older son and a ribboned rattle for her baby, Margaret Gordon heard it whispered again:

'He did not die at Flodden. When the time is right, he will be amongst us again. The King will return.'

'Wishful thinking,' said John Gordon forcefully, as they relaxed before a roaring fire in Robert's parlour that night.

Bella passed round a dish of almond fudge. 'But I've heard it said, too, up at the Market Cross, that the King escaped at Flodden and will return to lead the country to victory against the English.'

John Gordon shook his fair head. 'I saw the King's body myself. And my father Lord Huntly was one of those who officially identified it.'

'I don't see how,' muttered Robert, leaning back in Malcolm Laxford's carved oak chair. 'From what I heard there was an almighty row between Huntly and Home over whether or not that corpse was the King's. Home insisted it could just as well be Elphinstone. After all, there was no iron chain round the waist.'

'The King always wore the chain, we know that,' said Bella. 'But it could have been wrenched off in the heat of the battle, or taken by one of the English as a souvenir.' She sighed. 'Poor man. For a King of Scotland to die alone, unrecognised...'

Robert surveyed his guests as they gazed, unspeaking, into the fire. John Gordon, having proved himself at Flodden, had grown from restless youth into impatient manhood. Charming and impulsive, he was swift to draw his sword in anger, yet never churlish in his remorse. Mairead was sprawled on velvet cushions beside her husband, her black hair flamed auburn by the glow of the cresset lamps. Never the calmest of women, she appeared positively serene when compared to John. It was six years, reflected the Earl of Kinleven, since he had last met Mairead. He had been away at his castle in the Highlands when she married John Gordon and disappeared into the northern mists of Loch Kinnord. In that time, the pretty, wilful child had developed into a woman of resolution and rare beauty. She had mellowed, and it would be tempting to imagine that marriage and motherhood had endowed Margaret Gordon with a new quality of repose. But her eyes, bright blue, deep and wild, betrayed the passionate, rebellious spirit that still fired the blood of the dead King's daughter.

It was Mairead, never one to be squeamish, who broke the long silence of the group huddled round the fire.

'And what happened to my father's body?' Her voice was cool, steady, almost detached.

'We're not sure,' said Robert. 'They say Surrey took it back to Richmond Palace. But the King's plaid cloak was most certainly sent to Queen Katherine in England.'

'How could they!' shuddered Bella. 'Why didn't Queen Margaret demand it back?'

'She's a realist,' said John Gordon, draining his goblet of wine. 'What use the shadow when you have lost the substance? Besides, she was too busy establishing herself as Regent and organising the coronation of the young James V.'

'Everyone called it the mourning coronation,' Bella told Mairead. 'We all wore black, even the baby King. The bells were muffled, and instead of a fanfare of trumpets all you could hear in the Abbey was the sound of sobbing – men as well as women – when the child was crowned.'

Robert refilled their goblets. 'It was a bizarre business. We even had to sing the *Te Deum* in a whisper so we'd hear if Surrey and his merry men came charging through the city gates.'

'I wonder why he didn't press home his advantage?' mused Mairead, smoothing out a wrinkle in her white silk stocking. 'After Flodden, the whole of Scotland lay helpless at his feet.'

Robert said, 'According to Huntly, Surrey's orders from Henry VIII were to defend England, not to invade Scotland.'

'Added to which,' chipped in John, 'Surrey was eager to return to the action in France. There was far more glory in fighting alongside his King in Calais than skirmishing with a horde of barbarians in the marshes of Scotland. He just ordered all the bodies to be thrown into pits, and then hot-footed it back to London...' He paused, his face shadowed. 'Some of the men hurled into those trenches weren't even dead. The plundering English stripped them naked, took whatever valuables they could lay their filthy hands on, and left them to rot. God, the maggots...'

Mairead shoved a lump of fudge into his mouth as Bella gathered up her black skirts and ran from the room. Pausing only to thump her choking husband hard on the back, Margaret Gordon followed.

'I'm sorry,' she said, taking the sobbing Bella in her arms as she knelt on the bed. 'John is such a tactless creature. He didn't mean to upset you.'

Bella nodded. 'I know. And I still have Douglas. He's fourteen now, and so like his father...'

'Tom was always so kind to me,' said Mairead softly. 'Do you remember all those dashes through the night to escape the Queen? And how Tom used to tell me fairy stories about the Northern Lights to keep me amused? I wanted to come to you, Bella, when I heard he ... hadn't come back, but I was stranded up in Kinnord having my baby.'

Smiling, through sea green eyes shimmering with tears, Bella asked, 'Are you happy with John, Mairead?'

The younger woman shrugged. 'He is a good husband. And we are very alike in many ways. Too alike, perhaps. But we understand the desire to feel free, and try not to smother one another.' She laughed. 'Alexander Stewart says John and I are both as wild as weathercocks in a high wind.'

'But do you love John?' pressed Bella.

'Love?' the word echoed like a note from a cracked bell. 'No, I don't love him. But,' she rushed on, observing Bella's look of uncomprehending dismay, 'I respect him.'

Bella frowned. 'Then could you ... would you love anyone?'

'No,' said Mairead firmly. 'Not now, not ever. *Ne trop ne peu au cuer me sens frappee, Des dars d'Amour ... Par amour n'aim, ne amer ne voudroie.* My heart has felt no wound, severe or slight, from Love's arrows ... I have no lover, nor do I want one.'

'You're young,' said Bella, thinking of Tom, and the love they had known. 'You'll change.'

When the women returned to the parlour, they found the men totting up the most significant casualties of the war. Apart

222

from her King, Scotland had lost an Archbishop, two bishops, two abbots, eleven earls, fifteen lords and ten thousand men.

Bella voiced the wistful thought that had tormented every living Scot since the past September: 'I wonder what would have happened if we had won.'

'Nothing,' replied John Gordon flatly. 'We would have gained no advantage. How could we have mounted a successful invasion of England with winter coming on, and our army decimated by death, desertion and disease?'

Mairead gripped his arm. 'Desertion? You're not calling the Scots cowards, John?'

He prised her fingers from his embroidered silk shirt. 'Don't put words into my mouth, woman. The Scots were never cowards. But neither were we ever a nation to fight far from our own borders. Individually we can challenge the world at almost anything, and win. But force us to band together as an army, and you court catastrophe. Family feuds and squabbles flare up, and if the campaign drags on then we get to fretting about our farms, our animals, our lands and wives left alone and untended.'

Robert laughed at the resentful glares of Bella and Mairead. 'You must face facts, ladies. We Scots will fight bravely, to the death, for any cause, any principle we believe to be just. Provided, that is, the battle is short. Perhaps as a nation we are easily distracted.'

Mairead plumped up her cushion. 'Well the coming years will hold distractions aplenty with both England and Scotland effectively controlled by an English brother and sister.'

'You're forgetting the Queen's sister Mary,' said Bella. 'Her betrothal to the Prince of Castile is broken, and she is soon to marry King Louis of France.'

'Henry, Margaret and Mary,' chanted Robert. 'An unholy trio if ever there was one. Of the three, I think it's Margaret I fear most. Mary is unlikely to do us any harm as France is an old ally of Scotland's. As for Henry, well he has the virtue of being four hundred miles away in England. Headstrong he may be, but at least he's notched up a few years' experience as King, and I'll wager he's had his fill of vengeance against the Scots for the time being. But Queen Margaret is a complete novice at the art of statecraft. She may have learned a thing or two from King James, but I fear it's going to be a case of a little knowledge...'

Robert was right, thought Mairead. So far, the Queen had been hampered by pregnancy, obliged to lock herself away to await the birth of James IV's child. But last month, in April, the bells had rung out, signalling the safe arrival of Alexander, Duke of Ross, a brother to the two-year-old James V. He was born into a Court boiling with speculation and intrigue, with the nobles demanding another call to arms and revenge on the English. Margaret, realising that she must smooth her hawkish warlords' ruffled feathers, recovered quickly from the birth and was out of her bed within a week. Now all Scotland waited nervously for the Queen to make her move.

'She has the Council to advise her,' said Robert, thinking aloud. 'Lords Huntly and Arran will keep her in check. But she's lost a canny friend in Bell-the-Cat.'

'They say he died of a broken heart,' murmured Bella, 'when his son George was slain at Flodden.'

Robert stretched lazily in front of the sinking fire. 'He'd be leaping out of his grave in fury if he could hear the latest Court gossip. I hear our young widowed Queen is finding great solace in the company of his grandson, Archie Douglas, the new Earl of Angus.'

Mairead frowned. 'But Archie is spoken for, betrothed to Lady Jane Stewart of Traquair. It's a real love match ... if there *is* such a thing.'

'From what I know of young Archie Douglas,' said Robert, 'the Queen will have no trouble persuading him that the Lady Jane never existed at all, let alone that he was ever in love with her.'

'He's weak, and easily led,' agreed Bella. 'Soft as wax compared to his grandfather. He may have the Douglas good looks, but he hasn't inherited an inch of the old man's backbone.'

'It isn't his backbone our lusty Queen is interested in,' grinned John Gordon.

'How could she?' asked Margaret Gordon viciously. 'How *dare* she? After being married to a man like my father. With all Scotland to choose from, why should she favour a weakling like Archibald Douglas?'

'Perhaps,' suggested Robert gently, 'someone is doing the choosing for her.'

The man manipulating the heartstrings of the widow and the earl was none other than Lord John Drummond, the father of Margaret Drummond. After Margaret's death, he had judged it politic to play a passive role at Court. Now, twelve years later, he was just as ambitious, just as much an opportunist and, most important, he was Archie Douglas' grandfather. The boy was the offspring of John Drummond's daughter Elizabeth and her husband, the late son of Bell-the-Cat. With Archie inheriting the title of Earl of Angus, Lord Drummond told himself he would be failing in his moral duty if he withheld the paternal hand of guidance from the fatherless boy.

Lord Drummond had gazed with approval on Archie as he presented him to the Queen that bright May day at Holyrood. At nineteen, he was a trifle young, but Drummond calculated that the fire of youth was the vital element he needed to inflame the widowed Queen into impetuous action. Archie was handsome, amusing, socially acceptable and, thought Drummond grimly, totally malleable. The sugared wine of diplomacy was still John Drummond's favourite tipple. What he had hoped to achieve through the beauty and charm of his daughter Margaret he now saw within his grasp by means of the lusty persuasion of grandson Archie.

For once, Lord Huntly's magpie intelligence network let him down. Deeply involved in affairs of state, he paid scant attention to the chosen companions of the Queen. In any case, he argued later, when it was too late, Queen Margaret was still in mourning for her dear departed husband. That she should consider marrying again while still robed in grey for the late King was unthinkable.

John Drummond was able to think of little else. Hovering, as Robert put it, like an ageing God of Love he diligently fanned the growing flame of interest between the young couple. And when the Queen took her sons to Stirling for the summer, it was Archibald Douglas whom she requested to travel with her. The Drummond family star, it seemed, was set to rise again.

Two

Women do not like to be corrected,
But their minds are so fashioned
That they think they know their own business
Without being taught,
And let no one who doesn't want to annoy them
Find fault with anything they do.

                                          Jean de Meung

'My, how dull we are at Stirling without the men.' Lady Lennox gazed disconsolately round the knot garden. 'I confess I'm most impatient for Lord Angus to return from the hunt. Don't you find him the most charming company, my lady?'

Queen Margaret regarded Lady Lennox's girlish flutterings with disdain and mistrust. She had never revelled in the company of women. Even as a child, she had ignored sister Mary and confided her secrets to her favourite brother, Arthur. But since Flodden, the Queen and Lady Lennox had been forced together, not so much out of mutual grief as from mutual circumstances. They were both women without men. It was a precarious situation at the best of times, but with the cream of Scotland's manhood skimmed by war, and the Court festering with intrigue, the lack of a male protector made their position infinitely more vulnerable.

Seeing the Queen apparently absorbed in her *petit point*, Lady Lennox pressed on, 'Of course, the Earl is still very young. And, they say, rather too easily led.'

'That rather depends on who is doing the leading,' said Margaret blandly.

'Well, we all thought Lady Jane of Traquair had him by the nose,' said Lady Lennox eagerly, 'though that is perhaps unfair. Jane is a quiet, demure girl. She suits him well.'

'She suits him nothing,' snapped the Queen. 'Jane is

227

colourless, spineless and dull. If she marries Archie Douglas they'll resemble two peeled grapes drowning in the swamp of a milk pudding.'

'They say the Earl is deeply in love with her. And though her complexion is a little pale, she is certainly beautiful.'

'And I am Queen,' said Margaret, her smile razor thin. 'I have no doubt which attraction will prove to hold the greater allure for Archie.'

Lady Lennox cleared her throat. 'If I may say so, madam, there are many at Court who are bewildered by your patronage of the Earl. After such a great, brilliant man as King James, what possible appeal, they ask, can a nineteen-year-old youth hold for you?'

For a moment, as the Queen flung down her needlework, Lady Lennox thought she had gone too far. But fortunately, the Queen was in an expansive mood. She smiled indulgently, thinking of her shy, handsome suitor. 'Archie has much to recommend him, Lennox. You say he is young, but it is a mere five years that separates us. The King, remember, was forty when he died. Don't you think that after being married to a man seventeen years older than myself, I deserve some fun, a little freedom to enjoy myself now?'

Lady Lennox looked pensive. 'For my part, I shall always remember my time at the Court of James IV as the happiest I have ever known. We were merry then, my lady.'

'The King was merry, but he treated me always as a plaything,' sulked Margaret. 'Archie, now, respects me. He *listens* to me. And,' her eyes hardened, 'he would be faithful to me.'

Lady Lennox bent to her sewing, and murmured, 'You mean to have him then?'

Margaret sighed. 'I have to remarry, Lennox. And soon.'

'But madam, you are still in mourning. Why are you in such haste to seek another husband?'

'Because, Lennox, if I am not married, then I do not know who I am.'

The older woman laid down her tapestry frame. 'Of course you know who you are. You are the Queen, the Regent of

228

Scotland and the mother of the baby James V.' She suffered Margaret's mocking stare, and continued, 'Why, you have a more positive identity than any other woman in Scotland.'

'I am nothing, and no one without a husband,' Margaret insisted, brushing away a swarm of midges from her face. 'Any woman without a man to protect her is in a difficult position. For me it is worse. I am dangerous. As Regent, I can wield a considerable amount of power. I possess the key to my late husband's secret treasury. And, most important, I have in my care the two-year-old King. In Edinburgh, there are the earnest members of the Council, Huntly, Arran, Home and the rest, *advising* me what to do. In England there is my brother Henry and he, being Henry, will simply *tell* me what to do. Every bishop, every ambassador, every jumped-up courtier will feel it his duty to point out the right course of action to the poor, defenceless Queen.'

Lady Lennox could not reply. She had heard, as the Queen had not, the cynical song haunting the streets of Edinburgh, bemoaning their fearful fate with a wain as King and a weak woman at the helm.

Margaret was too absorbed in her train of argument to notice Lady Lennox's silence. 'Suppose I don't marry now, Lennox. Even if I wait a decent few years, eventually I shall have to choose a new husband. I'm young, attractive, rich and a Queen. I'm the most eligible woman in Europe. Scotland will soon be bursting at the seams with emissaries from every country you can think of, all begging for my fair hand. I shall be in demand, Lennox.'

Lady Lennox smiled at the acidity in the Queen's tone. 'I should have thought the idea would have delighted you.'

The Queen hissed. 'Stuff! When I was thirteen I became a virtual exile from my own country, and travelled here in a state of sick terror to marry a man I'd never met. I have no intention of being cast adrift again, alone in a strange land with uneatable foreign food and a language I don't understand.' She caught Lady Lennox's amazed glance. 'You've never thought of my position in those terms before, have you? I suppose you all fondly imagined I was delirious with joy and gratitude to be allowed to set my alien English foot on your sour Scottish soil?'

Lady Lennox wished the Queen would get back to the point: the Earl of Angus.

'No. Next time I shall marry a man I know, whose country I already live in and who won't dominate me. Having decided that, let us consider the choice.' The pause was momentary. 'There *is* no choice. The flower of our manhood was slain at Flodden. We are left with cannon-shocked wrecks, armless wonders and old men. Who will *you* marry next, Lennox?'

'I shall remain faithful to the memory of my beloved husband.'

The Queen laughed. 'So no one has asked you. Shame, Lennox. Of course, it must be hard to accept that you are now a little too long in the tooth to rival me for Archie's affections.'

Squirming like a fly impaled on a pin, Lady Lennox murmured, 'But why *now*, madam? The people of Scotland are fond of you. Yet if you marry while you're still in mourning for the King, you'll run the risk of alienating their affections.'

The Queen shrugged. 'I'm afraid I refuse to allow a handful of sentimental Scots to decide my destiny. And I'm *always* in mourning, Lennox, if not for one of my own family then for some corpse lying in state in some remote foreign country. I see no point in waiting. Until I marry I shall feel adrift. I'll be forever wondering what he will look like, what title he will hold, and whether he'll be English, Scots or French. A woman needs a man, Lennox, to give her life direction. Without him, she has no control over her own situation, but floats about like a dandelion seed, waiting for the wind to blow her back to earth.'

Margaret's face brightened as the yapping of dogs in the courtyard heralded the return of the hunt. 'Oh, here come the men! Quick, Lennox, how do I look?'

'Beautiful,' said Lady Lennox obediently, indulging in a sour reflection on the more unpleasant properties of a snapped dandelion.

The Queen and the Earl of Angus were married secretly in

a tiny church set amidst the glowing cornfields of Perth. Margaret neglected to inform her Council, her Court or her people until a full three weeks after the wedding. As Lady Lennox had predicted, their reaction was one of searing indignation and outrage.

'It's that scheming grandfather of mine who's to blame,' stormed Mairead, recklessly slapping one of Bella's beehives. 'I never trusted John Drummond. He manipulated my mother for his own ambitious ends, and now he's exploiting Archie Douglas. I hear the wedding was positively teeming with Drummonds, with grandfather beaming benevolently from the front pew, and my uncle Walter performing the ceremony. My mother will weep for shame in heaven.'

'Well the Douglases aren't exactly red eyed, that's for sure,' said Robert, leading Mairead to the safer pastures of the herb garden. 'The Queen has appointed Gavin Douglas Archbishop of St Andrews and Primate of Scotland. And that's just the beginning.'

Bella began filling a basket with aromatic rosemary, sage and thyme to be dried for the winter. 'I think the Queen was flattered by the verses Gavin Douglas wrote to her. He was a little sharper off the mark than old Willie Dunbar this time.'

Mairead snorted. '*Lily sweetly fair* and carrying a *sceptre of delight* indeed! She's overweight, pudgy faced and wears far too much French scent.'

Robert grinned. Privately, he considered Queen Margaret to be a fine looking woman, but this was clearly not the moment to say so. She would never acquire the slim, spritelike mien of Margaret Gordon. Nevertheless, the Queen had matured into a sultry, heavy lidded beauty of considerable appeal, Robert knew, to a growing number of men in Scotland and beyond. She could have played the field and taken her pick from Europe's most eligible nobles. Yet the silly woman had thrown out a glittering future with the washing water and married the engagingly weak-kneed Archie instead.

'She's as crazed as stained glass,' asserted Margaret Gordon. 'What good can come of this marriage? Huntly and the Council are spitting with rage. And between ourselves,' she lowered her voice, although the shrub-screened garden was totally secluded, 'John says they have sent Sir William Comyn to France, requesting the Duke of Albany to return to Scotland as Regent and Governor in place of Queen Margaret.'

'Albany!' exclaimed Bella. 'But he's more a Frenchman than a Scot. What do we want with some tasselled foreign courtier running our affairs?'

'He may have been bred a Frenchman, and even married a daughter of France,' said Robert, 'but he's never forgotten he was born a Scot. From what I've heard of John, Duke of Albany, he would welcome the chance to restore the honour of his family here.'

They all knew the shameful history of Albany's father. A brother of James III, he had plotted against the King and been exiled, ingloriously, to France.

'France,' commented Robert, 'appears to be the favoured dumping ground for all our traitorous dross. But the Duke of Albany is now one of their greatest nobles. He's a brilliant soldier, a wily diplomat and highly regarded by old King Louis. He is also, I would point out, a main contender for the title of heir presumptive to the Scottish throne should the King's baby brother die under the suffocating weight of the Queen's maternal protection.'

Bella frowned. 'But what about Albany's brother, Alexander Stewart? Surely he, as the first born son, would be considered heir presumptive?'

Mairead shook her head. 'No, Alexander explained it to me when we were fishing one day on Loch Kinnord. Alexander was born to his father's first wife, Catherine Sinclair. They were divorced, and when the old Duke was exiled and married his French wife, the children of Catherine Sinclair were considered illegitimate. So John, Duke of Albany, is regarded as the one true son.'

'And they have asked him here as Regent,' mused Robert. 'Do you think he will come?'

'Of course he won't come,' Lord Drummond reassured a nervously pacing Angus. 'In France he is rich, powerful and respected. He plays a leading role in a Court that is the most cultivated and elegant in Europe. Albany even, so I hear, appears devoted to his wife and family. Why should he want to leave such a gilded niche to come to a cold, battle scarred country and involve himself in gang warfare amongst a parcel of quarrelling nobles? The man has more sense. Mark my words, Archie, Sir William Comyn will return from France alone.'

Sir William Comyn, Lyon King-at-Arms, almost failed to return at all.

The Queen and her supporters danced till dawn when the news reached Stirling that Sir William's ship had struck a submerged reef and all but foundered.

'What did I tell you, Archie!' exulted John Drummond. 'Comyn knew all along that his mission was fruitless, and morally wrong. The man was shipwrecked on the rocks of his own conscience.'

But by February, Archie's boyish face was creased with anxiety. Had he been right, after all, to marry Margaret? It had all seemed such a glamorous adventure at the time. Margaret had made it clear she wanted him. She had positively pursued him. What peacock wouldn't be flattered, being hunted by the Queen of Scotland herself? And in all honesty, he had to admit he'd been glad of the furs, jewels and huge tracts of valuable land the Queen had lavished on him. Clearly, he had been bought. But for what purpose, other than pleasuring the Queen, he could not fathom. Nor would he try. Archie was content to leave the wearisome business of thinking to his grandfather, John Drummond.

Yet of late, Archie's bowl of milk and honey seemed to have curdled. The supply of money from the Queen was inexplicably drying up. She was becoming less generous with her presents; and her sudden shrill storms of temper sent him scurrying to his horse. But he fared even worse when he ventured outside Stirling Castle. The people greeted him with jeers and rotten apples, leaving him in no doubt that they regarded him as a usurper for daring to marry their beloved

King's widow. The Council, too, were openly hostile, treating him like a callow youth and refusing to accord him the proper respect due to the consort of the Queen.

Margaret merely laughed when at last Archie summoned enough courage to spill out his woes. 'At least they are united now, Archie. Before I married you the nobles were divided, bickering over whether to scream back over the border and seek revenge for Flodden. Now all that is forgotten in their common hatred of my poor husband.' She flung her arms around him. 'I love you, Archie. And I'm the one who matters. Don't ever forget that.'

Archie, feeling uncomfortably akin to the fatted calf, ran to his grandfather for sympathy.

'Of course the Council are peeved, Archie,' grunted Lord Drummond. 'They're furious with me for outwitting them and getting you into the Queen's bed ahead of their own kin. They're terrified of our Douglas-Drummond power. But there's nothing they can do about it.'

There *was* something the Council could do. Once again, they appealed to Albany to return. This time, circumstances were more favourable. Louis XII, gratefully exhausted by the youthful ardour of Margaret's sister Mary, had turned his gouty neck to the tapestried wall, and died. François I, his successor, was young, vigorous, and fully aware of the latent strength of the Scots-French Auld Alliance. With Henry VIII still breathing heavily across the Channel, François deemed it prudent to keep Scotland firmly on his side.

While they waited for Albany, and more significantly, François, to make up their minds, Archie found Margaret almost unbearable to live with. She was running desperately short of money, having plundered King James' secret treasury not on behalf of her children's welfare, but to buy gifts for her spoilt consort and his attendant Douglas family leeches. Never the most thrifty of women, Margaret managed in a few months to squander nearly all her late husband's fortune, and even with the coffers virtually drained, her profligacy continued: jealous at the thought of sister Mary flaunting her latest French fashions, Margaret ordered twenty new dresses,

234

while the huge wage bill for her retinue stunned even the hardened Council into awed silence.

Aware of her embarrassment, the Council refused to release more funds for Margaret's use. Choking down her pride, the Queen appealed to Henry VIII for help. He had already volunteered to take her sons into his protection, even offering to make James V his heir. Margaret rejected both these brotherly proposals. Henry raged at her ingratitude. Then, learning that she was bankrupt, he threatened to invade Scotland. Distraught, Margaret began scribbling a hasty reply, pleading that if the English soldiers crossed the border, the Council would seize on the excuse to snatch her children from her. Without the young King James by her side, Margaret knew she would be powerless, vulnerable as a new-laid egg. In her distress, Margaret had almost forgotten to read the last part of Henry's letter, in which he urged her most strongly to use all her influence in preventing the arrival of Albany in Scotland.

Margaret laughed bitterly. '*All my influence*. As usual, he's thinking only of himself. A Frenchman ruling Scotland would be disastrous for Henry, but he won't help by sending me some money. I'm a penniless, pregnant woman. Influence I have none.'

Lord Drummond spoke soothingly. 'You are a trifle depressed at the moment, madam. But I am confident that your financial difficulties are bound to be temporary. Huntly and the Council cannot withhold from you indefinitely the monies which are rightfully yours. And remember, you are not alone. You have the strong support of the Douglas family. Most important, you have in your charge the young King and his brother. There indeed, lies the basis for influence, my lady.'

The Queen gazed at him, her voice tearful. 'But for how long, Lord Drummond? For how long?'

As if in answer, the spring brought lilies to Scotland. White fleurs-de-lis, embroidered in silk on the blue and gold banner of France. On 15 May, 1515, the Duke of Albany landed at Dumbarton, with an impressive train of one thousand followers.

Three

A woman is a worthy wight,
She serveth a man both day and night,
Thereto she putteth all her might,
And yet she hath but care and woe.

                      Anon

Swiftly, the Queen installed herself, her children and her shivering husband behind the fortressed walls of Edinburgh Castle. She was five months pregnant and mortally afraid. But unlike the Earl of Angus, who visibly trembled at the mention of Albany's name, Margaret had never lacked raw animal courage. When at last she was informed that John, Duke of Albany, had arrived at the Castle, Margaret was ready. She had abandoned her dull grey mourning robes in favour of a dress of royal purple silk, thickly encrusted with jewels and silver braid. Flanked by her husband and his grandfather, and with her children playing quietly in the window alcove, Margaret felt confident enough to ignore Lord Drummond's advice to 'keep the foreign upstart waiting'.

Rising with difficulty from her chair, Margaret smoothed the silk over her swelling waistline. 'Admit him,' she commanded, and turned to face the man she feared most in all the world.

The man who entered her chamber and bowed low to kiss her ring was well built, elegantly dressed and spoke in low, fractured Scots.

'Madam, I am honoured to meet you. All France is aflame with talk of your beauty. I see we were not misinformed.'

Albany had not come alone. A party of six Italian lutanists accompanied him, followed by satin-clad pages bearing gifts. For the Queen's children they brought a rocking horse with a fortune in gold coins in its harness; and a musical box, its oak-carved lid filigreed in imitation of Venetian lace. While to Margaret Albany presented an exquisite belt, formed of six gold marguerites, each centred by a different jewel, a diamond, sapphire, emerald, pearl, amethyst and ruby.

Against her will, Margaret was charmed. Where she had expected blustering arrogance, she found a man of gallant sophistication with a warmth in his peat-brown eyes that softened the harsh line of his mouth. She waited while he exchanged the most curt of courteous greetings with her husband and Lord Drummond and then, watching his reaction carefully, Margaret guided him to the alcove to meet her children.

'May I present James V, King of Scotland, and his brother Alexander, Duke of Ross.'

Albany knelt, his embroidered coat trailing on the dusty floor as he smiled at the three-year-old James. 'He's a fine lad. I congratulate you, my lady. My only regret is that I was never privileged to meet his father. He would, I am sure, be proud of the way you are bringing up his sons.'

Lord Drummond looked on in disgust at the spectacle of the Queen being disarmed by a garlic-eating Frenchman. What a foolish woman she is, he thought. A few trinkets, and a flattering word or two, and she's won. She hasn't even noticed that Albany has completely ignored her husband. And me.

Albany, his broad back turned negligently to Angus, talked with earnest sincerity to the Queen. 'Strange circumstances bring us together, my lady. But I hope with all my heart that we may be friends. You are clearly a woman blessed with sound judgement and shrewd understanding. You must know that there are many in France, in Scotland and in England who would wish us to be enemies.'

Margaret faltered, as the heated letters of brother Henry came to mind. Henry would explode like cannon shot if she allied herself with this Frenchman. And yet, Albany was far from the ogre she had expected. His kindly interest in her sons had seemed genuine enough, betraying no darker intent of snatching them away from her.

She murmured cautiously, 'We can most certainly be

237

friends, my lord Albany. If you believe we have a common purpose.'

His gaze was direct. 'We both desire the unity of Scotland and the safety of the King. There are others,' his glance flickered to Lord Drummond, 'who thirst for power, and seek a personal advantage from Scotland's troubles. But together, if you permit, we can lead your country back to its days of former glory under your late husband, King James IV. And we can ensure that your son inherits a strong, peaceful, united nation.'

From the sudden spark of hope in the Queen's eyes, Albany saw that he had struck a chord. More than anything, Margaret longed for a return of the tranquil years she had known with James. If only she had realised her good fortune at the time, she thought wistfully, she would have enjoyed those golden days so much more. Yet here was Albany, standing stolidly before her, holding out the promise of a calm, secure future for herself and her sons. Could she, dare she believe him?

Before she could commit herself, Lord Drummond interposed crisply: 'My lord Duke, I fear you overestimate the extent of our nation's current difficulties. With respect, you are a foreigner to Scotland. You know nothing of our customs, our traditions, our people. The Queen, though born in England, has lived here for thirteen years and the people have taken her to their hearts, loving her for the loyal Scotswoman she now is. I would suggest that you could hardly expect them to accord you the same fealty on the strength of one month's residence in their country.'

With a movement deadly in its control, Albany turned on his heel and regarded the grizzled face of Lord Drummond. Margaret licked her parched lips. Angus was heard to swallow noisily.

Albany smiled, but the warmth stopped short of his eyes. 'I find your devotion to your Queen and country most touching, Lord Drummond. I shall bear your remarks strongly in mind.'

He was as good as his word. Six weeks later, with Albany declared the new Regent and Governor of Scotland, Lord

Drummond was imprisoned at Blacknest Castle, with his lands and estates forfeited to the Crown.

'That was a superb meal, Kinleven. You keep a table that would match the finest France has to offer.' Albany was in excellent spirits, savouring his after dinner Madeira as the guest of Robert Kyle.

'Albany enjoyed his roast swan all the more, thinking of the wretched Drummond dining on bread and water at Blacknest,' murmured Alexander Stewart.

Albany gazed benignly on his velvet capped brother. 'You know as well as I that the conniving old rogue will have bribed the guards to bring him in pheasant and a plentiful supply of burgundy.'

Robert threw a handful of cracked almonds to John Gordon and enquired of Albany, 'On what charge, precisely, did you arrest him?'

The Regent shrugged. 'Oh, some time ago Drummond took it into his head that the Lyon King-at-Arms had failed to address the Queen in the proper manner and was rash enough to strike the poor fellow in the face. Naturally, we cannot tolerate the nation's chief herald being treated in such a contemptuous manner. I had no choice but to arrest Drummond.'

'I can't help feeling sorry for Sir William Comyn,' laughed Douglas Fraser, forgetting for a moment to feel awed by the presence of the new Regent of Scotland. 'First he's shipwrecked in the Channel, and now Lord Drummond is using him as a punchbag. Remind me *not* to accept the job of Lyon King-at-Arms when I'm offered it.'

'Of the two, it's Lord Drummond who has my sympathy,' murmured John Gordon. 'He's an elderly man. And an old caged bird has little to sing about.'

Albany raised his eyebrows, '*Merde!* John Gordon, you've changed since we wrestled together in Orléans. I don't remember you feeling a shred of pity for anyone in those days.'

'Perhaps marriage has mellowed him,' said Alexander slyly.

John Gordon's fingers tightened round his glass. 'Lord Drummond happens to be my wife's grandfather.'

239

'And I happen to know she'd wish him to the Devil,' said Alexander Stewart, Dean of Dunbar.

Robert removed the glass from John's grasp, and slowly refilled it. It was one of a set of sparkling Venetian goblets presented to him by the Duke of Albany, and Robert had no intention of allowing John to incur Bella's wrath by heedlessly snapping the fine stem in two. 'How long do you intend to keep Drummond in custody?' he asked.

'Shrewd question,' smiled Albany. 'I realise I shall have to release him soon. Only this afternoon, I had the Queen herself sobbing and wailing on her plump little knees for his salvation. And the Council is certain to plead his cause as an old and trusted servant of the country. I merely want to give Drummond a fright, that's all, to knock some of the bluster out of him.'

Alexander meticulously peeled a grape. 'And what did you think of our *fairest of the fair?*'

'I was agreeably surprised by your Queen Margaret,' confessed Albany. 'She has not the pampered, coquettish airs of the French ladies nor,' he inclined his dark head towards John Gordon, 'the fiery, thoroughbred spirit of the Lady Margaret Gordon. But she is all woman, your Queen. Lusty and brave – though I fear a little too inclined to brood.'

'Why don't you just come straight out and say she's a good looking, sullen bitch?' demanded Alexander.

Robert stood up. 'Speaking of ladies, my lord Duke. With your permission, Annabella and Mairead will be waiting for us to join them.'

As Alexander rose to follow the others from the dining hall, he felt a hand on his shoulder.

'A word with you,' said Albany.

The Dean leaned gracefully against a walnut sideboard which smelt faintly of beeswax. 'Ah. You wish to seek my informed opinion on the state of the Church in Scotland today. Or would you like me to divulge the latest scandal from Rome? There was a masque, I understand, at which the Pope divested himself –'

'I wish,' grated Albany, 'to discuss a scandal nearer home.'

Alexander's eyes widened mockingly. 'No? Tell me more. You may rely on my absolute discretion.'

Albany's hand closed longingly round the brass candelabra. 'Your interest, my dear brother, in the Lady Margaret Gordon is all too apparent. The glances you exchanged with her at dinner were more than is seemly for a man to display towards the wife of his close friend.'

Alexander's smile faded. 'You read too much into too little, John. This isn't France, my dear, where a chance remark to one's dinner companion about the age of the cinnamon scones is immediately interpreted as an invitation to bed. We Scots may be a devious lot, but I'm afraid such heights of subtle nuance are beyond us.'

'Nevertheless,' Albany ploughed on, 'you can't deny that the Lady Margaret is attracted to you.'

'Margaret Gordon is her own mistress. If she chooses to smile on me then it is of her own free choice.'

'But you,' said Albany tartly, 'have no such choice. You would do well to remember your responsibilities, as a man of the Church and a servant of God.'

He opened the door, and motioned the impassive Dean to precede him into the parlour. Albany sank thankfully into the carved chair offered him by the Lady Annabella. He liked the capable, golden haired sister of Kinleven. She pushed open the casement windows onto the amethyst light of summer evening, and from the garden drifted the beguiling scent of roses, sweet herbs and fresh cut grass. Albany's jangled nerves began to quieten. Perhaps he had been too harsh on Alexander. After all, a man would have to be hewn from stone not to respond to the woman they called Mairead. He allowed himself, in the interests of fraternal solidarity, the luxury of studying the young woman stretched languorously on the cushioned settle. Her black hair was sleekly coiled, her dress fashioned of crocus yellow silk, and round her slender neck lay a carelessly knotted rope of pearls. Albany smiled, contrasting Margaret Gordon to the Queen, who on their first meeting had stood rigidly before him with the entire contents of her jewel box ranged like missiles on her gown.

Only once before had Albany known a woman with the primitive appeal of Margaret Gordon. But that was long ago, in the fragrant blue hills of Tuscany. By now, he told himself soberly, she was probably fat, forty and toothless.

A faint colour stained his cheeks as he met Margaret Gordon's amused blue eyes. Curse the woman. He'd be damned if he was going to give her the satisfaction of adding the Regent of Scotland to her list of admirers.

'I should be glad of your opinion, my lord Duke,' Mairead's cool voice lanced his heightened senses. 'We have been talking, Bella and I, about the insufferable position of women in our society.'

'By the Mass!' spluttered Douglas. 'I always thought ladies retired from the dinner table to loosen their stomachers and swop stories about babies.'

'Don't be impertinent,' warned Robert. 'Shut your mouth, open your ears and you may learn a thing a or two. Go on, Mairead.'

'It seems to me,' she said slowly, 'that the attitude of men towards women is most irrational. Take the Lady Annabella here. She is mistress of this house. The servants, the household budget, the management of food, supplies, light and heat are all in her charge. In different circumstances, Bella would work beside her man, tilling fields and tending crops. And yet,' the blue eyes blazed, 'Bella goes to church on Sundays and is informed that she, as a woman, is the instrument of the Devil and the gate of hell.'

'Though of course, the Virgin Mary is the Queen of Heaven,' said John Gordon.

'That's because she is a mother,' Mairead smiled. 'Once you bear a child you are venerated, but the worship doesn't extend beyond the nursery door. What appalls me more is the way men repudiate our proven intelligence and capabilities. Tell me, my lord Duke, do the women of France suffer a similar fate?'

Albany recalled the over-refined, painted ladies of the

French Court, feeding sugar plums to pet marmosets as they waited for their current lovers to come scratching at their doors. Then he remembered the woman of Tuscany, and the windows she had opened in his senses and his mind.

'There are women in France,' he mused, 'or there *were*, who think much as you do, Mairead.' The name slipped, unbidden, from his lips. 'There was the poet Christine de Pisan, for instance. She was very much a champion of her sex, and led an attack on the old-fashioned courtly love tradition of *Le Roman de la Rose.*'

'Ah yes, I know of her,' said Mairead. 'Didn't she form an order for the defence of women?'

Albany nodded, a trifle stunned by the turn the conversation was taking. It was impossible to imagine his pedigreed wife, Agnes de la Tour Auvergne, voicing such liberal views as those of Margaret Gordon. He smiled, realising that if Mairead could read his thoughts, she would most certainly accuse him of being patronising. He went on, 'Then of course, there was Jacqueline Felicie de Almania, a formidable woman who practised medicine in Paris.'

'Exactly!' exclaimed Mairead. 'And where are *our* women poets, writers and doctors?'

Douglas opened his mouth to pour scorn on the fanciful notion of a woman physician, then caught Robert's eye and quickly shut it again.

Alexander, Dean of Dunbar, adopted his vespers voice and chanted,

> *Who peyntede the leoun, tel me who?*
> *By god, if wommen hadde writen stories*
> *As clerkes han with-inne hir oratories,*
> *They wolde han writen of men more wikkednesse*
> *Than all the mark of Adam may redresse.*

'Chaucer had the right idea, but he was English and doesn't count,' said Mairead emphatically.

Bella frowned. 'But Mairead, I don't want to change anything. I'm really content as I am. After all, women are in many ways more fortunate than men. We don't have to go to war;

we're cherished and protected and our fathers provide us with dowries when we marry.'

'And what dowry, pray, did the Lady Annabella have to offer when she married Tom Fraser?' enquired Mairead silkily.

Bella flushed. 'None. But many poor girls of Edinburgh are given dowries by the burghers, as an act of Christian charity.'

'As a means of keeping the peace you mean, like mending the holes in the city wall,' muttered Mairead. 'The men must be persuaded to marry to breed children and preserve the fighting force of the nation.'

Alexander coughed. 'I feel constrained to point out that the sole argument St Jerome could find in favour of matrimony was that it served to provide the men of the world with sufficient virgins.'

Mairead kicked her husband who lay, eyes shut, clutching Robert's flask of Madeira. 'And what contribution have you to make, John Gordon, to this philosophical discussion?'

He opened one eye. 'I wasn't asleep,' he protested. 'I was just reflecting on the allegory of Chicheface, the mythical monster able to feed only on women obedient to their husbands. As I recall, the wretched beast starved for two hundred years.'

Robert took advantage of the relieved burst of laughter to divert the channel of conversation. 'To change the subject from obedient wives to wilful widows ... what, exactly, is to happen to the Queen's children?'

Albany stretched his silk hosed legs. 'We have chosen,' he said, selecting his words carefully, 'eight Scottish nobles who will take turns in serving the young James V and his brother the Duke of Ross.'

No one spoke. They all knew what Albany meant by *serving*. 'And tomorrow,' the Regent went on pleasantly, avoiding Mairead's eye, 'four of those nobles will proceed with an armed guard to Edinburgh Castle, to relieve the Queen of her burden.'

Faster than fire the word spread round Edinburgh.

'The Regent is taking the Queen's children.'

'They say she is not fit to bring up the young King.'

'Serves her right for marrying the Earl of Angus in such indecent haste. She's not to be trusted.'

'But it's heartless,' protested Nan to Blackpatch, as they pushed through the excited crowd. 'By removing her children, they'll tear away her last shred of authority. She'll be nothing more than a rag doll Queen.'

'They haven't got the young King yet,' replied Blackpatch.

The solemn procession began at the Tolbooth in the centre of the town. The four appointed nobles and the fifty-strong guard wound their way slowly up the hill towards the Castle, following by a mob screeching like a flock of gulls.

Nan nudged Blackpatch. 'There's the Queen, entering the courtyard. And, oh, look,' her voice softened, 'she has the child King beside her.'

It was an impressive spectacle, as Margaret fully intended it should be: the brave young Queen, with the hand of her son, the King of Scotland, held trustingly in hers. Behind Margaret stood a quaking Angus and a whey-faced nurse, carrying the baby Duke of Ross in her arms.

Fickle hearts faltered in the face of such a tender family scene. A man at the front of the crowd threw his hat in the air. 'Long live the Queen! God save the King!'

Some sections of the mob took up his cry, while others berated the approaching soldiers:

'Leave our King alone, you brutes!'

'A pox on you if you touch a hair of his precious head!'

'How could you take a woman's children from her? Have you no pity?'

Impassive, Margaret watched the steel ring of armed guards close tighter round the four alarmed nobles. As the people surged angrily forward, the dull growl of their outrage swelling into a vengeful roar, the Queen held up a jewelled hand. Instantly, the crowd fell silent.

Sure of herself now, the Queen turned to Lord Bothwell, the leader of Albany's party, and commanded, 'Stand! Declare the cause of your coming before you draw nearer to your sovereigns.'

245

Disconcerted by both Margaret's regal turn of phrase and the vicious hissing of the mob behind him, Bothwell's voice lacked conviction: 'We are deputed by Parliament, madam, to demand and receive our infant King and his brother.'

When the rumble of indignation from the people had died down, Margaret said, with icy hauteur, 'This Castle of Edinburgh is part of my inheritance. The late King, my husband, made me sole governess of it, and sole protector of my children. Therefore to no one can I deliver them. But, I respect Parliament, and I require six days to consider their mandate.' Her voice dropped, and as if speaking to herself, she murmured, 'For my councillors, alas, are few.'

Bothwell was allowed no time to consider her request. Turning to the chief gatekeeper, the Queen instructed, 'Drop the portcullis!' To the consternation of the nobles, and the delight of the crowd, the massive iron gate crashed down between the royal party and Albany's men.

'And while they were still blinking with amazement,' Nan reported to Bella later, 'the Queen turned her back on them and led the little King back into the Castle. Oh, it was magnificent!'

'And what part did our gallant Angus play in this drama?' enquired Bella.

Nan rolled her eyes. 'Need I tell you? He was first back through the Castle doors.'

'The rat,' muttered Bella. 'I'll wager he's boiling his pea-sized brain trying to work out how to make his peace with Albany while still keeping the Queen sweet.'

Bella was right. A week later Mairead brought news from Alexander Stewart that Angus had written to Albany swearing that he had prevailed upon the Queen to surrender the royal children.

'I fear his letter was premature and overoptimistic,' said Bella. 'For the Queen has fled to Stirling, and taken the children with her.'

'She hasn't a hope,' said John Gordon. 'Albany is hot in pursuit with one thousand men.'

246

Four

Where is thy chamber lavishly bedecked
With handsome bed and tapestries embroidered bold,
Spices and wines for thy delight
In cups of gold and silver bright.
The sweetmeats served on platters clean
With Saipheron salts, good seasoning.
The gay apparel of many a goodly gown
Thy comely lawn clasped with pins of gold;
All is gone, thy great and royal renown.

Robert Henryson

Bewildered and betrayed, the Queen restlessly paced the age-old battlements of Stirling Castle, ignoring the pleas of her ladies that, in her delicate condition, it was essential that she should rest. She was endangering, they twittered, the life of her baby, the Earl of Angus' heir.

To the Devil with Angus, seethed Margaret, scanning the horizon through sleepless, red-rimmed eyes for the first wisp of dust that would herald the arrival of Albany and his men. Just where was Angus now, when she most needed him? Amidst the flurry of their departure for Stirling he had hung back, muttering excuses about having to inspect his neglected country estates – land which Margaret herself, in the first foolish flush of love, had given him. Intent on rescuing her jewels, her clothes and her sons from Albany's grasp, Margaret had paid little heed at the time to Angus' nervous recital of one of his family's tedious proverbs: 'I'd rather hear the lark sing in the open country, Margaret, than the mouse cheep imprisoned within a gloomy fortress.'

He had followed his lark, leaving her, like an albino blackbird, to fend for herself. Had his grandfather been there, Margaret knew he would have stood and literally shouted some grit and guts into her husband's jellied bones. But Lord

Drummond still languished in Blacknest Castle. By the time Albany relented, and released him, Drummond would be a broken old man and of no use to her. Archie's grandfather had let her down, Margaret concluded unreasonably. Everyone had played her false. It was her own fault for believing in men, and trusting their judgement before her own. She rested her aching back against the warm stone wall wishing, not for the first time, that she were a man, like her brother Henry. No one dared cog Henry's dice. Yet Henry had done nothing to help her. He had sent no money, no promise of men and arms, not even a message of sympathy and consolation. He was so agitated at Albany's uncontested arrival into Scotland that he had turned on Margaret, accusing her of allowing him in deliberately to spite her brother. As if she could possibly have stopped Albany! It was so unfair. Henry seemed to imagine that she had enjoyed being compelled to abdicate her Regency to the Frenchman; that she delighted in the situation whereby Albany was now legally entitled to appropriate her Crown jewels, her palaces, her revenues. And her children.

A blush seared Margaret's tearstained cheeks as she remembered her first favourable impression of the Frenchman. How easily she had succumbed to his gifts, his smiles, his practised flattery. Even more humiliating than the memory of her past surrender, was the realisation that she still, despite his double dealing, found Albany attractive. There was something about the man's quiet determination and gallant manners that completely disarmed her. Perhaps, she thought sadly, because these particular characteristics reminded her of Albany's nephew, the late King James IV.

As the setting August sun set the sky afire, Margaret saw the first line of horsemen, galloping fast across the scorched plain below. Stirling Castle was the most daunting fortress in Scotland. But it could not, Margaret knew, withstand the might of Albany and one thousand men. She was beaten. But she was still Queen, and the daughter, sister, widow and mother of Kings. Even in defeat, she must make Albany respect her for that.

248

When Albany thundered through the castle gates, it was his turn to feel momentarily confused. Margaret stood waiting, robed in green shot silk, shimmering with emeralds and with the keys to the castle in her hands. Albany motioned his men to halt, and advanced alone. Elegant as ever in maroon silk breeches and a cream lace shirt, he bowed, gracious even in triumph, 'Madam, you know why I have come.'

Margaret's eyes flickered over the columns of steaming horses. 'Sire, I had gathered that your visit was not in the nature of a social call.'

Albany's dark eyes were kind. Margaret cursed the excitement that flamed within her as he murmured, 'Believe me, I have the best intentions of Scotland at heart. I wish you, and your sons no ill will.'

The Queen led forward the child King of Scotland whom she had dressed from head to foot in Stewart crimson. Watched by Albany, his men and her appalled ladies, Margaret gave the boy the keys of Stirling Castle.

'James, hand the keys of your castle to the Duke of Albany.'

Margaret's son moved towards the Frenchman, his small hands outstretched. Swiftly, Albany knelt. He removed the keys from the young King's sweating fingers, then impulsively took the boy in his arms, and hugged him.

Margaret could not still the tears as Albany returned her son to her.

'Please understand, madam,' said Albany smoothly. 'You are at liberty to stay here at Stirling with your sons. But I am compelled to inform you that you must accept that their legal guardianship is now in the hands of Parliament – although your wishes, as their mother, will naturally be respected. However, perhaps you would be so kind as to advise me if you wish to leave Stirling Castle.'

Margaret replied dryly, 'Of course my lord. After all, I am hardly a prisoner ... am I?'

As the Regent rode away she knew that in spite of his promise, she would not be allowed to remain long in Stirling with her sons. A mother could exert too much influence. Three days later her fears were realised: she was ordered by Parliament to return to Edinburgh, alone.

At Edinburgh Castle Margaret was greeted by her repentant husband who, dropping leadenly to one knee, begged her forgiveness for not accompanying her to Stirling. He had been ill advised, distracted by the unexpected turn of events. He had needed time to think, and refresh himself, in order to return and offer his wife the protection that was her due.

Margaret forgave him. He was, when all was said and done, all she had. Her children and her title as Regent of Scotland had been wrested from her. She had no friends. She was a powerless, puppet Queen. And, once more, she was pregnant. How ironical, she reflected bitterly, that in the early years of her marriage to James she had despaired of ever being able to conceive. Now it seemed her fate always to be heavy with child at the very times when she most needed all her strength and vitality. God how she hated being a woman, a mere useless beast of burden for nine months of the year. She wished her brother Henry could have a baby: that would prick his great bladder of wind. How would he like to preside over his Council after being sick every morning, to ride off to war with a distended belly, to hump a body carrying a weight so huge that sometimes it threatened to burst his rib cage?

Yet, ever contrary, Margaret remained fond of her brother – or what she could remember of him. It was thirteen years since he had kissed her goodbye at Richmond and whispered an assurance that if ever King James beat her he would gallop up to Scotland and personally give the barbarian a thrashing. Now Henry was King, and she was no more than a King's widow, without power, friends or influence in a foreign country. England, and her childhood, seemed a lifetime away. As she tasted the salt of her tears, Margaret gave way to a flood of homesickness. She was so tired of the forbidding mountain crags, bleak moorland and grey lochs of the country that was her adopted home. How she longed to walk among the soft lush fields of Richmond again. To see London, gay, alive and full of her own people instead of flint-eyed Scots who distrusted her and took her children away. She would have liked her boys to have seen London. Margaret suspected that Henry would have adored them all the more since he still had no male heirs of his own.

As the child moved within her, the wish crystallised into resolve. 'Why not?' she cried, out loud. 'Why shouldn't we all see London again?'

Angus was aghast at her plan. 'Oh, Margaret, you can't be serious. You haven't a hope of kidnapping your sons from Stirling Castle. And, in case you have forgotten, you are eight months pregnant.'

'Exactly!' flared Margaret. 'For once in my life I'm glad I'm with child. For once, I am going to use my condition for my own ends. For once, Archie, I'm pleased to be a woman. Because if I'm fighting men in a man's world, then I intend to use a woman's weapons.'

Margaret had judged her opponent well. Albany, the fearless soldier, the gallant courtier, the sophisticated diplomat, was as abashed as a green youth by the mystery of birth. When he was informed that the Queen begged his kind permission to retire to her Palace of Linlithgow with her ladies to prepare for the delivery of her child, Albany turned to Lord Huntly for advice.

Huntly was as embarrassed as the Duke. 'It is the custom, Sire, in Scotland for royal ladies to remove themselves from the prying public eye at this time. In such a ... fragile condition it is necessary for them to lie in complete darkness, with the windows shuttered and heavy tapestries lining the walls. For any men to attend the lady concerned is considered most improper. All the servants, everyone who attends the Queen will be women. Even her husband will not be admitted until after the birth.'

Albany sighed with relief. 'I can see no harm in it, then. Without a man to guide her I don't imagine that the Queen can indulge in any mischief. Tell her we consent to her withdrawal to Linlithgow.'

The Regent was not even suspicious when, a few days after Margaret's incarceration at Linlithgow, he received word that she was dangerously ill and pleaded for her beloved husband to be allowed to visit her. Albany not only agreed to the meeting, he even sent a message imploring the dear Queen to recover speedily.

Before the Regent's sympathetic note reached Linlithgow, Margaret had fled. Accompanied by Angus and two of her women, she escaped by moonlight to Lord Home's stronghold of Blackater Castle, just a few miles from the English border. She had to bully Angus into stealing the horses, and her ladies were sullen, resenting the undignified scramble down back stairs and through unguarded smelly ditches. In her stiflingly hot room at Blackater, Margaret ignored her complaining companions and rested her throbbing head on the barred window as she waited for news of Lord Home. Although her pregnancy had been a means of bringing her to Blackater, Margaret now found it an intolerable burden once more.

If only I were a man, she fretted, I'd be with Home now. Her thoughts soared out into the darkness, across the hills to the towns and hamlets around Stirling, which Home's men were setting afire. In her mind she heard the strident bells sounding the alarm, and Albany's men streaming from the castle to put out the flames. And there was Home, slipping through the chaos and swirling smoke at Stirling gates, dashing into the castle to snatch the royal children ... they were sleepy, confused, but at the mention of her name, instantly alert, riding flat out with Home towards the safety of Blackater Castle and the ultimate protection of England.

The minutes trickled by, but there was no sign of Home. As the sweat soaked the thin silk of her dress Margaret strained every nerve, listening for the gateman's shout, the clink of bridles and scurrying of stableboys that would herald Home's approach. Time and again she heard the sound of hoofbeats, only to realise that her fevered imagination was playing unkind tricks. And still Home did not come.

Angus, hollow eyed with anxiety, licked his lips. 'Something's gone wrong. He should have been here by now. I always said we should never have trusted him.'

'We had no choice,' said Margaret shortly. 'With Lord Drummond still imprisoned at Blacknest, there wasn't another noble in Scotland who would have supported us. It was Home or no one.'

'But he was one of the Council who sent to France for Albany in the first place,' gabbled Angus. 'How do we know he hasn't gone straight to the Regent and betrayed our – *your* – reckless plan? At this very moment, Albany could be riding here to –'

'Be silent!' hissed Margaret, craning once more towards the window. Surely . . . it must be . . . it *was* the sound of a horse.

Angus pushed her aside. 'He's come! It *is* Home!'

'Has he the children?'

'I can't see. There's no moon now.'

Impossible to sit and wait with dignity for Home to mount the stairs. Margaret raced down to meet him, tripping over her long skirts as she flung herself into the courtyard. Breathless, she pulled up short. Home was alone.

Wearily, the earl dismounted and flung his reins to a stableboy. 'It was no use, my lady. Albany wasn't fooled by all that fireraising. He sent only a token party of men down from Stirling and left the castle just as closely guarded as before. I had no chance. Believe me, it would have been suicide . . .'

Margaret slumped onto the cold stone cobbles of the courtyard. Before the blackness enveloped her, she heard Angus say with anguish, 'My God, Home. Albany will have us hung like blood puddings for this.'

When she awoke, it was not to the comfort of a warm bed, and the soothing hands of her serving ladies. Instead she was strapped like a sack of grain to her husband; they were riding a horse frightened near out of its wits by the furious pace to which Angus was lashing it. With the chill autumn air freezing her bones, Margaret gasped, 'Archie. Where are we going?'

'South, to Morpeth Castle. We can't risk Albany surrounding us at Blackater.'

Frantically, Margaret beat her fists against his back. 'But

253

Archie ... my clothes, my jewels. They are all at Blackater. We must turn back for them at once.'

Angus whipped the horse, forcing every last ounce of speed and strength from the unfortunate animal. 'Don't be so foolish, Margaret. I'm afraid I regard my neck as a far more valuable possession than your gaudy trinkets.'

Margaret screamed. Angus ignored her, and sped on across the rough stretch of gorse clumped moorland.

'My ladies,' protested Margaret faintly. 'Why are they not with us?'

'They were asleep, and there was no time to rouse them. They'll follow us to Morpeth tomorrow. Home is with us, though, riding a little way behind.'

For another ten miles, across streams, bogs and sheep tracks, the trussed Queen suffered the jolting and pounding of the terrified horse. The pains, intermittent at first, intensified to dagger-like stabs. She clawed Angus' unrelenting back. 'Archie. For pity's sake, you must stop. My baby is coming!'

Archie rode on.

'Archie, it's your son!'

He reined in the foaming horse, cursing quietly to himself as Margaret moaned in agony. 'Are you sure?'

She nodded, almost faint with pain. 'Oh Archie ... get me down from this damned horse.'

As Home cantered up to join them, Angus untied his wife and lifted her down onto the tough moorland grass.

Margaret whimpered. 'You must do something. I can't have this child here, now.'

Angus turned to Home. 'Stay with the Queen. Meanwhile I'll ride on a few miles to Harbottle. There's a fortress there. I'll have them make it ready for us.'

Home delicately averted his gaze from the woman lying writhing at his feet. He cleared his throat. 'Angus, I think it would be more seemly if you stayed with the Queen while I rode on ahead.'

'But I don't know anything about having babies,' stuttered Angus.

'Damnit, man, she's *your* wife. I don't see why I –'

Margaret groaned. '*Please...*'

Archibald Douglas, Earl of Angus, scrambled hastily up onto his horse. As he galloped away into the night, Margaret closed her burning eyes, convinced she would never see him again. Delirious with fear and pain, she knew that her husband would now take the road to Stirling, there to make his peace with Albany and save his own pathetic neck. While she, his wife, the first lady of Scotland, would bear his son on this deserted stretch of windswept moorland.

His son. She looked up at Home, kneeling beside her and ineffectually dabbing her forehead with his saddle cloth. 'No!' she cried with a venom that alarmed Home. 'I pray to God this child is a girl. I shall name her after me. And I swear to you my lord Home, my daughter may have the name of Douglas, but she'll grow up an English Tudor.'

But Angus did return. By dawn, much to Home's relief, Margaret was installed in the fortress of Harbottle, a crude barren stronghold, designed to harbour fighting men rather than a lady of royal blood on the verge of giving birth. The damp, rough stone walls were covered not with tapestries, but moss. There was no French wine or comforting dishes of cinnamoned egg custard to tempt her appetite: the Queen drank the soldiers' ale, and was grateful to share their rations of dried herring, boiled kale and dry rye bread. She was bereft of female attendants, for the ladies she had left sleeping at Blackater had crumpled under Albany's threats and refused to leave the castle to join their mistress. So it was on a rough straw mattress, infested with fleas, that the Queen delivered, alone, the child who would be known as the Lady Margaret Douglas.

By the middle of October Margaret was well enough to dictate a defiant letter to Albany, informing him of the safe arrival of her daughter. She also emphasised that she had moved to Morpeth Castle, on the borders of her own country, and had placed herself under the care and protection of her dear brother.

'But you haven't heard a word from Henry,' protested Angus, shaking sand over the wet ink. 'You promised me we could rely on his support.'

255

'And his money,' said Margaret wryly.

But Henry, uncharacteristically, was silent. Undaunted, Margaret wrote more letters – to the French King, the Venetian Ambassadors in London and, finally, to the Pope himself. They were touching, brave lines, painting a picture of a friendless, pregnant woman, torn from her children and condemned to a life of despair and destitution; of a young Queen usurped by an interloping foreigner, and forced to flee over the border to escape her own and her husband's enemies.

The civilised Courts of Europe were appalled. How could Albany behave so ungallantly? What was the man thinking of? Margaret hugged herself with glee when Home brought word of the Regent twisting himself into a knot of excuses and explanations in the face of the indignant outcry from Europe's female nobility. And at last came a message from Henry. Ever the opportunist, he treated the international expressions of outrage as a trumpet call to action, casting himself gloriously (if a little tardily in Margaret's eyes) into the role of guardian angel. In a fulsome letter to his sister, he expressed his undying affection and invited her to London in the spring, when the weather was more clement and she was fully restored to health.

It should have been a happy Christmas for Margaret, safe at last with her husband and daughter, secure in the knowledge that soon she would see the celandines flower in the fields of Richmond. Yet once again, unkind Fate held a dagger up her sleeve. As the Morpeth village children built their first snowman of the winter, two letters arrived bearing Lord Huntly's seal. Crouched before the acrid peat-block fire in her chamber, Margaret read that her younger son, the Duke of Ross, had died after a short illness.

I am satisfied, went on Huntly, *that there is no suspicion of foul play. Albany loved both your sons as if they were his own. His grief at the little boy's death, while but a shadow of your own, has been most touching to behold. Your son the King, I assure you, is in the best of health, and the most considerate of hands.*

Numb with despair, Margaret threw the note on the fire and ran through the connecting door to find Angus. He was lolling on the windowseat, shaking with laughter as he read Huntly's second letter.

Margaret shook him. 'Archie, how could you! I know he wasn't related to you, but can't you find it in your heart to feel the least bit sorry?'

Angus grinned. 'I should have thought you, of all people, would have found the situation highly entertaining.'

She snatched the paper from his fine-boned hands, and read that Lord John Gordon had been arrested, and was in danger of excommunication, exile and disgrace.

Five

He made, as rich as I could wish for,
A bed from meadow flowers and grass;
And as you walk the path which I walked
You'll smile, perhaps, there as you pass.
From the roses you still may,
Tandaradei,
See the place where my head lay.
Walther von der Vogelweide

It was Bella, escorted by Blackpatch, who galloped through the night to break the news to Mairead at her house in Perth. Margaret Gordon, clad in a loose, fur trimmed gown to conceal her third pregnancy, greeted her agitated dawn visitors calmly. Calling for mulled wine and fresh meats, she drew her friends near the fire in her colourful parlour, moving with the cool assurance of one whose childhood had been scarred with treason, hurried midnight flights and bad news at breakfast. She would not allow them to speak until the frost had melted from Blackpatch's eye patch, and the warmth from the blazing ash logs had returned the colour to Bella's pinched cheeks.

Spreading her fine wool skirts across the quilted seat of her chair, she enquired, with a touch of asperity, 'So. Tell me what my errant husband has been up to now?' She smiled as Blackpatch's mouth fell open. 'Well it's obvious that he was planning something. He insisted on going north to spend Christmas at Huntly Castle. I can assure you, there is nothing festive about that vast, sombre place at this time of year. Even our little son George yells in terror if we threaten to take him there. And then John was adamant that for the sake of my precious health, and my condition, I should stay here, snug and warm at Fothergill. What nonsense! He wasn't half so solicitous over the birth of his first two sons. A week before George was born I rode up a mountain with John to look at an eagle's nest he'd found. So what's he done?'

Bella pushed aside the dish of cold beef. 'You know he's been feuding for the past year with the Abbot of Kinloss over the ownership of some land?'

Mairead nodded. 'The Strathisla estates. The Abbot holds the deeds and is refusing to give them up. Alexander maintains that the wily old rogue hid the papers in Kinloss Abbey to stop John getting his hands on them.'

'The Abbot wasn't as shrewd as he thought,' said Bella. 'Just after Christmas, John and a band of mercenary ruffians broke into the Abbey. They forced their way into the vestry and smashed open the shrine of Lady Margaret Mowat where the papers were hidden. John is accused of stealing not only the deeds, but some of the Abbot's gold as well.'

Anxiously, Bella awaited Mairead's reaction of shock and dismay at such desecration. But Margaret Gordon merely said thoughtfully, 'I suppose John needed the gold to pay off his hired thugs.'

Blackpatch choked on a pickled walnut. Clearly, the poor lady had misunderstood. 'But madam, your husband wrecked and reviled the holy Abbey. Do you not appreciate what that means?'

'I understand,' laughed Margaret, 'that the Abbot and every man of God in Scotland, with one shining exception, will shriek with horror at the notion of their dusty holy relics being mauled by John's sticky fingers.'

'With respect,' murmured Blackpatch, 'it is the bones of Saint Margaret that lie in Kinloss Abbey.'

'The bones from the Abbot's dead dog, more like,' scoffed Mairead. 'Alexander tells me that there are, at this moment, scattered around the churches and cathedrals of Europe, no less than fourteen of our Lord Jesus' foreskins. Now I know He could perform miracles, but –'

Blackpatch hastily left the room.

'Oh dear,' Mairead sipped her wine, unable to meet Bella's unwavering gaze.

'John does not possess your ... advanced views on religion, Mairead. I could accept that *you* had broken into an abbey, but never John, hotheaded and reckless though he may be.'

'He was obviously drunk,' said Mairead, 'and his new friends must have encouraged him, knowing that even if they were caught, John would be the one to pay.'

'The price is high,' murmured Bella. 'He is to be excommunicated.'

Mairead shrugged. 'Oh, that! My own father was excommunicated for waging war on England, but I don't remember seeing Holyrood awash with his tears over it.'

'It meant the King was never afforded a Christian burial,' Bella reminded her.

'Do you think God cares how or where a man is buried?' cried Mairead. 'The King my father was acknowledged as one of the most devout men in Europe. Just because an ambitious soldier Pope signed a piece of parchment denying him membership of the Church on earth, do you imagine Saint Peter followed suit and clanged shut the gates of heaven? The notion is absurd. Excommunication means nothing.'

'If I may say so, it means that Lord John Gordon is under arrest at Edinburgh Castle,' said Blackpatch, returning to the parlour in a last attempt to impress the gravity of the situation on this strangely imperturbable woman.

Mairead was looking at Bella. 'It isn't possible, is it, that our Earl of Kinleven had anything to do with this raid on Kinloss?'

Impatiently, Bella shook her fair head. 'No, the whole affair lacked Robert's finesse. In any case, he spent Christmas teaching my son Douglas how to string a longbow. At the moment, Robert is arranging a ship to take John to France.'

Mairead's dark, delicate eyebrows lifted. 'France, indeed? Not Denmark, or Italy, or Spain?'

'John chose France,' said Bella.

'To be sure he did,' murmured Mairead, the glimmer of a smile touching her blue eyes. 'Of course, Malcolm Laxford is also in France. You would not know, but John and Malcolm were once in love with the same woman, a flaxen-haired beauty called Diane d'Éste. So naturally John would opt for France. I'll wager he can't wait to storm Paris and garrotte Mallaig's amours.' She stood up, and laid a blue-veined hand on Blackpatch's arm. 'It was good of you both to come. Will you wait for me while I change, and then accompany me back to Edinburgh? I will arrange fresh horses to be made ready for you. I want to visit John before he sails for France ... and admire the guileless sorrow in his face as he tells me that, much as he desires it otherwise, he must leave his loyal little wife behind.'

John Gordon glanced up in mild surprise as his wife swept past the guards into his room high in Edinburgh Castle. 'I'm not complaining, but I was under the impression that I was to be allowed no visitors. Don't tell me young Douglas catapulted you down a castle chimney?'

'I grew up in this castle,' said Mairead, lifting her face for his kiss. 'Every man at arms here is an old friend of mine.' She surveyed the canopied bed, the padded chair, the wine and sweetmeats laid out on the low oak chest. 'Hardly the bare prison cell. Are the dancing girls hidden in the garderobe?'

'I too, am no beginner at charming soldiers,' said John. 'Except in my case I find they respond to harder currency than my disarming smile.'

'Like the Abbot's gold?' suggested Mairead silkily.

He poured her a cup of wine. 'I'm sorry, Mairead. It was insanely irresponsible of me to try and steal those deeds. Forgive me.'

'I have never blamed you,' she said simply. 'And now I hear you are to grace Paris with your tainted excommunicated presence.'

'How can you jest? To be excommunicated is worse than being outlawed.'

'Rubbish. The jaded Court of France will be titillated by the scandal. All the royal ladies will come scratching at your door like cats hungry for cream. Then once you have been out of Scotland for a couple of years, you must come back and grovel to the Abbot of Kinloss. He will be so impressed

261

by your piety and contrition that he will forgive you and absolve the excommunication order.'

'You make everything sound so simple.'

Mairead scraped the mud from her riding boots onto the bedpost. 'I have learnt in my life to make the most of every situation. Instead of bemoaning your exile from Scotland and the musty Church, why not rejoice in renewing your acquaintance with . . . France.'

'I shall wish you were with me,' he said.

Margaret Gordon turned to the window. So he was not inviting, or pleading with her to accompany him. She gave him one last chance.

'Would you like me to sail with you?'

His gaze was direct. 'I think you will be happier at Fothergill. You are due to give birth in eight weeks' time, and even the great Barton brothers were fearful of the treacherous January seas. I should not like you to run any unnecessary risks.'

'As you wish,' said Mairead coolly.

'The children –'

'Will be safe. I shall have Bella with me until the baby is born.' She fastened her cloak. 'When do you leave?'

His tone held a trace of relief. 'Tonight. Robert is arranging horses, the ship, money, everything. And the guards will present no problem. I can't believe the ease with which it has all been organised.'

Because Albany wanted it that way, suspected Mairead. Far less embarrassing to let John escape quietly, rather than drag him into the full glare of a public trial. As she embraced her husband, Margaret murmured, 'Take care, John. And be sure to come home in a couple of years.'

He pulled the fur hood of her cloak up over her hair. 'I will. And in the meantime, I've told Alexander Stewart to look after you. He has my complete trust. If you are in need, promise me you will go to him.'

'I promise,' said Mairead.

'He's here again,' muttered Bella, watching the man in blue

262

guide his horse up the icy track that led to Mairead's hilltop house.

'Does he bother you that much?' asked Mairead, sweeping a chessboard from her bed to make room for her visitor to sit down.

Bella tucked the worn, crocheted shawl over the newborn baby girl sleeping in her crib. It was the same shawl on which Margaret Drummond had embroidered her personal legend: *Mérite*. But recently, in the large, ragged stitches of a woman who regards the art of needlework as a tedious waste of time, two words had been added, forming the new challenging motto: *Mérite et Désir*.

'I don't understand you, Mairead. Most women would have been smothered with shame at the excommunication of their husbands. But you cheerfully wave John goodbye to exile in France, and then instead of setting a shining public example of piety and sorrow, you immediately encourage the attentions of Alexander Stewart ... John's closest friend ... and a man of the Church!'

Mairead laughed. 'Come, Bella. You know my marriage to John was never a love match. We like one another well enough, but we are both aware that it was a union of necessity, arranged by my father because he knew he was going to die, and he didn't want me left unprotected and at Queen Margaret's mercy.'

Bella shook her head, fingering the faded gold silk of Margaret Drummond's finely worked *Mérite*. 'Your mother would never have allowed a man to call on her within forty days of her confinement, as Alexander visited you before little Jean was born.'

'I loved my mother dearly,' said Mairead, stretching lazily against the lace pillows, 'but she lived in a different age, when women had no choice but to remain slaves to convention.'

'She did her duty, and gained the respect and admiration of the nation,' insisted Bella.

'There's nothing admirable about lying respectably cold in your grave,' retorted Mairead. 'She should have married my father when he first asked her, instead of scuttling back home to Drummond Castle and a life of loneliness and longing.'

'And by selfishly disregarding the wishes of the Council, she'd have plunged Scotland into civil war,' said Bella angrily. 'Don't you remember the uproar when the Queen married Archie Douglas?'

Mairead twisted her hair into thin plaits, and tied them round her forehead. 'The Queen has no sense of timing. If she'd only had the patience to wait until she was out of mourning for my father, no one would have given a bean whom she married. My mother was in a far more advantageous position. The people adored her. With me gurgling prettily in her arms, the nation would have taken the new royal family to their hearts.'

'But the Council –'

'Would have been as impotent as the Pope's eunuchs,' declared Margaret Gordon. 'If it had been me, I wouldn't have cared about the outrage. I'd have presented them with my marriage as a fait accompli, sat back on my velvet throne and watched our illustrious Scottish nobility pecking one another to death like a clutch of mindless fighting cocks.'

Bella glanced out at the figure in blue advancing steadily up the hill. 'I suppose it's Alexander Stewart who's been filling your head with such treasonable fancies. And him a man of God, too.'

'He is his own man, Bella,' smiled Mairead. 'He didn't choose to enter the Church – it was decided for him, by his father, when Alexander was barely eight years old. Can't you see,' she sat forward in the bed, her face eager, 'we are two of a kind, he and I. We were both born outside society. I am illegitimate, and Alexander was disowned when his father divorced his first wife. He had no religious vocation and I had no desire to marry John. We feel strongly that if the establishment thrusts you aside, and then forces you along a path alien to your nature, then you cannot be expected to abide by traditional *mores*. For Alexander and I, the rules don't count.'

Bella shook her head. 'I must be getting old, Mairead. You shock me so easily these days.'

Mairead held out her arms, and said softly, 'Oh, Bella. We've been such good friends these last ten years. Don't desert me now.'

Before Bella could cross the room to her embrace, the door swung open to admit Alexander Stewart.

Glaring, Bella said cuttingly, 'I suppose, as a Dean, you consider yourself above the earthly convention of having yourself announced before you invade a lady's bedchamber?'

His blue eyes alight with laughter, Alexander bowed low. 'Lady Annabella, I crave your forgiveness. But all the servants are squabbling over a large box of quinces I brought them, so there was no one available to herald my arrival. And, not that it matters, but I am no longer a mere Dean, but a Bishop.'

Bella eyed the rough woollen cloak, creased breeches and torn doublet. 'Travelling incognito, no doubt?' she murmured.

He ignored the straight-backed chair she dragged forward, and seated his lithe frame lightly on Mairead's bed. 'Not at all. I prefer to leave the peacock trappings to my dear brother Albany.'

'Don't mind Bella,' said Mairead, her face flushed. 'She suspects you've come to lead me astray along the sinful paths of dalliance.'

Alexander grinned. 'Don't let me frighten you away, Bella.'

'*I* am not going anywhere,' retorted Bella, sitting down firmly on the cushioned windowseat. For two hours Bella chaperoned a man and woman whose relationship made her uneasy and whose conversation scaled ramparts far beyond her compass. They talked of astronomy, and the new art of navigation; they discussed the books he had lent her on philosophy and logic; they laughed over the fresh scandal from Rome, and whispered of rumours of a new Religion, which promised to discard the gaudy trappings and indulgence so long beloved of the Vatican.

Appalled, yet fascinated, Bella listened as the young pair explored the lush pastures of one another's minds. Gradually, like the flickering flare from a tinderbox, came a glimmer of

265

understanding. Seeing Margaret Gordon's lovely face illuminated with intelligence and excitement, Bella was reminded of the days, so long ago, when Mairead had worn the same exhilarated expression ... insisting on riding a horse that was too big for her ... tilting (an activity Bella had strictly forbidden) in rowing boats with Douglas ... in St Margaret's chapel, reading salacious, banned books hidden inside her Bible. Bella was accustomed now to regarding Mairead as a respectable wife and mother, a woman of title, property and responsibilities. It was easy to forget that Margaret Gordon had inherited the wilful lust for life of one of the most brilliant and democratic Kings Europe had ever known. She was nineteen, a married woman but still, at heart, a glittering girl in whom, like a mountain spring, bubbled the joyous wanton spirit of her father. In this dark troubled time after Flodden, when so much of the light, gaiety and laughter had been snuffed out of Scotland, Mairead was one of the blessed few who embodied the splendour and excitement of those old, golden days.

Only when Alexander had left the darkened room to return to Edinburgh did Bella chide quietly, 'I thought you were never going to fall in love? *I have no lover, nor do I want one.*'

'Yes, I did say that,' admitted Mairead, lazily watching Bella light the candles. 'But I have changed my mind. Do you blame me?'

Bella wrestled with her conscience. 'I would never deny you love. And I am beginning to see, now, why you are attracted to Alexander. In any other circumstances I would say you were well matched and give you my blessing. But he has his duty to God, and the Church.'

Mairead said gravely, 'And he fulfils that duty, Bella. In ways he dare not speak of openly, because many of his ideas are against the traditional code of the Church – the Church as we know it at the moment, that is.' She leaned forward, hugging her knees. 'If you listen to any priest anywhere in this country, he'll tell you more about hell than heaven. We are all damned, they tell us. We're going to burn in pits of raging fire and be tortured with red hot tongs for our sins.'

Bella nodded. Every church she had ever known contained reminders, in statues and stained glass, of the unavoidable purgatory to come.

'We who come to pray,' went on Mairead, 'are so crippled by the weight of our original sin that we aren't even allowed a proper glimpse of the altar. We're herded behind an ornate chancel screen, so as not to offend the sight of God with our impure presence. Now, Alexander doesn't believe in any that. Up in Moray, he preaches about the God of Love, not the God of Wrath. He conducts his services in *front* of the chancel and,' she lowered her voice, 'he speaks in plain Scots, not convoluted Latin that common folk can't understand.'

Bella swallowed. 'But what if he's found out by the Church authorities?'

'He knows he will be, in the end,' laughed Mairead. 'But by that time he hopes there will be enough like-minded clerics to support him. He calls himself a nonconformist.'

'And that gives you the freedom to take him as your lover?'

The woman in the bed reached down to stroke the downy head of the child in the crib beside her. 'Be at peace, Bella. I shall have no lover ... at least, not for a while yet.'

Yet, as the snow melted and the first new young hawthorn leaves uncurled to greet the spring sunshine, the visits of the man in blue continued. Together, he and Mairead roamed the green dunes of Perth, retracing the mossy paths that Margaret Drummond had walked in those lonely years of estrangement from King James. But still, Bella was sure, Mairead and Alexander were not lovers. What were they waiting for? Knowing the couple's sense of the dramatic, Bella was confident that the consummation of their obvious love for one another would never be a mundane matter of Alexander creeping into Mairead's chamber one moonlit night. This singular pair, who clearly regarded themselves as rebels against society, would scorn the traditional trysting places and seek out a more unique location for the fulfilment of their love. But where, and when?

On Mairead's birthday in March, Alexander gave her a

spinet, with ebony faced insets and accidentals inlaid with jade and silver. At Easter, he brought her a parrot, squawking in a gilded cage, while for Bella there was an ivory-framed looking glass, the first she had ever owned.

'He chooses such unusual gifts,' commented Bella uncertainly when she and Mairead were alone. 'Most men prefer to shower their mistresses with jewels.'

'I am not his mistress – yet,' replied Mairead, teasing the parrot with a peacock's feather. 'And besides, he knows I place no value on gaudy trinkets. I love only that which lives, like my splendid spinet, filling the air with sounds as sharp and fresh as summer rain.' She turned to face Bella, her eyes luminous. 'Do you know what day it is on Sunday?'

'You'd have to be blind and deaf not to know,' laughed Bella. 'All your unmarried girl servants have been in a pother for weeks wondering which of the village lads will invite them to the May Eve outing in the woods.'

'Well ... I have received *my* invitation,' said Mairead.

Impatiently, Bella threw a cloth over the jabbering parrot. 'You're not –'

'I'm going May gathering,' declared Mairead defiantly. 'I always wanted to as a child, but you'd never let me.'

'I should think not! It's hardly proper for the daughter of a King – let alone a married woman – to be seen capering in the woods with all the serving girls.'

'I shall disguise myself,' insisted Mairead. She hugged her friend. 'Oh, Bella, do come. I've told Alexander we'll both wear white peasant dresses with flowers in our hair. It'll be such fun.'

Bella took Margaret Gordon lightly by the shoulders and said seriously, 'What about John? Have you no thought for him?'

'As much as he has for me,' smiled Mairead. 'My husband is, at this moment, paying homage to his moon goddess – Diane d'Éste, *Queen of the sea and beauty of the night.*' Her face softened, and at that moment Bella saw her again as a motherless little girl. 'I too want the chance to push open an enchanted casement, Bella.'

268

Bella knew there was nothing more to be said. On Sunday, she and Mairead slipped from the house to join the villagers singing and dancing their way to the woods. A pack of children scampered on ahead, clutching blankets, for it was customary for even the youngest to be allowed to stay up all night on May Eve. In a clearing, the boys built a fire, leaving the girls to run through the violet twilight and strip the boughs from trees bridal with May blossom, to take home the next day as garlands for their houses. Feverish with excitement, Mairead twined a spray of white flowers into her hair, her eyes searching the shadows for Alexander Stewart.

It was not until the wicker baskets lay overflowing with snowy blooms, and the girls had gravitated, laughing, to the fire, that Mairead clutched Bella's arm. Dressed in a simple blue robe, and quietly occupied roasting a chicken leg over the flames, no one would have taken Alexander Stewart for a bishop. He grinned as Mairead slipped a May garland round his bare neck and flung herself, breathless, down beside him.

'You look like Persephone, fleeing from her prison beneath the earth to dance under the stars with her nymphs,' he said, winking at Bella. 'I feel I should be offering you figs and sun-kissed grapes instead of a sad piece of charred chicken.'

'I don't want to eat,' murmured Mairead.

His eyes gleamed in the firelight. 'Neither do I.'

Bella unpacked a stone flask from her basket and poured three cups of the elderflower wine she had brewed last year. As the woodsmoke hazed the air, a young girl began to sing a popular love song, and soon everyone, including Mairead, had joined in:

> *Kiss'd yestreen, and kiss'd yestreen,*
> *Up the Gallowgate, down the Green,*
> *I've woo'd wi' lords, and woo'd wi' lairds,*
> *I've played wi' carles and meddled wi' cairds,*
> *I've kissed wi' priests – 'twas done in the dark,*
> *Twice in my gown and thrice in my shirt;*
> *But priest, nor lord, nor loon can give*
> *Such kindly kisses as he gave me.*

As the sound died away, in a spatter of spontaneous applause, Mairead turned to Bella, her face flushed. 'I can't tell you how happy I am. Thank you for coming with me.'

In a whisper, Bella asked then the question that had been chafing her mind for months. 'Why have you waited all this time for him, Mairead? It isn't like you to be so patient.'

'Thank the Queen,' laughed Mairead. 'All the time she was at Morpeth there was the danger that she might return to Edinburgh. But now she's begun her journey south to London, and for the first time in my life I feel really free. There is no one left in Scotland, Bella, with reason or power to interfere in my life.'

Alexander gently lifted the dark haired woman to her feet, and Bella looked away, uncomfortable at the expression of naked desire in Mairead's eyes. She felt a touch on her arm.

'We are ... going now,' murmured Mairead. 'Will you be all right here for a while?'

Bella smiled. Around the fire many of the children were falling asleep, while their older sisters drifted off into the dark of the woods with their lovers. She drew her cloak around her. 'I'll go and watch the village boys choosing the tallest May tree to take back to the village.'

But she didn't follow the group of shouting boys. Instead she gazed into the glowing embers, and thought of Tom, her longing sharpened by the joy of the lovers all around her ... and the knowledge that Alexander Stewart was leading Margaret Drummond's daughter, with flowers in her hair, to a mossy kissing couch spread beneath a canopy of scented white May blossom.

Six

Alas for him whose sickness is love,
for what cause soever I should say it;
hard it is to be rid of it;
Sad is the plight in which I am myself.
Iseabal Ní Mheic Cailéin

When Margaret Gordon exultantly declared that she was free of all interference in her life, she was wrong. There still remained one man in Scotland who took an extremely close interest in her affairs, and who possessed the power to influence them.

The lovers were left in peace for six months. Then came an imperious summons from the Duke of Albany, Regent and Governor of Scotland, requesting his brother to attend him in Edinburgh.

Alexander Stewart, entering Albany's fastidious room in Holyrood Palace, found his brother uncharacteristically tense. The easy grace, the polished phrase had temporarily deserted him. Clearly, the subject of the interview aroused Albany's distaste.

'Damn it, Alexander. Margaret Gordon is the wife of a disgraced man. And you're publicly bedding her!'

'Not actually in the streets, John,' murmured Alexander, sitting down uninvited, on the tapestried windowseat.

His brother jabbed a manicured nail at the closely written sheets of paper before him on the table. 'You have both been seen joining in the local village fire-jumping ceremony at midsummer ... during haymaking the Lady Margaret Gordon was observed chasing rabbits from the cornfield – wearing only her shift ... and you stand accused, with the Lady Margaret, of encouraging her servants to,' he peered closely at the paper, 'to eat *blackberries* after October the tenth...?' His voice trailed uncertainly away.

'After that date blackberries are believed to belong to the Devil,' said Alexander helpfully. 'Come to think of it, they did taste a trifle bitter.'

The Regent struck the table. 'Midsummer madness . . . near-naked haymaking . . . inciting the Devil. Hardly activities seemly for a man of the Church, Alexander.' He surveyed his brother's rough woollen cloak. 'And why in God's name aren't you wearing your Bishop's robes? You're one of the richest clerics in Scotland, yet you look as if you've just mislaid your begging bowl.'

'*The habit doth not make the monk, nor fine robes a lady,*' quoted Alexander.

Albany swallowed, hard. 'Make no mistake. I have nothing against Margaret Gordon personally. She's a beautiful, amusing, intelligent woman. But you and I, Alex, are servants – I of the State, and you of the Church. It is vital that we set an example by observing the proprieties in our private lives. *Mon Dieu*, do you think I relish living in this uncivilised, barren country, when I have a sick wife pining for me in France, and fertile lands and a house I love there? I long for France. But my duty lies here.'

'Yes,' said Alexander conversationally, 'I noticed Home's head trussed like a potroast to the city gate.'

'While you were capering with Margaret Gordon over the buttercupped hills of Perth, I was fighting for my life putting down a rebellion led by Home,' said Albany grimly. 'I had no choice but to execute him. I did my duty. And if I can do mine, then you can bloody well do yours.'

Alexander shrugged. 'I regard my first duty as being to myself, John. And I didn't choose to become a cleric, you know.'

'Well you are one, so you'd better make the best of it,' snapped his brother. He stood up, smoothing the cuffs of his lace shirt. 'Surely you can see that for a Bishop of Scotland, my brother, to romance publicly with the wife of an excommunicated man is undermining my authority as Regent and Governor. I can tolerate your lascivious behaviour no longer.'

'Don't tell me! It's the rack!' exclaimed Alexander in mock

horror. 'Or am I to be hurled in a weighted sack into the Nor' Loch? The Scots have this quaint belief, you know, that death by drowning is humane.'

In a voice suggestive of a nail scratching glass, Albany explained that he intended to ask Parliament to confirm the old Duke of Albany's divorce from his first wife, thus legally illegitimising the offspring of that marriage. The most important of those children was Alexander Stewart.

Alexander fingered his velvet cap, and said lightly, 'Well, it is Martinmas, the season for the weakest beasts to be slaughtered to save the bother of feeding them over the winter.'

Extremely ill at ease, Albany hurried on, 'I appreciate that having to appear before Parliament and hear your heritage publicly denounced will not be at all pleasant. By way of compensation, I am arranging for you to become Bishop of Moray. I don't need to tell you that it is one of the most luxurious livings in Scotland, and will make you one of the nation's wealthiest men.'

It was also, thought Alexander wryly, five days' hard mountain riding from Margaret Gordon's house in Perth. By confirming my illegitimacy, Albany is guarding against me, his older brother, usurping him from the Regency. As if I cared. I have no desire to be Regent. All I want is the freedom to be myself. And by sending me north to Moray, he hopes to sever the tie between me and Mairead. But what Albany had overlooked, mused Alexander, as he took his leave from his brother, is that Moray is easily within striking distance of the Huntly castle on Kinnord Loch. Alexander thought it highly likely that Mairead would soon find it necessary to visit the Gordon family estates. She must have much business to settle there in her dear husband's absence.

The new Bishop of Moray spent Christmas with Margaret Gordon before riding obediently north. Mairead waited a discreet few months and then, bidding farewell to an anxious Bella, took her children to Kinnord in the spring. She was relieved to leave Perth, for it was strongly rumoured that the Queen was on her way back from London. Queen Margaret was taking her time, for she dare not re-enter Scotland while Albany was still in residence. But the Regent was making no secret of his longing to visit his beloved France once more.

The gardens of Edinburgh were vibrant with roses before Albany judged it safe to leave, for a while, the hostile land he hated so much. As a precaution against an outbreak of power fever amongst the nobility during his absence, Albany took with him to France as hostages the eldest sons of all the most important families in Scotland. Douglas Fraser, heir to the Earldom of Kinleven, was among them. Robert insisted on riding to Leith to wave goodbye.

They sailed in a fleet of French ships, newly fitted, freshly painted and liberally emblazoned with fleurs-de-lis. Albany, his eyes fixed firmly out to sea, took no notice of the barnacled *paquet* creaking past the flagship to weigh anchor at Leith. So it was in bright sunlight, almost under the gaze of the Regent himself, that Robert Kyle smuggled Lord John Gordon back into Scotland.

Robert and Bella accompanied him on the four-day journey up to the castle on Loch Kinnord. The weather was glorious. Bees hummed in the heather and fish jumped in the clear burns. Herds of shaggy, short-legged cattle grazed the tough, springy grass, tails and heads twitching rhythmically against the irritating swarms of flies. But taverns were few, and the tired and hungry trio were forced to beg grudging hospitality from suspicious crofters whose windowless turfed huts boasted no gardens or sheltering orchards.

'Why should we bother to plant trees or plan for the future,' a sour farmer demanded of John, 'when our lords only allow us to lease the land for five years at a time?'

Lord John Gordon, it was plain, neither knew nor cared. Fresh from the perfumed courtyards of Paris, he was brimming with news.

'All France was discussing Queen Margaret's visit to London,' he told Robert. 'Henry VIII laid on quite a show. Water pageants on the Thames, jousting, and a firework display at Richmond with Margaret's name blazoned against the night sky. Nevertheless, the Queen was hard put to explain the absence of her husband.'

Robert snorted. 'The little weasel. Two days out of Scotland, she turned round and found Angus had gone. Scampered back to Edinburgh, pleading with Albany to wipe his boots on his shivering face.'

'I'm surprised the Regent had the courage to leave Scotland at all,' commented John, spurring his horse through a cluster of hens enjoying a dust bath in the sun. 'With Lord Drummond released from prison, and Henry VIII's sister about to hot-foot it back over the border, Albany could well find himself *persona non grata* on his return.'

'Albany's no fool,' said Robert, his hair penny bronzed in the sunlight. 'He's hardly likely to let Drummond poison his own well. Edinburgh is stiff with guards, especially up at the Castle where the young James V is lodged. Neither the Queen nor Drummond will be allowed within shouting distance of the boy. And you'll have heard that your father Lord Huntly is one of the Council of Regency. We thought it better, by the way, not to advise him of the prodigal's return.'

John grinned, and the men's talk turned to the peculiar, though beguiling, eccentricities of the ladies of the French Court. Bella, riding behind, was absorbed in her own reflections on the behaviour of another noble lady. What were they going to find at Kinnord Castle? Despite all Mairead's calm assurance about this strange relationship between her husband, herself and the Bishop of Moray, Bella still felt it would be mortifying for John to surprise his wife and Alexander together at the castle. If only there had been time to send word! If only Mairead hadn't insisted on embarking on this bizarre adventure in the first place. What *was* John going to say, and do, when he found out?

It occurred to her that she should prepare him for the scenes of excessive indulgence and adulterous passion waiting for him at Kinnord. She could not save him from humiliation, but a tactful word, a graceful hint would surely minimise its sting. Yet as she urged her horse level with his, the warning message died on her lips.

'You may scoff, Robert,' John Gordon was telling her brother, 'but I know he's after your blood and your life. I have evidence that Mallaig is corresponding with certain parties in Scotland.'

'So have I,' replied Robert coolly. 'And I know who the certain party is. Every noble parent in the realm was screaming in anguish when Albany snatched their eldest and best to take with him to France. Yet Lady Lennox was observed to smile. Odd that, don't you think?'

There was no time for thought. They had entered the Valley of the Dee in which, hidden from sight by a circle of oak trees, lay John Gordon's family castle. He led the way, his eyes, like that of any man returning home after a long absence, searching hungrily for familiar landmarks.

Bella and Robert followed him in silence through the shade of the oaks, and down a dry rutted track until ahead they saw the wide waters of the loch, reflecting like a bronze shield the light of the setting sun. Bella slid from her horse and gazed at the grey stone castle rising on grassy banks from its smooth girdle of water. Skylarks swooped between the turrets, and only the cawing of distant rooks disturbed the peace of this remote haven where Margaret Gordon had brought her lover. Dry mouthed, Bella waited while John exchanged pleasantries with the ferryman waiting to take them across.

She should have spoken, Bella thought, as she clambered into the rocking boat. She should have given him some word of warning, a premonition of betrayal. Bella glanced nervously at Robert, but her brother sat immersed in his own thoughts, a hand trailing carelessly in the cold water.

Halfway across, Bella summoned up her courage. 'John, I must talk to you for a moment. About Mairead. You see, she –'

His face brightened. 'Look! There she is! Sitting in that hollow by the reeds.'

Bella stared at the tableau on the bank. Mairead was dressed in the pale gold flowing robes of her grandmother's day, with filmy head veils fluttering softly in the evening breeze. She was spinning, the wheel of her loom turning in precise counterpoint to the dip and lift of the ferryman's oars. With the castle forming a perfect backdrop she resembled, Bella realised, a figure in one of Holyrood's finely worked French tapestries, depicting the life of ladies in bygone days.

'Penelope at the loom,' murmured Robert, amusement creasing his lean face.

'Behold my wife!' shouted John exultantly, his voice echoing across the loch. 'My loyal, devoted, *faithful* little Mairead!'

Still shaking with laughter, he refused to wait for the boatman to secure the ropes. Jumping out, he splashed through the shallows into the outstretched arms of his waiting wife.

'John! My wild, reckless one. You've defied them all and come home.'

'Didn't I promise you I would?' He held her away from him. 'How well you look, Meg. And what were you spinning – a cloth of gold tabard for your lord returned from his odyssey? I had hoped to surprise you.'

Over his shoulder her eyes held Robert's in a smile. 'Travellers are rare in this part of the world, John. You should know that. I heard of your coming three days ago.'

As Bella's knees buckled with relief, John Gordon looked round expectantly. 'But where is Alexander? Why isn't he here?'

'He'll be coming across the water tonight,' said Mairead, taking his arm. 'But first, there are two young boys, and a daughter you have not yet met, bursting at the seams to greet you. Oh, and we've arranged such a party for you tonight! Better than anything you ever knew in stuffy old France.'

Exchanging a wide-eyed glance of mutual bewilderment, Robert and Bella followed the woman in pale gold as she swept her husband up to the castle. By eight o'clock, cleansed and freshly robed, they had gathered in a Great Hall heady with the scent of rose petals and rosemary strewn on the flagged floor. Servants loaded the long oak table with flagons of wine, dressed fresh salmon, chicken in aspic, chilled almond mousse and spicy cinnamoned pears. Bella, reclining against a heap of satin cushions, revelled, unashamed, in the luxury of being waited on. She tidied her coil of shining hair, conscious that the chapped red hands of which she had been so ashamed eight years ago, were now smooth and nearly white. The hands, she thought wryly, of a cosseted lady of leisure.

In the gallery, a group of local minstrels were playing country airs, with what had to be admitted was more enthusiasm than talent. Musicians, mused Bella, must be thin on the ground in a place as remote as Kinnord. Mairead was seated below, plucking at the threads of her silvered Venetian lace dress as John and Robert argued over a story about King François tilting at a barrel full of boiling pitch. They were all nervous and ill at ease, Bella realised. They were waiting for the missing guest, breathless to see how John Gordon would receive him.

It was a noisy argument amongst the minstrels that prevented them hearing the commotion of Alexander's arrival. So no one had time to prepare expression or mind as Alexander Stewart, Bishop of Moray, entered the Great Hall of Kinnord, resplendent in the silks, velvets and heavy jewelled chains that were his to wear by right.

In the racking silence, no one moved. Even the vitriolic tongues of the musicians seemed to have grown green mould. Then John Gordon pushed back his chair and ran at full pelt down the Hall to embrace his friend.

'Alex, how good to see you! But why all the tinsel and trimmings? I'm fair skewered on the rubies across your chest.'

In Mairead's clear blue eyes Bella recognised a flicker of relief. It was all right. There would be no strain, no bitterness or mistrust between her husband and her lover. Every nuance of the delicate situation was intuitively understood between the three of them. Alexander's bones were not, after all, to be fashioned into Gordon knife handles.

That night, the five friends flung themselves into an unstinted frenzy of merrymaking. They demolished the salmon and chicken, then persuaded Robert to demonstrate his juggling expertise with the salt cellar, an empty cream jug and a carving knife. Alexander, his gold chains of office thrown in a clanking heap on the floor, climbed into the gallery and insisted on leading the giggling minstrels in a lively rendering of a song he could never have learnt at vespers. Everyone joined in the rollicking chorus. Intoxicated with wine and high spirits, the group joined hands and danced, spinning out of the Hall in a wheel of breathless laughter, to play hide and seek on the winding steps of the dark castle stairs. Finally John, in borrowed Bishop's robes, led them all in a demoniac dance round the ramparts, with the silvered lace of Mairead's dress sparkling like frosted cobwebs in the moonlight.

It was well past midnight, with the servants dismissed and the musicians collapsed in a stupor of ale, when Mairead led her guests to a small parlour furnished with bright silk hangings, gold tooled books and heaps of soft velvet cushions. Here, at last, they could talk in private about John's future. It was vital, they agreed, that as a first step to having his excommunication order revoked, John should pay an immediate call in sackcloth and ashes, on the Abbot of Kinloss.

'You won't have any trouble with him, John,' promised Alexander. 'I've been sowing silver seeds around the barren cloisters of Kinloss for months.'

Bella was shocked. 'Surely the Abbot would never take a bribe ... ?'

Alexander smiled. 'Not a bribe my dear, merely a not inconsiderable contribution towards treating the woodworm in the Abbey roof. All that remains is for me, as Bishop of Moray, to honour the Abbot with a visit and deliver a little homily on the Christian virtue of forgiving repentant sinners.'

'It was a stupid thing to do, desecrating the Abbey like that,' muttered John, his fair hair damp with sweat. 'The Abbot had no choice but to excommunicate me.'

'Don't fret about that now,' urged Mairead, wiping his brow with her scarf. 'My, you're hot.'

'It's a stuffy night,' said John.

Mairead, who had been about to slip on her shawl, glanced at him sharply. Then she took his hand, and said gently, 'I'm afraid I have some sad news for you, John, about your aunt, the Lady Catherine Gordon. She died last month, in London.'

279

'I'm sorry, of course,' said John slowly, 'though I hardly had the chance to know her well. She married Perkin Warbeck when I was still a boy, and then after the King of England had him executed, Aunt Catherine stayed on in London and managed to get through two more husbands. She must have been quite a woman.'

That she certainly was, thought Bella, gazing over her wine goblet at her brother. Bella still had no proof, but she was positive that at the end of their affair, the beautiful Lady Catherine had given Robert Kyle a purseful of gold with which to set himself up as a saddler.

Robert made no comment on his former mistress. Mairead, too, said nothing about the book which earlier that evening she had placed in Robert's room. A maid had found the well-thumbed volume in a locked chest belonging to the dead Lady Catherine, and had tactfully sent it to Margaret Gordon. It was a book of Spanish love poems, and on the flyleaf, in the distinctive strong hand Mairead had recognised as Robert Kyle's, were the lines,

To God I commend you, and to the heavenly Father;
Now we part; God knows when we shall meet again.
Weeping from his eyes, you have never seen such grief,
Thus parted the one from the other, as the nail from the flesh.

It was two days before Bella and Mairead were able to snatch the opportunity for a private talk. While the men were busy composing John's repentance speech to the Abbot, the two women walked arm in arm along the reedfringed shore of the loch.

'I'm concerned about John,' Mairead confided, her voice low, although there were only Bella and the rooks to hear her. 'He isn't well. He seems feverish, yet his eyes are dull, sometimes almost unseeing.'

'Perhaps it's a summer chill,' suggested Bella. But she too had noticed John Gordon's high colour, and the perspiration permanently pebbling his brow. 'Do you think he returned to Scotland because he is ill, and needs your comfort? Or is he genuinely sorry about the Kinloss episode?'

Mairead flung a stone into the water, frowning as she watched the ripples spread. 'I think he was homesick. John thrives on fresh air, and a landscape of mountains and lochs. I'll wager he felt like a man in corsets amidst the formal gardens and paralysing etiquette of the French Court.'

And yet, as the oak leaves turned russet and floated into the loch, John Gordon showed none of his old desire to fish and hunt with his friends. Increasingly listless and irritable, he was often to be found sitting up on the battlements, lost in thought and impervious to the chill autumn winds.

'And his skin is always clammy, and he's constantly fatigued,' Mairead told Alexander. 'It's as if he's plagued with worry and self-doubt. But why?'

Alexander shook his head. 'The Abbot of Kinloss has forgiven him, and received him back into the Church. I can't imagine what else can be tormenting John.'

In December, John took to his bed. He seemed glad to have his wife and friends around him, yet he hardly spoke, spending most of his time gazing vacantly up at the rafters. Beside herself with worry, Mairead arranged for physicians, faith healers and astrologers to be rowed to the castle on the loch. John refused to see any of them.

At last, one freezing winter morning, Margaret Gordon entered her husband's chamber. He was lying on his back, staring blankly into space, his bedlinen soaked with sweat. Firmly, Mairead closed the door. 'I think it's time,' she said, 'that you told me all about it.'

John Gordon died in his wife's arms, two weeks before Christmas. He was buried, at the Abbot's insistence, in the Abbey of Kinloss. As Mairead and Alexander knelt, side by side, at John Gordon's tomb, Bella and Robert walked briskly round the Abbey gardens to keep warm.

Robert was still deeply shocked. 'It was all so quick. And we still don't know what was wrong with him.'

'John Gordon died of a broken heart,' said Bella, holding her ermined hood close against her face as the first flurry of snow began to fall.

Robert blew on his hands. 'I always thought it strange, that business between him and Mairead and Alexander. Of course he was jealous. Cuckolded by his closest friend, and having to pretend he didn't know. Beats me why he stood for it, poor bastard.'

Bella took his arm. 'No, no – you don't understand.' And then she told him what Margaret Gordon had revealed to her. 'John Gordon was passionately in love with a beautiful French girl called Diane d'Éste. But shortly before he left Paris, John heard that Diane had just been married.' Bella looked her brother in the eyes, 'To Malcolm Laxford, Earl of Mallaig.'

Seven

All is hazard that we have, there is nothing biding,
All is hazard that we have, there is nothing biding,
Days of pleasure are like streams, thro fair meadows gliding.

Anon

'I want a divorce!' shouted the Queen.

Lady Lennox raised a single, sparse eyebrow. Was the Queen deranged? *I am happy to my heart to be home,* Lady Lennox recalled Queen Margaret declaring on her return to Edinburgh in the summer of 1517. Now, eight months later her royal mistress sat huddled in blankets before a roasting fire at Holyrood, complaining about the bitter February weather, her head cold, and her errant husband Archie.

Margaret had been prepared to be gracious over his desertion of her on that nightmare flight to London. She had been looking forward to receiving his grovelling apologies for the cowardly way he had run back to make his peace with Albany, leaving her with their baby daughter to struggle on alone to the English capital. After a few days of dignified, injured silence, she had intended to forgive Archie and bask in his eternal gratitude at the reassurance of her love.

But Archie had not come and thrown himself at her feet. With Albany still away in France, the Earl of Angus had joined forces with wily Lord Drummond to challenge the power of the Council of Regency. On one issue, however, the rival factions were agreed: Queen Margaret was a meddling, irresponsible woman who must on no account be allowed near her son James, under heavy guard at Edinburgh Castle. Margaret was frantic. By now the boy's tutors would have persuaded the young King that his mother had abandoned him. James would grow up hating her.

Yet Margaret knew she was impotent against the warring nobles who sought to control her son's destiny. She was so impoverished, she couldn't even afford the expense of bribing James' guards. On her visit to England, brother Henry had lavished affection, entertainments and advice on Margaret. But no money. The Queen had returned to Scotland in a dress borrowed from her sister-in-law Katherine, to face yet another sickening setback in the news that Archie Douglas had seized the revenues from her most valuable properties at Methven and Ettrick Forest.

That February, Lady Lennox hastened to Holyrood with even worse tidings: Archie Douglas, Earl of Angus, was living on the Queen's lands at Methven, with the Lady Jane Stewart of Traquair.

'*My* husband is residing on *my* lands, and spending *my* revenues on that fancy bitch Jane Stewart,' raged Margaret. She blew her reddened nose. 'He married a Queen. He is one of the most influential men in Scotland, thanks to me. And in return he steals my money and sidles back to the stringy arms of his childhood sweetheart.'

Lady Lennox had never forgiven the Queen for her remark after Flodden: *It must be hard for you to accept that you are now a little too long in the tooth to rival me for Archie's affections.* She drew breath to impart the next blow.

'I understand, my lady, that there is also a child of the, er, relationship. I believe she is known as the Lady Janet Douglas.'

'The more you stir a dung heap, the more it stinks,' exploded the Queen. 'I shall definitely divorce him.'

Lady Lennox was enjoying herself. Clearly, the Queen was going mad. 'I hardly think divorce is possible, madam. And it is hardly proper.'

'Oh, go away!' yelled Margaret. 'How can I think when you're prattling on about what I'm not allowed to do. I'm Queen, and I can, and I will!'

Lady Lennox, wilting under the full gale of Tudor temper, hastily withdrew.

The following spring of 1519 brought forth not a gale, but a positive hurricane of Tudor displeasure. This time, the blast was blowing from the south, with Queen Margaret herself as the target. Henry VIII, King of England and Defender of the Faith, was appalled, disgusted, outraged. Divorce? The notion was insupportable, he wrote. It was the duty of kings and queens to remain loyal to their partners, otherwise the whole foundation of monarchy would be undermined. Margaret was strongly urged to cast out all monstrous thoughts of divorce and concentrate her energies and charm on winning her husband back. Henry concluded his letter with the information that his dear wife Katherine had been so grieved at Margaret's intention that she was sending one of her own friars to Scotland, to reason with her unhappy sister-in-law.

'Pious, interfering cow,' ranted Margaret, conveniently forgetting Katherine of Aragon's many kindnesses to her in London. 'I need a strong man to help me regain my son and assume control of this country. Not a sanctimonious Spanish friar intent on bringing me to my knees.'

'I think it's sweet of Queen Katherine to feel so concerned for you,' murmured Lady Lennox. 'I am sure you will find Father Bonaventura of great solace. He is the only man who can lead you from this dark valley into which you have blundered.'

'If he thinks he's going to lead me on a happy journey back to Archie, he's due for a crushing disappointment,' retorted Margaret grimly. 'I shall be rid of Father Bonaventura within six weeks.'

In the event, she needed only four. Defeated and disillusioned, the gentle, well-meaning friar returned to London and bowed his tonsured head before the unmitigated fury of the King.

'We shall have no more pussyfooting around,' stormed Henry. 'I've tolerated Margaret's whims for long enough. If she won't be persuaded to return to her husband, then she must damn well be frightened into it.'

Shortly before Margaret's thirtieth birthday in November, Henry VIII despatched Henry Chadworth to Edinburgh. He too, was a friar, but where the meek Father Bonaventura had been a disciple of the Lamb, Henry Chadworth was an apostle of the God of Wrath. For two months the rafters of Holyrood trembled under his thunderous denunciations of divorce, until Margaret complained that every inch of her flesh seemed seared with fire and brimstone. She had never in her life been brave enough to defy her brother for long. With the might of England and heaven ranged against her, Margaret surrendered, and allowed Henry Chadworth to arrange a public reconciliation with her husband. Chastened, the Queen retired to Stirling Castle for the Christmas festival, forcing herself to remain silent and unrecriminative when Archie disappeared for days at a time to visit Jane Stewart at Methven.

The change in the Earl of Angus bewildered Margaret. The man she had once decried as witless as a wild goose was now baring the teeth of a lion. Confident in the love of Jane Stewart and the prospect of seizing power from the Council of Regency, Archie made it plain that he no longer needed Margaret's help or influence. He had deployed the revenues from her estates in raising and training a private army which would answer only to him. Even the death of old Lord Drummond, his grandfather and mentor, failed to shake Archie. With his army at his back, he intended to make the House of Douglas supreme again in Scotland.

Margaret was to remember 1520 as the year in which she realised that she was married to the most unpopular man north of the border. Nobles and commoners alike had grown to dislike and distrust Angus, and to fear and resent the growing menace of his troops. Edinburgh, simmering with intrigue and suspicion, boiled over into violence as soldiers from Angus' private army clashed with rival forces led by Lord Arran. The confused citizens cowered behind locked doors, uncertain where their loyalty lay. Was it with Lord Arran, Huntly and the Council of Regency, representing the Governor Albany? But the Duke was still in France, and who knew when, if ever, he would return. Or should they support the Earl of Angus, husband of Queen Margaret and head of the powerful Douglas family? Yet Archie Douglas was a proven coward, with no experience of leading a nation.

Margaret was horrified. She was safe, she reasoned, behind the fortressed walls of Stirling Castle. But for how long? As

Angus' wife she could not avoid for ever the storm of the people's hatred for Archie. Somehow, she must publicly disassociate herself from the tyrant she had unwittingly married. Their reconciliation must be revealed as the farce it really was.

Divorce was the only answer. But to defy her brother Henry she needed the help of a man who ranked equal to England's formidable sovereign. With anyone of lesser distinction beside her, Margaret knew she would crumble before the full torrent of Henry's anger. In all the world, she knew only one man who possessed that vital authority. And she was aware that to earn his support, she would have to swallow her pride and beg him to return to Scotland.

Her letters to Albany were long, disjointed and highly emotional. The country was in desperate need, she wrote, of his firm guiding hand. And she too, bitterly unhappy woman that she was, craved his forgiveness for her foolish rebellion against him. She had been wrong to run away to England. Now she saw the error of her ways, and desired above all else a divorce from the Earl of Angus. Could Albany find it in his heart to write to the Pope on her behalf?

Albany's reply was charming, witty and evasive. He told her a great deal about the current fashions favoured by the ladies at the French Court, and the enchanting antics of his children at Christmas. But on the subject of the Queen's divorce, or his return to Scotland, Albany was significantly silent. Had he refused outright to help her, Margaret could have accused him of a disappointing lack of gallantry. Even a few lines of threadbare excuse would have given her something with which to challenge him. Anything, she thought bleakly, even flagrant lies, would have caused her less dismay than the lord Duke's chosen policy of benign neglect.

Margaret heard nothing more of, or from, Albany for almost a year, until in November 1521 she learnt that his fleet had been sighted off the coast of Garvlock, a town on Lady Lennox's estates. The lady herself brought the news to the Queen at Stirling, adding brightly that Albany had most courteously sent his herald ashore, requesting permission for his master to disembark onto her lands.

'Such chivalry, Your Grace! I was quite overwhelmed. It is so reassuring, don't you think, to see such evidence of the Regent's care and concern for us?'

'They say the Queen and the Regent are lovers,' Bella told Margaret Gordon.

'I thought Albany had better taste,' murmured Mairead. After John's death she had returned quietly to her house in Perth, declaring that she would never again cross the loch to Castle Kinnord. She went on, 'When the Duke left Scotland five years ago, he and the Queen were about as compatible as a pair of fighting cocks. What did he do, force a love philtre down her throat?'

Robert carefully drew a pan of roasted chestnuts from the fire, and tipped them into the chafing dish at Alexander Stewart's slippered feet. 'Nothing so crass, my dear. He simply took her to visit her son, King James. She hasn't been allowed near him, remember, for six years. I was privileged to witness the charming scene at the gates of Edinburgh Castle. Albany bowed, and handed her the keys. She curtseyed and gave them back. He hesitated. She wiped a tear from her downcast eyes. Oh, the suspense was awful. I was on the verge of rushing to grab the keys for myself, when they swept into the Castle, side by side. Most touching.'

Alexander grinned. 'I should imagine the crowd enjoyed it. At least Albany's return will mark the end of all this gang warfare between the nobles.'

'Not quite,' said Mairead, her hand resting lightly on Alexander's shoulder. 'There remains the slight problem of the Earl of Angus. His troops are still stamping about in Edinburgh. And Albany can hardly risk Archie leaping out from the bedchamber arras to discover him, lute in hand and breeches down, serenading the Queen.'

Alexander peeled her a chestnut. 'Precisely. Which is why my tidy-minded brother arrested Angus on a charge of high treason and despatched him to France.'

'Where else?' murmured Robert dryly.

'The lad was not, as it happens, at all eager to broaden his mind with a spell of European travel,' laughed Alexander. 'He sat in Albany's dainty chamber at Holyrood and simply refused to budge. The Regent was reluctant to call out the guards, for fear of alerting Archie's band of armed thugs. An uncivilised tug of war over the noble person of the Earl is hardly Albany's style. So he slipped a powder into Angus' wine, and while the Earl was still inconscious, Albany had him dumped on a cargo ship at Leith. Archie will wake up to find himself lying in a tub of salted herrings – at Dieppe.'

'I hope my son doesn't tangle with Archie in France. He wrote to say,' Bella told Maircad, 'that he had not returned with the rest of Albany's Scottish hostages, because he wanted to stay on in Paris and perfect his French.'

Everyone burst into derisive laughter.

Bella said defensively, 'Well, Douglas is nearly twenty-two years old. It's time he was wed.'

'But I always thought,' exclaimed Mairead in mock despair, 'that it was *me* he was in love with.'

Robert glanced at the Bishop of Moray, comfortably clad in his customary plain blue shirt and breeches. 'Talking of which . . . aren't you taking rather a risk, visiting Mairead with your brother less than a day's ride away?'

'He isn't visiting. He's living here,' said Mairead defiantly.

Alexander smiled. 'Officially, I am paying a series of courtesy calls on all the local abbots. Unofficially . . .' he looked into Mairead's eyes, his face alight with mischief.

Margaret Gordon kissed the back of her hand, and pressed it against her lover's face. 'Don't worry, Robert. Albany will be too busy reasserting his authority over Scotland to bother about us.'

'They are practically living together as man and wife,' Margaret protested to Albany.

Wearily, the Frenchman laid down his knife. He had endured a trying week presiding over the Spring Assizes in Edinburgh. The complexities of Scottish law were still a mystery to him and Lord Huntly, present as adviser, had served only to muddy even more the cloudy waters of Albany's mind.

Why, the Regent had demanded, was he forced to sentence a man convicted of killing his wife, to be hung, whereas a murderess was sent to the stake? Huntly had thought the matter over and then gravely announced that death by burning was kinder than the rope. As if, thought the exasperated Albany, there was something aesthetically pleasing about frying in your own fat.

And now it seemed that Margaret had chosen this peaceful Sunday suppertime to make him sit in judgement on his brother and the Lady Margaret Gordon.

Albany shook out a starched linen napkin and meticulously wiped his mouth. 'They have been in love for years. Frankly, I hardly think the sleeping arrangements at an insignificant house in Perth are likely to cause a major international incident.'

'But you don't understand – it's a scandal!' exclaimed the Queen. 'You are French, my lord, and accustomed to scenes of considerable licence amongst your nobility. Here in southern Scotland, we take a more . . . traditional view. If the Bishop and Margaret Gordon had stayed up in the wilds of Kinnord, they could have danced naked on the ramparts and no one would have known about it. But what is permissible on a remote castle in the middle of a loch is likely to cause outrage in the mannerly parlours of Perth.'

Albany could not deny that he had heard the incredulous whispers, and the shocked laughter. He had also, on his way to the Assizes, caught a snatch of a scurrilous street song, to the effect that the corns on the Bishop of Moray's knees had been caused by his kneeling too long not in praise of God, but at the shrine of more earthly delights.

'Of course my brother's indiscretions reflect badly on me as Regent,' admitted the Duke. He sighed. 'I suppose the only course left open to me is an ultimatum – he'll have to give up either the mistress or the cloth.'

The Queen fluttered onto a silk cushion at Albany's feet, aware that she must choose her next words carefully. The Regent, she knew, liked and admired Margaret Gordon. Why, she could not imagine, but men were ever irresponsible in their affections. 'I feel, my lord, that your brother may have been led astray,' she began. 'He was, after all, a very good friend of the late Lord John. How natural, then, that he should seem to befriend and comfort his companion's widow?'

Albany nodded. 'Perfectly proper. But did he need to cultivate such a captivating bedside manner?'

Margaret hurried on. 'My lord, I have known Margaret Gordon since she was a child. As the daughter of the King it was inevitable that she should be totally indulged and spoilt. And I am afraid the wilful girl has grown into a headstrong woman who believes she can have any man she wants. It is she, I fear, who is responsible for luring the good Bishop into her lagoon of lust.'

The Regent choked, to smother a gasp of involuntary laughter. *Lagoon of lust* indeed! That was rich, coming from the lips of a married woman who had brazenly enticed him into her bed. But her words had struck a chord. It did seem extraordinary that Alexander should choose to jeopardise his considerably privileged position in life, merely for the sake of one woman. Of course, everyone knew that bishops experienced physical desires just like anyone else. For heaven's sake, he had them himself, and very pleasant it was too enjoying the charms of this pliant Queen, all in return for one simple letter to the Pope about her divorce. Also, it had to be conceded that Alexander was not a cleric by choice. *I would rather have been a navigator and explored the oceans*, Albany had once heard him tell the Earl of Kinleven.

The Regent shifted restlessly in his chair. Alexander's position was, in some respects, too like his own. Had he not himself been born of the blood royal, yet fated only to serve a Crown, never to wear one? In France he was hailed as a brilliant soldier, but Scotland forced him to play the role of diplomat. No one knew better than he the cost of committing yourself to one course, while your heart lay in another.

If only Alexander had been more discreet. The Queen was right: no one much cared what bishops got up to in the savage lands beyond the Grampian mountains. But for a man of God to flaunt his relationship with his mistress – to be seen, riding

291

together, laughing and joking through the prim streets of Perth – that was too much for society to overlook. Society ... Albany suddenly recalled that night five years ago at the Earl of Kinleven's home, when Margaret Gordon had openly mocked the traditional tenets of morality which he as Regent was committed to uphold. Could the Queen be right again? Was it Margaret Gordon who played the pipe, and Alexander who followed?

He saw now that he had been wrong to tell the Queen that Alexander's affair was of no importance. Of course it had to be stopped. That was clear. But as neither the Bishop nor the widow constituted a threat to the safety of the State, surely they could be dealt with by the Church authorities. Yes, that was the answer. Relieved that the decision was made, Albany made a mental note to contact the Archbishop of St Andrews first thing in the morning.

The kitten-soft voice of the Queen broke into his thoughts. 'Naturally, you are worried about the possibility of Margaret Gordon bearing a child, a son, by the Bishop.'

Albany reached for his wine. Stupidly, he had never given the matter a thought. But he considered it now, and it was not a prospect to relish. If the daughter and nephew of James IV produced a son, and if by any ghastly chance the young King James should sicken and die ...

'It's impossible,' he burst out. 'Both Margaret Gordon and Alexander are illegitimate. No child of theirs could possibly have a claim to the throne.'

Margaret raised her eyebrows, watching the Duke's feverish calculations on who, precisely, was James V's heir.

'There is, of course, the Lady Margaret Douglas, my daughter by the Earl of Angus,' said Margaret. 'She *is* the legitimate granddaughter of King Henry VII of England. But as a mere girl, it might be difficult to establish her claim against a *son* of Margaret Gordon's.' She waved her hands. 'This is all speculation. The worst may never happen. But Lady Lennox did mention how pale Margaret Gordon looked when she called on her in Perth recently.'

It was a lie. In fact, Lady Lennox had been at pains to point out that the Queen's rival was brimming with vigour and good health. But Margaret could see that the suggestion of a prize bun in the Gordon oven had unnerved Albany. She could do no more – at least, not at the supper table. Rising to her feet, Margaret held out her arms to him. 'You are fatigued, my lord. Come to bed now, and let me kiss away the tension from your dear face. By the time dawn breaks, I am sure you will have resolved the vexed problem of Margaret Gordon.'

Eight

*What if a day or a month or a year, crown thy delights with
a thousand wish'd commentings.
Cannot the chance of a night or an hour, cross thee again with
as many sad tormentings.
Fortune, honour, beauty, youth, are but blossoms dying.
Wanton pleasures, doting love, are but shadows flying.
All our joys are but toys, idle thoughts deceiving.
None have power of an hour, in their lives bereaving.*

Anon

'Albany has Mairead confined under armed guard at Drummond Castle!' Distraught, Bella slipped off her cloak. 'Everyone was talking about it up at the Market Cross this morning.
She's a virtual prisoner, Robert.'

'Not for very long, I'll wager,' said her brother, absorbed
in restringing his bow. 'There isn't a castle in Scotland that
could contain Margaret Gordon once she'd made up her mind
to get out.'

Bella sank into her rocking chair by the parlour fire. 'This
is serious, Robert. The Archbishop of St Andrews has ordered
Alexander to return to Moray immediately. Which means
Mairead has no one to defend her.'

'Alexander is not on his way back to the Highlands,' said
Robert. 'The Bishop is down at the saddlery, entertaining
Blackpatch with stories that would make a sea captain blush.'

Bella sighed. 'What are you all up to now?'

'Nothing . . . yet,' replied her brother. 'There's no point in
showing our hand until we know what conditions Albany has
stipulated for Mairead's release. But you may rest assured that
Alexander Stewart will not go north until he knows that
Mairead is safe. Meanwhile,' he forestalled Bella's next question, 'you are the obvious person to pay a call on the lady at

Drummond Castle. It would be a waste of time me going, as the Regent is bound to have forbidden her any male visitors. Ride to Perth at first light, Bella, and find out what the Lady Margaret's plans are.'

'I don't see,' muttered Bella gloomily, 'that she's in a position to formulate any plans.'

Robert smiled. 'Then you don't know Margaret Gordon as well as you thought.'

By mid afternoon on the following day, Bella and Nan were crossing the celandine-starred fields of Perthshire. On the hill ahead, rising ninety feet into a bright blue sky, lay Drummond Castle. It had been built by Mairead's grandfather, Bella told Nan, from a reddish sandstone renowned for its strength and durability.

'Pity,' mused Nan, anxiety creasing her plain, angular face. 'No chance of crumbling mortar or rotting woodwork giving the Lady Margaret a hole to escape through.'

Bella shook her golden head. 'No. Robert says some of the walls are ten feet thick.'

'How can he be sure?'

'He nearly got caught here once, removing a few barrels of Lord Drummond's finest Rhine wine,' explained Bella.

Nan laughed. 'He always did have expensive tastes. I remember in the old days, before I married Blackpatch and turned respectable, you'd never find Robert the Red prepared to share a common street girl's pallet. But we used to see him sneaking out of Janet Kennedy's house at dawn, his purse all a-jangle like the bells on a lady's bridle.'

Bella smiled, her eyes distant. 'It all seems such a long time ago. Another world.'

'Aye, it was a hard life, yet everything seemed simpler then,' said Nan. 'You were a serving girl, I was a bawd and we were ruled by good King James IV. Now you're a lady, I'm a shopkeeper's wife and we've a Scottish King, an English Queen and a French Regent. At least under James IV you knew where your loyalties lay.'

Bella giggled at the unintended pun. 'You wouldn't want to go back to earning a living on the streets, though, Nan?'

'I'd hate to be that desperate again. But,' Nan cast an experienced eye over the castle guards. 'I had some fun you know. A different man every night, learning new tricks, living on my wits. I miss it, sometimes.'

Bella saw what was in her mind. 'Tell you what. Why don't you stay and amuse yourself with the guards, while I talk to Mairead.'

'Always providing the soldiers let you in,' muttered Nan, smiling with her mouth closed at the Captain of the Guard to conceal the gaps between her remaining four front teeth.

The Captain had emerged from a guardroom fetid with the smell of sweat, leather and urine. Soured by years of low male company, plain army rations and the screams of the convicted murderers he was required to accompany to the gallows, he gazed on Bella now with the air of one suddenly afflicted with a raging thirst. She was, granted, no longer young. But weren't the ripest apples the sweetest? When she moved, he caught a drift of lavender from her dress, mingling with the scent of honey, new baked bread and roasted almonds from the wicker basket she carried. The Captain closed his eyes, and indulged in a brief moment of fantasy about the comforts of marriage to a fragrant woman, in a little house with roses round the door. Then, ignoring the grimacing Nan, he pulled in his paunch and led the Lady Annabella up the winding stairs to a room on the third storey. He apologised profusely for the embarrassingly large lock on the Lady Margaret's door. But the Regent . . . the angel's mouth curved. She quite understood. She would be glad if he would accept a small token for his trouble. Dazed, the Captain palmed the piece of silver and stumbled down the stairs, too much in love to remember about relocking the door.

When they had hugged and kissed, and Mairead had declared for the tenth time that she was healthy and unharmed, they sat down near the window to discuss her plight.

'Need I tell you that it's the Queen who is behind it all,' said Mairead cheerfully, spreading honey on a hunk of bread. 'But poor Albany! He may have set off from Edinburgh fired with the Queen's fervour of spite against me, but by the time he reached my house he was limp with embarrassment over the whole mission.'

'Where was Alexander?' asked Bella. 'I think certain parties at Court were most disappointed that there wasn't a brotherly confrontation on the doorstep.'

Mairead licked her fingers. 'Alexander had already been called back to Edinburgh for an interview with the Archbishop of St Andrews. Stupidly, we thought he was merely going to wag an arthritic finger at Alexander for living with me. We had intended, henceforth, to be more discreet – at least for a while. But I suppose he's been strapped to a mule and whipped back to Moray?'

'Not yet,' said Bella. 'Robert is hiding him in Edinburgh until you are released. So what did the Regent say when he arrived?'

The blue eyes danced. 'He came striding up the garden followed by a score of clanking soldiers. Naturally, I pretended to be delighted to see him. How did he know, I cried girlishly, that today was my twenty-fifth birthday? If his men would care to leave their noisy swords in a heap in the porch, I was sure Cook would be able to find them each a slice of my birthday tart.'

'By this time Albany must have been beginning to wish he'd never left France in the first place,' laughed Bella.

Mairead nodded. 'He wouldn't look me straight in the eye. He gazed over my left shoulder and gabbled that it was his sad duty to escort me to Drummond Castle, where I must remain until I signed this.' She rummaged under the honey pot and waved a sheet of parchment bearing the Regent's seal. 'It sounds very frightening and official, but in effect I am to promise the Regent never to see or contact Alexander again.'

'Oh Mairead,' said Bella sadly. 'Whatever will you do?'

'I shall run away and enter a nunnery.' Mairead looked aggrieved as Bella stifled a shout of laughter. 'I'm *serious*.'

Bella wiped her streaming eyes. 'I'm sorry ... it's just that I can't quite imagine you as the wimpled wife of Christ.'

'I shan't actually take vows. But the convent up near Moray

would be an ideal place for me to hide. I know the nuns there would give me shelter.'

'Moray is the first place Albany will look for you,' warned Bella. 'And what about those innocent nuns – won't you be placing them in an invidious position, by making them lie to the Regent on your behalf?'

'Those innocent nuns, Bella, entertain the local monks in their cells and have pawned all the convent spoons and knives to buy themselves silk stockings.'

'Hardly surprising with Alexander Stewart as their Bishop,' murmured Bella. 'What's that they say about *the monks think it lawful to play when the abbot brings the dice?*'

'Exactly. From the sound of it, I shall find the convent a real home from home,' said Mairead. 'I intend to spend two or three weeks here at Drummond Castle, quibbling with Albany over the wording of his moronic document. I may even pretend to be ill, and too weak to sign my name – anything to delay matters and set the Queen's nerves on edge. Then, if Robert will help me, I shall escape and ride to Moray. But first, I need to see Alexander one more time.'

'That's impossible,' frowned Bella. 'Albany has forbidden you any male visitors. Anyway, I can tell Alexander what your plans are.'

'But there's something else he should know before he leaves Edinburgh. Something I must tell him myself. As he can't come here, then I must go to him.' Mairead grasped Bella's hands. 'It's the Easter Day fair in the village on Sunday. Let's all go, Bella, and meet Alexander there.'

'Robert knew you'd be cooking up something,' sighed Bella. 'All right. Let's just see if I've got this straight. On Sunday, Robert and I smuggle you from the castle. You have your talk with Alexander at the fair, and then slip back here. Presumably, we have to devise a way of making you vanish for a few hours without the guards realising you've gone. Then the Bishop will return to Moray while you chew the fat with Albany. After you've stalled him for a few weeks, you tear up his ultimatum, jump out of the window and gallop north to join Alexander.'

'Something like that,' nodded Mairead, her eyes brightly intense. 'Let me assure you, Bella, that no paltry piece of parchment is going to come between me and Alexander. No one can make me sign it. And nothing on this earth is going to come between me and the man I love.'

Knowing that all Mairead's visitors would be reported to Albany and the Queen, Bella stayed away from Drummond Castle in the week preceding the Easter celebrations. But the guards could find nothing suspicious – in fact they were rather charmed – when Nan stopped at the castle gate to leave an armful of freshly-picked flowers and herbs for the Lady Margaret. The sweet smelling bouquet was secured in an old crocheted shawl. Nan also brought two flagons of extra strong ale, for the Captain of the Guard, with the Lady Annabella Fraser's compliments.

As Bella rode up Drummond Hill on Easter Day, she found the Captain basking in the warmth of the late afternoon sun, his arms clasped round the bewildered head of the soldiers' pet sow.

'She'sh my friend,' declared the Captain thickly. 'The only true friend I ever had.'

'Please don't stand up,' said Bella. 'I can find my own way to the Lady Margaret's room.'

The Captain stroked the pig's ear. 'The guards outshide her door will let you in. The Lady Margaret ishn't well. Perhaps you'd better shtay the night with her.'

'I'm afraid that won't be convenient, Captain,' Bella demurred. 'My brother the Earl of Kinleven is expecting me home to play hostess to his dinner guests.'

The Captain's bloodshot eyes filled with ears. 'I thought you were her friend,' he sobbed. 'My little Daisy here wouldn't leave me, would you my precious?' The pig snorted. 'Why won't you shtay with that poor ill lady upshtairs?'

'Oh, very well,' murmured Bella meekly. 'I'll ask the guards to lock us both in for the night.'

'That'sh right,' nodded the Captain, wincing as Daisy sat down heavily on his foot.

Bella ran lightly up the stairs, and let out a sharp sigh of relief as she saw the two guards slumped, glassy eyed, on the floor outside Mairead's room. Already, a line of tidy minded ants was marching across the flagstones to clean up the honey smeared round the soldiers' mouths. Swiftly removing the keys from the larger man's belt, Bella unlocked the door.

'Safe in the arms of Morpheus!' laughed Mairead, peering past Bella at the two prone men. 'I don't know what those herbs were, Bella, but they certainly did the trick. I chopped them up into a paste of honey and almonds like you said, but when I offered it to those loons the fat one refused, saying sweet food made his teeth hurt. The only way I could persuade him to eat it was by spreading the paste on tiny pieces of ale-soaked bread. It was like cosseting a sick child. How long do you think the drug will work?'

Bella hustled Mairead from the room. 'They'll sleep for about six hours. You'll be safely back inside by then.'

Margaret Gordon locked the door and, keys in hand, led the way back down the stairs, pausing for a moment outside the guardroom on the second storey. 'They're all pickled on your ale,' she whispered, listening to the sounds of ribald laughter, argument and song.

'Sow drunk, you might say,' muttered Bella.

The women hurried on to the safety of a large, cool store-room immediately below the guardroom. Bella sniffed, savouring the mixed aromas of the corn, salt, meat, spices, almonds and sugar stacked in sacks and chests all round the walls.

'Look, it's still there,' called Mairead, gazing down into the centre of a huge disused well. Bella followed her pointing finger and saw a small door about ten feet down from the opening.

'I found it by accident when I was a child,' said Mairead softly. 'This storeroom used to be the kitchen then, and my grandmother Drummond was forever scolding me for playing with the scullerymaids.'

'What's the door for?' asked Bella.

'The well was fed by an underground stream,' explained

Mairead, 'and after especially heavy rain, the door would be opened to release some of the water along a tunnel and out down the hillside. Otherwise it would have flooded the kitchen floor and Cook would have hung himself rather than face my grandmother. The stream has dried up now so this well hasn't been used for years.'

As she spoke, Mairead slipped out of her gown. 'Be reasonable, Bella,' she said, forestalling her friend's protest. 'I can hardly crawl along a narrow chute all cluttered up with gathered silk skirts and fancy ribboned sleeves. Quick, take your dress off, too. It would be silly to ruin it.'

'Now I understand why you wanted Robert to bring us fresh clothes,' muttered Bella, shivering in her thin shift. She crammed both dresses into a bucket, and tucked the bunch of keys underneath. 'How do we get down the well?'

'There are rungs,' said Mairead. 'I just hope they haven't rusted up. I'll go first.'

She scrambled over the edge of the wall, and lowered herself slowly down into the gloom, testing each rung with the ball of her foot before putting her weight on it. To Bella, the wait while Mairead fumbled with the stiff doorcatch seemed endless. Then a blast of cold, dank air and an echoing shout of triumph drifted up to her as Mairead disappeared from view into the tunnel.

Bracing herself, Bella slid backwards over the edge and began her descent. She was heavier than Mairead and several of the rungs were loose. The well must be about fifty feet deep, she reasoned, and probably littered with discarded cooking pots and spits from the old kitchen. If she fell ... for a moment a wave of sick panic enveloped her. She clung with sweating hands to the rough iron, aware that it was quite impossible for her to move another step, up or down.

'Come on, Bella!' Mairead's voice, distorted and distant, pierced the icy grip of fear clamping Bella to the wall. 'Robert is here, with horses and dresses.'

Breath and courage miraculously returned. Climbing steadily down now, Bella quickly discovered the entrance to the shaft and wriggled inside. It was musty, filthy and running

301

with rats. But there was light at the end, and her brother's face, grinning encouragement.

Within two minutes her shoulders were free of the tunnel, and Robert pulled her clear onto his horse, laughing as she took great gulps of the fresh evening air.

'It's all right,' whispered Mairead. 'We're on the other side of the castle from the guardroom. And that thicket of thorn bushes gives us excellent cover.'

Bella rubbed her goose pimpled arms. 'I want nice soft wool covering me, not a thorn bush. Where's that gown, Robert?'

When the two women had changed into the plainly styled dresses and shawls he had brought, Robert led them stealthily down the path that led to the village. Once out of sight of the castle, Bella's spirits lifted as they mingled with the laughing crowd making their way to the fair.

'Now, where in God's name is Alexander?' asked Robert, tethering the horses to a water trough.

Mairead jumped onto an ale barrel, and surveyed a village green fringed with stalls, booths and rowan trees garlanded in red and white bunting. Children darted between the brew stands, boys blowing toy trumpets and girls selling posies of forget-me-nots, windflowers and glowing marsh marigolds. Under a star-strewn sky, the air was filled with the music of gipsies' pipes and tambours, the chatter of caged parrots and the mouthwatering smell of ox roasting over a sage-scented fire.

'He's over there, by the stocks,' Mairead exclaimed at last, pointing to a familiar figure in a blue cloak, who appeared to be haggling with the burly official locking a struggling youth into the pillory.

'Poor wretch. I suppose he's been caught picking purses,' commented Robert.

Bella craned for a better view. 'Knowing Alexander, he's paying the man in charge to wipe the lad's face when the fun starts and everyone starts throwing rotten fruit. I've seen grown men suffocate under the weight of all that slime and filth.' As she spoke, she turned to Mairead. But the younger woman was gone, running across the newly scythed grass to greet her lover.

Feeling unaccountably bereft, Bella gazed bleakly up at Robert. 'Well! What do we do now?'

He slipped his arm around her shoulder. 'I'm taking you to the fair, of course. What shall we try first – hoop-la, skittles, or the bobbing apples in the barrel?'

His enthusiasm was infectious. For three enchanted hours they stepped back into the realm of their childhood, feasting on sticky buns and custard tarts, giggling at the antics of a performing monkey, and falling over, breathless with laughter, at the end of a blindfold three-legged race. Occasionally, they caught glimpses of Mairead emerging, bright eyed, with Alexander from the woods, or joining hands with him in a kissing game, her flying dark hair spangled with firelight.

After a particularly energetic Highland jig, Bella flung her arms around her brother. 'Oh Robert. It's been such fun. If only we could always be as happy as this.'

As he hugged her to him, a polite cough sounded behind them. 'I'm sorry to interrupt,' said Mairead, 'but I'm afraid we moles have to burrow back up that tunnel to Drummond Castle, Bella.'

'Has Alexander gone?' asked Bella.

Mairead nodded. 'It won't be for long – only a few weeks – before we're together again in Moray.'

Taking the hands of the two women in his, Robert guided them across the crowded green to the horses tethered by the water trough. They found not only horses waiting for them. As the trio crossed the road towards the trough, a group of guards stepped quietly out of the bushes. Their swords were drawn, and on their tunics they wore the crest of John Stewart, Duke of Albany, Regent and Governor of Scotland.

Mairead dropped her hand from Robert's and, as Bella stifled a cry of protest, walked steadily towards the soldiers. But they ignored her, and moved instead to surround Robert Kyle, the Earl of Kinleven.

'My dear,' said Robert, rising gracefully from his straw mattress, 'I had fondly imagined you lying in a permanent state of swoon at Drummond Castle, too weak to lift your hand to sign Albany's ultimatum.'

Margaret Gordon paced agitatedly round the small bare room. It was set high in Edinburgh Castle, heavily guarded, and windowless. Albany, Mairead reflected, was giving Robert no opportunity to exhibit his proven skill at rooftop escapes. She turned to the man whose hair, once bright red, time had mellowed to a glowing russet. 'Robert, ever since I was a child, I've always been able to rely on your support. Twice, you've saved my life. When my father married the Queen you turned endless upheaval and dawn flights from a nightmare into a thrilling adventure. You came to the aid of my husband, spiriting him away to France, and smuggling him back into Scotland two years later. And you have been a tower of strength over my friendship with Alexander.' She took a deep breath, and said in a rush, 'So as soon as Bella and I crept back into Drummond Castle last night, I signed Albany's document. Bella has taken it to the Regent.'

Robert was silent for a moment. Then he said gravely, 'You mean, for my sake, you have promised the Regent never to see Alexander Stewart again?'

Mairead nodded. 'In the circumstances, there was nothing else I could do. Don't you see, I had to give him up, in order to be free to repay my debt to you. It is my turn now to offer help.' She hurried on, before Robert could protest. 'The Captain of the Guard at Drummond Castle said he didn't know the precise nature of the charge against you, but that he had heard it was serious.' She grasped his arm. 'Robert – I'll beg or bed or steal or murder. Whatever you ask, I'll do, if it will secure your release.'

Robert lifted her smooth, blue-veined hand and gently kissed it. 'I thank you lady,' he said softly. 'I don't quite know how to tell you this, Mairead ... but ... well, I'm afraid your sacrifice has been in vain. I am beyond salvation.'

'Nonsense!' exclaimed Margaret Gordon. 'You, of all people, must have some plan, either for your defence or your escape. If not, I'll think of something for you. What crime are you to be charged with?'

304

'I don't know, at least not officially,' frowned Robert. 'I shall doubtless be informed, at length, during the enquiry Albany is conducting tomorrow. But I know *who* is bringing the charge.' He drew a piece of paper from the inside of his shirt. 'This arrived for me today. Do you read Spanish?'

Margaret Gordon hesitated. Five years ago, at Castle Kinnord, she had been sent a book of love poems which Catherine Gordon's maid had found amongst the possessions of her dead mistress. Mairead had placed the book, without comment, by Robert's bed. Neither by word nor gesture had she ever revealed that she had read — and understood — the lines on the flyleaf, written in Spanish by Robert Kyle when Catherine had left her saddler lover to marry Perkin Warbeck, the Pretender to the throne of England: *Thus parted the one from the other, as the nail from the flesh.*

Robert said blandly, 'As the King your father was such an excellent linguist, Mairead, I naturally assumed he would have taught you a smattering of Spanish. However, I'll translate.' He unfolded the paper, and read,

Since when might we receive honour from my Cid of Vivar!
Let him go now to the River Ubierna and look after his mills
And be paid in corn as he used to do!

Mairead sat down on the thin straw mattress. 'I don't understand.'

'Then do you recognise the writing?' asked Robert, tossing her the note.

She held the paper close to a guttering candle. Yes, she knew the owner of this bold, spiky hand. She remembered a note tied to the collar of a kitten he had given her, long ago, in this same castle. 'Mallaig.'

Robert nodded.

'But what does it mean? Why has he written in Spanish? And what's all this about mills and corn?'

'Because at a joust once, I caused Mallaig severe public embarrassment by posing as a Spanish nobleman,' laughed Robert. 'The verse he has chosen is from the *Cantar di mio Cid*. The hero of the song, El Cid, was an adventurer of humble birth who rose to a position of some fame and prestige in Castile.'

Mairead's eyes cleared. 'I see. So this is Mallaig's way of announcing his intention to have you stripped of your title and reduced to a commoner once more?'

'Precisely.'

'You're taking it all very calmly,' said Mairead. 'Had you any idea then, before your arrest, that Mallaig was plotting against you?'

'Naturally. Your own husband was good enough to warn me, years ago, that Mallaig was after my blood. And I've received a score of interesting letters from my nephew Douglas in France. He tells me, incidentally, that Mallaig has brought his beautiful wife Diane with him to Scotland. I'm sure you'll be fascinated to make her acquaintance at the hearing tomorrow.' When Mairead failed to reply, Robert went on pleasantly, 'You will be there, I take it? Personally, I can't wait to see what kind of woman would have fallen in love with such a monster as Mallaig. And it must have been a love match, because Diane d'Éste was a wealthy woman in her own right. She had no need to marry our Malcolm for his –'

'Why have *you* never married?' broke in Mairead sharply.

Caught momentarily offguard, Robert recovered quickly. 'I *am* married – in spirit – to several women.' He laughed softly at her disappointed expression. 'Come, now, Mairead. What did you expect me to say? That I was waiting for you to grow up?'

She flushed. 'Don't be absurd. I might have known I'd never get a straight answer from you. I've no doubt you'll be just the same at the hearing tomorrow, standing before Albany and Mallaig with that infuriating smile spread across your face.'

Robert leaned against the cold stone wall. 'Well, you must admit, the situation does promise a certain degree of entertainment. The Regent, as a former guest in my home, will be crucified with embarrassment. The Queen will be busy pricing her jewels against yours and Diane's. Huntly –'

'Wait a moment.' A sudden misgiving clouded the moment of light relief. 'Just why did Albany send word that *I* must attend? Surely no charge of Mallaig's against you could possibly involve me?'

Robert's tone was reassuring. 'No, but Mallaig is still exiled from Scotland which means, by law, that he isn't entitled to bring a public charge against me. Your presence is a legal necessity if the circumstances of Mallaig's banishment are to be officially explained to the Regent.' He laughed. 'I'm sure Lady Mallaig will be enthralled by the story of her husband's attempts to murder you.'

Mairead stood up. 'And what do you think will be the outcome of the hearing?'

'I shall be found guilty,' said Robert flatly.

'How can you be so sure, when you don't know the charge?'

Robert shrugged. 'Mallaig would never dare show his hand unless he was positive he held four aces – maybe five, knowing our Malcolm. You have to remember, it's his life's ambition to watch me die.'

'Die! But I thought . . . you said you'd merely be stripped of your title.'

'After which . . .' Robert drew a finger across his throat. He did not tell her what else they would do to him before they allowed him the release of death.

After a long while Mairead said, in a voice that was barely a whisper, 'Then I will never see you again, alone?'

'It's conceivable that you may see my head decorating Mallaig's front door.'

'For God's sake, Robert! *How can you joke?*'

Robert smiled, and said gently, 'Perhaps because I've always regarded my talent to amuse as an instrument for survival. Until now, that is. It's just that the habit of living is a hard one to break.'

Mairead moved slowly across the room and laid her hands lightly on Robert's shoulders. 'I want you to do something for me,' she said, looking into the depths of his sea green eyes. 'I want . . . will you . . . please will you kiss me goodbye?' She turned away her head as he bent to brush his lips across her cheek. 'No, not like that. Kiss me the way you kissed Catherine Gordon when you said farewell to her.'

Robert was very still. 'My dear, this is hardly proper. I have always liked and admired Alexander Stewart, you know.'

'He would not mind. You know he would not. Besides,' she smiled, 'you have always liked and admired me, too.'

She had guessed. The beautiful, bewitching Mairead had found him out. When or how, by intelligence or intuition, he dared not ask. But she knew. Mairead ... the child he had always protected. Margaret Gordon ... the woman he had always desired, yet never allowed himself to embrace in anything but the most brotherly fashion. He looked down on her lovely face. She was standing so close that he could feel her warm breath on his mouth, and smell the lingering traces of her perfume. He wanted this woman. God, how he wanted her!

As her hands tightened on the thin lawn of his shirt, Robert said softly, 'I've just thought. Perhaps there *is* something you can do for me after all.'

Nine

'Now that I am oiled, keep me from the rats.'
Last words of Pietro Aretino, after receiving Extreme Unction

Never had the Regent Albany longed more passionately for
France. The wife he loved was ill, and needed him. To his
growing children he was now a stranger, with his paternal
authority flaking like the tempera on his locketed portrait
hanging from their mother's neck. In his orchards outside
Paris, the apple and pear trees would soon be in flower, mile
upon mile of pink and white blossom brocaded under a rinsed
spring sky.

In Edinburgh, the April showers had turned to sleet, and
the atmosphere in the Regent's orderly room at Holyrood was
rancid with hatred and mistrust. Instead of enjoying a lei-
surely canter through his lush French estates, he now faced
the prospect of sitting in judgement on a man he liked and
respected – a man whose hospitality and friendship he had,
in happier times, been glad to accept.

The Earl of Kinleven stood on Albany's right, flanked by
the guards who had deliberately placed him furthest away
from the door. The Regent could not bring himself to look
the accused man straight in the eyes, but he was uncomfortably aware that of all those present, Kinleven was the most
relaxed.

Lord Huntly, who had just dropped an armful of legal
documents, was bobbing between floor and table like a
squirrel gathering nuts. Mallaig, seated with his French
wife Diane at the opposite end of the room to Kinleven,
appeared outwardly composed. But already the edges of his
beard were matted with sweat, and his aquamarine eyes had
the poached appearance of a man bedevilled by sleepless
nights.

Albany directed his gaze at the two women who sat across from him – the Queen, regal in dark violet satin, and Margaret Gordon, defiantly gowned in glowing red velvet. Since their arrival, they had exchanged not so much as a look, let alone a word, an exercise in stiff-necked hauteur which, under different circumstances, Albany would have found highly amusing.

The Regent cleared his throat. 'If you are ready, Lord Huntly, I will begin the proceedings.'

Huntly hastily retrieved the last roll of parchment from the floor and subsided, breathing heavily, into the chair beside the Governor.

Forcing himself to look directly at Robert Kyle, Albany said clearly, 'Robert Kyle, Earl of Kinleven, you appear before us today to answer a criminal charge brought against you by Malcolm Laxford, Earl of Mallaig. I must make plain that these proceedings do not constitute a trial, but a private hearing. For reasons of which we are all aware, but that Lord Huntly will declare officially in a moment, the accuser, as a Scottish exile, is not legally entitled to demand a public trial of one of our noblemen. However, because of the serious nature of the charge, we have decided to allow the Earl of Mallaig to state his case before us so that you,' he gestured towards the implacable Robert, 'may be given the opportunity of rebutting the allegations.' The Regent paused as Huntly whispered in his ear. Then he nodded, and raised his voice, 'Lord Huntly kindly reminds me that it is essential for everyone in this room to realise that although this investigation is being held in private, it still carries the full weight and authority of the law of Scotland. If the Earl of Kinleven is found guilty then I, as Regent and Governor of Scotland, am empowered to sentence him as the law demands.'

Two of the guards shuffled their feet. Albany silenced them with a glare, and then turned to Huntly. 'If you would be so good, my lord, as to outline the events which led to the exile of the Earl of Mallaig.'

Huntly rose slowly to his feet, and began, in a voice as dry as a week-old crust, 'In August 1503, during the festivities

310

attending the wedding of our late King James to the gracious Queen Margaret, it was brought to my attention that an attempt was to be made on the life of the King's natural daughter, the Lady Margaret Stewart. As a consequence, I decided . . .'

While Huntly rumbled laboriously on, Mairead continued her cool appraisal of Lady Mallaig, the beautiful woman who, as Diane d'Éste, had captured the heart of the young John Gordon.

Flaxen haired, and quietly dressed in sage green silk, she sat demurely by her husband's side, her delicately boned face impassive as Huntly retold the story of intrigue, deceit and attempted murder. Only once, as Huntly explained the blood tie between the Earls of Mallaig and Kinleven, did Diane raise her eyes; and then it was not to contemplate the King's daughter whom Mallaig had tried to kill. When Diane's subtly painted eyelids lifted, it was to look with candid interest on the man who had humiliated her husband.

Margaret Gordon would have understood if Diane's level gaze had displayed the loathing and contempt of a loyal wife anxious to defend the man whose name she bore. But the expression in her dove grey eyes conveyed something start-lingly different to antipathy: a strange excitement and, when Robert Kyle boldly returned her stare, the suggestion of a challenge.

A man's life was at stake, reflected Mairead, yet this beauti-ful, marble-hearted bitch was actually enjoying the sport. She was like a Roman Empress, amusing herself by flirting with the handsome gladiator in the last desperate moments before the lions came roaring into the arena. And this was the woman whom her own John Gordon had loved and lost; the temptress with whom he had planned to sail to the New World, before he had been obliged to wed an illegitimate daughter of the Scottish King. Poor John, thought Mairead sadly. What liv-ing hell she must have put you through. But you would have been out of your depth married to Diane. She's deadly, and dangerous, and more than a match, I'll wager, even for a man as ruthless as Malcolm Laxford.

Across the table, there was a loud rustling of papers as Lord Huntly resumed his seat.

'The preliminaries having now been completed,' intoned Albany, 'I call on the Earl of Mallaig to state his case against the Earl of Kinleven.'

Mallaig rose slowly to his feet, savouring the air of mounting tension. 'The charge,' he said, in a voice laced with malice, 'is murder. I accuse you, Robert Kyle, Earl of Kinleven, of murdering and savagely mutilating our father, Malise Laxford, the first Earl of Mallaig.'

In the stinging silence that followed, Robert's impassive expression betrayed no hint of his reaction to the charge. The Queen's enamelled bracelet scraped the table as she urged Mallaig, 'Continue!'

He inclined his head, only too anxious to oblige. From his first confident words it was obvious to Mairead that his speech had been well rehearsed. No doubt, she thought viciously, the calculating woman at his side had suggested a few cut-diamond phrases of her own.

'I have to take you back in time,' the bearded earl was saying, 'to the year my mother took me as a young boy from Mallaig Castle over the sea to her native France. You have heard Lord Huntly tell how Malise, my father, then attempted to re-establish a parental relationship with his two estranged children, Robert and Annabella, who were living with their aunt Lilith.'

Mairead restrained a shout of indignation. What Huntly had actually said was that Malise had cast out Robert and Bella when he had married the Frenchwoman. And that on her departure, the drunken earl had harassed the youngsters so much that the formidable Lilith had been forced to set her wild cat on him. Mairead was rising to her feet, determined to voice her protest, when she caught Robert's eye, and was forestalled by his almost imperceptible shake of the head.

'Lilith and Malise,' went on Mallaig, 'died within a month of one another, when Robert Kyle was fifteen. Lilith passed peacefully away in her sleep, but Malise was not so fortunate.'

His eyes burned into Robert's. 'Before you and your sister scuttled off to Edinburgh, Kinleven, you spread the cruel lie that Malise had been drowned on a fishing trip. But you were in too much of a hurry to turn your back on the silver sands of Mallaig. A few days after your departure, our father's body was washed ashore two miles up the coast, and was identified by a crofter.' He paused. 'Malise had not only been stabbed to death . . . but his testicles had been severed and sewn, very neatly, one to each lip of his mouth.'

The Queen hurriedly left the room, her face blanched. Mairead clamped her hands over her face, restraining an insane desire to laugh. Peering through her fingers, she noticed that Diane was calmly plaiting the silken threads of her tasselled girdle.

Albany cleared his throat. 'How did you acquire all this information?'

'As I said,' the earl continued, plucking at his beard, 'I was taken to France as a very young boy, and I never had the opportunity to become as well acquainted with my father as I should have liked. Naturally, I had heard all manner of strange tales about him. Some months ago I determined to make a pilgrimage to my home at Mallaig, to collect the revenues from my estates and try to discover what kind of man my father really was.'

Liar. Mairead glared at him. You were desperate to find some flaw in Robert's story of his birthright. You returned with the express purpose of unearthing evidence that would discredit and dishonour the man who had exposed you.

Albany frowned. 'But as an exiled man, Mallaig, you were surely breaking the law by setting foot on Scottish soil?'

'Er . . . no,' murmured Huntly, scrabbling amongst his rolls of parchment. 'It says here, if I can just find the place . . . that, and I quote, the Earl is permitted to enter Scotland once every five years, for no more than three months, to attend to his estates.'

'Quite so,' said the earl. 'In Mallaig, I made it my business to talk to everyone who had known my father. And it was then that I came across the crofter who had found his body.'

313

'And why had the crofter not brought this very serious matter to the attention of the authorities?' demanded Albany.

Mallaig shrugged. 'He is a simple man, my lord. He had himself been convicted of one or two minor acts of violence, and he was afraid that *he* would be accused of the earl's murder. So he buried my father in the sand and said nothing to anyone.'

'Strange, then, that after all these years, he should feel the need to unburden himself to you,' remarked the Regent.

'He is an old man now,' said Mallaig sorrowfully, 'and anxious to clear his conscience before meeting his Maker. When he learnt that I was Malise's son, he seemed glad to reveal the truth to me.'

Glad, more like, of the gold pressed into his trembling hands, thought Mairead.

'Thoroughly alarmed by what I had heard,' went on Mallaig, 'I thought it my duty to interview all the local fishermen. They insisted at first they could tell me nothing about the night my father died. But later, one man asked to speak to me privately.'

What was it that loosened this one's tongue, wondered Mairead. Bribery or threats?

'The fisherman admitted to me that he had helped Robert Kyle load Malise's dead body onto his boat. They had rowed out to sea and dumped it overboard. Robert Kyle had paid him handsomely, and the fisherman had asked no questions. I am afraid, my lord Regent,' Mallaig's face was pained, 'that to these rustic Highland folk, money talks louder than morality.'

'Have you the witnesses here?' rapped Albany.

Mallaig nodded. 'They are outside. With your permission, I will call them –'

'There is no need,' said Robert loudly. 'I plead guilty to the charge. I murdered Malise, our father.'

This was worse than Albany had feared. 'I imagine,' he said, looking pointedly at Robert, 'that you wish to enter a plea of mitigating circumstances.'

314

'No, my lord,' replied Robert calmly, his hands clasped loosely behind his back. 'I just wish you to know the truth. Malise came hammering at the door one night, and refused to go away. We had a heated argument on the front steps, and in a blind rage I drew my dirk and stabbed him repeatedly. I slung him over a horse, and took him down to the beach and paid one of the local fishermen to row us out to sea. I have only one thing to say in my defence – that Malise was an evil, cruel man who deserved to die.'

'I can think of many men I'd like to see dead, Kinleven,' said the Regent sternly, 'but these are civilised times, and unjustified violence cannot be allowed to go unpunished.' Damnit, this was too much. He had done everything he could to help Kinleven, but there were limits. If only the man had taken his hint and invented a valid reason for killing his father. But he seemed obstinately determined to condemn himself.

Albany stood up, perplexed by the commotion the guards were making outside. It was bad enough having to pass judgement on a man whom he had liked and respected as his friend, without the added indignity of the antechamber to his room sounding as if war had just broken out.

'Robert Kyle, Earl of Kinleven, you have admitted a charge of murder. I therefore have no choice, as Regent and Governor of Scotland, to sentence you ...' Albany felt his voice fading to a whisper, and summoned all his will to make himself audible, 'to sentence you to death by exe –'

The door was flung open to reveal a flushed and extremely dishevelled Lady Annabella Fraser.

'Get out!' Robert shouted fiercely to his sister, displaying his first show of emotion since the hearing began. 'You can't do any good, Bella. For God's sake go!'

She ignored him, bestowing instead a glance of reproach on Margaret Gordon.

Albany, who knew more than anyone realised about what passed between the numerous prisoners of Edinburgh Castle and their visitors, was able to interpret that look. He had taken the precaution of stationing one of his most trusted men outside Robert Kyle's room when Mairead had come to see him yesterday.

'*I've just thought,*' *Kinleven had said.* '*Perhaps there is something you can do for me after all ... You can make sure that Bella doesn't come within sight of Holyrood Palace during the hearing.*'

'*She has a right to be there,*' *Mairead had responded, after a lengthy pause.* '*You are allowed to have a member of your family present.*'

'*It would be too distressing for her,*' *Robert had insisted.* '*And, selfish though it may sound, it would be unbearable for me. Will you help me to keep her away, Mairead? I'll tell you the best way to do it ...*'

And now Bella was saying silently to Margaret Gordon: *Did you honestly think you could drug me with my very own herbs? How foolish. You should have known that nothing, but nothing, would have prevented me from coming.*

Mairead turned to Robert, her blue eyes signalling apology.

'How dare you burst in like this?' blustered Huntly. 'Why were you not stopped by the guards?'

'They tried – very hard,' said Bella, still breathing heavily. 'I'm afraid I was obliged to inflict certain injuries on them which may give their wives, and future children, cause to complain.'

Albany hid a smile. 'Why have you come?' he asked.

Bella faced him across the table. Her dress had been torn in her struggle with the guards and her tangled golden hair streamed almost to her waist. 'I came to tell you the truth about Malise,' she said. 'All Robert has told you is a lie. It was I who murdered our father.'

Robert was the only person in the room not shocked into silence.

'Oh, *Bella,*' he sighed.

Albany said gently. 'You may sit down, Lady Annabella.'

Bella subsided thankfully into the chair the Queen had vacated.

'Now,' Albany continued, 'Will you tell us, first, *why* you killed your father?'

Bella's face was scarlet. 'Because ... because ...'

'Because,' said Robert icily, 'he raped her.'

Bella found her voice.

'Robert was out, stabling the horses for the night,' she said jerkily. 'Usually my father would come storming up to the house, swearing and yelling, giving us plenty of warning and time to bar the doors. But on this occasion he slipped in through a side door, quietly. I was in bed. The first I knew that he had entered the house was when I awoke and saw him locking my chamber door. Before I had time to move, or shout he was ... upon me.'

'How old were you?' asked the Regent gently.

'Thirteen.'

Even that, Mairead noted, failed to move the implacable Diane, who was looking at Bella as one would contemplate a new variety of exotic fish.

'I'm sorry,' said Albany. 'But I must ask you to tell us everything, Lady Annabella, in detail.'

Bella nodded. 'Malise had been drinking, of course. I must have fainted, for when I regained consciousness. I found my nightrobe ripped and bloodstained and my father lying half naked on top of me. He was snoring.'

Lady Mallaig hurriedly converted a laugh into a yawn.

'I wriggled away from him,' Bella continued, 'terrified that he would wake up and attack me again. But he was so drunk it would have taken a thunderbolt to rouse him. I saw his belt and dirk lying on the floor. I must have been in a deranged state of mind. The next thing I knew, the dagger was in my hand and I was plunging it into his chest, again and again. I don't remember, but I suppose I was screaming while I did it, because Robert heard me and broke down the door.' Bella buried her face in her hands.

'The rest you know, my lord Regent,' said Robert.

'Er, not quite,' muttered Huntly, peering at the notes he had taken during Mallaig's evidence. 'There is the question of the...mutilation of Malise's body. I find it hard to believe that such a delicate piece of surgery could have been performed in the blind rage Lady Annabella states she was in when she stabbed her father.'

'Bella was not even aware that it had ever taken place,' said Robert. 'She didn't lay another finger on Malise after I arrived in the room. The disfigurement was carried out by the wife of the fisherman who helped me dump the body overboard. Bella was not the only girl the earl had attacked: some weeks previously, he had also raped the fisherman's daughter. This kind of mutilation is a traditional form of Highland vengeance, although usually the act is performed while the man is still alive. I may say,' he added viciously, 'that if the fisherman's wife hadn't done it, then I would.'

Albany poured himself a glass of wine to soothe his shattered nerves. By God, these Scots were a barbaric lot. He decided to draw the proceedings to a hasty conclusion, before either Kinleven or Mallaig dredged up any further acts of unspeakable savagery.

He gestured towards the bearded earl, who had sat silent and palefaced since Bella's timely intervention. 'Well, Mallaig, the matter now rests in your hands. By law, you have the right to demand that I pass a sentence of death by burning on the Lady Annabella Fraser, and a penalty of some severity on her brother for aiding her, and concealing her crime.'

'If I may be allowed to say,' rasped Lord Huntly, 'that to press charges would seem to me to be the very depth of inhumanity. I recommend, my lord Mallaig, that in the name of Christian charity, you drop your accusations against the Lady Annabella and her brother.'

'But it is my right to demand justice,' murmured Mallaig.

'Yes,' Albany was forced to agree. 'It is your right.'

Bella lifted her tousled head and looked Mallaig straight in the eyes. Sea green eyes that matched hers, and Robert's exactly. What she read there gave her little comfort and no hope. Mallaig was a ruthless man who would harbour a grudge for a lifetime, especially if crossed by a woman. Margaret Drummond had twice made a fool of him, and for that he had persecuted, and tried to kill her daughter. Bella shivered, remembering an incident on the Castle gallery, when Mallaig

318

had tried to kiss her, and she had responded by giving him a bruised knee and a sprained finger. He had not forgotten, and he would never forgive. For that, he would be willing to send her to the stake.

Bella closed her eyes, gripping the table as a dizzying wave of terror enveloped her. She had heard the shrieks of the women they burnt on Castle Hill. Already, she could feel the flames singeing her feet, and smell the sickening stench of her own roasted flesh. When the searing heat seemed almost unbearable, and her head fit to burst from the blaze of red hot light, she felt comforting arms around her and Margaret Gordon saying softly: 'Keep faith in the Regent, Bella. He is a just man, but he is kind, too.'

The Regent felt as weary as a lathered old workhorse. I can't do it, he decided. If that monster Mallaig insists on pressing charges then I shall intervene with a plea of mitigating circumstances. Damnit, the girl had been raped by her own father! No one, not even a man as mentally calloused as Mallaig could demand her death in exchange for that of an incestuous drunkard. But, reflected the Regent uneasily, it wasn't the Lady Annabella's blood that Malcolm Laxford was after. He had come here today determined to take his revenge on Robert Kyle and nothing Albany could say was likely to deter him from seeing his enemy broken. Mallaig would argue, with justification, that Kinleven had not only failed to report Malise's death to the authorities, but that he had wilfully concealed his sister's crime, and even condoned it by taking upon himself the disposal of the body. Mallaig would further claim that Kinleven was an unfit person to bear the illustrious title of Earl. He would demand, first, that Robert's title be stripped from him; and second that his right hand be branded and then severed. This was the punishment the law decreed for such a crime, and Albany knew he would have no choice but to authorise it.

Albany drained his glass. Why was Mallaig taking so long to make up his mind? The Regent glanced down the table and saw that Diane was gripping her husband's velvet sleeve, preventing him from rising with dignity to announce his decision. A low, heated exchange was taking place. Although the Regent could not hear what was being said, it was plain from Mallaig's livid expression that in less exalted company he would have beaten his wife's lovely face to a pulp. Undaunted, Diane dug her long nails deeper into Mallaig's arm, anger firing her grey eyes like lightning striking slate.

The Regent toyed with his damascened paper knife, politely ignoring the domestic dispute at the end of the table. Clearly, the lovely Diane could not be pleading for Bella's life – on the contrary, she would probably have found it amusing to climb Castle Hill and watch the goose fry. No, it was the Earl of Kinleven who was the object of her petition. But if she succeeded in saving him, mused the Regent, it would be with the sole intention of marking him with her own, personal brand. Yet if the Earl of Kinleven felt intimidated by such a prospect, there was no sign of it in the amused aquamarine eyes fixed unwaveringly on his brother's wife.

The Regent's suspicions were confirmed as Mallaig's hissed whispers erupted into a roar. Shaking with rage, he shot to his feet and towered over Diane. '*Merde! Espèce de putain!* Do what you will.' And shouldering his way past the guards, he flung himself from the room like a frenzied wild animal robbed of its prey.

Diane sat with her hands in her lap and waited – until the sound of her husband's running footsteps had receded, and Albany was twitching with curiosity and impatience. Mairead bit back a laugh, reflecting that before her marriage Lady Mallaig had been Diane d'Éste, a member of a family renowned for their patronage of the drama.

At last, with easy grace and consummate timing, Diane rose to her feet and addressed Albany in charmingly accented Scots: 'My lord Regent, my husband has commanded me to inform you that, upon careful consideration, he wishes to drop the charges against the Earl of Kinleven and his sister.' She smiled then, not at the woman she had reprieved, but at the red-haired man whose face was etched with relief, and gratitude.

The Empress, thought Mairead, had exercised her preroga-

320

tive and saved the gladiator. But you may be sure, Robert my dear, that she will make you pay for your freedom.

While Huntly formally declared the hearing to be closed, the Regent allowed himself a rare moment of relaxation. This unsavoury business, *Grace à Dieu* was over. While his other pressing problem, that of his brother's romance with Margaret Gordon, had been solved by her promise never to see Alexander Stewart again. The Queen was his willing mistress, and would remain a docile ally in return for his assistance in obtaining a divorce from the Earl of Angus. He, and Scotland, were at peace. With luck, in another year or so, he would be able to think seriously about returning to France.

The sound of a body slumping to the floor made hay of his complacent reverie. Margaret Gordon lay face down on the flagstones.

Albany was always ill at ease when confronted with female weakness. 'The poor lady,' he said nervously, as Bella knelt beside the woman in red. 'The whole affair must have been a great strain for her. Naturally, the Lady Margaret is over-wrought.'

Bella looked up. 'The Lady Margaret,' she said quietly, 'is with child.'

Ten

Dearest, delay not,
Ours love to learn,
I live not without thee,
Love's hour is come.

Anon

'Lennox, bring me my looking glass!' shouted the Queen. 'And don't forget to tell me the moment there is any news about the birth of Margaret Gordon's child.' Margaret sank back on the sweatsoaked pillows in her chamber at Linlithgow, irritated by the sound of children singing carols outside. 'How dare they warble of joy and goodwill, while I am lying here, dangerously ill?' she fretted.

At first she had ignored the dusky red spots on her face, imagining them to be a harmless winter rash brought on by an over-indulgence of spiced meat. But as her skin swelled and erupted into clusters of angry pustules, Margaret realised with horror that she had smallpox. Within a week, her face had been so inflamed that even Lady Lennox could hardly recognise her. Now, on the thirteenth day, the sores had become dry and itchy, and Lady Lennox was trying to muster the courage to suggest bandaging the royal hands as a means of stopping the Queen's incessant scratching. Even when in the best of health, reflected Lady Lennox, the Queen was never the most reasonable of women. But when the first lady was sick and delirious, her chatter bordered on the insane.

'I am going to marry Albany,' the flushed Queen repeated, for the tenth time since she had fallen ill.

Lady Lennox struggled to control her rising impatience. 'Madam, we have discussed this matter before, at considerable length. Not only is the Regent already married, but he is in love with his wife. The Frenchwoman, Lady Mallaig, was able to confirm that fact before she and her husband departed for Paris in the spring.'

'The Duchess of Albany is a sick woman, Lennox. She is going to die. I know it. And when she does, I shall have secured my divorce from Archie and be free to marry Albany.' The Queen sat still for a moment to allow Lady Lennox to bathe her swollen eyes. 'It is the only solution. I can't imagine why it never occurred to me before. We are both of the blood royal. It will be an excellent match. I shall bear him strong, vigorous sons – legitimate children who will stand before any bastard offspring of Margaret Gordon's in the line to the throne.'

'And has my lord Regent,' enquired her companion slyly, 'expressed any desire to marry you?'

'Why shouldn't he want me for his wife?' demanded Margaret. 'I'm the first lady of Scotland and mother of the ten-year-old King. Albany will not be slow to realise the advantages of our uniting to govern Scotland until my son comes of age. No one would dare oppose our combined strength. Together, we will rule the nation in peace.'

Lady Lennox persisted. 'All Scotland knows that you and the Regent have been lovers, my lady. But are you quite sure, after all this time and after all that has happened, that he will wish to enter into marriage with you?'

'What are you talking about?' snapped the Queen. 'He's lusted after me for years. Why should he stop now? I may be thirty-three, but my body is still firm, I have all my teeth and every poet in the land has written verses praising my hair, my eyes, my flawless complex...' She choked, clawing at her cheeks. 'Oh no. *No!* Lennox, bring me that looking glass.'

But she had no real need of the glass. The terrible truth was mirrored plain in Lady Lennox's mocking eyes.

For over a year the Queen hid herself away at Linlithgow, shrouding her ravaged face with veils, medicinal lotions and cosmetic pastes. Miserably, she waited for Albany to call, dreading his expression of disgust and disinterest when he set eyes upon her. It was with the utmost relief that she learned that the Regent was too involved in a fresh bout of bickering with her brother Henry VIII to come wooing afresh his former mistress.

Henry had offered Scotland a five-year truce, and his daughter Mary as a bride for the young James V. When the Regent Albany refused, explaining that Scotland would continue to ally herself with France as a means of protecting herself from English domination, Henry promptly retaliated by burning the border towns of Kelso and Jedburgh. Reluctantly, Albany led a small Scots force over the border and into battle. It was a disastrous expedition. Although Henry had sent only a token party of men, they were more than a match for a half-hearted Scots army tired of war and unwilling to soldier through the ice and snow of winter. Disillusioned, the Regent had no choice but to retreat and settle for an uneasy truce with the triumphant English monarch.

As Albany's depression deepened, so the Queen's spirits began to lift. Gradually, she had been coming to terms with her changed appearance, until in the clear spring light of 1524 she found the courage to study herself in the glass without flinching. She accepted that even the most practised flatterer could never again call her beautiful. But although her face was pitted here and there where she had scratched the smallpox scabs, the skin looked healthier now, even blooming, with the aid of a little tinted powder. It was her right eye that caused Margaret most distress. Her illness had left the lower lid marked by an ugly growth, known as a pearl. A bitter irony, the Queen reflected, for one who had all her life worshipped her jewels, and whose very name, Margaret, meant a pearl.

Nevertheless, in every other respect she was still a robust, healthy woman. And, conveniently, Albany's French wife had recently died. The Regent, Margaret reasoned, would be in low spirits, mourning his wife and his defeat at the hands of the English. Would he not welcome the soothing, loving presence of a woman who from past experience understood his every mood, his least desire? Surely, if she approached him with tact and sympathy, he would overlook her pitted face, in return for tender words and gentle caresses. After a few nights in her arms, with the candles extinguished and the curtains drawn, it should be a relatively simple matter to persuade him to make her his wife.

The Regent, Lady Lennox informed the Queen, was conducting his annual inspection of the royal castles in Perth.

'Then we shall join him there,' declared Margaret, buoyant with confidence and resolve.

Later, she was to wonder how she could have forgotten that Perthshire was Drummond country. The aura of her late husband's mistress still had the power to curdle the Queen's blood, and reduced her to sullen silence as she rode past the castle where Margaret Drummond had died so horribly.

Had she been chattering or laughing with Lady Lennox, she might not have heard the man singing nearby.

Margaret clutched at her companion's arm, craning to place the source of the sound. 'I know that voice, Lennox. It's Albany. I'm sure of it.'

The Lennox lips tightened. 'But what is the Regent of Scotland doing here, my lady, in the middle of the countryside? And *singing*! Hardly a seemly activity, I would have thought, for a man in mourning. Just listen!'

The words rose loud and clear into the still May air:

> *'Here is the table spread,*
> *Love to invite thee,*
> *Clear is the wine and red,*
> *Love to delight thee.'*

The Queen was shaking with suppressed excitement. 'Don't be so stuffy, Lennox. Can't you see – he's *glad* his wife is dead. Albany is rejoicing at his release. Oh, don't just sit there, sniffing. Come *on*!'

Spurring her horse, Margaret followed the sound of voice and lute down the narrow track leading through the rowan trees. As the jennet delicately picked a path into the grassy vale, Margaret suddenly tugged on the reins, dragging the animal to an abrupt halt. Lady Lennox, behind her, let out an outraged breath.

The carefree minstrel, they saw, was not the Duke of Albany, but his brother, Alexander Stewart. He was sitting on a plaid rug, with a laughing Margaret Gordon sprawled beside him. Strewn round a small fire were flasks of wine and hunks of cheese and bread, while on a tattered multicoloured shawl crawled a near naked, dark haired child.

Smiling, the Bishop of Moray retied the cloth round the child's waist. 'Where are your manners, my dear? Exposing your bare bottom to our exalted visitors in such a brazen fashion.'

The Queen was so angry she could hardly speak. 'What . . . who . . . how dare you . . .' she stuttered impotently.

'How stupid of me,' said Mairead pleasantly to the Queen, lifting the child into her arms. 'I'd forgotten that you have not yet been introduced to our daughter. May I present the Lady Sybilla Magella Stewart.'

Lady Lennox could not restrain herself. '*Magella*?'

'After Magellan,' explained Alexander. 'Surely you've heard of his expedition which has sailed all the way round the world?'

Seeing Lady Lennox's nonplussed expression, the Bishop went on, 'But it's so enthralling. Just imagine, when this child's grandmother was born, our knowledge of the world had remained the same for centuries. We knew nothing of the lands and people on the other side of the earth. But by the time Margaret Drummond's granddaughter arrived, eighteen months ago, the globe had been circumnavigated and a ship had sailed on every ocean. Naming her Magella was our own way of commemorating the event. It's rather apt, don't you agree?'

The Queen had taken in only two words of his discourse – Margaret Drummond. 'Enough!' she exploded. 'I demand an explanation for your presence here together.' She leaned intimidatingly over Mairead. 'You, Margaret Gordon, gave your solemn promise to the Regent of Scotland that you would never again associate with this, this . . . with the Bishop of Moray. Have you any idea what Albany will do to you when I tell him you have broken your word? At the very least, he

326

will have you thrown into prison. And I shall make sure you stay there, to rot.'

Mairead calmly settled the gurgling child back on the shawl, and said, 'I gave my word to the Duke of Albany in his position as Regent of Scotland. As he no longer holds that title, I consider my obligation to be invalid.'

'Don't be absurd!' spluttered Lady Lennox. 'Of course Albany is still Regent.'

'Haven't you heard?' Alexander asked. 'The Regent sailed yesterday for France.'

The Queen said impatiently, 'Of course, he has to bury his wife and console his children. But when his affairs are settled, the Regent will return to Scotland.'

Margaret Gordon shook her dark head. 'No. Lord Huntly and the Council told him they were dissatisfied with his running of the country's affairs. They said that under Albany's rule, Scotland had become a mere vassal of French foreign policy. The Duke responded by saying that if the Council had lost faith in his judgement, then he had no choice but to lay down the burden of the Regency and sail for home. He declared that he would never come back to Scotland.'

It couldn't be true. They were lying. They wanted to make her suffer. Dry mouthed, the Queen stared at the couple standing arm in arm before her. The self-assurance, and pity in their faces confirmed her worst fears. Albany, the man she had intended to make her third husband, had abandoned her.

'Then who,' enquired Lady Lennox hesitantly, 'will lead our country now?'

'I shall,' declared the Queen, her mind galloping along new paths. Perhaps, after all, Albany had done her a great favour, not a disservice, by leaving Scotland. 'I was Regent before he came here, so by right the title must revert to me.' She fell silent, absorbed in thoughts and plans undreamed of ten minutes ago.

'Well, Mairead and I will cause you no embarrassment," Alexander told her. 'We are travelling to the Highlands, to join the Earl of Kinleven at his castle.'

'I hope you're taking his ill-bred sister with you,' said Lady

327

Lennox, who had never been able to countenance the elevation of a common serving girl to the title of Lady Annabella.

'No. She is staying in Edinburgh to prepare for the homecoming of her son Douglas from France,' replied Mairead, ruffling Magella's mop of dark curls.

'Speaking of France,' said the Queen, her voice carrying an authority which had been lacking in all the years of Albany's rule, 'I think it only fair to tell you that when I am once more invested as Regent, I shall pardon the Earl of Mallaig and invite him back to the Scottish Court. I shall also,' she glared malevolently at Mairead, 'insist that you sign another document, assuring me that you will renounce your association with Alexander Stewart. I warn you here and now, I absolutely refuse to allow this affair to continue.'

The glimmer of a smile lit Margaret Gordon's face. 'You may assume the title of Regent, but I can assure you that the Council will never again allow you the luxury of total control. If you try to come between Alexander and I, then I shall approach my grandfather Lord Huntly and ask that he and the Council overrule you, by enforcing the existing exile order on Mallaig. As it was I whom Mallaig tried to murder, I feel sure the Council will uphold my plea.'

'Of course,' said Alexander genially, 'if Your Grace would care to give us your word, in writing, that you will not molest the Lady Margaret and myself, then we will withdraw any objection to Mallaig's return. As I said, Mairead and I will not be troubling you with our presence, as we are going to Kinleven.'

The Queen plucked at the folds of her dress, mentally weighing one option against the other. On the one side, there was her deep rooted desire to humble Margaret Gordon once and for all; on the other, was her desperate need for an ally. Margaret Gordon was right, damn her. The entire Council was likely to take against her. When she became Regent, it would be essential to have by her side a man of proven loyalty and ruthless determination. Mallaig was the ideal candidate – in fact, the only candidate.

Regally, she inclined her head. 'Very well. As long as you

both stay out of my sight, I will allow you to live in peace, and sin, together. I shall send you my written permission when I return to Edinburgh.'

Alexander's voice was equable, but firm. 'We shall have departed for Kinleven by then ... and you know how slow and unreliable the mail horses are to the Highlands. Let us seal the bargain in writing now.' He took a sheet of music from the case of his lute. 'Here, we can use the back of this, and a piece of charcoal from the fire.'

The Queen waited fretfully while he scribbled the words that would remove Margaret Drummond's daughter from her power forever.

'There we are,' he said at last, handing her the paper and charcoal.

'*I, Queen Margaret, Regent of Scotland,*' she read, '*hereby promise that under no circumstances whatsoever will I interfere in the relationship between Margaret Gordon and Alexander Stewart, nor attempt any ill deed against either of them or their child Magella.*'

With a muttered curse, the Queen signed her name.

'Perhaps,' suggested Mairead smoothly, 'Lady Lennox would care to act as witness?'

The Queen laughed. 'Don't you trust me?'

'No,' said Mairead coldly, passing the document to Lady Lennox for her signature. Without another word, the Queen gathered up her reins and turned the jennet back up the track towards the road. When the two women were out of sight, Mairead smiled at Alexander. 'How long will it be before she finds out?'

'Soon,' he said, tucking the paper the Queen had signed safely into his shirt. 'But not soon enough. That's why I included the phrase, *under no circumstances whatsoever.*' He kissed her. 'She can't touch us now, lovedy.'

Margaret Gordon lay back on the rug, tucking her daughter into the crook of her arm as Alexander picked up his lute and resumed his song. She felt a passing pang of pity for Lady Lennox, who would be the one to bear the full brunt of the first lady's rage when she discovered the truth. For what they had not told the Queen was that Mallaig was already back in Scotland, in furious pursuit of his wife.

The unpredictable Diane had deserted both her husband and the gentle pastures of her native France and sailed for Scotland. To the rugged grandeur of the Western Highlands, and a mellow sandstone castle called Kinleven. Two years ago, this lovely, lethal woman had granted Robert Kyle his freedom. Now she had come to exact her price.

Robert and Diane, face to face on the silver sands that fringed Kinleven. It held all the promise, reflected Mairead, of an unforgettable confrontation. Especially when Mallaig caught up with them.

And closing her eyes in the warm May sunshine, Margaret Gordon hummed a descant as her lover sang:

> *'Mistress mine, come to me,*
> *Dearest of all.*
> *Light of mine eyes to me,*
> *Half of my soul.'*